The Discovery

Being the first volume of

The Magic Pawn

By

SIMONA M. DIACONESCU

Cover design by Maria Spada
Translated from Romanian by Andreea-Elena Gînju

To my lovely, little brother, Raul and to the two women in my life: my mother, Angela and my aunt, Elena. They helped me be who I am today. I am forever grateful to them.

"The first step to moving forward is to finally be aware of what you feel and to have the strength to accept it no matter how burdensome it is. You need to learn from your own mistakes no matter how many times you fall. Because this is the only way you will become yourself, your best self."

The Discovery

CONTENTS

Prologue:
"Eric"

The suspect was still unconscious as he sat in the chair we had previously thrown him on. His hands were chained tightly with duct tape onto the chair handles. We had left his feet loose. This guy was not a problem for us. He was just a man who did not have any magic powers; another puppet.

I could not make any further mistakes and let escape any information that would help me find the Magic Pawn. Who else knew that she existed? Who was after her; who was trying to get her involved in their egotistical plans where power took precedence over everything else? How could I protect her from these people when I did not even know who she was?

The only thing I knew was that the Magic Pawn had to be a girl in her early twenties. It had been difficult for me to squeeze out this piece of information from a man; I had used the best method for such circumstances: torture. Some of them eventually gave in, but others did not say a word. Absurd abnegation. More specific: death by torture.

Was Baldric involved in any way? If so, then it means that he knew about the girl. He had connections that I could never aspire to. Perhaps one of his creatures told him where the girl was hiding. But, is she hiding? Does she even know how important she is to us? Is she even aware of the powers she has? Does she know that her importance is absolute both in protecting the magic world and in destroying it? Or was she simply oblivious to this? Perhaps she went about living her peaceful life being unaware of the burden that had fallen on her shoulders once she became the bearer of powers that exceed even the imagination of wizards. I had to help her and make sure she does not fall into the wrong hands. Unlike me, the others wanted to use her as a pawn in a game they called life. A dangerous game where the reward was the power, one got by sacrificing the lives of others. If that were to happen, then the magical world will no longer be the way we know it. Nothing is more dangerous than a magic pawn that has been touched by darkness.

As the game furthers and comes to an end, life and death will be only inches apart. Then there is her; she appears to alter the end of this game, of this harsh reality that should have developed differently.

In a way, it all happens because of her. If it were not for her, then these greedy people would not have been able to carry their plans into effect. This cold war over who gets the main pawn would not have existed. The world of magic would have gone its own way just as it has until now. Far too easy problems would have been left for me to solve. And Baldric...

My brother was not dead, as we had thought. This would have been much too easy. He only wanted to deceive those far too naive. He had always intended to show up in the midst of chaos, since he was a big part of creating it in the first place. I did not know exactly what, but I knew that Baldric was up to something. The solution? To kill him.

But even with Baldric out of the picture there was still another problem: should the pawn be taken out of the game?

-He's waking up, Mystic said. Finally, some action.

She was anxious. Although she seemed calm and steady, I knew she was only pretending. Just as it was for me, her mind too was repeatedly pleading for something: "Let's hope we find something out this time".

There were very few moments like this when she would seem confused. This woman knew exactly what she wanted out of life. Her facial expression was usually that of a though person but it had now been replaced by another one which made her seem slightly vulnerable. She was tired and afraid we would hit yet another dead end. Two years had passed since we had started to look for the Magic Pawn. Every time we came close, something would happen and we would have to start everything all over again. We knew that we had to find a girl in her twenties, but we felt further than ever from that. I at least had had enough of running after her. If it had not been for Mystic, I would have probably given up a long time ago. However, this tall blonde woman, with her blue eyes and a body that would rock any man's world, had all the right words when you needed someone backing you up. She was only two years younger than I was; this twenty-seven year old woman was now my closest relative.

We knew each other from when I was ten years old, when all the chaos on Kaeillindor had begun. She was left alone among strangers. Since then, she had been in the care of my family.

She was not the frightened girl anymore. She was a strong woman and was not afraid of the consequences as long as it got her what she wanted. She was the best partner I had, the only person I trusted.

We had never been romantic with each other. The idea seemed strange to both of us.

'Alright', I said eventually as I snapped back into reality. 'Let's see what we are up against.'

The suspect tried in vain to get up from the chair. Seeing him gesticulate in desperation like that only made us laugh.

'Who are you? Why were you hovering around the campus?' I asked him.

'What campus? I already told you. I am a backpacker, that's all. And...'

'Forget it. This won't work with us.'

We were in the forest in the secret basement of an old hut. The hut looked uninteresting and that should have kept all meddlers away.

'Look...look at me', he whispered.

He was so typical: boots, jogging suit and a big...and empty rucksack; just a bottle of water and a bag of food. It would have been a lot more plausible if he had had a sleeping bag with him, some extra clothes and all the other things a backpacker needs.

'It seems your boss did not train you very well', Mystic said sarcastically. 'And by the way, this is private property.'

She went to the stranger, smiled at him, took him by the chin and looked him straight in the eyes.

'You are a bad liar', she scolded him. 'Who did you say you are working for?' She put a finger on his trembling lips. 'No, don't rush to answer that. You see, we have two ways for this: the easy way or the hard way. Which one do you choose?'

The man tried to make sense of the stuff in one of the corners of the dimly lit room and then sighed. It was a sigh of relief.

'What did you expect? A Middle Age type of torture? No... that would be too complicated. I have news for you: the world has evolved.

You have two options. First: you tell us everything you know and Eric will make you forget about all of this. Second: this is not so pleasant. How about slow death by suffocation? You know...that's not a very nice feeling, when you'd give anything to at least be able to beg for air.'

His long hair was covering his eyes. He was probably praying to wake up, and he hoped this was nothing but a nightmare.

In a split second his face turned back to Mystic; her eyes could be truly frightening ones. She pushed her fingernails deep into his cheek, leaving thin blood tracks all over it. Horrified, he whined. He could not say another word.

Mystic had to go on intimidating him.

'Or do you prefer to feel deep stings through your entire body? You will feel them one after the other and each time it will hurt so much more. How would it be if you caught fire but not really be on fire? Let's say that you are not in flames but you fell as though you were? Do you want me to explain this to you?' He shook his head and Mystic started to laugh. 'Ha! And you call yourself a man. Trust me, it is incredibly painful!'

'Yyy...you are crazy! Completely crazy! What do you want to do to me?'

'I don't think you are in any position to be asking questions. So? Is it the first or the second option?'

I could no longer stand to wait. I had been waiting enough. Enough with the threatening! We had to do something. I wasn't going to waste my entire day being here. Without giving much thought to it, I used my special power. I began drawing shapes into the air and pushed them his way with a gentle blow. He was about to face his deepest fears. Fact or fiction?

The duct tape strips came loose. The man screamed, ran to the corner of the room and hunkered down.

'How did he manage to rip the band? And what has gotten into him?' She looked at me. Realising what had happened, she said: 'I haven't told you about this. Your worst fears. How would it be if someone were able to bring out all your fears and turn everything into reality? Or illusion...'

The man pulled his knees to his chest and leaned on them. He began to twitch convulsively. I had to finish the intimidation and Mystic knew that. She got herself in front of the stranger just in time.

'Enough! His heart might stop at any time.'

I remained with my hand hanging in the air.

'Move out of his way!'

'Why? So that you will kill him?' She shouted and seemed as if she'd had enough of all this. 'We need him alive!'

One last scream and then silence.

'Are you happy now?'

Irritated beyond belief, Mystic left room and pulled the door hard behind her.

This day could not have been any better. I had lost my last source and it had taken me a lot of time to find the information. I went next to him and leaned down to check his pulse; the man blinked. So he was not yet dead, there was still a chance.

'I need a name', I said to him while grabbing him by the neck.

'I don't know', he said in coarse voice. 'I don't know her name.'

'I need a name', I shouted at him; I was pissed off.

'Meya, her niece', he whispered.

Mystic had already been out of the forest when I caught up with her.

'Can you just stop for a minute?'

'He is dead!' she shouted. You killed him and now we have no chance of finding anything out. And don't tell me about next time because this is not the first one you've lost control over. And don't you dare deny it!'

'Can you just listen to me?'

'Don't interrupt me!' She snapped at me. 'Yes, I know you can control your powers. It's just that...sometimes you act as if you go into psychological overdrive. Like some apprentice who has lost touch with reality, acting on impulse. He did not even have any powers. He was just a man. Just a simple man!' She repeated. 'Oh...and another thing. I am not taking care of his body!'

'I already called Jamie.'

'Two years, Eric. Now I am the one who feels like giving up. I am sick and tired of always ending up in the same dead spot.'

Mystic knew me very well. Sometimes she knew me better than I did myself. Tough, indifferent and too scared to ever show my true feelings. I knew that my vulnerability would have made an important weapon for my enemies. But Mystic was not my enemy. Then, there was fear. Having been brought up by so many nannies that did not linger for too long in my family's house, I was never the sentimental type. I was afraid. I was afraid that someone would eventually get to know my fears, my weaknesses...I had weaknesses.

'I found her'.

'What? You are joking, aren't you?' She asked me and looked completely shocked.

'No. I am dead serious. I know who it is.'

'I cannot believe it. After all this time...'

'It's Meya's niece. It seems we have to go to Kaeillindor.'

I knew this was a sensitive topic for her. That island had only caused her unhappiness. You could read the sadness on her face. She was a tough woman. She should not behave like a whining girl. This was her motto. Life had not been exactly easy for her. She has been on roads with too many obstacles and she has had to learn how to overcome them by herself; this had made her the woman she was.

'Are you alright?'

'You have never been there...in the midst of all that chaos', she reminded me. 'But I am alright...how will you get on the island? You cannot cross over the barrier.'

'You will go there first. In the meantime, I will see if I can meddle in Meya's business. She will help me get on the island if I make her believe that she needs me.'

'And how do you think you'll manage to do that? That wretched Meya is not so easy to fool.'

'Let's just say that I know her weaknesses.'

'And what will you do about the prophecy?'

I had completely forgotten about that. Destiny had played a hoax on me and it seemed that now it was also controlling my love life. The Magic Pawn and I would be sharing a special connection. Nonsense! I did not want to believe this, although the prophecies were as rare as they were true. One could not fight his destiny. But it was impossible for me to think that I would be falling in love with a girl whom I had not met and whom I already did not like. I had my reason not to like her already: everything that was happening was because of her.

'Well Mystic, this is not going to be a problem', I said. A part of me knew already that I was only lying to myself.

Chapter 1:

"Radical changes"

I didn't know where I was heading. Encroached by fear, I was running through darkness in a desperate attempt to escape the ever-growing myriad of people that were after me.

I knew this was a dream. It had to be. But I had no ability to control it. As usual, the only thing I could do was to hide in the darkness. Although they could also find me there, it was still the only place where they could not tell who I was and where they could not touch me. It was as if a force beyond any reach – a fathomless power, one that I could not see but I felt floating into the open air – pushed them away, as they were getting too close to me. And then, there was he: the tall blue-eyed guy, the only one who didn't frighten me and who gave me a sense of security.

But it was the protection I felt in darkness that really gave me the shivers and augmented all my fears. And I hated that just as much as I hated not knowing what was happening to me.

And just when I thought it couldn't get any worse, things took a completely new turn, as I woke up with aunt Meya in my room.

'What are you doing here?' *I checked the clock on my nightstand.* 'I am happy to see you but it is 2 o'clock in the night. And you could have said something before turning on the lights'. *I told her as I was shading my eyes.*

'We need to talk!'

'Now? I know you are crossed with my parents but couldn't you have chosen a more reasonable hour?'

'Just listen to me!'

She appeared to be agitated. Her hands were moving steadily.

'Talk to my folks', I babbled. 'Let me get back to sleep!'

The blanket that was covering me just rolled over by itself. By itself! I didn't see Meya moving.

That's when I realised things just weren't right. I instantly snapped out of drowsiness.

Something was happening.

'Put some clothes on you! You have to come with me'.

I stared at her baffled. After all it was 2 am.

'Your parents have been trying to keep you away from me because we are alike. But I cannot give up on my niece when she needs me. Don't tell me you are not at all curios to know more about yourself, you little witch?'

I jumped out of my skin as the cabinet doors opened noiselessly all by themselves. The clothes and some of my stuff shuffled into a suitcase that was not mine and in less than a minute my luggage was ready.

I was in shock, watching the entire scene, unable to tell if this was a dream. It was happening much too fast for me to get a grasp of anything.

'But...this is impossible', I whispered in trembling voice.

'Anything is possible', said someone behind me.

It seems Meya was not alone. A girl, whom I thought to be my age, was also invading my privacy. She was tall and slender; hair down to shoulders, straight and jet black, triangular face shape and eyes the colour of the hair.

'And who are you?' I asked revolted.

'Christine, I told you to wait in the car.'

What did my aunt want? Did she want me to run away with her? To leave my parents and... No way. I realised I knew very little about this woman, too little to trust her much. And this girl just kept smiling. She was in such a merry mood and so energetic that it infuriated me.

I went towards the door.

'I am not going anywhere with you.'

'I thought you said she would be easy to convince. '

Just one look from aunt Meya made that girl swallow her words.

I yelled as loud as I could and my parents stormed into the room. They did not seem too surprised to see my aunt – as if they were expecting this. Were they?

'You have kept all knowledge about her roots away from her', said Meya. And she wasn't asking.

'They have told me all I need to know', I interfered. *The girl standing next to my aunt seemed extremely amused.* 'Does this seem like a show to you?' *She stopped laughing and looked at me sympathetically. I didn't need this.* 'Leave! Just leave, both of you!'

They didn't budge.

'What is it that you want? What are you after? Go back to where you came from', *dad told her, his voice colder than I have ever heard. Never before had I seen him struggling to keep his cool.* 'Enough already! We won't let you use Kate for your personal goals. She is too important to let her...'

A long discussion followed, the two sides at odds with each other over "who deserved me more and who not". I couldn't keep up. My head hurt so much that I could focus on nothing else.

'What truth are you talking about?' I asked at some point, having had enough of hearing the word "truth". I cannot even tell which one said it last.

'Don't you dare!' My mom threatened.

'It's her choice', said my aunt calm as she was.

'You'd better not!' The girl said. 'Look at her! She doesn't seem well.'

'I already said I'm not going anywhere with you', I interfered.

'I'm sure you'll change your mind after I've told you what I have to say. If you come with me I will tell you the entire truth and I will help you. If you stay here you will just be living in a lie.'

'Please', said mom with tears in her eyes.

I was listening baffled, trying to figure out what was happening. Again they started screaming at each other until two words were spoken; two words that would change everything.

'I... I'm...add...adopted?'

I could barely murmur the words out. I walked unsteadily away from my parents. I looked them in the eyes begging them to say this was just a lie, but none of them said a word.

Aunt Meya showed me three DNA results. No match between mine and any of my parents'. The last one was hers. According to the DNA, Meya was indeed my aunt. No wonder my parents didn't want her around me. They were afraid that she might tell me the truth. They

knew how much I hated to be lied to. Why had they not been honest to me from the very beginning?

It all fell to pieces in just one night. Just another one of those nights that would change everything.

I knew I could not take the right decision now but I felt the need to escape. Flooded by bitterness, I left with aunt Meya on the spur of the moment without even glancing back. I didn't care about their tears and words.

Everything...my life up till then...slowly passed by...slowly...as sand grains in an hourglass, leaving utter emptiness behind it.

While turning the hourglass – way too soon and without any consideration for the consequences - I decided to take a different path – a new one – because the path I believed to be mine all those years was now closed. Whether this was going to be the right one or not, only the fine and slow-moving sand grains would give me the answer.

And thus, I found myself in a strange car together with aunt Meya, Christine, and her son Edward.

'I thought you weren't coming anymore cousin', *he said with a large smile on his face.* 'You have no idea how much I have missed you'.

We had been very close during our childhood, and he had been my best advisor as a teenager during a tormenting period in high school, but I had not seen him for over a year.

'I am happy to see you, too', I said, trying to mimic a smile.

I did not feel like talking. I curled up near the window and looked as this absent street that was so familiar to me was now fading behind me.

'Can you drive faster? Let's not forget that we have a flight to catch', said the girl.

We are flying? I wanted to ask but my voice could not push through. Where are we going? I tried to ask again but it was to no avail.

I wrapped my jacket into an improvised pillow and placed it under my head. I fidgeted a bit until I could get comfortable and shut my eyes closed. I stood like that, inert, overwhelmed by this avalanche of feelings enhanced by the sheer image of solitude and carelessness.

My escape had come into being. Would it be one without return?

Katelyn Lambert, how did you put yourself in this situation? I scolded myself. For someone who was twenty-three years old I had different expectations of my life. Or at least I expected to be a normal person, one who has worked extensively to get her bachelor degree in biology. I was supposed to think about what Master program to take, but I was no longer sure I wanted that. In fact, I was no longer certain of anything.

Not until long before I had always been surrounded by friends...anyway...by those I thought to be my friends. Envious girls who probably wished I would go somewhere far away. That type of people who are over-preoccupied with how they look, to consider caring for anybody else except for themselves. Yes, I was one of those self-absorbed persons.

Most of the boys only saw the sexy girl in me, slender body, long, finely shaped legs and beautiful breasts. The long hair down to my waist and slightly curly, flashy blonde, round-shaped face and large deep green eyes that would shift to purple-blue in the sunshine. The girl they desperately had to have. I liked to be in the limelight. I flirted back – but only if the guys were good looking – and it all came down to this and nothing more.

Now things have changed. I have changed. When I look back I feel as though a stranger found her way into my memories. And in order to acknowledge that, I had to take part in all the strange happenings in my life.

I cannot stand my parents making sure they remind me almost every day that I am different. I hate just hearing the words "special", "different".

What can be so special about not knowing yourself anymore; the dreams; the headaches that sometimes feel as if they'll never stop; my sudden changes of behaviour; the vulnerability of my feelings? I keep shifting from being irritated to feeling normal. When I am angry I burst out at whoever is with me at that time. And now the weather is also starting to flip. Grey clouds darken the sky. Lightning gets much too close while thunders crack afar. The wind begins to blow hard. As soon as I snap out of this state, the weather calms down as well. When I cry it happens often that it rains outside. It must be only a coincidence. I mean...it has to be a coincidence!

Nature understands me as if reacting to everything I feel, and this drives me crazy, sometimes. And then there are all these persons I do not know but whom I have actually seen before. Things I know for sure will happen in one way or the other. And I know it is more than déjà-vu.

Last but not least, there is the memory of that wretched night in March - four months ago – that changed everything.

I was at a party that James, my former group colleague, had organised. A selfish guy spoiled by his parents and filthy rich. His parents were away in Paris for some highly important business meeting and so we had the entire house to ourselves.

When I got to his place, I was surprised to see that he was the only one I knew so I turned to walk away. James stopped me and we began to fight and as he grabbed me by the waist and pulled me to him something changed. He pushed me so hard that, unless a guy who was behind me had caught me, I would have landed straight on the floor. He looked at me with fear and horror.

'Your eyes', he said.

And then fell on his knees unable to finish his sentence. People began crowding around us. I panicked. I could not think rationally. Damn it! I ran in fear.

I can say that that was the turning point for my change. It was James' turning point also. That night was the last one I would see him and also the only one whose details I will keep to myself. Ever since then I have been wondering what James had seen in my eyes that scared him so much and how had I managed to hurt him by simply touching him.

I got the creeps every time I recollected this sad event. I wanted it erased from my memory but it just continued to hold on to me desperately.

The truth is that as much as I wanted to learn about the reason for all the changes in my life, I was more afraid of what I could find out. Yes, I know...it is hilarious and, at the same time, depressing to be frightened by your own self. No matter how hard I tried to deny the truth, it starred me right in the face. And I hate, hate that there is a part of me that enjoyed the fact that I was a freak.

Unfortunately I got to the point where I realised how the power of one's thoughts can suddenly lay bare the fact that a person can have opposing thoughts at the same time; as if torn between two individuals with different feelings and goals, always at odds with one another.

The solution was not denial but acceptance. I had always wondered whether I would make anything important in life – something special. I did not however expect to turn into a freak...well...a witch. The monotony of life looked like a pretty good option at this time.

I admit. I am really scared. Damn it! But I must not let fear run my life.

The first step to moving forward is to finally be aware of what you feel and to have the strength to accept it no matter how burdensome it is. You need to learn from your own mistakes no matter how many times you fall. Because this is the only way you will become yourself, your best self. You will end up falling many times in life, but you must learn how to get back on your feet by yourself.

My new motto in life: Listen! Embrace! Fight!

You cannot run away from what you are! I told myself with the bare minimum optimism, and then I sighed at the thought of my parents.

'We are here Kate', I warm voice awoke me from my drowsiness.

I put on my jacket and got out of the car. I gazed at the big airport lying before me wondering if this was the right thing to do.

'Where are we going?'

'Greece, the island of Crete', said Christine all cheered up.

So far from home...I tried to clear my throat.

'I didn't know you live there...'

'I don't live there sweetie. And I don't live where you thought I did.' *Now it's so much clearer for me, aunt.* 'From Corfu we will be heading to a wonderful island, one you've never heard about before in your life.'

'It is a secret place', said Christine.

24

'What is this? You're joking, aren't you?' I commented maliciously. 'There is no such thing as an island in the Mediterranean Sea that people don't know about.'

'Just like there is no magic', added Christine.

What could I say to this?

I slept on the way there, unable to resist the fatigue.

As soon as we got out of the taxi I could feel the sea breeze and its smell that was so particular and so comforting.

We arrived on a motorboat that troubled the water behind it a bit too much although it did not seem to be going at a very high speed. "Magic" was my aunt's reply. Although I was very curious I did not insist on knowing the topic.

I tried not to think too much about the fact that I was surrounded by water. I was not a very good swimmer. And to be at sea, heading to...nowhere? That frightened me terribly.

Two pairs of eyes turned towards me.

'What are you doing?' Christine and Edward said at the same time.

'I'm not doing anything?' I mocked them.

I don't know what they found so funny but they both started to laugh.

'She is sea sick. And you two stop with these comments and let her be!'

'But we didn't say anything', they protested.

'No...I mean I am not sea sick.'

'Yes...right. Me neither...'

'Christine Ebenzer!' My aunt shouted at her.

There is something wrong with this place. I have a very unpleasant feeling about it; a strange sensation that's giving me a massive headache. Anxiety and fear and...

'Do you trust me?' *My aunt's warm voice had an immediate calming effect on me.* 'Listen to me!'...*She took my palms into hers.* 'I understand how you're feeling. I know what you're going through. You are also tired now and everything is much too new and happening much too fast. It will get easier with time. There is really nothing wrong with the place we're heading to. That's where you were born, my sweet Kate...'

I stopped myself from sighing.

'I don't understand', I said all confused. 'Where is this place? I now find out that I was born on some deserted island – apparently one that does not even exist...'

'Look over there Kate!' She pointed to the sea.

'What do you expect me to see?'

'Look closer!' She insisted.

'Nothing.'

'Really, sweetie? Do you really not see?'

Alright; now she's mocking me?

'I'm sorry aunt. I forgot to take with me my ultra-sight glasses...'

'Look closer!' She insisted.

Pissed as I was I crossed my arms over my chest.

'Sweetie...'

'Really, Meya? Really? 'And stop calling me sweetie!' I snapped at her.

She let me be. But then that strange feeling appeared again. I flinched, feeling the cold invading every part of my body. It was as if I were in the middle of a snow storm. I found it difficult to breathe on account of a wind that was blowing too strong, although it was apparently inexistent. And the cold had made me unable to move.

And all of a sudden everything disappeared; as did that strange sensation amplified by the nausea. I could feel my body and I could breathe again.

'What was that? And don't tell me none of you felt anything because no matter how crazy you think I am, the pain caused by the cold was very real;' too real, even if only for a few seconds – which went by much too slow.

'We just passed through a magic portal. Because this was the first time for you, it's normal for it to cause a not-so-pleasant sensation for you', my aunt replied. 'The island of Kaeillindor is where magic was born; this is where its essence resides. The portal was created to protect it. That is why people do not know about its existence. They cannot see it.'

'You mean to say that we are in a different dimension?'

Everyone started to laugh. What was so funny?

'No sweetie. Imagine you are in a cave. Getting to the exit depends on the road you chose to take. Every road is like a portal taking you from one place to the other. Remember before when I was showing you the dim golden light coming from the portal? You had to look really carefully and know exactly where to look in order to see it. Moreover, the portal is surrounded by protection spells. Do you understand now?'

'I think I do. I am trying to assimilate all of it although there is a part of me that's waiting to wake up from this dream any moment now.'

Chapter 2:
"The Island of Kaeillindor"

The island really did have amazing places. The forested mountains descended straight into the clear sea. The luxuriant vegetation seemed to coat the entire island in a green cloak. The ever-present palm trees, the olive trees, the fruit trees, and the cypresses of a green so deep that it made it difficult not to stop and stare at them, curios about whether they are real or not.

And in that wilderness, the wonderful species of orchids with their dazzling perfume and the colourful carpet they lay made you daydream and never want to get up from that dream.

Then we reached a cliffy area, full of trees and shrubs some of them with shapes as strange as they were interesting.

Some of them were shaped like mushrooms with slim branches uniformly positioned to form a green hat.

'Wow... it looks strikingly similar to the dracaena cinnabari', I said as I realised that I was thinking out loud.

Edward and Christine gave me a strange look.

'I was talking about that tree over there', I said, as I was pointing to one of the numerous trees in the shape of sunken hat mushrooms. *The same look.* 'Dragon blood, if I have to spell it out for you. The extremely bizarre tree whose red-coloured resin drips off the trunk when it is wounded? Come on...you live here and you've never been interested in knowing this?'

'Wounded?' They all asked, and then started laughing.

'I'll lead the way, my aunt interrupted. 'I have something that needs to be done.'

After she left, the other two continued to tease me.

'What's so funny?' I retorted.

'A wounded tree?' Edward asked once more.

This was becoming very annoying. I looked at them both. Christine gave him a shove before he could say anything else.

'I didn't know you were so smart', he said, while keeping himself from laughing.

'Really? I have always been passionate about nature; the most bizarre wild places; the strangest rock formations. The unique trees and...'

'But this is definitely not blood...what blood?' Edward shouted behind me.

'Of the dragon', Christine replied much too loud although she was standing right next to him.

'I did not say it was blood', I retorted while stopping. 'I only said it looked like blood. I cannot believe that this superb scenery doesn't move you even a bit. It is unique and...'

'This was our reaction in the beginning...but we are starting to get bored with the scenery. The trees that have strange shapes are frightening.' *Christine became serious again.* 'That tree that you were telling us about has black resin as you can very well observe, and silver threads drip off it during the night. Trust me...you don't want to come close to it when that happens.'

29

'And what about the screaming tree?' Edward pointed to a specimen that seemed very familiar to me.

The trunk in the shape of a bulb, thin branches with numerous flowers all coloured differently, unscented and in the shape of funnels. The tree did not have any leaves.

'Screaming?' What a strange name...

'We named it like that.'

Aaa....ah it began with the letter a...

'Everything happens at night. The flowers just seem to come alive. They make a truly deafening noise and...'

'That's it', I burst. 'Adenium obesum – the dessert rose. I knew it! Aaa...you were saying what?'

'If the first part of the island is just like any other, welcoming and full of superb scenery, this one is far from that', Edward said.

I felt a chill down the spine.

'That's just stupid', I added in mockery.

'I think that...'

'That we should just get going. This place scares me', Christine said.

'Then we should have taken the other road. We can still go back, you know. You still have time to change your mind.'

'No thanks, Edward. The dead area of the island frightens me more. Even Meya avoids it and you know that your mom does not scare off that easily.'

Although a part of me was curious to see what Christine was talking about, I realised that, in fact, it was better I didn't know.'

We walked away from that area and came across another stretch of thick vegetation.

When we finally arrived to the inhabited area I was very pleased to see a combination of various architectonic styles. The predominantly white modest houses combined with the more vivid colours of the big pompous buildings. The large yards and enormous gardens embellished with all sorts of statues and fountains placed in the middle of fields of flowers – each more different and special; the meticulously pruned hedges which kept company to the various fruit trees.

People were already hustling and bustling on the narrow and busy streets that sprung from the main street. Although it was still very early in the morning, the entire community was up and running. Even children not more than twelve years old saw freely to their activities. Shouldn't they be sleeping at this hour? It was holiday time. Waking up early had always been a problem for me.

Christine answered my questions as though she would be a mind reader. Or perhaps she just checked out my face which definitely showed total confusion.

'People here work hard to make a better future for them of just for having what to put on the table the next day. If there is a lot that needs to be done then those families have their children working also. Living here is a lot more difficult.'

'Yeah...not many can afford to just stay and do nothing', said Edward while starring at Christine. She turned her back at him and ignored him.

'I'm guessing there's no telephone reception here...or is there?'

'No, there is no reception. We use our own methods...'

I sighed. There is so much that I have to learn...

I looked around at the crowd wondering how they all got to live in a place like this. I assume that most of them were born here.

'Your room is already prepped', Christine said. 'I chose the colour and all the decorations although Brysena took care of everything else. Brysena is one of the many employees of father's;' she cleared it for me before I even had the chance to ask.

That's when we stopped in front of a huge building, truly impressive.

'Is this where you live?'

'Yes, it's wonderful, isn't it?'

'Wow...' that was all that I managed to say.

The gothic style building was no doubt the size of a palace: tall walls, not too thick and supported on the outside by buttresses that finished in sharp arches; numerous windows, tall and wide with flare-like frames and divided longitudinally by see-through stained glass columns which allowed light to enter the room abundantly. A beautifully coloured rose window framed the door on top. On the last floor of the building – out of the three – a bas relief representing the phases of the moon stood out.

A large garden surrounded the building probably covering a wider area in the back of it. The front part was filled with flowers some of which had been carefully planted in large pots of different shapes. There were also small garden statues. The water ran as clear as a bell as it flowed out of a marble fountain centred by a sculpture portraying the nude bust of a woman.

The vestibule presented a big arch on which there lay inscribed several meticulously drawn stars. Then there was the long hallway with its huge golden chandelier shining in the sun light; supporting poles covered in clamberers bearing multi-coloured flowers. The marble floor was made of rhombus stones of different sizes positioned as such that they would please the eye.

As we were walking down the hallway that was much too long and mazy I felt as though I were in a labyrinth. There were far too many doors that were hiding who knows what, and corridors coalescing with one another.

'How much time do you think it takes someone to move through the house without getting lost?

'Too much time', Christine replied with a smile on her face. 'If we consider the underground area also...and those secrets rooms that I am sure dad has been keeping away even from us, his children. Although I think my sister Maggie is close to discovering one of those rooms... if she hasn't already...'she sighed.

So Christine also had a sister.

We went up a spiralling staircase and stopped at the second floor where my room was being prepped for me.   Several other small hallways followed until – eventually – we got to our destination. Edward had cleared off – I think he went straight for the freezer – leaving Christine in charge of helping me with everything else I needed.

The room was very spacious with a large bed in the middle of the room that could have easily taken four persons. A painting stood above the bed portraying a blonde woman with gorgeous green eyes. The walls were painted in a shade of light purple and there was a mirrored nightstand across from the bed. By the window there was a small table accommodating a large orchid in a pot, and a desk in the corner.

'Are you the only ones... aaa...' I felt I was losing my breath, unable to say the word – this was absurd by all accounts.

Christine gave me a strange look.

'Aaa... Do I really have to say it?'

'You don't like the room...?'she asked appearing to be a bit disappointed.

'No, no, it's not that. The room is beautiful. It is even more welcoming than I would have expected. I like it a lot. But we can talk about it later...Are the rest of the inhabitants also... I mean... can they also do aaa...'

'Why is it so hard? Wizards? Witches? No...' she replied unmoved. 'It is only Maggie, Edward, Meya and I. And no one must know about this. OK?'

'I wouldn't even know what to tell them, if I wanted to.'

'Dad doesn't know either. This is...'

'A very serious thing and extremely important...yes, I know...'

'Magic is not a thing!'

'Ok.... so we are wizards...do I need a twig like the one in Harry Potter or what?'

'Like in what?'

I started to laugh.

'Harry Potter?! Come on... everybody knows about...' but Christine interrupted me and didn't let me finish my sentence.

'No, we don't have twigs. And try to remember that we live on an island in the middle of the sea; the secret island.' *The irony in her voice made her sound funny.* 'We don't have television, internet connection and no mobile phone network.'

'What can I say?...if you can do the cool stuff I have seen in movies then all those things that you just listed will seem to be nothing compared to this. '

Christine insisted she gave me a hand unpacking although I didn't need the help – I only had a suitcase, too small for all the things I would have wanted to put in it. Before I could even open it Christine beat me to it and my clothes started flying through the room heading for the wardrobe. I was shocked by the large number of things flying through the room and how everyone got placed properly. Exactly how I had them placed at home.

'Wow...now this really is a helping hand.'

'I cannot believe this...how did they all fit into that small rotten suitcase?'

'What can I say? The contrast between what's essential and what appears to be dominates when magic is taken into the equation.'

'Will I also be able to do this? And how did you do it?'

'This and many more...' *She shrugged her shoulders.* 'You just need lots of concentration and a few words.'

'So anyone can do magic if they learn the right magic words?'

She burst into laughter while heading slowly towards the door.

'Oh Kate... you have so much to learn.'

'Wait! You still didn't answer my question.'

'Only if you are gifted.' *That's the only thing she said and then closed the door behind her.*

Alright... this girl could be really strange sometimes.

I wasn't going to stay in the room. I took a hot shower and then I decided to go and explore the house a bit, in an attempt to find the kitchen – my stomach really needed some food.

As I was rushing to find a way out of this labyrinth I was "lucky" enough to run into a guy.

He pushed me out of his way and seemed to be quite nervy about the little incident.

'Move out of my way!' he snapped at me.

'Alright...There is no need for you to shout or to push me away like that', I told him, but he ignored me and went on his way. 'A "sorry" would have been a lot easier', I shouted behind him.

He stopped walking but didn't come towards me. I waited for him to say something. Nothing.

'Aaa... what are you doing?'

'I am waiting', he said in a sharp voice.

'What?'

'For you to apologize.'

Although my indignation grew with every second I spent with "Mr. Cranky", this was too much. I burst into laughter and that made him even angrier.

'What's so funny?'

That's when I froze. A shadow flashed across his face. But his face seemed numb. An eerie sensation descended the room. The coldness in the air full of despair, fear and also...

I screamed unable to pursue my thoughts. Everything around me was turning into an icy marble.

As I was trying to pull myself out of this surreal feeling I began waving my arms and feet like a madman resisting his straightjacket. I was uselessly fighting the air around me; that force beyond the tangible. The thought that I was at least trying to do something soothed me. A desperate voice resounded in my ear. Although I could not understand anything it was telling me I continued to hang on to it until finally, with one last scream from me, it all ended.

With my eyes tear-filled I managed to get back to reality. I was still in the hallway and the guy was holding me by the arms. Christine was also there looking very serious.

I shuffled my eyes from one to the other unable to say anything.

'Are you ok?' he asked.

I pulled myself from his arms and gazed into his deep blue eyes. He could hypnotize any girl with that look. I found myself imagining how it would have been to just take a taste of those fleshy lips and grab him by his scruffy brown hair. He was tall, around 1.90 and well-built but not like those who overdo it in the gym. This was the first time anything like this was happening to me and I know it's more than just physical attraction. I saw myself in his eyes and I knew then that I would never be able to live without those eyes; those blue eyes that I seemed to know. Something about this guy seemed familiar. I know it's crazy.

I am going crazy. It cannot be that I see a guy for the first time and think that I could never again be without seeing his deep beautiful eyes. Ok Kate...Come to your senses!

The guy was also scanning me head to toe, waiting for me to say something. He probably thought I was crazy. I nodded and came out of my daydream back to reality.

'Are you well Kate?' Christine asked me.

'Sure...aaa... I'm sorry.'

'This is Eric', Christine said. 'He is also a wizard. He is friends with my father and Meya and is here visiting.'

'Is she a witch?' The guy asked surprised. 'I didn't feel anything coming from her.'

'That's because she has never used her powers. Not intentionally. This is something completely new for her.'

'I'm Kate. Katelyn Lambert', I said and put out my hand.

He remained perplexed and left me hanging.

'Katelyn Lambert? Are you sure?'

'There are many things I am not sure of but I think I know my name', I said, trying to pull a joke.

He put out his hand and, strangely enough, gave me a large smile.

'I am Eric Balfour and you have no idea how happy I am to meet you.'

The next day, at breakfast, I met the rest of Christine's family. Her father Aaron was a tall man, big around his waist and completely grey. He was in his fifties. Maggie, her sister was twenty years old, shorter than me and very beautiful. She had curly dark hair down to her waist. Her green eyes and dimples made her look very adorable despite the fact that she always looked serious.

I didn't feel comfortable. Eric avoided looking at me and chose to ignore me. Since we had been introduced we hadn't talked again. He did say that he was happy to meet me but now he was ignoring me. And I had to refrain myself from looking at him. Now and then, he glanced over at Meya, who was mixing her food with the forks; she appeared to be lost in her thoughts. For a moment I wondered what these people must have been thinking about until I realised that I actually should not bother about that. The only one who was in a good mood was Edward who was teasing Maggie over her body.

-You're trying a new weight loss diet? He looked with fake-hungry eyes at her fruit salad. I didn't know he liked anorexic girls... Ok, I'm done, he said, cowering at her sight.

Before it got even more awkward for me, Christine stormed into the room. I was wondering when she would pop up.

'Good morning, everyone. Yes, I am sorry I'm late. It seems time has finally managed to pull a trick on me too. Maggie is the one who is usually late.'

'You are ten minutes late. I am never late for more than five minutes.'

'Yes, but you do this almost every morning', Aaron said uninterested. 'I have to leave. I have something to take care of. Meya, if you are done, I would like for you to accompany me somewhere.'

'Eric, I'll see you later this evening.'

'Sure', he replied and gave my aunt a smile which she seemed to like although I felt to be a bit forced.

I was wondering what their history was.

'Of course...'Maggie commented after the two had left. 'They never have enough time for us. Not to mention that "somewhere". She never tells us anything, absolutely nothing...'

'Why don't you try to find that out yourselves? I mean...you can always decide to follow them if you want.'

They all turned and looked at me.

'Maybe I should not have said this...'

'But you did say it', Eric replied.

This was the first time when he was talking to me and I felt worse than a teenager because I was unable to find my words. I just looked at him without saying anything.

'I don't think this is a very good idea', Edward said. 'After all, it is none of our business what they are doing. And it should not be your business to know that either. I don't know about you but I for one don't think that mom is keeping things away from me. And if she is doing it, then it is surely for my own sake. I mean...'

Maggie raised her hand in protest.

'Just give it up, won't you? I am really not interested in your relationship with Meya. And if you like to go on without knowing, well then that's your business. So please go on living your colourful life filled with innocent people.' *Then she added as if for herself.* 'Pff... As if there is such a thing...'

'Listen sis, don't you think this was a bit too harsh?'

'It's alright, Edward said. 'This is just how Maggie is...'

She puffed but said nothing. I could not tell if Edward was disturbed by her behaviour or not. He seemed to be his own self as he had been until then.

'Eric, I almost forgot. Is it alright if we move the training for tomorrow at 3.30 pm? I cannot make it today.'

'Sure, I have some business I need to take care of today anyway.'

'Training? What kind of training? Soccer?' I asked in an attempt to make some conversation.

Eric started to laugh and I didn't understand what was so funny about that.

'No, not that. But if you really are curious then you can stop by and watch us. You might be surprised. I don't think you would manage it anyway.'

I didn't understand what he was referring to but I felt that he was challenging me and I wasn't going to back down.

'Sure. I will be there tomorrow at 3.29 pm. I can hardly wait to see you in full action', I told him and winked at him as I was trying to hide the irony in my tone of voice.

Chapter 3:

"Dream or reality?"

I was already in bed dressed in some very short pink pyjama pants and a tight white tank top when someone knocked on my door. I opened it without even thinking to ask who it was and when I saw Eric my first reaction was to run my hand through my scruffy hair. How childish of me... as if he would pay any attention to me.

But he was. He scanned me from head to toe for a few seconds without saying anything.

'I have something for you', he said as he was pulling something out of his pocket. 'Meya wanted me to give you this. This belonged to your mother.'

A tone of questions flooded my mind when I heard about my mom. Why had she given me up for adoption? How did she look? What about my father?

I took the necklace and I sighed. I looked at the crystal locket in the shape of a half-moon. Eric offered to help me put it on. I turned my back at him and jumped out of my skin when I felt his fingers touching me. He brushed my hair aside and locked the necklace. That is when we both remained quiet but you could cut the tension in the air.

'Aaa...Thank you. But why didn't Meya bring it to me herself?'

'She was on her way to see you. Since my room is right next to yours, she gave it to me. Oh, and also...She hopes that your lessons can start next week.'

'Why so late?'

'She is pretty busy. She has many things to do.'

I sighed. Maybe this was just my impression – and a wrong one – but Meya seemed to be avoiding me as much as she could. Or perhaps she was really busy. Aaron always got her doing things.

'That's all. Sleep tight Katelyn.'

'Good night to you, too', I told him as I was trying to force a smile.

I was going to have to wait for at least another week before I would be initiated into the art of magic.

'And stop being sad! P.S.: nice pyjamas', he said and then left.

'I am not sad, I shouted behind him although I knew this was a lie.

I admit that Eric intrigued me. But it would have been superficial of me to stress out about him. So what if he looked incredibly hot? So what if he told me that I have nice pyjamas? He was probably just trying to be nice, just that...And then I let myself go to the world of dreams. A world created by my own feelings starting from the most hidden fears to the most powerful desires.

I woke up facing the half-moon. I pulled up in a seated position and felt the soft sand under my palms. The air was cold and my hair was blowing powerfully in the wind. As I was checking out the place I got frightened.

How did I get so close to the beach? Is this some incredibly stupid joke? No, it could not have been.

And yet I was not in my bed, in my room. I was on the beach. I got up on my feet and stared at the most beautiful sight I had ever seen. The

sense of fear soon vanished and was replaced by a feeling of pleasure. The fear had turned into excitement. This combination of colours, this indescribable mixture where the lightning bolts took on different shapes and gave a fine shine to the veil stretching from one side of the beach to the other, was more than my eyes could stand.

It seemed to surround the entire island. It was striking how it seemed that the mixture of colours touched the sky turning it into a coloured glass city. I felt hypnotised by that surreal beauty. Unable to resist temptation, I came close to it. It was turning instantly from deep yellow to a strong red and had black-golden stripes imprinted on it which seemed to form some kind of a labyrinth. The lightning bolts that were crossing it from above made it come alive.

I was caught in this magical place which attracted me terribly. The only thing I cared about then was the constantly growing desire. All my senses merged into one. Should I get close to it? Should I run my fingers through the veil and feel how the specks of light gently rub my skin? All other things meant nothing compared to this irresistible desire.

It is not as if everything was perfect in this state of reverie. Deep down there was a voice that bugged me. It tried to pull me back into reality begging me to get as far away from this place as possible. As if I was stupid to listen to it. The temptation and the desire were much too strong. I ignored the voice which went on shouting louder and louder, beckoning me not to touch the veil.

One last sound and then I abandoned myself to temptation, to the magic.

When I touched the veil my fingers did not run through. It was like some sort of a barrier. What was it hiding?

The shine of the colours got stronger and stronger until it became too shiny for my eyes. Damn it...I could not pull my hand away from there. The voice inside me had warned me but I was too cowardice to try to fight the desire to touch that veil.

My senses were now fully alerted. I was paralysed with fear. Or was it more than that? It was something beyond my will. It seemed as though there was something or someone who was trying to control me. All of a sudden, tens of white lightning bolts flashed from my palm extending towards the veil and making deep cracks in it. I felt how every bolt was sucking all energy out of me little by little. Although the amount of energy each bolt took from me was minuscule, there were just too many lightning bolts. I wasn't going to be able to bare it for long. They slowly drew all energy out of me and this was as painful as it was frustrating. I could do nothing. I watched where they were heading and that's when they came together as one. I heard a powerful noise after that, like an explosion. I howled and slowly managed to pull my hand away from that shattering veil whose dazzling beauty was just a mask hiding its true nature.

'Monsters with a lovely face – yet there are still monsters nonetheless.'

I continued to scream until I woke up in my bed. Tears were running down my cheeks. I was sweating and shaking. The pain in my palm was still pulsating.

There was someone in the room with me. This person was holding me. A worried voice implored me to calm down.

'And last but not least, there is hatred, revenge', I added.

I got hiccups from all that crying and I could not control the shivering.

'I...I...'

What should I have said? That I am sorry? Would this have made any difference?

The one who was holding me was Christine. Maggie and Eric were also there. His face did not look like someone's who was about to wish me anything good.

'All of this because of a stupid nightmare? Do you have any idea how you scared us? You are not five years old. And next time before you start screaming like a crazy person in the middle of the night please try to remember that you are not at your home. Some of us have important things they need to do the next day. That is to say that they need sleep!!!!'

I startled at the tone of his rough voice. I was such a naive to think that Eric liked me. But he was right. Did it even matter that I felt as though it had all been more than a nightmare? No matter how impossible it must seem to be, the stinging in my hand and my weakened body confirm what I suspected. And this is just the beginning of consequences.

I was pulled away from my thoughts by Maggie who was defending me.

'You don't have to be a jerk about it.' She looked at me and seemed worried. She was also aware of the fact that this had been more than a nightmare. I gave her a meaningful look. She and I had to talk. Urgently!

'I know... and I am sorry. Aaa, I am alright. You can all leave now. And thank you. Christine...'

'Let's talk tomorrow, alright? You have to rest now.'

As if this was something that I could do. How could I wait until the next day without knowing anything? Before I even got to say anything else the door closed behind them.

When I got up from bed and used my hands to support my bodyweight I jumped in pain as I felt the deep stings in my left palm. I quickly went out on the hallway and called for Christine.

'What do you think you are doing?' Eric asked me.

'I have to talk to Meya. Aaa, do you have any idea where her room is?'

'At this hour? Try a normal hour, Lambert.'

From Katelyn he had moved to Lambert. Nice... Eric seemed to like me more and more.

'Didn't anybody tell you that Meya is out tonight? Dad is also leaving tomorrow. I don't know what it is that they have to do, but it is definitely something important. I have no idea how long they will be away but dad told me that they are not coming back until they have solved the matter. Three days, one week, two, a month...' she shrugged his shoulders. 'The longest that dad has been away is one month. Meya however...has been gone for as long as a year. And no, I have no idea where they keep going.'

'I hope it's not going to be longer than a week. Meya was just telling me that we will be starting the lessons. Chris, why didn't you tell me that she's leaving?'

'I'm sorry. I forgot.'

'And you didn't think it would be important enough to try to remember to tell me?'

'I doubt it', Maggie said. 'I mean that Meya is going to come back in a week's time.'

'Chris, we need to talk! Now!' I said in a very serious tone and she began to laugh.

I felt I was going to explode at any moment.

'You are very funny when you are angry. Alright, tell me what you want to know.'

'Yes she is', Eric seconded that.

'You know what? Just forget it. I don't even know why I am here on this mysterious island. I am tired of all the lies and the secrets. I will find out myself!'

'Lambert, why don't you try to calm down? Come one. I'll make you some tea. You and I have some talking to do. And you girls should get back to sleep.'

Although I wanted to refuse him and even if all my senses were telling me to do so, I finally accepted.

'Tea sounds very good. Sleep tight girls and forgive me for having scared you.'

'I'll see you tomorrow', Christine said.

'Sleep tight and take care Kate. Come on sister, let's go!'

Eric proved to be a disaster in the kitchen. It took us some time before we could find the tea bags and the sugar. It was pouring outside and, on top of it, it roared and flashed constantly and that made me unsettled.

'Don't tell me you are afraid of the rain?'

'I am afraid of thunders and lightning bolts.'

'Why?'

'I don't know why. They just make me jump out of my skin.'

'There must be a reason. Why?'

'What?'

47

He came next to me and took the tea cup from my hand. He put a hand on my face and patted my cheek. 'You have beautiful hair. You should let it loose', he said and took off the rubber band that was tied around my hair. 'Don't keep it in a ponytail anymore!'

I was trying to figure out what he was doing. Eric was an experienced wizard. It cannot be that he wanted anything from me or perhaps he just wanted sex. I shook my head puzzled and pushed him away.

'I don't know what it is that you are trying to do but I think I'd better go to bed.'

I got off the chair and as I was passing him by he caught me by the arm.

'What is Meya hiding? She is your aunt. I am sure you know more than you say you do. You are a good actress, no doubt about that.'

'Excuse me?'

I don't know what he wanted but he was definitely delirious.

'Come on...stop playing innocent, you little magic pawn.'

'What are you talking about?'

'I just want to know what Meya is up to and to see your true powers. Although there is a slight possibility, it's still hard to believe that you didn't know about the magical world until now. I have to make sure you're telling the truth and that you don't work for Meya. I have to make sure you are really the Magic Pawn.'

'You are scaring me', I told him and I was getting ready to leave but he grabbed me even harder by the arm.

He then put both his arms on my shoulders and fixated me.

'Look me in the eyes', he said, and when I refused to do that he grabbed my chin and lifted my face towards his.

I wanted to resist him. All my senses were going crazy but I did the stupid thing of looking into his deep blue eyes. I was lost. In that moment I only wanted to please Eric and nothing more.

'And now that we are all calm, tell me everything you know about Meya.'

He patted my cheek and continued to stare me in the eyes. He was wonderful. The most beautiful man I had ever seen and I would have done anything for him. But something was screaming inside me.

"Wake up!"

I shook my head and removed myself from this reverie where all I wanted was to please Eric, and I pushed him away from me.

'What's wrong with you?' I yelled at him.

'This is impossible', he said shocked.

I moved back a few steps until I reached the table.

'Listen. I don't know what you are talking about. I don't know anything about Meya and nothing about magic and this freaks me out. Please leave me alone because you are scaring me. And what scares me the most is that for a brief moment I wanted to do anything for you.

'That's because I used one of my special powers on you. I still don't know how you managed to resist it.'

'Special power? Now you really got me confused.'

'You really don't know anything?'

'Does it seem to you like I would still be here, on an unknown island, in an unknown house, together with strangers, if I knew?'

'Ok, I get the point.'

'So, a special power?'

'Hypnosis; but it comes with a twist. It only works on wizards. I still don't understand how you managed to resist me.'

49

'I cannot believe that you tried to hypnotise me!' I said angrily to him.

'It didn't work anyway, so stop fussing over it.'

'What was that?' I asked as I heard a noise.

I wanted to say something else but he signalled me to be quiet.

'Someone is coming', he whispered. 'Quickly, come this way!'

He had barely finished talking when he jumped out the window at an impressive speed. I went up on the window case and looked down. I stopped.

'There is no way that I am doing that!'

'Come on Lambert! We are on the ground floor.'

'I still don't understand why we have to hide!'

'Hurry up and stop commenting!'

I could hear footsteps coming closer and closer on the hallway. I closed my eyes and jumped right before the door opened. I slipped on the soft mud and fell on my back getting dirt all over me.

'Ouch.'

'You could have kept your eyes open.' He grabbed me by the hand and almost pulled me behind a rose bush.

'It's pricking!'

'That's perfect. We can hear everything from here and they cannot see us. It's too dark.'

'But did we really have to stay behind the...?'

He covered my mouth with his hand before I could finish. Meya was at the window looking sceptical around. She was checking the perimeter. I squatted next to Eric getting as low as I could.

We were both soaking wet and were looking at each other with the same question running through our minds.

Wasn't Meya supposed to be away?

Eric was right. Meya was hiding something. I could not trust her, nor could I trust him. No way.

'And yet...What do you think my aunt is hiding?'

'Just keep quiet! I am trying to hear what they are talking.'

Really? How could he understand any of it? Everything that I could hear were the large rain drops. And how could I concentrate in this situation? I was soaking wet. My left palm still hurt but not as much. I don't want to be the one who complains but it seemed like it was raining heavier and heavier.

'Damn it', I said pissed. 'Just stop already!'

And it stopped. Just a few second after that it stopped raining. What a coincidence, right?

'But...'

'Perfect', Eric said. 'Now shut up and listen!'

Alright...I would leave all questions for later. Now I was going to listen to the mysterious conversation.

'Too late', I heard Meya saying very clearly.

'...will suspect something?' The other voice belonged to a man.

'...in the care...'

There was no way that these few bits of conversation were going to help me...Concentrate Katelyn Lambert!

'...tonight...beginning...the moment we have been waiting.'

'Can you promise me that there will be no consequences?' The man's voice could be heard very clearly.

I tried to hear some more but nothing. Then I saw Meya with her back against the window. She was passionately kissing this mysterious man. Their hands were frantically touching each other as if they were

about to take a bite of one another. Before we could see anything else –
although I definitely would not have looked at more than this – one of
them pulled the drapes.

'Yuck... you mean to say that my aunt has been lying to us only
because of this romance? I can almost laugh thinking that we went
through all of this just to see her...'

'It's Aaron', Eric interrupted me.

To be honest, I didn't care about who my aunt was having an affair
with.

We walked quietly side by side until we got to my door.

'I want to help you', Eric said. 'I want to know more about you. You
intrigue me, mysterious girl.'

I laughed and that made him seem troubled.

'You are kidding, aren't' you? What makes you think that I would
ever accept your help? I don't trust you just like I don't trust Meya.'

'It seems to me that you are not in a position to refuse anyone's help.
I am not saying that you should trust me. That would be stupid from
you. And no, I don't want to help you because of your beautiful legs or
because of the sight of your wet tight tank top. You should get into your
room quickly. I am guessing you feel cold.'

'Good night to you too, Eric.' I closed the door and then I found
myself smiling like a young girl in love.

Slap yourself Kate and snap out of it! I told myself while I was
checking myself out in the mirror. Don't you dare let your hormones
dictate how to run your life! Eric is a mysterious wizard who is much
too good looking and that should keep you away from him.

I was having my best sleep when an incredibly annoying voice
managed to wake me up. I didn't open my eyes hopping that whomever

that person was she would give up. Of course she did not give up. She continued to call my name until I eventually shouted.

'Let me sleep! And turn off those lights!'

'I need you!'

It was five in the morning.

It was Maggie and she seemed very unsettled. She was pale and her red puffy eyes had deep dark circles around them. She looked as if she had been crying all night long. And there was something else. She looked scared. I got up and made some room for her next to me. She was shaking. She didn't protest when I took her into my arms – although normally she would have. In fact, I don't think she even realised it.

'You need to sleep!'

Every time she attempted to shut her eyes she twitched and that made her open them again. It was as if the images in her mind frightened her. At some point she started to cry.

'They'reee. They're dead', she said while she was sobbing.

I already started to hate everything that was happening. She burned with fever and was delirious.

'I am going to get some help.'

She grabbed me by the hand as I was trying to get out of the bed.

'No...It's important.'

'Later', I said. Now it is more important for you to get better.

'But I saw them. Dead. Blood everywhere. You have to believe me. I know you two saw Meya tonight...with my father, I mean Aaron... They are all liars. Don't trust any of them.'

'Try to calm down! Please.'

I ran into Eric's room. I turned on the lights and shouted at him to wake up.

Nothing.

I pushed and pulled him and shouted until he eventually woke up. He shaded his eyes while swearing.

'Eric, I need you!'

As he was waking up, he got out of bed and only then could I see that he was naked from the waist up and had only a pair of shorts. Eric looked good, but almost naked Eric looked even better.

Not now Kate, I admonished myself for the thoughts I was having.

'Look, I am flattered that you broke into my room and that you tell me you need me but you could have woken me up in a nicer fashion.'

'Come on Eric, I am not in the mood for your jokes now. Maggie isn't feeling well. Call someone, a doctor! She is in my room.'

'Why didn't you tell me this in the first place?'

I wanted to answer him but he interrupted me.

'Never mind now', he said and then ran out of the room.

I assumed he was going for the doctor. And as it turned out, he was doing just that. Fortunately there was nothing serious going on with Maggie. The fever was just from an early stage cold that she was developing. After we made sure that she was alright, we went our way and let Maggie rest. Christine was sleeping. Eric insisted that we didn't need to worry her about that.

Chapter 4:

"Looking for answers"

Christine and I were heading towards Edward and Eric's training place. She looked very nice in a short fluffy summer dress with a flower print. I had chosen to wear a pair of jeans, a turquoise polo shirt and my hair in ponytail. Christine was in a very good mood today. Ever since we met that day she had been talking constantly. She was enthusiastic about the nice weather, about her favourite sport – volleyball – and about how she was planning to redecorate her room. In any case she was talking about everything except for what was important. I don't know...MAGIC maybe!!! After all, this is why I was here. To discover myself and learn about what I was capable of doing in a way less known and less normal. I tried to talk to her about the dream I had the night before but she just avoided the topic until she eventually changed it. I was under the impression that she loved magic and that she would like to talk about it. At least that's how it seemed until recently. But now...she behaved as if she was hiding something.

I tried many times to see Maggie but every time there was someone by her room who was telling me that she was asleep. "She needs a lot of rest", the doctor told her. I believe his name was Philip; an old man, short and heavy with grey hair and flap-eared.

'Are we there yet? We have been walking already for – I checked my watch – twenty minutes, and that seems like forever in Chris' company who won't stop talking. '

'No. We will be there shortly.'

Eric and Edward were training in archery. The training consisted of an obstacle race on a field where traps had been set. This was a nice surprise but a bitter one to swallow and it made me think of the past.

I was ten years old when I started this sport; metric rounds archery. Unlike field archery, the metric one takes place on a flat terrain where the archer has to shoot a certain number of arrows. I knew this was a method for mental, moral and spiritual development. It's such a wonderful feeling when you stretch the band of the bow, aim and release. That is the moment when it is just you and your target, nothing more. It is so quiet and then the arrow reaches its target. The joy of seeing that you've managed to hit the target as close as possible to the centre. I will never forget how enthusiastic I was during my first day at archery. First of all they presented to me the equipment and then they told me how I should hold my arms and in what position I should keep my body when I am getting ready to shoot. I was so anxious. When I took the bow for the first time, I knew that this was the thing that I wanted to do for the rest of my life. My dream was to become a professional archer and participate in the Olympics and win as many medals as possible. I had practiced a lot and I was working a lot. I wanted to become a better archer by the day. Mister Garret who was my teacher and who initiated me into the secrets of this less-known sport played a great role in my successes. He always supported me. He trusted me more than I trusted myself. He always said I had a natural talent for this activity. I was like a daughter to him and he was like my second father. I participated in many competitions thanks to him. My biggest win was when I was seventeen years old. But I never really got to enjoy wining the first place in the national championship and the fact that I was going to go the Olympics. Just a month later, the misfortune happened. I quit after that. I swore I would never touch another bow again. It was difficult but I had to quit.

Even now as I see the arrows going straight for their targets and the archers who move on to the next marked spot from where to shoot their target, the feeling of guilt comes back.

'Are you alright Kate?'

'Why wouldn't I be?'

'I don't know why but I have the feeling that you are about to burst into crying. Your face is poker-like but I can feel that you are not alright.'

I started to laugh.

'You are just imagining it.'

'If you say so...'

We went to say hi to the boys. They were sitting on a bench waiting for the juniors to finish their training. Eric looked down beat but seemed to cheer up when he saw me. Edward ran towards Christine and took her by the shoulders.

'I cannot believe what I'm seeing. Tell me Kate, how did you convince her? This is the first time when she's come to see me. She never comes to see me, not even during the competitions and that's really not nice of her. She says she prefers to keep her fingers crossed from back home, or from anywhere else but not from here. She is completely against the idea.'

'It's not that I don't want to. I just cannot. This place has such a strange energy... There are certain feelings that I get from being here.'

'These are the feelings about which you have been talking with mom. This is all in your head.'

'In any case it makes me feel agitated.' She looked at one of the archers and twitched. 'And please just hold your horses. I do not plan on staying here for too long.'

I was the only one who noticed the sudden change in her state of mind. She was no longer the same happy and cheerful Christine from before. One minute of tension and then she could breathe again relaxed. She seemed sad and then smiled. She refused to watch the archers during their training. She was fighting something, but what?

I remained absorbed in my thoughts until a name passed by my ears.

'Why does this have to be my fault? Can't it be the fault of our renowned professor Garret?'

Life was really mocking me. Why is it that everything around me keeps reminding me of the biggest mistake in my life? Although I will never get past this, the feeling of guilt had become bearable as time passed. Now...it felt as if I was going back in time and that hurt. Garret had no business being on the field. But this did not matter. It was my fault. Even if indirectly, he was still dead and it was my fault.

'Are you alright?'

'Why does everybody think there is something wrong with me today? Is there a reason? No...of course not because everything...' *I stopped before I could say anything that I would regret. I was letting off steam on the wrong person when I was the only one who was to be blamed.* 'I am sorry Eric...I am only tired but thank you for asking.'

'You are not at all a good liar Katelyn. We both know that there is more.'

I didn't say anything and that is only because Eric was right.

'Kate! I am going with these two great archers' – he bowed to them – 'to grab their equipment. Are you coming?'

'Sure.' *I said, but then I saw her standing on a bench not far from me and I changed my mind.* 'Actually, why don't I wait for you here?'

'However you want' Eric said. 'Let's go!'

'The hall is not too far from here. We'll be back shortly.' She gave me a quick embrace. 'I really hope you are alright', she whispered.

'I am alright Chris. I really am.'

The reason why I decided to stay behind was a little girl who was about the age that I had when I started archery. Long curly blonde hair and her white skin...for a moment I pictured myself as a child. But the difference was that I was always so happy during the training. No one paid any attention to her and she seemed sad. Everybody minded their own business and there was no trainer in sight.

I went to her.

'Are you alright?'

She turned to me and looked at me with her big green eyes that resembled the emerald. She had tears in her eyes.

'I like it a lot; very much, even if I am only a beginner. Today I found out that my coach got ill. No one knows when she will be back. She was so good to me and did not even ask me for money – she enjoyed teaching me. Mister Garret charges a lot from beginners and my parents cannot afford that. I am sure that he is asking for a lot of money also because he cannot stand children...'

'That's not true', I interrupted her.' Everybody loves children. And who wouldn't love a girl as beautiful as you?'

'But it is true...And now. I am sorry. I don't even know why I told you this. I don't normally talk to strangers. And I have never seen you around before.'

She started to cry and I could not resist taking her into my arms. She didn't budge.

'I'm going to tell you a secret but this has to stay between us, alright?' I took a tissue out of my bag and wiped off her tears. 'I have just one condition. You stop crying.' She agreed. I know I am going to be sorry about this but I just could not sit back and let her be so upset when I knew I could have done something to change that. Everybody needs hope to cling on in order to follow their dreams.

'What if I were your coach? But it is going to be a little different. I am going to help you with all the theoretic information you need to know and you will get all practical aspects from your colleagues when I tell you to do something. I... Let's just say that I am not that good of a practitioner...Which means that you will not get to see me shooting. And there is one more important thing. Except for your parents, no one must know that I will be coaching you. So...'

'I agree', she shouted in happiness and gave me a wide smile. 'I do not know why but you look like a person I can trust. Nobody else here would have done this for me.'

'Now I want to hear some details about you. I need to know what level you are at.'

'My name is Melissa. I am twelve years old.' *She looked younger.* 'This is my second week. I don't really understand much of the theoretical part and...'

'You will do just fine. Don't forget that I am here to help you.'

'Thank you. Aaa, you didn't tell me what your name is.'

'Kate. And now let's get down to business.'

I helped her put the finger protector on her right hand and the forearm protector on her left one. The quiver was far too big for her to put on her back. For a moment I held my breath when I saw the bow so close to me. It was a recurve one.

'First of all, the distance should not be that big if you want to reach your target. After much training you will manage to hit from long distances. You place the arrow with the coloured feather in the direction you want to shoot and you nock it on the bowstring. Lift the bow to a vertical position.' *She did what I told her to do.* 'Now keep your left elbow rotated to the outside so you won't get it hit by the bowstring as you release it. Grip the bowstring with your right hand; just with three fingers with the exception of the thumb and the pinkie' – that's right I encouraged her – 'you pull it and bring your hand to the cheek close to your ear. It is as if you would pat your face. Then you concentrate and shoot. And another secret that I don't think you knew: hold your breath as you are getting ready – breathe in and hold it and breathe out as you release. Got it?'

She was excited but she was also scared. She was afraid that she won't do well.

'Calm down! You don't have to be good at it from the beginning.'

'I am calm', she said but her red cheeks and scared eyes said otherwise. She was overwhelmed. 'Can you...can you repeat that last part you just said?'

'Sure, of course.' But I stopped as I saw Eric and Edward standing behind me. Damn it, I hope they just got here. I had forgotten about them. Christine was on the bench. She waved at me to go to her.

'What are you doing here?' Eric asked.

'What do you mean?'

'He was referring to the field. You should not be here. Not you either little girl', he said to Melissa. 'The juniors' training will end in about five minutes.'

'It's not over yet', Melissa said thus proving she had a though character.

'We feel sorry for you but we have a competition in two days' time.'

'Eric! She is only a child. Do you really have to be so unfriendly all the time?'

'You still didn't tell me what you are doing here.'

'I asked her to hold my arrow quiver.' *What a smart girl. I could not have come up with a better answer myself.* 'It broke...'

'Never mind. She should not be on the field and neither should you' – he looked at Melissa – 'not without a coach. You are a beginner.'

'And now can you just let her shoot in peace?'

'Go ahead.'

'Remember that it is like you would be patting your face. And remember also our little secret.' *Why was Eric paying so much attention to me all of a sudden?* 'The breath...Alright, alright...stop looking at me like that. I'm leaving.'

Melissa finally took the shot. It was not a good shot, not even for a beginner. The arrow did not go very far and landed in a completely different place than she had aimed – by the feet of some huge guy.

Melissa was overwhelmed and started to cry as she left running. I would not have been able to catch up with her. We left only after Edward had promised me that he would try to find out about her. Christine was very agitated and she almost jumped with joy as we were getting further and further away from the archery field. This was a girl who was really afraid of archery and I was not less afraid either.

It was past ten in the evening and I had still not been able to catch any glimpse of Maggie. There was always some muscle man by her door. "You cannot get in.". That was everything they said and no other comments. What could I do in that situation? Start an argument with him? What good will that do? I would not have solved anything.

I had been trying to sleep for two hours and still nothing. I got out of bed and went down the hallway. There was still someone in front of her room and that made me completely mad. When had it got to be so warm in my room? I opened the windows. The lights were still on in Eric's room. I shouted and shouted until he finally heard me and came out on the balcony. He was topless and wore only a pair of training trousers. It took every drop of will I got to stop myself from starring at his pecks and his six-pack.

'We have to talk.'

'I know. You're just in time.'

Now this was something that I definitely did not expect to happen. No comments? Something was surely wrong and I don't know which one of us had realised that.

'I have to see Maggie. What are we going to do with that big guy standing outside her door? We cannot get out without him seeing us.'

'Mysterious girl, this is not a problem. I can get rid of him in a second. It's just not the right time to get on the wrong side of Meya and Aaron. And I would have done it if you had not stepped in.'

'And how does that change things? What could you possibly want from me? Because if there is anything I've learned, it is that no one helps anybody for no reason at all.'

'This is a discussion that I am afraid we will have to leave for later. For now I just need you to help me create a diversion.'

He explained his plan to me but I did not like that last part – the one where I was going to stay in my room while he would leave in hiding. So I was going to change the plan a bit. I changed my clothes, got into bed and then I started to scream. One, two...it took five seconds for that muscle guy to come to my room and turn on the lights.

'Are you alright?'

'It is awful', I told him in trembling voice and then I started to cry.

'Miss, what...ah...' – *you could tell that he is not good at that sort of things* – 'why are you crying? Is everything alright? Can I bring you anything?'

'Turn around!' He looked baffled at me but did as I told him.

I the meantime I got out of bed and put on an overall. No way should he have seen me getting out of bed in my jeans and t-shirt. I pretended to be blowing my nose.

'You can turn now!' *I looked at him with a scared child-like face while I was wiping off my so-called tears with my overall sleeve.* 'I...I had a nightmare that no one would ever like to have.'

This guy who was not older than twenty-five years old, short and very well built refrained from laughing.

'And where are you going now?'

Shall I put on the hysterical girl act or should I go straight to having a nervous breakdown?

'Where am I going?' I yelled at him. 'Do you think I plan on staying in this room after the nightmare I just had? Do you want me to tell you about it?' He was about to answer when I interrupted him. 'No, you don't want to. What do you care? And now move out of my door frame! I cannot stay one more minute in this room. When I think that...never mind.' The guy looked at me without budging. 'Are you deaf?'

'But Miss, you are not well. Shouldn't you...'

I was not going to let him finish any sentence.

'Nothing', I flashed out at him. 'I am going to Edward's room.' *His eyes got bigger and he gave me a look as though I had told him that I am going to sleep with him.* 'He is my cousin, you moron.'

'But what...'

I interrupted him, again. It was becoming funny to play with this guy's nerves.

'He won't dare comment that I'll have him sleeping on the floor. Get lost!' I yelled.

He left immediately as he babbled something inaudible and returned to his watch post. I am sure that he would have gone on his four and started to bark like a dog if that would have made me shut up.

Eric was outside when I finally managed to track him down. He had managed to enter Maggie's room but she was not there and that got us worried. He commented when he saw me and told me to get back to my room, but of course I did not listen to him. I continued to follow him as he went around the house seeming very interested in its walls – he kept touching some spots on the wall. Although I was not too far behind, it took some effort from me to keep up with him. The dim light of his flashlight was not of much help for me nor were the big rose bushes – ouch. I could hear something moving behind me. I turned for a few seconds and when I turned back I saw that Eric was not there. The light was gone and I found myself in the darkness.

I could feel a foul smell in the air. When it filled my nostrils, I realised that it had a slight smell of something dead. I stretched my arms forward and started walking slowly, making sure I was not going to hit something and that I would avoid falling down. I had a history of stumbling and the darkness only amplified the feeling of insecurity; the fear of the unknown.

A fluorescent beam kept moving around the house coming lower and lower until it disappeared – had it gone down into the ground? I pressed my eyes in a blink thinking that it was all in my head but when I opened my eyes the fluorescent beams continued to appear one at a time in the same spot I had seen the first one. It was a deafening silence. I could hear my breath.

Then it became chilly. The clear sky was filled with starts and not a breeze – no way was it going to rain. I got goose bumps from the cold. I wrapped my arms around my chest and I could feel the cold getting deeper and deeper. Then, without being aware of my actions, I started to walk towards those strange beams of light.

Were they fireflies?

It didn't take long before the lights started to get bigger and bigger until they got to take on ghost-like shapes. I felt like I was about to lose my breath as if a strong blizzard had hit me straight in the face. Despite all that my feet continued to move. I wonder if they would have stopped if I had told them to walk. And the more I struggled to stop, the colder I felt my body. This was the third time this was happening which means that I could not have imagined it – first on the boat and after that on the hallway when I met Eric. Captured by fear I could feel my heartbeat getting faster and faster. When I got closer to them I managed to see what they were – it's not as if I could make any sense of this. Through those fluorescent lights mixed in the fog you could see something that vaguely resembled a human face. The body seemed to be human-like but you could barely see anything because of the fluorescent lights that were much too strong and because of the fog around it. It was clear however that they seemed to be moving around something. Two blue areas were more obvious in one of these spots...ghosts? The spots approached me and they looked more and more like human eyes. Although I could not see very well, there was one thing that I was certain of. They inspired a sense of sadness like I had not felt before. It was only a meter away from me. Should I panic or should I start to worry about the fact that I was not panicking? The ghost was trying to show me something. It pointed to the ground underneath it and then it vanished into that spot it had just showed me. One after the other the ghost-like shapes followed it and disappeared together with the cold and the smell from before. I took a big breath in. I could breathe again without having to turn my nose.

And now what, what should I do? And where was Eric? Why had he not seen anything?

'I want answers!' I said out loud as if nature would have understood what I was saying. I was agitated and I started to stomp my feet like a child.

I screamed when I felt the earth shaking under my feet until it disappeared. And just like that, in a fraction of a second, I found myself dropping deeper and deeper into the unknown and in the darkness until I hit on something hard. I cannot approximate the distance. But the fall was definitely painful. I landed on my back and I could feel how I was losing my breath. I hurt everywhere on my body as if I were someone's boxing bag. I had a tingling sensation in my left arm and my feet were in pain. My cheeks burned. I barely managed to get up. I pushed my hair aside and I could feel ... blood.

Don't panic!...don't panic!

I was desperately shouting for Eric hoping he was still outside.

Chapter 5:

"More and more madness"

Eric had almost fallen down and he was now cursing. He turned the flashlight towards me and cursed again when he saw me.

'Do you want to blind me or what? Take that light away from my eyes and do something!'

'Right away', he said and it got dark around me once more.

I could not help myself.

'Are you serious? Without any comments? Really nothing?'

And the last spot of light above us disappeared.

'Eric', I shouted even louder just to get a big fat nothing from him.

I don't really enjoy being alone – and definitely not in the dark in some cave somewhere. And as it always happens when we want time to go by quicker it seems to be passing in slow motion.

One second ... two seconds ... as if captured by the darkness...full of despair...fear...how long until sunrise?

Without moving I waited...and waited...ten minutes...one hour...how long had it been? Damn it, I cannot stand to be in this place anymore.

Ah...and the pain just won't stop. I cannot remember when was the last time I whined so much...and I feel the need to keep whining.

'Someone please help me!' I yelled in despair although I knew it was in vain.

Some people where probably now rolling in their beds sunken deep in their dreams. Some were probably squirming over some nightmare and some were sound asleep enjoying the soft mattress and the fluffy pillows, while others – me – well – were struggling not to fall into despair while longing for a way out of some cave.

In a short while it started to get lighter. I startled when Eric showed up behind me. I was so happy to see him that I could have hugged him.

'I...I thought that...you abandoned me here', I told him in trembling voice while struggling with the tears that were going to give away my true state of mind.

'You though wrong. Can you walk?' He asked and then offered me his hand to help me get up.

'I guess so.'

We moved towards a partially lit area and I felt slightly awkward as we were facing each other. He was checking me out and stopped when he saw my face. He frowned as he was pointing to my forehead.

'That doesn't look very well. We are going to see Doctor Phill right now.' He grabbed my hand and pulled me after him without giving a damn about the fact that I was protesting against it.

'I'm alright', I said again and again. *I took my hand to my forehead.* 'Look, see? It's just a little scratch.' He offered me a tissue. 'Done, it's solved!' He gave me that same look. 'Well...it could have been better but I guess it will just have to do. Wait a minute...you didn't tell me how you got here. And what is this place?'

He stopped in front of a big iron ladder propped against the wall.

'We'll have time for this later', he said vocally.

'And why not now?'

'You go first!' He said calmly and pointed me to the ladder.

I took the flashlight from him and looked around. I stopped and looked at a

hole in the wall from across.

'A tunnel; an underground tunnel. I am curious about what it is hiding', I said and then screamed when a mouse appeared where I was flashing my light. This made Eric laugh.

'It's not funny. Rats scare me.'

'Everything scares you.'

'And where does this ladder take us?' I asked him while ignoring his comment.

'To Aaron's office.' He pulled a key out from his pocket. 'I managed to make a copy a few days ago. I was suspecting for a long time that he was hiding something in there. I found one of his vaults. It was pretty difficult to find out his password - but that's a different story. Inside there were some papers with some combinations. Put together they gave clues pointing to the library in Aaron's office – behind it there was the key to a storage room. Under the hideous purple carpet that he got from Christine was the entrance to this place.'

I wanted to kick myself.

'And if you are so smart to discover all these then why were you hovering around the house?'

'It's only when I saw you here that I realised that something had to be in that storage room.'

He ran his hand through his scruffy hair and sighed. He seemed tired. I was also tired but this did not mean that I was not going to listen to him and then be on our way. I could not wait until next time to find out what this tunnel was hiding.

'This is none of your business anyway.'

'You are free to leave if you want.' *Perhaps it was none of my business but I was not going to admit that.* 'Oh, and I assume that you don't need the flashlight anymore.'

I went into the tunnel at a slow pace but it was difficult for me to walk. My feet hurt and for sure I would end up with some nice bruises. Eric obviously came after me babbling something about how I should have stayed in my room as we had planned.

'You could have told me that you were planning to come back and that it would take you some time', I told him after about five minutes walking. 'I could no longer bear the silence between us.'

'I was back in about ten minutes, if not less.'

'I could swear that it had been at least one hour. In any case, thank you.'

The tunnel seemed to date long back. Every now and then we would see fragments of drawings on the walls, dusty paintings that had been worn out by time. The moon, a cat's head, twisted lines, half of something that looked very much like a very large diamond, a crystal globe, parts of people and many other things.

Not long into our walk we ended up at a split of roads.

I sighed.

'What do we do now, Miss Mysterious?' Eric asked.

'I haven't the slightest idea. Shall we just take our chance? There are four roads. How do we know which one is the correct one?'

'You are joking, aren't you?' He refrained from laughing. 'The right road? What do you expect to find? Come on, let's go back!'

'I don't know', I shrugged my shoulders. 'Perhaps you are right. Let's go...'but I stopped as I felt a chilly airflow. 'Do you feel that?' *He looked at me and didn't understand why I was asking that.* It's coming from here – *I showed him the road on my right hand side. I got that same look from him.* 'Come on. It's like an air conditioning blowing towards us.'

'Are you alright?'

'Do you mean...that you...' – I refrained my words – 'aaa ... you don't feel anything?'

'Are you sure you didn't hurt your head worse than you think?'

Was that possible?

'I have to see something.'

We started walking towards the draft and had the strange sensation that this was going to be the answer to some questions, as well as the chance for me to ask some more. I kept hearing how Eric shouted for me until his voice vanished into an echo. Our only source of light was the flashlight that I now had. I was afraid to be alone but every time I attempted to go back to Eric, there was something that stopped me before my mind could put things in motion.

A fluorescent light flew before my eyes. I knew what was coming next. I could already feel how I was getting goose bumps from the cold air. I should have left but since I was already here, I continued to walk until I could no longer feel my legs. I had to stop for a short while. I leaned on the wall and that's when I heard a sound.

I was scared. I moved away. A part of the wall moved to the side opening up an entry into the unknown. It was a narrow hole through which you could only crawl.

I didn't think about it too much. I thought that this had to be a sign. I grabbed the flashlight tightly to make sure I wasn't going to drop it and I went through slowly. I dropped closer and closer to the ground as I advanced. My back hurt terribly and it was getting harder and harder to breathe.

I clenched my teeth. I had to do whatever was needed.

Not very long after that I could see the light at the end of the tunnel. At first I thought I was only imagining it. My eyes hurt from how tired I was and I probably would have fallen asleep had I closed them even for a few seconds. I heard the echo of some voices but I could not understand what they were saying. As I got closer I realised that someone was having an argument.

At the end of the tunnel there was a big room that was strongly lit. I could tell that I was in a ventilation shaft.

My heart pounded and I was breathing heavily as if I had just ran for six kilometres – not that I could actually run that long. I stayed on the ground with my face down as I was trying to calm down. I did the only thing that I could possibly do at that time. I opened my ears wide and listened.

'There will be more', said a man with a coarse voice.

Then a trembling voice followed.

'But...is five not enough?'

A powerful laughter. Silence and then another voice – this time a woman.

'Don't tell me you are backing down? Because once you have decided to do this you cannot come out of it – not alive. And you know that a few extra inert bodies don't mean a thing to us.' *I flinched when I heard this.* 'We will do anything to meet our goal. Do you understand? That's what I was saying.' *The tone of her voice became relaxed all of a sudden. It was a sign of falsity.* 'Aaron' – *please tell me that this is not who I think it is* – 'dear, you have sent your best people and they still haven't returned although they should have been back by now. I hope they did not fail in releasing the morh. You do understand what this means, don't you?' *Her voice resembled that of someone who was almost crying.* 'I don't even want to think about it. The first part came out perfectly. It could not have been any better. The veil is sending only faint signals that it is weakening – lines, ruptures that are invisible to the human eye. But this is just the beginning. We need the morh that escaped and I still don't understand how he did that.' 'For your sake' – *she yelled again* – 'I hope that he is the injected one. This way we will see if our experiments are working or not. Next! She commanded.'

I was trying to get a better view so I crawled a bit on my elbows until I got to the very end. The place looked like a huge laboratory fitted with the latest technology – all sorts of devices and big screens on which there were drawings, sketches and different calculations. On this island that apparently did not even exist, there was a secret laboratory – go figure – an underground one. Many people were moving around avoiding as much as they could some tall glass tubes covered with a black cloth so that you could not see inside.

Five white cloths were lying on the ground. Given their shape I had a pretty good idea what they were hiding.

I could hear meaningless words being said which resounded in that room. It sounded like an incantation. Three of them stuck into my mind – morh, noctis and blood.

After the incantation was done, one of the bodies covered with the white cloth started to float – I blinked several times hoping I was imagining it. The body kept lifting up into the air and then disappeared leaving a sort of fine dust behind it – or was it fog? – that evaporated immediately. A powerful noise – like a wallop – came out of one of the big tubes that were covered with the black cloth.

Then the crowd applauded.

'Enough', said the female voice from before. *I tried to see where it was coming from but there were too many people.* 'You should applaud when we have a real victory. Now, the next body!'

The white cloths moved aside. The impulse of running away from that crazy place was so strong that I had to bite my lip in order to refrain from screaming. I clenched my teeth hard and it hurt – the result of cruel reality. As I was expecting it, the white cloths were covering dead people, inert bodies covered in blood. The women who had said the incantation leaned down and began moving her fingers on the body of one of the victims leaving silver tracks behind. A man came close to her and he – ah, disgusting!!! – he sucked her bloody finger. The woman let her head fall back and I froze. It was Meya.

'Ah...yes...that's it', she said as she moaned.

I cannot believe this! She moaned! She was completely mad! She babbled something and a shield made out of shady glass formed around her and around the man next to her who was probably Aaron. As if nothing had happened, the rest of the people continued minding their own business. The bodies were taken into another room.

I could not stand to see whatever was coming next. But that is when I felt the cold. The ghost-like shapes appeared before me one at a time in the middle of the room. It seems that I was the only one who could see them and this did not make me feel any better. One of them came close to me. It had the size of a child who did not seem to be more than eight years old. I got to see those sad eyes again; the constant crying, the kind that cannot be comforted. The ghost pointed to Meya and Aaron. I refused. I wanted to leave. I suspected what was going to happen next and I definitely did not want to witness that. But every time I was more and more convinced that I wanted to leave, the cold got to me; it froze me and would not allow me to go back. I didn't stand a chance. In order to be able to leave I had to watch the next scene of a very bad movie; a reality that provokes nothing more than disgust.

Meya was in the same position. She seemed to be in a trance. During this time, Aaron had taken off her blouse and was now working on the pants.

I turned my eyes towards the ghosts.

'I beg you ... I don't want to see this!' Their eyes were just as sad but they could not be convinced. I was either going to freeze to death or to continue watching.

Aaron was sucking her breast and was moving frantically his hands all over her body. He squeezed her butt strongly and then slipped his hand in her panties. Meya moaned and arched her back even more. Aaron grabbed her by the waist and put her down. He kissed her all over her body stopping at the intimate area. When he was done, he took off his clothes and just before he got deep inside her, Meya woke up and moved her lips. Aaron was thrown to the side.

'The pleasure that the partner has to offer; his strong desire to penetrate a witch; the disappointment of not being satisfied; the taste of the blood of the right victim and my own fluids on his tongue.'

Meya began rambling sentences with words that I had never heard before.

'Apesta fioni dare kalku.'

A dark circle formed around her. Hazy lights began spreading through the room until they circled every person there.

77

The black cloths moved aside by themselves and before I could see what was in those glass tubes I lost myself.

I woke up facing Eric and I had a terrible headache. I wanted to ask him where we were, but despite my efforts, I could not. I was so powerless as if someone had drained almost all life out of me. The images flashed before my eyes – we just passed by a marble pole. I blinked strongly a few times and then the mist went away. I was in Eric's arms. His eyes were sparkling and he looked sad. Why was he so sad?

'We'll get to Doctor Phill any minute now. You will be alright. I promise.'

I was struggling to keep my eyes open. Why did he seem even sadder when he looked at me?

'The doctor is...'

'No', I shouted and I felt that my forehead was going to explode in pain, as if every inch of it were struck by arrows. 'The tunnel?'

'This is what you're thinking about now? I should not have let you go there in the first place. But if this will make you feel better, then we'll go back when you get well.'

Every inch of me screamed for me not to go back. This had been real...

'We have...to talk.' I had to fight off the pain that got stronger towards the middle of my forehead.

'Just a bit longer and we'll get there.'

I wanted to get away from here but I could barely feel my arms and legs.

'NO!' *I said with as much determination as I could. Damn this headache, damn everything. I had to say something.* 'Why don't you just feed me to the rats? It's just the same as bringing me here.' *Eric stopped in front of the door and looked at me as if I was delirious.* 'I am not crazy. I am only shocked by what I have just seen and I am tired. I only need to get some rest. I beg you. No one has to know and especially no one close to Meya.' *He raised his hand and he was preparing to knock on the door. I grabbed him by the collar of his t-shirt and I begged him to look at me and to listen to what I have to say.* 'If you do not take me back to my room right this instance then you can just as well consider me dead to you. I am leaving this island the first time I have the chance and I am going to save my ass while you all are going to sink deeper and deeper into the ground. Do you understand? They were dead! And, think about it. He is the one who saw Maggie and now she is a prisoner in her own room. Why aren't we permitted to see her? It's clear that the doctor is in cahoots with that mad Meya and her acolyte Aaron.'

'I know we should not trust them. And now I know that you are not a part of their plans. I am sorry I thought this about you. I will take you to one of the guest rooms – someone is probably still guarding Maggie's room. But you should know that I don't agree with this.'

He sat me carefully on the bed and returned with a first aid kit after five minutes. He first offered me a glass of water and a couple of pills.

'One of these is precisely for your headache and the other one is meant to help you sleep better.'

I took the pills and I thanked him with a weak voice. He smiled at me bitterly and then cleaned my face carefully with a cloth dipped in a colourless liquid that smelled strongly of lavender. He did the same for the scars on my hands. My palms were worse – especially the left one. He looked at my left palm with great interest.

79

'What is it?'

'Your sign is a bit strange ... have you had it like this since you were born?'

'What?'

There was a half-moon tattooed on my left palm. The half-moon was vaguely contoured in silver.

'So it was real, but it was not. The dream...'

He looked at me and seemed more confused than ever. And he had good reasons to feel like that. Even I could not make sense of what I was saying. Everything sounded much too strange.

'I am sleepy', I said. I felt how my eyes were shutting but I was fighting to stay awake. I was afraid that if I closed my eyes then all sorts of shattering images would come to my mind.

'Try to sleep! We'll talk more tomorrow.'

I did as he told me to, but I almost instantly saw bloody spots.

I am afraid, I told him trembling and I grabbed his hand.

That's when I saw myself in front of that veil and I saw a lot of blood and I saw Eric as he was struggling to get past the veil and Meya...she was trying to kill me.

I screamed and I let go of his hand. Eric looked at me shocked. He sat by my bedside and ran his hand through my hair.

'It's you, he said. 'After all this time I finally found you. And now I am sure that it's you. The Magic Pawn...is...is right here...'

'Eric...I...I don't know what you are talking about.'

'You had a vision and you led me there also. You are the wizard who's born every other thousand years. You are so innocent and so new to the world of magic and you have no idea how important your role is.'

'If this is a vision does it mean that those things will happen? I am scared', I told him trembling.

'I am here and as long as I am next to you, nothing bad will happen to you. And now that I found you, we must leave this island. Thanks to Meya I managed to get past the barrier. If she finds out about this, she will take away my access and I will be sent back behind the barrier.'

'I don't want you to leave! I do not know you but I feel safer with you; safer than I have felt with anybody else.'

He covered my cheek with his hand. I did not expect that to have such a calming effect.

I laughed a bit and that made him confused.

'This is the first time when you are calling me Kate...'

Chapter 6:

"Word of the day: panic"

I woke up in my room. My body was numb as if I had slept through the entire day.

'Two days actually', said the big guy who had been guarding outside Maggie's door. Until now at least, because for some stupid reason he had moved his watch post a few doors away.

'Is this a bad joke or what?'

He looked at me with a face resembling a scared puppy.

'I don't understand what you mean.'

I was about to snap. Two days had just flown by. Who knows what had happened; important stuff maybe? No, definitely important. And I have been spending these past two days in bed like a dumb, during the worse time possible.

'What are you doing here?'

He looked at me puzzled.

'I am working?!'

This is clearly not the best day for me.

'Yes, I can see that.' *I wanted to leave but he positioned himself in front of me.* 'Is there a problem or what? Move aside! You've caught me in a bad mood today.'

'I'm sorry but I was told to...'

'I don't care what you were told but I do not need some guy standing outside my door. Go and guard something else! You're obviously wasting your time here.'

'Your aunt Meya' – *I flinched at the sound of her name* – 'she asked me to let her know when you woke up. She wants to talk to you before you can exit the room.'

'Good choice of words. The room! Not the cell!'

I looked at him angrily and signalled him to leave but he would not budge. He was serious about his job. He really wanted to push my nerves to the maximum.

'Do you really not understand that I cannot let you leave the room?'

'Get out of here!' I yelled at him.

'Enough, Kate!' A voice resounded in the hallway.

Meya; she was the one I was actually furious with and not this guy that I had just latched out on.

'I am sorry...'I said to him, realising that he was only doing his job.

When Meya showed up before me I just froze. I simply blocked not knowing what to do. She no longer had that loving and caring aunt expression on her face. She looked down at me as if I were the lowest being in the world when in fact it was the other way around.

When she got closer to me she made this face as if I had a bad smell or something. Seriously? 180 degrees flip in her expression. And this is her real face; that of a truly evil crazy and despicable woman. There was so much I wanted to say to her but I was sure that my voice would have trembled had I attempted to say anything. This woman really frightened me.

'I am not going to hide behind words so I'll get straight to the matter. I know all your moves Katelyn Lambert. Don't think that I do not know where you were two nights ago. I am glad that you assisted my show' – *'Thank you', she said and then bowed* – 'but I also wish you had not found out. Not yet at least. Now this is how it's going to play out. You keep your mouth shut and no one will get hurt. You were not there, do you understand dear? Oh, I almost forgot. You can say goodbye to Eric.'

'What did you do?' I shouted at her.

'My dear Kate, I think it's best if you'll be a good girl, or else...'

'Or else, what?'

'I don't think you want to find that out', she said and left pulling the door behind her.

During the days that followed I had to behave naturally as if nothing had happened. And this was not really an easy thing to do. I had to do something but I did not have the slightest idea how to start and who to trust. My "dear" crazy auntie was up to something and she would not lose the sight of me.

And then there was also Eric. I did not know anything about him and I was going crazy at the thought that Meya had done something to him.

Although I had come here to discover more things and to learn more about myself, I had only managed to become even more confused. Edward and Christine did not seem to want to teach me any spells, or anything. And they did not seem to have the time to do it either. What was the big rush? If you asked Meya, there was no rush. I could not stand the smile she put on when someone else was with us. Breakfast became the worst part of the day. I could not eat with her starring constantly at me. *"You have not been eating lately, Katelyn. Is everything alright sweetie? You look a bit pale."* And I had to answer her smiling: *"Everything is alright auntie, don't you worry!"* After that

I would have to grab a few bites just to please her. How could she imagine that I had any appetite with her next to me and Aaron across the table from me? Mealtime conversations were perfectly normal. Just like a family and a happy one nonetheless.

It seemed I wasn't going to sleep yet another night. This was the fourth night that I was kept awake because of the thought of not having a plan. Time passed by too quickly and I still had no idea what to do. I had no idea when, how and what I should start with. Solitude and insecurity can bring you to the verge of desperation in such a situation. I went out in the middle of the night hoping the cold air would help me clear my mind. I was in the yard in front of the house when I ran into Christine.

'You cannot sleep either?'

She did not reply. She signalled me to join her on the bench. It didn't seem to be one of her best days; or her best nights.

'Are you alright?'

'I don't know.'

We sat together in silence enjoying the silence of the night and the fresh air.

'Any moment now', she said.

'What?'

'No...It's getting closer...' She curled down on the bench and took her hands to her temples. 'I am afraid...I just want it all to be over and that will only happen when I have confronted them.'

'Damn it, Chris. What are you confronting? What is happening to you?'

'The feelings...they are so strong. They are revolted, angry, sad and about to break. And they are all afraid by that thing that caused them so

much suffering; that thing which makes the fog so dense and so dark.' *She looked desperately at me trying to find some support from me.* 'You do know what I am talking about, don't you?'

Seeing her like that I definitely could not tell her that she seemed crazy. But then I looked into her frightened eyes and I saw myself.

First I had to calm her down.

'There are many things that I do not understand but I trust you. Christine, you are a strong girl and you will manage to get out of anything that is happening to you. And hey...I am there for you. And now let's wipe those tears off. Maggie would not stop laughing if she saw your face right this instance. She wouldn't be able to mend the problem even with her professional makeup case.

She forced a smile and wiped off her tears with the sleeve.

'I think I can say the same thing about you too. How long has it been since you've slept?'

'I feel better than I look.'

'Thank you.' *She gave me a hug and I was a bit surprised by that.* 'It's for believing in me, you know? They are here. Let's go and I'll confront my fears and we'll find out what is happening here.'

I did not have the slightest idea what she was talking about but I followed her nonetheless. We went to the orchard in the back of the garden and we stopped not too far from a crowd of people. We hid behind some tree trunks and we listened.

There were about twenty people – men and women. Just one familiar face: Aaron. Christine did not seem surprised to see him.

'Did you really try it?' A woman in her thirties yelled at him. She was short and her hair was scruffy. 'Where are the results?'

'Talk quietly!' Aaron said to her. 'The others should not hear us.'

'But perhaps it is time they knew', a man interfered.

'And what exactly should we tell them?' Another man asked.

Then they went about coming up with ideas for and against it. A whole hullaballoo and nothing concrete about it. The only real aspect about it was that these people were hiding something. They were afraid about something.

'My daughter is dead Aaron, do you understand? And many others like her. And you are telling me that your logic is correct? People have been killed by this thing, whatever it is, for the past two weeks.'

'And what do you suggest? That we tell them? This would only cause even more panic and it will lead to complete chaos. And Georgina, we would not even know what to tell them because we have no idea what is happening.'

'We will recommend a curfew. We will think of a reason for that.'

'But attacks have been happening also during the day lately.'

'Since when?' Aaron asked.

'For the past two days. The most frequent ones are in the forest and around it. This creature has not come close to the town yet. It doesn't seem to like crowds.'

Christine showed up behind me. She looked horrified.

'There is someone else here watching. I can feel it. Her rage is so big that it covers any feelings coming from the others. And she is here for one thing only. 'She stopped for a second before saying the word; revenge.

'Are you sure?' I didn't see anyone else.

'This is a complex hiding spell. Let's go before someone sees us!'

'But perhaps...'

'I've heard enough, Kate.'

'Just a while longer.'

'No', she said and grabbed me by the arm.

'Ouch.' I pulled myself away from her. 'I am coming. You don't have to be like that. You are as cold as ice.'

'Well...try feeling that with your whole body. The feeling of revenge can be really painful.'

'Chris, now I am completely baffled.'

'We don't have time for stories now but I have recently found out that I can feel people's feelings. I know it's strange. All things aside, I will talk to Edward to stop training for some time. I don't care about that stupid competition. I don't want to know him out there in the forest.'

'You're not going to tell him the truth, are you?'

'And what is the truth?'

Oh no...Melissa. How will I be able to explain to her why I won't be able to coach her anymore? I wonder if she will listen to me if I tell her to take a break from training. The only useful thing I had been doing since Eric disappeared was to coach Melissa. Her enthusiasm and her laughter made me forget about my problems. She did have a secret talent. She was perseverant, willing to learn and full of dreams and had good chances of becoming a great archer.

And just like that, the night walk that was going to help me clear my mind, had turned into a situation that made me have even more questions. How ironic.

'It just is...too much...'

'Edward. I am going to talk to him now. Meanwhile you could use some sleep. And Kate...Stop lying to yourself! You look better than you feel.'

I didn't contradict her. I don't know how I looked but the truth is that I wasn't feeling well.

'Take care!'

'You too, Kate.'

I didn't manage to get much sleep. When morning came I could barely stand to be in bed. I got to the archery field an hour before and I was surprised to see that Melissa was already there. She smiled when she saw me.

'What do you think you're doing here little girl?' I snapped at her. 'Do you always come here an hour before me? And why are you by yourself? Is there really no one with some sanity around here?' God, I was the same when I was twelve years old. 'Did you expect me to be proud of you?'

I felt my anger getting bigger and bigger...I don't even want to think about what would have happened if ...if she would have ran into...whatever that creature was. I was angry and Melissa did not deserve this. I wish there were a different way but there is none.

'Starting from today all training is stopped. And I don't want to catch you here by yourself again. Promise me!'

She looked at me confused, barely managing not to cry.

'But ... I don't understand.'

'At least for some time. And no...I do not know for how long. You had better promised me because if you plan on continuing then I will talk to your parents and I will make sure they never let you do this again.'

I was angry at myself for this ugly attitude and because I had to be so harsh to her but I had no alternative. I could not possibly tell her to keep away from this place because there is a creature that's killing people.

'They have never forbid me to...'

'But they will as soon as I have told them about...Ah, never mind. You cannot possibly understand. To put it simply, you either stop coming here for now or your dream of becoming a great archer is gone.'

I hated myself for what I had said as soon as I stopped talking.

She clenched her fists and gave me a mean look. I knew what was coming next. Every child rebels when he's asked to do something he doesn't want. She was to tell me everything that upsets her, feelings that she really did not have, but she would eventually accept the situation.

But it wasn't like that at all.

She looked at me for a few seconds and then ran. I shouted after her but she did not reply. She didn't look back. She wanted to be by herself, to cry, to blow off steam. This has to wait for later. Now I had to make sure she got home safe and so, without further thinking it, I ran after her.

I found her soon after in the forest, leaning on a tree. She sat with her feet to her chest and was crying heavily. I was the only one to be blamed. I sat next to her but she did not pay attention to me.

'I'm sorry, it's just that...Everything is going to be alright, I promise. I didn't want things to go like this. I just went insane thinking that something might happen to you.' I took her into my arms and we stayed like that until she calmed down.

'But nothing is going to happen to me. Why should it?'

'No! I will make sure of that. Come on, I will take you home.' *Fortunately she did not fight me on that.* 'But first let's go and get your equipment.'

'Alright.'

I was going to make up to her. Melissa deserved it. And again I felt how something broke inside of me. She was disappointed and afraid that she would not be able to pursue her dream. I was the same after the accident although I already had some successes that got me closer to my dream; but at what cost? Someone died because of me.

'What are they doing here?'

Edward was training with some guy I did not know. Didn't Christine say that she would make sure that he cancelled his training?

I felt something was wrong.

No, everything is alright. Look around you! There is nothing wrong. But this feeling kept pressing me. I am scared. Why am I scared? Calm down Kate! You are just being paranoid.

Edward waved at me as he was coming towards us with this guy I didn't know.

'Meli, what are you doing here, little girl?'

'When will you stop calling me that?'

He took her up in his arms and gave her a spin.

'Not any time soon.'

Melissa acted miffed but then smiled at him. They seemed to be pretty close.

'I'm Ress.'

'Katelyn. Nice to meet you!'

He was tall, about 1.8 metres and so thin. He had a nice face, big black eyes and a wide smile.

They started to tease each other. It seems Ress was Melissa's brother's best friend.

'Let's go!' I told her.

'But I want to stay. Ress will take me home, won't you?'

She put on her angel face, smiling and flashing her eyelids. Sometimes I wish I was a child again and be able to quickly push aside all negative feelings and all unpleasant happenings.

'I thought I told you something. Let's go now before I lose my patience. You two should do the same.'

'No, we shouldn't', Edward said. 'What has gotten into you?'

Oh no. That feeling of panic came over me again.

'Damn it. What's so hard to understand?' I snapped at both of them.

'What's wrong with her?', Ress asked.

'It's not safe for us to be here.'

I grabbed Melissa's equipment and virtually pulled her away from them and we left. I could hear them babbling behind us when this smell got into my nostrils. Melissa could feel it also and she looked at me puzzled. It resembled the smell coming from something dead, by a rotting body. It was so intense that we had to refrain from vomiting. A noise came from the forest and it became louder and louder. It was a combination of sounds and human screaming. Was this the creature that everybody was talking about? No, this could not happen now, not now. Edward and Ress came behind us. With their bows ready they looked around with precaution. After less than a minute the noise stopped although the smell lingered for a while. Melissa asked the big question.

'What was that...? Yuck... and that smell...'

'I have no idea', Edward said. 'Ress?'

'I don't know but this cannot be good. And I am not referring to this awful smell.'

Then they looked at me waiting for an answer.

'Aaa, let's get away from here!'

'I don't think it's anything serious. Perhaps it is an animal?' Ress asked. *I gave him a look.* 'Alright, maybe it is not an animal. Wait for us to get changed and we'll go.'

'You are joking, aren't you? I am not going to stay here another minute more. I don't know about you guys but I made a promise to someone that I will get her home safe. I don't plan on waiting for that creature while you two get changed. No, no...no way!'

Edward looked at me amused.

'Creature? Don't you think you are overreacting a bit?'

'Shut up both of you', Ress said revolted. 'Didn't you notice anything? It's too quiet.'

He was right. It was as if everything had gone to sleep all of a sudden. I could even hear myself breathing. That didn't last long. I heard Melissa scream as if to announce the chaos that was about to happen. Before I could realise what was happening I felt a strong pressure on my shoulders and then I was thrown to the ground.

Chapter 7:

"Run and don't look back"

Everything had happened so fast that I did not have time to realise what or who had thrown me to the ground. I got up and I stood in front of Melissa to shelter her. She was crying.

The moment when I saw this creature holding Ress down, I froze. It stood above him with its mouth wide open and its teeth coming out filling him with a black slimy liquid. This creature looked worse than everything I had ever seen in my nightmares – and I have had many. The feeling of fear that it provoked me was simply paralysing. It was much taller than me, and definitely strong; Very strong. Its body was almost human-like. Head, hands, body and feet, all purple. Its presence gave you the shivers. It was a body so rotten. A living-dead with its wings coming out from its back like those of a moth. They were like membranes covered in this dead transparent skin through which you could see dozens of red stripes. Its long fingers were so skinny that you could see the bones and they ended in claws instead of nails. It was a monster; a failed experiment of nature. A very agile one which seemed to hold not a human being but a puppet – that's how light Ress was for it.

Edward recovered from the state of shock. He realised that his friend's life was hanging by a thread.

This creature was getting ready to have a taste of Ress and it would have done so if Edward had not shot an arrow at it hitting one of its wings.

A few seconds of waiting followed next. For a brief moment the monster was off beam but as it realised what had happened it pulled out the arrow in no time.

'Take Melissa and run!' Edward shouted at me.

Some vines appeared around the creature all of a sudden, and wrapped themselves tightly around its feet, holding it in place. Edward was using his affinity on earth.

'Run!' He yelled at me seeing that I was not reacting.

I took Melissa by the hand and we started to run without looking back. Melissa was losing her breath and could barely keep up. We didn't have time to go back to town to get some help. It would have been too late. I had to go back for Edward and try my best to help him. Although I had no idea how to do it, I hoped that the adrenaline would make my magic surface. I could not just sit and do nothing while my cousin was fighting that creature. Damn it, Katelyn, think!

'The locker room; that's where you should be safe.'

Melissa tried to protest against me locking her in there. I promised her everything was going to be alright but I had serious doubts about that.

As I had expected it, when I got there it was too late to do anything for Ress. His body lay in a pool of blood and the creature stood above him.

What did I think I was going to do?

'What are you doing here?' Edward shouted at me as he was trying to hurt the creature.

'There's no point, we have to leave.'

'I'm not leaving my friend here', he said with tears in his eyes. 'I have to find its weak spot.'

'If there even is one.'

I got in front of him and stopped him before his next attack.

'There's no point, do you understand? He's dead!'

Edward pushed me aside and took the shot. To my surprise he hit it in the head. I was expecting for the arrow to come out through the back but it did not. Instead, the creature was howling. It stood above Ress and then it was instantly next to Edward. It took the bow from him and broke it, then threw Edward next to Ress. After that, it came and faced me for a few seconds. I felt my soul cramming inside of me and how I got smaller and smaller before that terrifying face and that foul smell. Its big eyes were red as blood and had cracks all around them. Its ears were pointy and sharp. My heart pounded. I was shaking but I did not know if it was so because of the fear or because of the cold. I was going to die. The thought that everything was coming to an end so sudden was horrible as was the thought that everything I had fought for my entire life was for nothing. Nothing in my life mattered anymore.

Was anyone going to cry for me? Did I matter to anyone? Oh please God, promise me that Melissa will be alright. Hopeless, I closed my eyes and waited. Was it going to take long? Is death painful? Or is it a release from everything that you've struggled for in life? Is it a way into a new life, one that pertains entirely to the soul?

But that did not happen. I felt cold air around me, and then a strong wind blow took the creature up into the air and threw it away from me. Then the vines appeared again and began wrapping themselves around it at an incredible speed.

'Thanks, Edward', I said to him.

'I thought I told you to run! I cannot keep it away for too long and my spells don't really work against it.'

'How can I help you?'

'You can help by taking shelter!'

'And what will you do?'

'I will manage.'

'I cannot leave you alone with that thing!' I said to him and then made a face as I heard it howling.

And just when I thought nothing else could go worse, it came.

Melissa. She was running towards Ress.

'Are you insane?' I yelled at her. 'Where do you think you are going?'

'Ress...'

'He is dead. And your silly childish behaviour won't bring him back to life.'

'No! He cannot be dead.'

'Stop, Melissa! Don't take another step'

'Damn it Melissa. Do you want to get yourself killed? Why didn't you stay in the locker room?'

'He is not dead', she said.

'He is dead!' I shouted at her.

'Ress', said Melissa. 'He is not dead. See?'

His still body was lying on the ground. No movement.

'He is calling for me', said Melissa crying. 'He wants me to go to him.'

'Stop, Melissa! Don't take another step' I yelled at her seeing that she was heading towards the creature that would soon escape from under Edwards' vines.

But it was too late. I did not manage to stop her and it all happened so quickly. I only got to see the tracks left by a shadow. One moment, the creature was down on the ground, and the next one, it lifted Melissa up. I heard Edward saying some words I did not understand. It was most probably a spell. I saw a red light coming out of his palms and then two spirals headed towards the creature, making it howl. But it would not move. It did not let go of Melissa.

I was desperate and so I did the only thing that struck my mind. It was so difficult to perceive this thought that it almost seemed as if it was not me thinking it. I ran to the quiver, took out an arrow, and poked my finger with it hoping that the smell of blood would entice the creature.

Edward came next to me. He said something but I could not pay attention to him. The creature went stone-like again as it stood above Melissa who was now on the ground. It took more blood to entice it. But now the problem was Edward. Although I tried to fight him off he still managed to grab the arrow from my hand and throw it away. I tried to run towards it but he grabbed me by both arms and held me back. I shook my hands and feet like a desperate person until my knee went straight for his crotch. He cursed. Two seconds. That's all the time I needed. I pulled myself away from his grab and I ran towards the creature leaving him behind.

'Stop!' He kept shouting behind me. 'What do you think you are doing?'

To be honest, I had no idea what I was doing but something inside me told me that this would help Melissa. Perhaps it was just false hope but I kept on holding to the thought that I was not going to be disappointed with my decision. Not this time. I grabbed the tip of the arrow and pressed it on my right arm. I bit my lip until I could feel blood in my mouth.

The creature twitched and made the strangest sound that resembled a pitched scream.

And then it happened. It let Melissa go. It stumbled and seemed perplexed. You could see both fear and pleasure on its face as if my blood had given it a state of frenzy.

'Come on! Let's get Melissa and get out of here!'

'No', I said.

For a moment Edward gave me a flabbergasted look and then yelled at me furiously.

'Why don't you stop playing the hero for a moment and listen to me at least once!'

'But you don't understand!' I yelled at him. 'The creature will come after me. My blood has given it this state. And damn it. Do not ask me why and how I knew how to do this.'

'I don't care', he yelled.

'And Ress? 'Melissa asked as she came next to us.

'It's too late for him', Edward said. 'We are leaving now!'

'No', I yelled. That's when I felt something stinging in my right cheek. Edward's slap got me back to reality. I looked at him and he also seemed shocked by his gesture. But desperate situations demand desperate measures.

What was I trying to be: a hero? There is no such thing. My arm hurt terribly.

'Run, Kate! The creature will come after you shortly. The blood.' I will try to hold it in place for as long as I can, but you have to run! Melissa, you stay next to me. As soon as this monster comes out of this state of frenzy, it will go after Kate.

I did as Edward told me and, without realising it, I began running towards the opposite side of the town.

'Run and don't look back!', I heard a voice that sounded so familiar.

I realised that that voice did not belong to either of the two I was with. Could it only have been in my imagination?

'Go into the forest and go east! There is a shortcut to the barrier'

A shortcut to the barrier? Why would I want to go to a dead end? But that's not what's most important. Who was talking? I could not see anyone.

I kept running until I felt I could not run anymore and not because my feet couldn't. My arm hurt and blood kept flowing.

I was gasping for air. I took off my t-shirt and wrapped it around my arm tightly to stop the bleeding.

The creature was surely after me. I had managed to get it away from Melissa. And now what? What was I supposed to do? I didn't have the slightest idea. It was as if someone else had taken control over me and dictated my every move. A power I could not understand and could not see but I felt deep inside of me as it was trying to take control over me. All of this was probably the result of fear and despair. I was probably hunting the wrong hare, a product of my imagination. But what other alternative did I have? No other idea came to my mind. I was aware that the creature was going to eventually catch up with me. How much time did I have? It did not matter. I had to take advantage of every second. Time had never been so precious for me before. When your own life is at stake you move rapidly and you feel no pain and no tiredness. I was hanging to the thought of survival and adrenaline rushed through my veins.

The forest was now behind me. I stopped when the voice inside my mind told me to. No life form lived on this part of the island and it was truly frightening. It was a rocky desert. What should I do now?

"Wait!"

Clearly.

I was going crazy.

What could I wait for? To wait for that creature to come after me? Because there was nothing else in sight. There was no escape if I continued to walk forward.

And then it happened.

That incredibly beautiful coloured veil appeared in this waste land. It was just like in my dream only this time it was for real. The irony of life...we keep fighting for our dreams to come true and then when that happens, with or without us wanting it, we wish to come back to that state of sleep.

"Keep walking!"

I did not understand anything of what was happening. Right now everything was too much for me to understand.

When had I started to cry?

"Go through the veil!"

This thought took me to the way out of this crazy place where I should never have come.

The veil was just a few metres away from me and just as I thought that my escape would become a reality, those few metres turned into hundreds of kilometres. I felt the smell and then a strong blow on my back. I felt the hard sharp claws of the creature poking my back. Damn it. That pain. It hurt so badly. It was that kind of pain that makes anyone go crazy.

The pain went through all my body as if the creatures' claws had been poisonous. I was unable to move my lips to at least scream because of that pain. I was paralysed.

The only thing that came to my mind was that veil that was so close to me. It was just a few steps away from me; a few steps that I could not take. The creature was on top of me. Its mouth was wide open and I could see the disgusting saliva and then I felt it dripping down on my face and hair.

I had to channel my energy on the most important thing: my life. All my thoughts had come together as one: I have to survive. I am young and I have a long road ahead. This cannot be my destiny. If now I know that I am a witch, why should I depart from this world before I can find out more about what this means? Why did I have to find out that I can do magic if I won't have the opportunity to do it? And I did not deserve to end up being this creature's meal.

My head was spinning and my sight became blurred.

This was going to be the end of me after all.

"Come on Lambert! Hang on just a while longer!"

I flinched when I heard my family name because I knew that voice.

I looked towards the veil. It had now lost a bit of the intensity of its colours and that's when I saw Eric.

Eric was alive, I kept saying to myself. I recovered hope although my life was hanging by a thread.

Eric was alive and blue flames came out from his hands. He flashed these flames towards the veil but the barrier did not allow him to come to me. Meya had taken away his access to the island.

My back burned and I felt how life was slowly but surely leaving me. Everything around me began to spin and then it all turned into mist. I closed my eyes and abandoned myself to darkness.

It did not happen. Although I had lost all my strength I continued to be conscious. My back had gone so numb that I could no longer feel it. The creature was still on top of me and seemed to be in a trance.

The only thing I could feel was a maddening pain, so strong and burning that it made you wish you were dead. I preferred death at this point but my conscience kept me alive and a prisoner to this painful world. I eventually managed to scream. I was screaming hopeful that someone might hear my desperate cry. I knew no one was going to come. This waste land accommodated only this creature and me.

I finally felt I was going to faint and that the pain was going away. That is when the creature got off from me as it made deafening sounds. It stopped and burst into flames. The smell and the rotten fried flesh was the only thing left of it.

I could breathe in peace realising for the first time ever the importance of life, that feeling that comes with the joy of living.

We have to learn how to enjoy everything life gives us; to see the beauty even in small and seemingly unimportant things.

Now I know that I have a long way ahead of me and that I have to fulfil my destiny. I will find out what my destiny is along the way. For now, however, I had to enjoy the luxury of being alive.

With my last strength I pulled myself all the way to the barrier. When I touched it, I could feel a veil of energy flooding my entire body. It was different from the dream. The veil, this immense curtain was now working with me and not against me. Then, all of a sudden, it disappeared. I could now see the beach, the sea, and also Eric, who caught me just before I was about to fall.

'I...I thought that Meya had hurt you.'

He did not reply. He looked at me with this shocked expression on his face. It was true that this was not one of my best appearances. I was dirty, covered in blood, bruises and scratches, with my hair all over the place and only in my bra. But did any of it really matter? I smiled from deep down inside of me and I felt happier than ever. That confused him even more.

'I am alive', I murmured.

It was difficult for me to talk. I had to make an effort to do it. I coughed and spit blood. The nausea came in waves. I swallowed and tried to breathe between the flashes of pain and nausea.

A lit narrow tunnel lay before me. The darkness was swallowing the light and I could not do anything.

'I thought I had lost you', he said with tears in his eyes.

Eric was crying. Eric was crying for me. Why? There were so many things I did not know about him. But even if we had just met, it felt as if I had known him my entire life. A part of me longed for him, while the other part was scared of the connection I felt we had. I know it was the same for him.

'You were so close to me, you were hurt and...I cannot even say the word out loud...and I could not do anything to help you. The thought that I could be so helpless is...'

-What do you think you are doing?' A woman yelled.

Then I heard my name being called by numerous voices. Someone was crying, another one was yelling and some others were fighting over something, revolted and worried. There were steps approaching us and stopped in front of the barrier, except for some.

'Meya', I said and my voice was trembling. 'Don't you dare let her take me away! I'll never forgive you if you do that.'

'I am here for you and I am not leaving anywhere without you.' Then the last beam of light vanished.

I woke up in a hospital room feeling as though I had just woken up from a nightmare with the exception of the fact that my body hurt. I had a cannula on my left wrist.

A nurse was in the room with me and she was reading a book.

'What are you reading?' I asked.

'You are alright', she said and then stopped reading.

'How do you feel? Do you feel any pain?'

I did not reply. I did not feel well at all. I did not know how I possibly could have described the past events in my life.

'You have been very weak and dehydrated. I've given you a glucose venous solution. I am going to let your aunt know that you are alright.'

I froze just hearing her name. I was so close to dying and I could only think about Eric's betrayal. This is what hurt me the most. I don't know why it did. I had just met the guy and my soul longed for him. He left me alone with crazy Meya after he had promised that he would never go anywhere without me.

The nurse left the room immediately and short after Christine showed up.

'What's with the worried face?'

Without any answer she rushed to me, took out the cannula and threw some clothes on my bed.

'Put these on and let's go! Maggie is waiting for us in the library.'

Chapter 8:

"Trapped"

'I have been doing some research lately and this is what I came up with.'

She showed us a book the size of an encyclopaedia. The cover read: "Mythical creatures".

'I have to check something out. I will be back soon', Christine said and then left running.

'Wait, it's not time yet!' Maggie shouted after her, but it was too late.

She went through the book and stopped at the chapter entitled "The morhs, our ancestral terror".

'I wanted to show this to her before she left.'

It was a black and white picture, a bit worn out by time but which portrayed them very clearly. I shook just thinking about my encounter with that creature. Even now, I could still feel its claws on my back and that terrible breath.

'Do you see this hideous thing in the picture? I still cannot believe that such an aberration of nature exists but all evidence until now has proven the contrary. The way they looked when they were found, the autopsies: don't ask me how Chris managed to get hold of those. Their bodies had been completely drained of blood. If you thought vampires did not exist, well...I cannot think of any other explanation. Not to mention that the wounds on their bodies match perfectly the way that morhs act. The cuts they make with their claws full of bacteria. I mean...It has to be that or vampires. I don't know why exactly but I tend to think it was the morhs. Although there were instances of attacks happening during the day and that goes against any theory. These creatures are animals of the night and the sun is supposed to harm them. Or at least this is what this book is saying.' *Maggie sighed.* 'It cannot be vampires. I mean, if I were to believe in the existence of morhs, why would I not believe that vampires exist also? Oh, my head will explode. I could not find much about them but I have read the information at least three times. Morhs, their name comes from the living-dead. Ironic, isn't it?'

'Yes', I whispered.

'They were once human', she said, 'but they sold their souls to the Devil and they became monstrosities, animals of evil. They ooze the smell of death. They feed on blood and on the chaos of their prey. They like to suck all life out of any living being. You cannot really get away alive from an encounter with a morh. If sucking all your blood won't kill you, then its bite will. That way, it will infect you with a poison so strong and complex that there is no cure for it. Bacteria are so deceiving. At first, they give you the impression that you've managed to make it out alive, but they stay inside and hurt you until they've drawn all the energy out of you. This creates a connection between the morhs and the victim, and so they will be able to track them down later on. We have to find out how they can be defeated, and this book doesn't give any information about that. Perhaps I should just keep looking.'

She looked around her and sighed.

'There are too many books and we don't have much time. And what are you doing? Help me! I didn't bring you here for nothing.'

I could hear her talking but I could not grasp what she was saying. I heard my name over and over but I was unable to answer her. I sat in the same position with the book about morhs in my hand, starring at the picture portraying them. Maggie came next to me, took me by the shoulders and gave me a good shake. From being angry she now sounded worried. I was not planning to do that, but somehow I pushed her hard. The push got her off balance, she tripped on the books that were lying on the floor and she landed on her ass. I wanted to run and find a bathroom but I did not make it in time. I stopped and vomited. Maggie wanted to come next to me but I waved at her to stay put. She did not have to see this.

'Oh, no...trouble.'

'What now?' I asked disgusted by the bitter taste in my mouth.

'Meya. She is on her way here. And she's not coming alone.'

'Let's go and hide!' I took her by the arm but she did not move an inch.

'Too late. She is right behind that door. There is a guy with her that I do not know. We have nowhere to hide and nowhere to run. The only way out of here takes us straight to Meya.' *I looked at her surprised.* 'You and Chris are not the only ones with magic tricks up your sleeves. I have got some of my own.'

Meya entered the room and she was with...I held my breath...a morh. She had given that guy she was with to the morh to eat. I turned my back on them. This was not something that I wanted to see. I took Maggie by the hand and I told her to shut her eyes closed.

'It's all going to be alright', I told her before the room filled with smoke.

Maggie fainted and then I also blacked out.

I woke up surrounded by dark clouds and a terrible back ache. It did not take me long to snap out of it. I was lying on a tall rock with my wrists and ankles cuffed tightly with some metal rings tied to a chain that was fastened in the ground. I was in the middle of a circle marked with a thick red line – I hope it is not blood. There were lit candles along the circle. The dry ground was filled with skulls. This "beautiful" picture could not be complete without Meya, of course. She stood outside the circle. Aaron was next to her and so was the scary morh.

PANIC!!!!

What could I do? How did I get myself in this situation? I felt my heart pounding and my stomach clenching. I tried to get up, to rip the ties apart but those chains were extremely well fastened to the rock. The only thing I got out of it was probably some nasty bruises. My wrists and ankles hurt. Those stupid metal rings were tight.

'Hey, auntie! It's not as if I'm complaining about this treatment but do you think you could have tied these bracelets a bit looser?'

I lifted my arms as much as I could – the stupid chains weren't very long – and I showed her the rings. Of course this was a stupid question; a completely stupid thing for me to do. I was so stupid to try and act brave when I was in fact shaking unstoppably. How many times had I used the word stupid?

'Oh, you are awake', she said to me in an annoyingly calm tone.

Panic...her voice made me even more panicked.

'Well...let the show begin', I said softly and shacking.

'Your enthusiasm pleases me', said Meya while the creature was walking around the circle.

I thought it was going to enter the circle. With every attempt I could feel my soul getting smaller and smaller; so small that it could probably have been easily eaten up by a tiny mouse. But every attempt it made failed. This invisible force that was protecting the circle pushed it away. Should I have felt safe? No...we are talking about Meya after all, and that pretty head of hers was definitely "cooking" something.

I did not have the slightest idea what was going to happen. I suspected it wasn't going to be good – not for me at least. I had failed but I thought that I should at least know what was going to happen to me. My only hope was that at the end of all of this I would still be alive.

You know that expression: "Curiosity killed the cat"?

'Oh auntie, you had better not leave any scars, not on my pretty face. And what is all this?' I asked.

'I am doing you a service.'

'Great – I can hardly wait to see what your sick mind can come up with.'

Aaron was about to say something to me, probably something nice, but he stopped when he saw that Meya was laughing.

'What' so funny? Don't laugh without me!' I told them.

'My niece is very funny, isn't she, Aaron?'

Her puppy nodded in agreement and looked at me.

'Are you going to tell me what the deal is with this morh and what I am doing here? And I'd like an answer today because the last time I checked my schedule you weren't in it. So I don't have much time to spend with you, auntie dear.'

I felt like a current going through my body, deep stingy tingling sensations.

'I'm glad you enjoyed that.'

'Is that the best you've got?'

This time I screamed. I could feel my entire body electrocuted. I saw it. I saw the blue forms entering my body. I screamed and I struggled on that rock until someone said stop. That was Aaron.

Meya gave him a look and I think he almost shrunk under her sight.

'Don't forget why we are here', he said.

'Come one. I was only playing a bit.'

'You were playing? How can someone's pain give you satisfaction?' I asked her in a hoarse voice.

For a brief moment I thought that Meya was going to do the spell again but she abstained.

'Now look! You are here because I want to help you get rid of your magic powers.'

'Help me? And who told you that I wanted to get rid of my powers; powers I haven't really been using because someone did not stick to their promise? And I am guessing that the magic lessons are out of the question.'

'Can you really tell me that you don't want to lead a normal life? If you get rid of the powers you will be able to enjoy your life freely: boys, friends, going out, clothes; without being afraid that you might hurt your boyfriend if you get too close.'

I wondered if she was trying to fool me.

'I'm sorry for you but I am really not interested. You see...having a normal girl life is not what I plan. I was not born normal. Why should I be normal now? In fact, I actually like knowing that nature can go crazy around me without me wanting it.'

And then I saw it. I stopped any further stupid comments. Of course I wanted a normal life but I was not going to have Meya know that. It could barely be seen, but the barrier from my dream and from my encounter with the morh was just a few metres away from me. It looked different. It did not entice me. It did not have that attractive combination of shiny colours. There was no strange shape drawn on it. It looked like a dense fog cause by a searing heat, except for the fact that it cannot have been more than 25 degrees Celsius outside.

And then I saw him. On the other side of the barrier there was Eric struggling to go through it. Meya and Aaron didn't seem to be aware of his presence. That was a good thing.

'So, are you going to keep me here the entire day? You know, I have other plans too. And no, I don't plan on giving up my powers to you. And I am guessing that they are good ones since you want them so badly. Oh...too bad I don't know how to use them. Although most of the times they act by themselves on my behalf. You know...like a protective shield that activates by itself when it senses danger.'

'It doesn't matter', Meya said. 'The circle is protected by spells that inactivate your powers. Not even the eldest wizard could make a spell. But you may go ahead and try' – she winked at me – 'because you are special.'

I looked over at Eric. He used his magic to write in the air with thin black lines. When he was done, I could read this message: "Don't use any spells! There are consequences."

'How long are you going to keep me here? I can see that you like games but I have had enough of them.'

Eric wrote another message: "Stall for time!!!" That's exactly what I was not doing.

'Or...what's the big rush?'

Could they sense the fear in my voice? Was I really brave? No...just too stupid to think about the consequences.

'I know you. I was sure you were not going to give away your powers to us willingly. But you see, the spell is a very complex one and I have been working for too long on it, only to be happy with a no from you. I am not stupid Katelyn. I always have a backup plan'. Maggie appeared as if from thin air –probably a hiding spell. She was afraid and did not know what was going on – just like I didn't know either. You could see that she could barely abstain from crying out. It took a sign from Meya and the morh approached her. Maggie screamed and tried to run but the morh went after her and grabbed her by the arm.

'Let her go!' I yelled. 'And you, Aaron, you are such a bastard. How can you do that to your own daughter?'

'No need to panic', Meya said. 'You see, it takes blood offered willingly by the victim in order for the spell to work. You do that and Maggie will not be harmed. And then we let both of you go and everybody is happy.'

I could not believe what was happening. I was in shock. Aaron had just given away his daughter freely. How could he use her as bait to get to me? Did he not care about how she must have felt? To know that your own father would not give a damn if you are killed; killed because of him.

'Don't listen to them!' Maggie shouted.

That's very brave of her, but stupid nonetheless. Perhaps she was thinking that her own father won't be so wretched after all and he won't hurt her – not truly.

'Shut up', Aaron yelled at her. 'I'm guessing you don't want the morh to have a bite of you.'

'You make me sick', Maggie said. 'I don't even know who disgusts me more; this stinking morh – oh God how he stinks – or the two of you?'

Meya came close to the circle. I could see her face. Her lips moved slowly.

'No', I yelled. I realised she was getting ready to make a spell.

'I'm glad you got the message.'

'She is your daughter, you bastard. How can you hurt her like that?' I yelled at Aaron, while ignoring Meya.

'No, she is not', he said uncaring. 'Not her and not Christine either.'

Shock! I wanted to hit him so badly, to make him suffer. If I could feel those words hurting me, I could only imagine how Maggie must have felt. I knew how much it hurt to find out that your parents...are not really your parents. I had found out that in a nicer fashion than she was finding out. I was wondering when Maggie would burst out. I know I could not have abstained myself. She was probably too shocked to react in any way. She was still taking everything in and I just wanted so much to make Aaron suffer. I felt the rage flooding my body. My soul had become cold and had emptied of any positive feeling. I hated him. I hated Aaron perhaps more than I hated Meya. I wanted both of them dead. This was the only thought that mattered.

I pulled the chains so strongly that they broke and it was not because of my strength, but because of magic. I came down from the rock, ignoring the multitude of skulls I was stepping over. I concentrated on those two, thinking how much I wanted to see them hurt and I let negative feelings flood me. I tried to get out of the circle but every time I touched it I was pushed back.

'Stop it!' Meya commanded. 'Anything that you try to do will turn against you. You are going to get yourself killed and I have no use of you dead.'

'The only one who is going to die is you', I told her and my voice did not seem to be mine.

The sky turned dark and I saw blue lightning bolts heading towards Meya and Aaron. Victory was mine for a moment until the bolts changed their trajectory and came towards me. Meya babbled some words and they stopped right before entering the circle. She looked exhausted.

'Stop it! You are going to get yourself killed.'

But the lightning bolts continued to come towards me and there were more and more of them. They headed my way like the flames coming out of a dragon's mouth. That dragon was me. I was causing all of this. But I could not stop myself. I felt something inside of me. I felt victorious. I liked using the powers. And it made me even happier to know that someone was going to get hurt by them. It was like a soft tickle inside of me. Eric kept writing messages telling me to stop.

Every good feeling I had, vanished when one of the lightning bolts went straight towards Maggie. The morh positioned himself in front of her to shield her. A terrible noise was made when the blue light touched it. But the morh was alright. I cannot say the same thing about Maggie. Another bolt was coming behind her. It was just a few centimetres from her and Meya was struggling to keep it away. When had I become the bad guy?

That is when I felt that I was becoming a prisoner of my own powers. I had fallen into darkness and had let myself taken by cold feelings. I was not capable of doing anything. Something had taken control over me. That dark force inside me was waiting to take any opportunity to come out to the surface. It was a devouring force that was feeding on negative feelings; a fierce thirst for power.

'I cannot control myself.'

'Hang on to the thing that matters most to you', Maggie shouted at me.

She was so tired. That is when I realised that Meya was not the only one who was fighting this flow of lightning bolts. Maggie was helping her.

'I cannot', I yelled again. 'I am a puppet at the mercy of my own powers.'

'Try', Maggie begged while she continued to fight off the lightning bolts.

'Stop! Both of you! Someone has to die, someone has to be hurt or else this won't stop', I found myself saying.

'But it's not going to be you who gets hurt', Meya said and directed the lightning bolts towards Aaron. Maggie screamed, ran towards him and placed herself in front of him. The morh followed her and positioned himself between her and the bolts thus protecting Aaron.

'Damn it', I yelled. 'Meya, let's make that stupid spell of yours. I want to get rid of them. But please, I don't want anyone to be hurt.'

'Alright.'

The lightning stopped. The light took over the darkness and the clouds disappeared in the sky.

'You vile woman', I yelled. 'You could have done this before. You pretended all this time.'

Maggie was really exhausted. She could barely stand. The morh did not budge from her sight. It was like a very dedicated bodyguard.

'This is the first and last time Aaron. Next time I will let your little lover hurt you.'

'You know I wasn't going to do it', Meya said.

'Yeah right', Maggie said and moved away from Aaron.

Meya took out a knife from her purse and pushed it inside the circle. It was made from silver and the snake-like handle had a word inscribed in italics. It seemed to be in Latin: "Fatifer".

'You have to splash some blood on the skulls', Meya said.

'Do what?' Maggie shouted. 'No way.'

Another message from Eric: "Just stall for time! Don't listen to Meya!"

I still had the half-moon on my palm. I pressed softly with the tip of the knife, clenched my teeth and cut the half-moon. Blood spout out.

'Don't waste it! Meya shouted.

"Don't you dare!" Eric wrote. He was angry and seemed ready to hit anyone who had dared to approach him. There was also Maggie who was scared and exhausted, but would not stop fighting. She kept trying to get rid of the morh, but it was too fast for her. Meya and Aaron gloated. I went around the rock and I let blood drip over the skulls.

'Enough', said Meya. 'Now we wait.'

The blood continued to drip. I took off my t-shirt and was left in my bra. I tore a piece of the t-shirt and wrapped it tightly around my palm to stop the bleeding. During this time, the skulls turned red and I felt as if I were in a horror movie.

'What does all of this mean? Actually I don't really care. What must I do?...'but I stopped. Maggie managed to go on the other side of the barrier. The morh hit the barrier and could not pass through.

'It doesn't matter', Meya said. 'Let her go! She is of no use anyway.'

Eric seemed to be amazed by the fact that Maggie had managed to go over the barrier. I felt relieved to see her there safely. Everything I had to do now was to wait for this witchery ritual to be over and then go home. In fact, it was a relief for me to know that I would be getting rid of my powers. I did not want to know what Meya was going to do with them once she had them. I know I was selfish, but I wanted everything to be done as soon as possible. I cared about my wellbeing and that of my friends' before anybody else's.

Chapter 9:

"Almost dead"

Meya began to say an incantation and then Aaron handed me a goblet that contained some liquid which smelled strongly of sulphur.

'Are you serious? I'm not going to drink that.'

They both looked at me angrily. Eric continued sending me messages. He had even begun threatening me. I was going to have to deal with him if I listened to Meya.

'Alright...'

I held my breath and I drank the liquid from the goblet in one sip. It did not taste as bad as I had imagined.

But the effect was instant. I got dizzy and I could no longer stand on my feet. I fell over the skulls being unable to even move a finger. I was paralysed from the neck down. Meya continued her incantation and the red skulls started to slowly lift into the air. They merged together into a skeleton. I was watching this and I was terrified. My fear grew bigger and bigger as I was becoming aware of my inability to run from this place. I saw a skeleton shape forming rapidly. It came above me, turned into a red dust and entered inside me. The moment of impact was absolutely terrifying. I felt as if something was tearing the flesh off me. I shifted from burning to feeling how the cold was aiming for my chest. I wanted to scream hoping that would take away some of the pain, but the cold had taken my voice away.

When you are in pain you almost involuntarily want to gasp, to move, to do anything but to stay in one place. And I was paralysed. I was being offered on a tray to the pain and it was biting me merciless. Tears were pouring out from my eyes as if they were telling of the pain that was going to invade my entire body. I felt like something was being ripped from my guts. My magic powers were abandoning me and Meya just continued with her incantation. Lights in different colours were coming out of me and they turned brown just before entering Meya's body. Every thread of light was like blood dripping out from me. The brown spots representing my magic that had become impure from Meya's touch, began heading for the barrier. The crazy woman stopped the ritual and went on cursing. The pain was all gone, but I continued to be paralysed.

'It's not working. My dark magic is not doing anything to the barrier.'

So she wanted to destroy it. Was that even possible?

'Maybe you should take more from Kate?' Aaron said.

Was he referring to my magic? Did he think that was not enough?

'No, it wouldn't work anyway. How could I have been so careless? She is the chosen one. My sister was the one who made this barrier. Kate, you are the only one who can destroy it and I am sorry that you are going to waste your magic on this. I would have liked to have a taste of it all. Aaa, it is possible that you might die along the way', she said without giving a damn.

The next thing I saw was an explosion above the barrier, followed by a few others, until Eric stopped. He was aware of the fact that his magic was not going to suffice.

"I am sorry" he wrote in the air. "I've let you down".

And just when I thought that it could not get any worse, I felt that excruciating pain again and saw my magic heading for the barrier, which became visible on the impact.; an immense curtain that became real when it was touched by my magic. Its colour was now navy-blue and started to develop black strips that were widening. The strips multiplied constantly and I was getting closer and closer to death.

I looked over at Maggie and Eric. They were watching helplessly how I was about to die and how the barrier got weaker. I wanted to see their faces up close, to look into their eyes. My magic helped me do that. Maggie's big brown eyes were in tears. Eric held her in his arms while she was struggling to come to me. What a goof. Didn't she realise that I was a lost cause? She would only be getting herself in further trouble. I could see the sadness and disappointment on Maggie's face, but Eric looked absolutely desperate. His blue eyes were just too beautiful to be so sad. His face was covered in tears. Why would someone who hardly knew me, cry so much for me? He could not have been older than twenty-seven years old, but the sadness made him look even older.

I don't know what hurt more: the pain that Meya was causing me, or seeing Eric suffer, who was practically a stranger? It was as if someone had torn him apart just like I was being torn apart. I looked at him and I felt the strangest sensation. I had a connection with him. I know I was not only imagining it. He was so sad as if all his dreams had fallen to pieces; as if all the dreams he had, had been thrown into the pitfall of past. I could feel him so close to my soul. I could sense that the feelings he had were a mix of pain, sadness, disappointment and hatred, but it was fear that was the most dominant of all feelings.

I could feel a wave of heat coming from him; like the warm touch of love that makes you feel comforted and safe although that's not how I was at that time.

Things happened very quickly after that and they took on a completely different turn. Christine came. She was together with a tall blonde woman. A battle of lights deployed before me, much too fast for me to keep up. The morh also seemed to be disoriented and did not know what to do. It was waiting for a command from its master. Aaron was held down to the ground by Christine and the stranger was fighting Meya. They both seemed to be of equal strength. A green light passed just millimetres away from the blonde. Aaron took out a gun and shot Christine – no fuss about it – in the shoulder. The morh became even more confused. It was struggling between the incontrollable lust for blood and the need to listen to its master. But she was too busy to remember it. Just a brief absence of mind and the blonde took a hit from Meya. She was thrown into the air and then dropped to the ground. Chris was perplexed and looked at her father in shock. He took another shot, but this time he missed.

'Hit him!' The blonde woman shouted at her.

But Chris was not doing anything. Maggie ran towards her and made a spell which threw Aaron's gun away from him. She was preparing for another one when Chris placed herself before her.

'Don't you dare touch him!'

'He is my father also, she shouted. 'Do you think it's not difficult for me too?'

'I don't want him to be hurt', she said crying.

'You are so stupid', Maggie said angrily.

While they were arguing, Aaron ran for the gun. I wanted to scream to warn them, but I could not.

The gun unloaded and hit the blonde woman. She was shaking but she ignored the pain in her leg and continued to fight Meya. What a brave woman. Maggie pushed Chris out of her way and was about to hit Aaron with another spell. Stubborn Chris just continued to protect their so-called father.

'What do you think you are doing?' Maggie asked desperately.

'I won't let you hurt him, I cannot.'

'I don't want to fight with you.'

'Neither do I.'

'Then move!'

'I cannot', she said.

'You're so stupid Chris, and you Aaron...this is not over.'

She ran to the blonde woman who was now lying on the ground.

Meya came to me and I could feel again the world collapsing around me. The barrier continued to get weaker but not weak enough to permit strangers to come in. Eric was still trying to pass through it. Chris put Aaron in a space-limiting spell so that he could not go away. Both she and Maggie then turned their magic against Meya who wouldn't stop the incantation. She was probably protected by some spells, because the two girls could not get to her. Their powers were not as strong as the ones of the blonde woman.

I got that strong nausea once more. That was the feeling I always got around the morhs. Damn it. I was not mistaken. The creatures appeared again one at a time. They were thirsty for blood and were bringing death with them.

'What are we going to do, Mystic? Christine shouted.

So this was the stranger's name.

'Come next to me', she said to them.

They went to her and Mystic did a protection spell. She shut a glass globe around them. The morhs could not go through. The girls screamed and for a moment I thought that the protection was gone. But this was not it. One of the creatures was eating up Aaron. I turned away. I did not want to see this.

It was done. We had lost. Damn it. We had really lost. I looked to see Eric, but he was not there anymore.

Then I saw a purple spiral hitting Meya. Because she had been taken by surprise, she took the hit hard. It was Eric and he was angrier than ever. He kept attacking Meya.

But the morhs were still there. They were hovering around him waiting for a signal from their master.

'I want him alive', Meya said, 'but you can have a little snack.'

I felt this incredible desire to protect him. I felt so connected to him that I probably would have also suffered if anything had happened to him. I could not think about anything else except for this sudden urge to protect him. I got up with great difficulty. I had no idea what I wanted to do.

I made it. I managed to come out from that circle, from that awful prison. This could only mean that Meya was seriously hurt because there was nothing holding me back from escaping. The morhs felt my blood and started to become numb falling into some kind of a trance. I took advantage of this situation and I ran towards Aaron's lifeless body. Perhaps I only thought I was running, because my feet were barely moving. I refrained from vomiting when I saw the body and I took his gun that was by his side. I had to do something and since magic was not my strong suit – if I even had any magic left in me – then I had to use human powers.

Alright...how do you use a gun?

Damn it. The creatures woke up from the trance and they were coming straight for me. Meya was busy fighting Eric and was not paying attention to me anymore. I ran closer to them; I aimed and pulled the trigger. The noise was so deafening that it made my ears hurt. Luckily the gun was loaded. The bullet hit her straight into the chest. I did not expect to have such good precision. Or perhaps magic had helped me.

Meya dropped to the ground. The next thing I saw were the morhs falling prey to the sun. They all burned in an instance. It seems Meya was the only reason why the morhs could walk during the day. But now she was dead.

I had killed her...

I could not move. I still had the gun in my trembling hand. I was crying and I was too traumatised to let it go. Eric came next to me and tried to take the gun away from my hand, but I held on tight to it. Chris ran to her father's body. She was virtually screaming. That's when I let the gun drop and I fell down on my knees. Maggie went after her. She was the younger sister, but she proved to be so much stronger than Chris who was 24 years old. She took her in her arms like a mother who is trying to soothe her crying baby.

Meya is dead. I had killed someone. I had taken someone's life. A life I had no right to take. Why had I done it? I knew Meya was a really despicable person, but I should not have been the one who...

'This was the second time...' I said in trembling voice.

'It's going to be alright.'

Eric squatted in front of me. He probably did not know what to do. He did not seem hurt. Mystic came next to us. She did not look alright. She was exhausted and had scratches and bruises on her arms. Luckily Aaron was not a good shooter and the bullet had just grazed her right leg.

'She is in shock', he said.

I looked up from the ground and pushed my hair aside. Something was going on with Mystic. When she looked at me she reacted as though she had seen a ghost.

'Where did you get it from?' *I looked at her not knowing what she was referring to.* 'Where did you get it from?' *She asked again, this time louder.* 'The medallion.'

I looked at the half-moon hanging around my neck. I had completely forgotten about it.

'Not now Mystic', Eric snapped at her. 'She needs peace of mind and privacy.'

But I did not want that. I wanted someone to hold me tight, to look into my eyes and to tell me that it had all been a dream, a damn nightmare.

'But you don't understand. I have to know.'

'Mystic, go to the girls and see if they need anything!'

She sighed and left.

'It belonged to my mother, or at least that is what Meya told me. However, after all that happened, I don't know if I can trust her', I replied. *Mystic stopped and turn to me but did not say a thing. For a moment I thought that she was going to run and take me into her arms but she refrained.* 'Why?'

'Never mind ...' she said and then walked away.

I got up. The pain and the tiredness were the only things I could care less about at this point. I had to escape from this place.

'You should sit!' Eric said. 'You are exhausted. Help will be here shortly.'

'I have to leave.'

'Why are you so stubborn?'

'I have to get my thoughts straight. This is just too much. Don't you understand?'

'No, you don't understand. I am not going to let you play around with your health. Where do you want to leave by yourself and in your condition? Listen to me, Kate! It took me a long time to find you. I've already let you out of my sight twice, but it's not going to happen again. I am not letting you leave anywhere without me.'

He was so down beat and tired. He made a spell and released me from the cuffs. I felt relieved to get away from their grip. He examined me head to toe. He took my arm that had an improvised cast on it and looked at the cut.

'This half-moon of yours is very strange. Since when have you had it?'

'I got it once in a dream, I think. Not long ago. It was after I came to this island. Damn it. My entire body hurts and my hand even more so. This half-moon is a nuisance whenever I'm close to the barrier. Can't you do one of your magic tricks and make this pain go away?'

'I'm sorry', he said. 'Magic doesn't work like this.'

'Alright, then can you tie my arm back again because I want to leave.'

'Are you always like this?'

'Like what?'

'So difficult. Did you really not understand anything that I have been telling you?'

'Damn it', I shouted at him. 'I just killed someone and this is not the first time I've done it. I need to be alone!'

He went silent after that.

I was lying. I did not want to be alone. In fact, there was nothing that I wanted more but for Eric to take me into his arms and tell me that everything had just been a nightmare. I don't know what was wrong with me. I wanted him so badly, but I only pushed him away from me. And I managed to keep him away. He went to check on the girls and just told me that he was giving me some privacy. I guess I was going to be his prisoner after that. Alright, maybe I am exaggerating about being his prisoner.

But this was not important now.

The first time I had killed someone had been during one of my many archery lessons. Some people had said that it was just an accident, but I knew it was not. I had not been on my best behaviour for some time. All that partying had been keeping me up for several nights in a row. I was extremely tired and dizzy when I got to the lesson. He had just told me about it. I was at a pool party when the coach phoned me. The competition had moved a week before. I was careless, a big idiot and that got my coach killed. It did not matter that it was unintentional, or the fact that he wasn't supposed to be on the training field. I should have double-checked before shooting the arrow that killed him. And that was why I had given up archery.

I went slowly towards the barrier. I wanted to leave from this place and never come back. Chris was absolutely devastated, but she had Maggie by her side and she would help her go through this. Eric and

Mystic had risked their lives for me, although I was only a stranger to them. They were always going to have my gratitude.

I went past the barrier and that's when I felt this familiar warmth. I took one last look at them. The blonde and Eric seemed to be having an argument. Maggie was still holding Chris.

The last thing I wanted was to be alone but still I left. I was too scared and traumatised to take any good decision and yet I was doing it. Kaeillindor: too many secrets, too many questions. I did not want to know anything more. I just wanted to forget everything that had happened and start a new life. And this would only have been possible if I stopped seeing those people that reminded me of this nightmare.

I saw Eric and Mystic struggling to go through the barrier but they could not. I was now connected to it. I could feel this and the half-moon on my palm was that connection.

I was lucky enough to find a boat on the shore. This was probably Eric's. Without overthinking it, I got on and left to wherever the wind would take me. I hoped it would be to civilisation.

Chapter 10:

"Face-to-face with Baldric"

I woke up on a hospital bed with a blonde nurse staring at me. She was short and had her long hair tied in a bun. Her smooth face did not have any makeup on it. She had brown eyes and freckles and she did not look older than twenty. She was a nice sight.

I had a cannula in my right arm. My palm and wrists had bandages on. Those chains had been really tight, no joke about it. I nearly jumped out of my skin just thinking about that bad memory. I was in a blue hospital gown which was absolutely hideous.

This girl said something which appeared to be in Greek and I could not understand any of it.

'English?' I asked her in hoarse voice which did not even seem to be mine.

'Yes. How are you feeling?'

'It's strange but I don't have any pain.'

'That's a good thing.'

'Where am I?'

'Palaiochora.' She could probably see how puzzled I was because she went on explaining. 'It's a small town south of Crete.'

'Great...I said to myself.'

'I have to go. I'll let everyone know that you are awake. A...the policemen have some questions for you. Do you think you're up for a discussion with them now?'

'I have nothing to talk to them about...'

'It's obvious that something bad happened to you. Who were you trying to run from? Some fishermen found you. You did not look so good when you got here. We only want to help you.'

'Do you really want to help me?' I asked.

'Of course. You have nothing to worry about. Everything is going to be alright. The policemen are going to find the people who tried to harm you.'

Yes...exactly how I had imagined it. I probably looked like a girl who had just escaped from the hands of the kidnaper.

'Aaa, can I borrow your phone? I have to talk to my parents.'

'Of course. Give us their phone number and we'll let them know where you are and what happened. By the way, what happened to you? And what is your name?'

'Aaa...'I shrugged my shoulders. 'I don't remember. I just want to go home.'

'You really don't remember anything?' She asked looking very sceptical. 'And how is it that you remember your parents' phone number?'

Damn it! She had figured it out. I was not good at this at all.

'I mean to say that I do not remember how I got in this state. I remember everything else; my memories have not been affected. My name is Katelyn Lambert and I came here on vacation with my parents. Please, I just want to make a call.'

'Make it a short one', she said. 'And I don't know anything about this.'

Go figure, none of my parents answered their phone. Perhaps they were in one of those missions that they never talked about.

This was very sad. Now that I needed them I considered them to be my parents.

I admit that I am selfish and that I have let down the people that raised me from a young age. I chose to play the victim and to trust the wrong person. I did not deserve their help or their forgiveness. It did not matter if they were my biological parents or not. "I am sorry. I am so sorry", that's how I started the message that I left to my father as I was trying not to burst into tears. I knew that words were not enough. Father always used to tell me that words are just the first step you take. It is the facts that matter. "You were right all along and I screwed up. I cannot talk for long. I need your help. I am in Palaiochora, south of Crete. Aaa. And I am in the hospital but don't worry, I am alright. Now...I think...Aaa...I have to go."

I deleted the call history and gave her back the phone. She offered me a tissue.

'Thank you. Thank you so much.'

'I am going to tell the policemen that you are not well enough to make a statement yet. But you cannot postpone this forever.'

'I know. What is your name?'

'Zoe. It means life in Greek.'

I felt the need to talk to someone but I did not have the courage to do it. And who would believe me? I could not say out loud everything that went through my mind.

I had been so wrong. But how else can you learn to move forward? Mistakes are essential for becoming mature. It doesn't make any difference if you are told as a child not to touch the stove because you'll get burned. Sometimes, you have to try it yourself; to see that it hurts so that you won't do it next time.

And here I was, alone, a stranger in an uncomfortable bed in a small and cold room, in a town I did not know and far from home.

Sometimes I just let my guard down. I cannot be strong all the time and pretend that nothing happened; pretend that my life has not changed so radically in such a short time.

I should behave like a mature person but I cannot and I don't want to. I am not ready for this.

I am twenty-three years old, damn it

I just want to have a normal life.

Dreams...

This is everything that I have left. Pointless dreams; I know they won't come true. And yet I cannot give up on them. I have to fight but I have just started and I am already tired. My soul is troubled by this feeling that time has not altered. I want to be alone in the middle of nature. I want to shout, to scream out my problems, to release myself from everything that is pressing me. Oh God how I want to get rid of this pain in my chest.

I woke up in total darkness. I could only hear the clock ticking. That's a bit strange when you are not in your own room. Someone opened the door and I managed to see the figure of a man. I heard steps approaching the bed and I shut my eyes pretending to be asleep. Shortly after that, the door opened again. I heard the nurse screaming and something breaking.

The lights were turned on and strange faces began entering the room one at a time. A flower vase was in pieces on the floor and the nurse that took care of me kept rubbing her shoulder. She had tears in her eyes.

Somebody had hurt her and that somebody was probably going to hurt me too.

A discussion in Greek followed after. The nurse was scared and she gesticulated while talking to a tall fat guy. There were two other nurses in my room who had probably come to see what was happening.

'Someone tried to kill you', Zoe said to me angrily. 'I caught him trying to inject you with something', she said and pointed to a syringe that had fallen on the floor. 'And I don't care that you don't want to talk to the policemen. You will talk to them! Now! And you are going to tell them about everything that happened to you.' She shouted at me in a protective manner. I almost had the impression that it was my mother scolding me.

Was this ever going to end? I wondered.

'But they won't believe what I have to say...and...I still hope that my parents are going to show up.'

Zoe sighed and then left my room together with the other two nurses, but not before letting me know that we are on the second floor and she had someone guard my door. So...no attempt to run. That's what she thought.

Let's recap! Why had I run from that island in the first place? Was it impulsivity? Fear? No... The answer was stupidity! I am definitely not better now. Someone had just tried to kill me. And that person knew where to find me next time. He knew who I was. I know I am not running for first place in "Girl of the year' award but still... to be a target? I am curios though...what's the bounty on my head?

I got out of bed. The nurse was not lying. I really was on the second floor but luckily my magic was not gone. I took the blanket from the bed, tied the four corners together, held on tight to it and jumped with my eyes closed...I let myself flow into the strong wind, a wind that had appeared from "nowhere".

'Thank you magic', I said when I landed safely on the ground. 'And now... where to?'

I felt a tingling sensation in my chest. The medallion around my neck had a dim shine. It felt warm to touch and I remembered that Meya had given it to me. I took it off and threw it away.

Then something strange happened. It was as if I was watching images from a video projector. Mystic and Eric were coming to life before my eyes. I got close to them hoping that I could touch them; hoping that they were really here. But just as I feared, my hand went through them.

They were in a forest and I could tell from their gestures that they were having an argument. Mystic kept waving her hands in agitation as she was probably trying to explain something to Eric. Eric looked down and seemed to be preoccupied counting the leaves more than he was paying attention to what Mystic was saying.

And the medallion proved to have even greater powers when I could hear what they were saying. That is probably why Mystic had given me that look when she saw me wearing it. It might be a rare object used for communication in the magic world. Who needs a telephone when you have this? I don't think that the two could see me. Was this thing working one way only? Because if that was true, then I think I would rather prefer to have a telephone...

'But Eric', we need a plan!

'No! You need one! I have had plenty. They never work out.'

'But we cannot give up.' Mystic shouted and you could hear the despair in her voice.

Eric looked at her suspiciously and then said:

'What's with this sudden change? You were the one who kept saying that we should quit until not long ago.'

'But now we have found her.'

'And we have lost her!'

'Not for long. Christine has agreed to come with us to the campus. She is special. She will learn more about herself and she will help us. She wants to.'

'I don't see how a girl who is still very much affected by her father's death will be able to help us.'

'She can feel what is in people's hearts. She can read their intentions immediately. You know that, don't you? In the campus she will learn more about herself; how to control the gift she has and what else can she get out of it. She will be able to sense the presence of people. This way she will be able to help us find out where Kate is.'

'This will take too long time.'

It seemed that Eric had a counterargument to anything that Mystic was saying.

'I know', Mystic sighed, 'but it's all that we can do. Kate cannot be too far'.

'She is definitely not on the island. My men have been looking everywhere for her. Maybe she got lost at sea.'

'Eric, stop talking nonsense! You know very well that you would have felt if anything bad had happened to her. The connection between you two...Remember how you felt when Meya tried to take her powers away from her?'

'I don't want to think about that.'

'Why Eric? Because it caused you pain seeing her hurt and you were afraid? And you are not at all used to these two feelings?'

'Mystic, you are testing my patience.'

'And you are testing mine', she shouted at him. I don't want to fight with you. This is not the right time. The barrier is unstable now and we do not know how it works and in what way Kate is connected to it. It's a good thing that at least the two of us managed to get past it. But I do not know how.'

'It's invisible. It just feels as if you are fighting air and that is incredibly frustrating', Eric interrupted her.

'It must have been very difficult for you, wasn't it? To stay on the other side of the barrier and see how chaos develops before your eyes and how you are unable to do anything. I mean...we have been looking for Kate for such a long time and she was standing right in front of you and needed your help and you...'

Mystic stopped, realising that she was being inconsiderate.

'I'm sorry...'she said.

Eric clenched his fists and seemed to be tormented by that memory. He was angry and was pushing the leaves with his foot.

'I feel we are missing something. Perhaps we should get back to the island. Baldric was very interested in it.'

'No. We risk not being able to get away from there. The barrier is very unstable. I have never had any problems with it. My mother was one of the wizards that created it. But now...I don't think I have to remind you what we had to go through to get away from that island. And, please, try to forget about your crazy brother. Baldric is dead and that's it; the battle between you two is done.'

'Yeah...and now we go on our mission: "finding The Magic Pawn". Oh, wait. It has a new name: "finding Lambert" ', Eric said ironically. 'Such a stubborn teenager – impulsive, unable to see beyond her own selfishness. She has no control over her powers. She deserves an award for bad decision-taking. I am still wondering what she could do to help us, because I really don't see her able of anything useful.'

As Eric continued to add more and more "compliments" about me, I felt so ashamed that I just wanted to vanish into thin air.

'Hey, I am right here', I shouted, although I was aware that no one could hear me.

I noticed a dim light on Mystic's wrist.

'It's just a nuisance. And I am sure that even if we do find her, she will not help us. She is shallow and too dumb to realise her own value. She probably wants nothing more right now, than to get rid of the magic...since she was so eager to offer it to Meya.'

'You don't know me to be talking like that about me', I shouted angrily. 'Oh Kate...congratulations! Now you are crazy on top of everything else; you are shouting at nothing.'

It was ridiculous. I was talking to myself. But...if the shouting seemed to be making me less angry, then it must have been a good thing, right?

'And yes, maybe I do want to get rid of the magic; because I did not even believe it existed until recently. And I am not selfish or shallow, damn it. I am only scared, scared of myself, scared of what I could do.

139

In fact, I am truly terrified because I can feel it. The magic is there...and...and it wants to come to the surface and take control over me. And it feeds on meanness. And then, there are the dreams also...and...'

I could not take it anymore and I started to cry.

I did not wipe off my tears because I needed this. I sat down, pulled my legs up to my chest and leaned my head on my knees. I let my feelings out and cried until I could feel I had no more tears.

I don't know how long it took. It might be that I was doing it for half an hour but it might also be that it was just for five minutes.

When I got up I stumbled a bit and felt rather dizzy. I had just run away from a hospital.

The medallion was still shining. I looked at the two and I could see them starring...at me?

Oh...no, don't tell me that they just witnessed my breakdown. I turned to leave not wanting to find out, but Mystic called for me.

'Kate, are you alright?'

I had no choice but to talk to them. Leaving would only have proven my immaturity...and would have given Eric extra arguments to continue not to think highly of me. And again...what do I care?

I decided I was going to be honest...

'No...'I answered.

'I cannot believe it...'said Mystic. 'How could I have forgotten about the medallion? This was our trick...and...'

She did not continue. Eric looked sceptical at her and after that "I had him all focused on me"

'Where are you? And what were you thinking to leave like that? Do you have any idea in how much trouble you've got us? How could you be so irrational? I promised you that I would never leave you alone.'

'Yes, alright...I already know what you think about me. You don't have to say it every time you get chance. And no...I have no idea what got into me...I just panicked; I let myself captured by fear. It was too much... The magic simply terrified me...and yes...I want really badly to get rid of it.

Eric sniffed.

'You have no idea what you are talking about, little girl. Just tell us where you are already. Do you want answers? Let us help you!'

'Now you call me "little girl", seriously?'

'Forgive him. He is angry', Mystic said. 'He has been a mess ever since you left. He is upset that he could not keep his promise to you.'

'Let's not exaggerate. And you Mystic, you need to learn when to keep your mouth shut. Lambert, where are you?'

'I will answer your question, but first you have to answer mine.'

'Kate, please, we don't have time for this now', Mystic said. 'You are in danger...'

'I don't know you; why would you want to help me? Why are you being so nice to me? If there is anything I've learned, it is that nobody helps you without wanting something out of it. Why am I so important to you?'

'Such a stubborn and unaware teenager', Eric said. 'Just tell us already where you are!!! Or we will let you deal with everything by yourself. After all, you are making it difficult for yourself. With this attitude and with the few things you know about magic, you won't get too far.'

I felt his words like a slap on my face.

'Eric, you are not helping', Mystic scolded him.

I heard a noise behind me and I turned.

'Just a dog', I said as I caught my breath.

Or at least that's what I thought until I could hear some strange yowling.

'What happened?'

'Nothing...' I said ironically...'Today's order of business: Target – Katelyn Lambert.' *My bad sense of humour in critical situations.* 'Someone tried to kill me this evening. Aaa...and I think I have company...'

'What?' Mystic shouted.

'And you're just telling us this now? Where are you?' Eric shouted and seemed to be pissed off.

Several dogs came out of the bushes; some were bigger than others...they were growling and their eyes were red...I really love dogs but only the small and fluffy ones. Then the air became filled with the deafening croaking of crows that had red eyes as well.

I was in trouble again...I don't know how...but trouble seemed to stick to me like glue.

'Crete', I shouted. 'Palaiochora.'

The figure of a man appeared from among those dogs and crows. Then the sense of nausea became overwhelming and the air got filled with the smell of death. First I thought it must be from the morhs. Balls of fire were coming out from that stranger's hand. They remained suspended into the air and lit the place up. I screamed as it became clear to me where the smell was coming from. The dogs and the crows were dead...I mean...they were alive...but also dead. The dogs' flesh was rotting and large pieces from their bodies were missing and you could see inside them. They were full of blood. Their mouths were crooked and their big fangs were sticking out. The crows' feathers had been plucked and they were full of blood just like the dogs were. Their claws were big and sharp just like their beaks. The creatures were coming after me. I kept moving backwards until I hit a tree. They continued coming after me and they were getting closer and closer. I covered my eyes with my arm and I began to scream hoping someone would help me.

'Easy now, children', said the stranger as he stepped into the light.

The creatures stopped and went back to their master. He was tall and well-built and had short dark hair. The expression on his face reminded me a lot of someone.

'Baldric!' Eric and Mystic shouted.

And then I put two and two together. They had mentioned him earlier. Eric's brother, the one who was supposed to be dead.

'Stay away from her!!!'

'And what if I don't, little brother?'

'I will kill you with my own hands! And this time I will make sure that you stay dead!'

'It's been such a long time and this is how you welcome your brother? Why don't we put this threatening aside?! There is no point in doing that and... anyway...these threats are useless.'

Eric wanted to say something else, but I interrupted him.

'What do you want from me? In fact, what does everybody want from me? Was it you who tried to kill me this evening?'

'Kill you? I could never hurt you.'

He came closer to me with his followers by his side. Their smell was truly unbearable. I felt sick to my stomach. I could not resist that smell anymore and I vomited.

'Stay away from me!' I said felling very weak.

I got away from him and from the place where I had just vomited, until I realised that my feet were of no use anymore. I didn't take more than ten steps until I became too dizzy to do anything. I could feel how my body was falling to the ground. Baldric grabbed me by the waist and helped me stand.

When he touched me, I got an instantaneous feeling of cold as if I had just stepped in Siberia in the middle of winter. His pets – if I could even call them pets – moved away from us.

'I'm sorry', he said as he finally became aware of the disturbing smell oozed by his living dead. He patted my cheek and I flinched as I felt his ice-cold hand. Although I almost started to tremble from that cold, the wave of cold soon disappeared and with it so did my dizziness.

In that icy embrace it was difficult for me to focus on what was happening around me. I heard Eric cursing and shouting at Baldric to get his damn hands off me. That's what I also wanted. I could feel the fear deep in my bones...or perhaps it was just the cold...But I did not actually feel the cold and I was not shivering either. It was a different feeling and it just kept taking over my chest. I was definitely scared and I wanted him as far away from me as possible. I looked into his black eyes and that's when something strange happened. I could see through him. I could read so much hatred but also pain and fear in those dark eyes. Baldric was suffering and he was even more frightened than I was.

'Why are you so frightened?' I asked.

I had used all my strength to get those words out, but they could barely be heard.

He looked at me puzzled.

'All that pain and fear...you are more afraid than I am.'

That is when I thought he was going to drop me. I could not yet stand on my feet by myself.

'It cannot be', he said as he looked at me completely shocked.

But it had happened. I had looked him straight into his soul. Those dark cold eyes had been so easy to read and I think that I was the only one who could do that.

I screamed when I felt how all that coldness caused by an avalanche of meanness and hatred was invading my soul. Baldric did not react. He took his hand to his heart and felt the warmth that I was giving him. He was flabbergasted and seemed to be fighting his own frenzy. The more warmth I gave him - warmth coming from positive feelings – the more coldness I got from him. It was as if I had invaded Baldric's memories for a short while; betrayals, lies, meanness, hatred, selfishness, shallowness and death.

'This is just too much. Stop it!' I begged him and my eyes were in tears.

He reached for my face to wipe my tears off but realised that his touch was only causing me even more pain. He woke up from that frenzy, let me go and moved back a bit.

'I...am sorry.'

'I'm sure you are', Eric shouted at him. 'Don't you dare use your dark magic on her soul to take away its essence and hope that perhaps then you will feel something human! I have news for you brother; you have tried this too many times; the bodies left behind stand proof of

that. And it seems that you still cannot do it. You are just another psychopath unable to feel anything resembling love.'

Baldric ignored him and became focused on me.

'I would never hurt you. And I promise you that the person who tried to kill you this evening will pay for it.'

Whatever moment of weakness he might have had earlier was now gone. He oozed fear and chaos once more. One of his crows came next to him and he whispered something to it. The crow disappeared leaving a streak of black dust behind it.

'And now what?' said Mystic with despair in her voice.

'For now, we negotiate. This is the only thing we can do.'

Not really the only thing. Something told me that Eric's people were already on their way to me. They just had to stall for time.

'Negotiating with Baldric is never a good thing. There is always too big of a cost. The man's soul is frozen. He doesn't feel anything and he doesn't care about anything else but himself.'

A man approached Baldric and bowed to him.

'Master, you called for me?'

'Did you try to kill this young lady earlier?'

I sniffed.

'I...I thought that...'the man began to stammer.

He was a short man, skinny and had black hair. He seemed to be over forty years old.

'You thought wrong!' *He signalled the dogs.* 'It's dinner time, children! And you don't have to see this.'

He took me into his arms and I became a prisoner of his cold soul.

I closed my eyes. I was terrified. The man's howling became silent and vanished into the darkness of the night. It was too much...and although the cold had a strong impact on me at first, in the end it made me feel sort of good. When you are a complete mess, when you can no longer control your feelings, when the emptiness in your heart becomes bigger and bigger, you let yourself controlled by the pain growing with each day that passes; you end up in a moment of despair when all you wish is to be done with all of it. This coldness seemed to be decreasing some of the intensity of this avalanche of feelings and that made want to accept it. What do I care if I cannot feel love anymore as long as there is no more suffering either?

'Take your hands off my daughter, you bastard!'

This familiar voice made me wake up from my state of frenzy. It was my father. The shock was even greater when I saw my mom. She had a shiny bow in her hand which she used to shoot down Baldric's crows one at a time. I took advantage of the fact that Baldric, who had been taken by surprise, was not paying attention, and I ran to my parents. I knew they had many secrets but I never would have expected this. Father held something that resembled a spear in one hand and a gun in the other one. He was fighting off the dogs and they did not stand a chance. The spear shined so bright that they were afraid to come close to him. All he did was to shoot his gun and, just like mom, he seemed to have a very good aim. They both behaved as if they were professional fighters. They were not wizards but their weapons where definitely magic ones.

This moment of glory went on until Baldric began to fight back. He sent several spells against my parents who were now in front of me. More and more coloured lightning bolts were coming towards us, each representing a different spell. Mother began to shoot arrows at them and that made them burn down, leaving sparks behind. This was similar to a fireworks show. She was so fast at shooting the arrows that I could barely keep up looking at her. Baldric's dogs were all dead but the crows just kept multiplying. Father was fighting them off with his spear; but this was not going to last for a long time. Mom did not have many arrows left and I don't know for how long dad would be able to fight off those damn crows that just kept multiplying. I was standing behind them and I was unable to do anything. I could not help my parents who were fighting for my life. I had been thinking of different ways to hurt Baldric but nothing happened. I was too panicked to make any magic just by focusing on it and I did not know any spells.

Baldric seemed amused. This was all a game for him. He could not care less, and my parents were not going to resist for long. When I saw my mom thrown to the ground by one of Baldric's spells, I became infuriated and let magic take control over me. I let the other side of me come to the surface; thirsty-for-power-and-consumed-by-anger Kate who was capable of using all the magic that she had been keeping hidden. I went next to my mother and all the anger I had accumulated against Baldric turned into magic. I was led by one thought only and I fought back using spells that I did not know what they meant. I felt my body burning when one of his spells hit me. Baldric had managed to block all my spells but, when his spell hit me, Baldric stopped fighting back. He seemed to be taken by surprise and could not fight off all the green flashes that I was sending towards him; one of them hit him in the chest. I felt the pain as soon as it hit him, and we both screamed at the same time. That is when I understood why Baldric had been taken by surprise earlier; the moment that his spell hit me he was also affected. In a very weird manner and through some strange mistake made by the universe, the two of us were somehow connected. But his spell had been an easy one. The burning sensation did not last too long and was not that intense either. Baldric did not want to kill me. If he would have wanted that then he would have done it. But my spell, however, was incredibly painful. The pain started from the chest and extended rapidly through the entire body. I could barely breathe with all those stings I felt in my chest which were growing in intensity. I kept sending green flashes from the half-moon in my palm.

'Stop!' – Baldric yelled. 'You are going to get us both killed.'

'I don't know how!'

Then everything came to a halt and I dozed off into the sweet smell of a chemical substance. Chloroform?

Chapter 11:

"New beginnings- The Barbara Balfour Campus"

I could feel my entire body numb after an eight-hour long drive that would end soon, or so Eric said. We were heading for the Barbara Balfour campus and this was going to be my new home. Mystic, Chris and Maggie were also with us.

Some past unfortunate events had made magic school begin at 18 years of age when you are legally an adult; this was something I would be learning more about in history classes. You could not be taught complex magic spells until that age. If used wrongly, magic can become dangerous. Many children and teenagers had been injured or even died from silly games. Normally, even if you are a wizard, there is not much that you can do unless you know spells. Only the greatest wizards, those who you read about in books on the history of magic, have managed to create magic without having to say any spells.

It seems I was one of them and, according to the prophecy, I was destined to do great things and to become a great witch. I wanted to find out what exactly the prophecy said but they dodged that question like a bullet every time I asked, so I dropped it; and anyway, I thought this was silly. I do not believe in prophecies or other stuff like that. But I did not believe in magic either and yet it proved to be real.

Finding me was like finding the needle in the haystack. At first they did not have much except for the words of an old wizard who had been dead for long time; but they did not have anything certain.

So there I was, heading towards a new road, a new life. The Magic Pawn... I felt I was going to hit them when I heard them referring to me like that. I am just Kate. My name is Katelyn Lambert; no Magic Pawn or anything like that. I did not want to hear that because, to be honest, it scared me. It's not easy to find out that you are the most powerful wizard that is born every thousand years. When Meya died, the magic she stole in that crazy ritual, returned to me. But all that power comes with a price. I don't even know what I could start with...maybe with the fact that there was probably a bounty on my head. There were so many who wanted to get their hands on the Magic Pawn. So, I was going to be a target my entire life. I had to hide. No one had to find out who I really was. Moreover, I did not have the slightest idea how to control all this power I had. The magic that flooded me had to be used, else it would become harder and harder to control. That's the reason why Eric and Mystic were so interested in me. Unlike the others, they did not want to exploit my powers, but to help me control them.

There were however people who had a special power and who did not need a specific spell to use the gift they had. It seems that Christine was one of them. She could read people very well and thus she could figure out what their intentions were. This took time, of course, but with a lot of work and focus she could look into people's souls, feel their emotions and figure out when they lied and when they were being honest. Eric had the power to hypnotize wizards and to make them do whatever he wanted them to do. He had tried to do this to me because he thought that I was hiding something and that I refused to tell him the truth. But his power did not work on me. Maybe because I was the Magic Pawn...anyway, I don't understand anything anymore. I had so much to learn. Eric's other special power was slightly more complex and truly painful. He could make you face your deepest fears. It was all an illusion, of course, but one you could die from.

Some others had the gift of controlling one of the four elements of nature: earth, air, water and fire. And there were all sorts of other powers about which I would learn in the campus. Unlike her sister, Maggie did not possess any gift.

Two weeks had passed since the episode in Greece. Mother held a cloth soaked in chloroform over my mouth and nose to make me become unconscious and thus stop the spell. Baldric had run away threatening that I would eventually "be his".

Everybody was now excessively protective of me because of that. This is why Eric and Mystic insisted that they took me to the campus themselves. My every move would be observed. This was just great!

My parents turned out to be professional hunters. They were always fighting all sorts of magic creatures. This was one of the reasons for which I had been given into their care. They were in Kaeillindor when a woman begged them to take care of me, because I was very important. She told them I was a witch and that there are people who will try to hurt me at some point. She was very scared and she was injured. She put me in my mother's arms and then she ran away. Ever since my parents told me this story I have been thinking about what could have happened to that woman; if she is still alive or not, and why she was so scared. I promised myself that I would do my best to try to find out more. No one knew anything about my father.

When they saw the half-moon in my palm they told me that my biological mother also had a similar one, but on her cheek.

In order to see the island of Kaeillindor you must pass through a magic portal. That is why I felt that chill when I was on the boat with Meya, Edward and Christine. In addition to that, it appears that the island was surrounded by a magical barrier, one that became visible after touching it in that dream that seemed so real. As far as the barrier goes, it seems that it had not always been on the island. It was created later in order to protect the island from the strangers who were trying to steal its secrets. They say that a Grimoire might be hidden on the island; it contains the strongest and darkest spells. It would be unstoppable if it got into the wrong hands. It could destroy the island. Kaeillindor is the essence of white magic; this is where it all came to life. The name of the island comes from the Latin word *candor*, which means purity, and *ilustris* that means brilliant.

One of the reasons for which I am so connected to the barrier is that my mother is one of the wizards who created it. Another reason could be the fact that I am the Magic Pawn…Only the families of those who helped create the barrier can pass through it without any problem. Eric had managed to do this with Meya's help.

Something happened when I touched the barrier; the half-moon in my palm shows that a connection was established. I am the reason why it is so unstable now and why you cannot always cross it. When I ran away from the island it took several hours before anyone could use it again. Why? I do not know…Perhaps the reason was the connection that I had with the barrier, and because I wanted so badly to be alone at the time. Eric's people have been trying to find out more about the mysterious barrier with the help of Edward who has barely recovered after the news…

It seems that Eric and I have a psychic connection, one based strictly on feelings. We are drawn to each other like magnets and it's not just physical attraction. According to my parents, we are meant to be together. Or at least this is what is said in a different prophecy. My attraction to him was obvious but it was just physical attraction. And I was definitely not on Eric's list of favourite people. The only thing that interested him in me was my powers. We had not been talking much during the past two weeks. We just avoided being alone by ourselves. Eric was not meant for me. Both of us refused to believe this.

The fact that there was a physical connection between Baldric and I was obvious after the fight I'd had with him. The moment he touched me, an exchange of energy took place between us. He fed on my white magic while giving me a small part of all that coldness in him. Baldric was a man filled with hatred, lacking any feelings that make someone human. He was not aware of the gravity of the consequences when he sold his soul for power. And now, it seems that he was willing to do anything to be able to feel again. It's not easy to live in a block of ice. It did not take me more than a touch to realise the battle that went inside Baldric. Eric seemed to be even unhappier with this than I was. He became very touchy every time I talked about it.

As for Meya, it seems she had a secret laboratory. There they were attempting to modify the structure of the morhs; they wanted to control them and make them survive day light. No one knows who was working for her. After she and Aaron died, their project was abandoned and Edward destroyed the laboratory.

Christine has taken their father's death more difficult than her sister, who believed Aaron had it coming. Maggie suffered a lot but she kept that to herself. She is not the type of person who lets her feelings out. These were her feelings and she had to learn how to face them by herself. To know that the person whom you adored has managed to crush all the good things you saw in him is not an easy thing to do. He was their father and he had let them down brutally. He had turned into a murderer, a psychopath, a man without feelings. And now, just like me, Maggie and Christine had no idea who their real father was or what had happened to him.

The girls were relieved to leave the island. It was too much for them to continue living there after everything that had happened. Just like me, they needed a new beginning and this was the Barbara Balfour campus. It looked quite nice in the brochures. It's huge, surrounded by forests and hidden somewhere in the mountains. It was probably placed in the middle of nowhere to make sure that no one tries to escape. There are two large gyms and special athletic fields for different sports like tennis, volleyball, basketball, handball, football, etc. I was never good at any of these sports but I like basketball and volleyball. There were also two swimming pools, an indoor one and one outside; the students had access there not only during the polo and swimming lessons but also during their spare time. I did not read details about the classes or such. I was going to find out anyway.

I became slightly afraid as we approached the campus. I was entering a new world. Who knows what obstacles I would be running into and whether I would be able to overcome them. More importantly, who knows if there even was a future for me. There is a possibility that I became infected with the morhs' bacteria. There was no cure for it and the inhabitants of the island were the ones most aware of that. They had to watch helplessly how those dear to them died, falling prey to those wretched bacteria. Not more than two days after being infected, the symptoms began showing. The pain became harder and harder to take. They had to spend their last days alive being unconscious under the effects of strong pain killers. Two weeks had passed and I was feeling relatively alright. Yes, I was a bit drowsy at times, but that was because I was not eating. Had I been infected, then I should already have been in terrible pain. In all the cases from the island, the people had been bitten by the morhs. This was not the case for me. That thing only shoved its claws deep into my back. It shouldn't be that big of a deal, right? Perhaps I was safe. Maybe their bacteria were transmitted only through biting. At least this is what was said in the book about morhs that Maggie had found. In any case, I did not want to share my fears with the others. If through some sick joke of life I had been infected, there was no reason to tell them anyway. There was no cure so they could not help me. It would only make them look at me with pity. This was the last feeling I wanted others to have about me. For now, I was alright and this was all that mattered. I pushed away all negative thoughts. I had made a promise to myself before I left home. In this new life I would slowly rebuild myself and become my best version. And what better way to start if not by stopping the whining and trying to be a bit more optimistic? The thought that I would end up moving things with words sounded great. I could do a lot of things just slacking in my bed. Magic has its advantages and I would be discovering them slowly. It takes time and patience.

Time solves everything!

The silence in the car was becoming heavy.

'Hey there, future roommate', I shouted at Christine interrupting her from her daydream.

'What it is?' she asked suspiciously.

But before I could say another thing, Mystic discouraged me. She had kept her mouth shut until now. Why didn't she keep doing that?

'You two won't be sharing a room.'

'What?' Both of us yelled.

'I said that you won't be sharing a room.'

'Oh, I got that part.'

'I thought that we will all three be sharing one room, Maggie interfered.'

'Why can't we do that?' Chris asked.

'It's very simple. As you already know, the campus is divided into two categories. Normal wizards, like Maggie and Kate, and special ones, like Christine. Therefore you will be living in different sectors of the campus. You will probably have some classes together.'

'Is this what you call normal?' I pointed to myself in mockery.

'Katelyn', Eric interfered. 'You cannot stand out; therefore we cannot put you in the special sector.'

'Don't you think that you are overreacting?' I asked revolted.

'No! And you had better not cause any problems. The more you integrate, the safer you will be. Oh, and you will be doing extra classes with Mystic and I because you have a bit of a problem with controlling the magic. We will talk about this later.'

'Great. That's exactly what I needed.'

I mean to say that I am super-excited to learn more about magic even if it scares me. And I want to learn how to control it, but to take lessons

with Eric will be very difficult. I admit that he intimidates me and I am very much attracted to him. I am officially screwed.

'At least you will be sharing a room with Maggie' Christine whined. 'Whereas I, I don't know anybody…'

'We're here', Mystic said.

And then it became silent.

We went to the main building where the headmaster's office was. Mystic and Eric took us on a long and twisted hallway. The place looked so cold and so hostile. Various weird shapes were inscribed on the tall ceiling. A few sinister paintings portraying some very strange people drew my attention. Their red eyes stood out in that dark background. There were also paintings that were meaningless – just some tenebrous images mixed together.

I was expecting something else. Couldn't they have lit this hallway a bit more?

'Oh, what is that deafening noise?' I asked as I was covering my ears.

'It's the bell.'

Yeah, I probably should have guessed that by the doors that started to open one after the other. Students of different ages exited impatiently their classrooms and the silence on the hallways soon vanished.

A short red-headed boy was in a rush and very careless, and bumped straight into Mystic. He looked at her with his big scared eyes. He babbled an apology while his colleagues were laughing silently and were probably making fun of him.

'Fun's over', Mystic snapped at them. 'And you, Sam, stop staring at me! Get lost unless you want to get detention.'

Detention!!!Where am I? I thought I was done with the rigour of primary school. I was going to find out later on that detention was not exactly what I had imagined.

The boy didn't say anything more. He lowered his head and moved away from this woman who seemed to be freaking them out. Mystic had never given me the impression that she was such a cold person, so authoritarian – and definitely not one that I would be scared of. That is why it seemed quite funny to see her in this position.

'And why are you laughing?' She asked as she tried to keep that authoritarian tone of voice; but the smile gave her away.

She was blonde, blue eyes, straight hair down to the shoulders, tall and very long legs; it was impossible for men not to turn their heads. Not to mention the breasts that stood out through that décolletage she always had. She gave me the impression of a Barbie doll and it made it difficult for me to imagine that people would be afraid of her. But I am sure that this was just the surface. Mystic was far from being a Barbie doll. Xena, the Warrior Princess suited her better.

We finally arrived at the headmaster's office, where we were welcomed by a middle-aged woman, a bit chubby and wearing a red dress which, in my opinion, was much too tight for her body shape. On the wall behind her desk, hanged a portrait depicting a group of smiling people. The happiness on their faces was in fact annoying. Or maybe this was only my impression. Just because I felt miserable every time I thought about the possibility of having been poisoned by the morhs' bacteria, it did not mean that the rest could not be happy.

'These are the new students: Katelyn Lambert, Christine and Maggie Ebenzer', Eric said.

'Is either of them special?' Lady in Red asked and scanned us head to toe.

'Only Christine is.'

After that, the lady whose name I had not yet found out gave us each our schedule, a map of the campus and the keys to our rooms. Although classes had already begun that day, because of some problems that Eric had, we arrived later.

We went out of the building were classes were being held and from there we split. Mystic left with Chris to the east part of the campus, while Eric accompanied Maggie and I to the opposite side. We walked among the students and I was feeling more and more embarrassed. I felt as if all eyes were on me. I felt as I was being examined from head to toe. Of course, this is what happened to any new student. Very embarrassing. If I could, I would have become invisible while passing them.

They are paying too much attention to me, more than they should. One of them just got stuck staring at me like a dope. Was there something on my face? Had I changed in any way? As far as I know, I was still the same Katelyn. At least on outside.

'Are you going to move out of the way or do you plan on staying here the whole day?' Eric snapped at him.

'Ee…excuse me' he said embarrassed, and moved out of the way.

Maggie poked me and looked at me giggling.

'What is it?'

'He likes you', she whispered to my ear.

'Ha?'

'It's obvious', she said while pointing to Eric.

She wanted to say something else but she stopped when Eric came next to us.

The thought that he might like me made me smile. But Maggie was just teasing me because she knew that I was attracted to him. I mean, who wouldn't be?

Just before leaving the main courtyard, Eric asked us to wait for him for ten minutes because he had something that needed to be done quickly.

'I cannot believe this', Maggie said after he had left.

'It's only ten minutes.'

'No, Kate, look behind you!'

A group of students were watching the charade put on by some chicks who probably thought they were important if they teased this red-headed girl who had her hair tied in a bun and was short. She was wearing a long wide skirt and a flowery blouse that was also wide. Alright, what is their problem?

'Their stupidity is beyond belief.'

I cannot stand this sort of things so of course that I could not keep away. I went towards the group; Maggie came after me.

A blonde girl, shorter than me and with a very straight hair that was long down to her waist, made a sign and the red-headed girl's books instantly fell to the ground. This was obviously followed by a series of laughter.

'What's so funny?' I asked, while the girl was collecting her books off the ground.'

'Hm...Annie, isn't it obvious? Or better said Granny by the clothes she is wearing'. Laughter again.

'Stop it, alright? What is wrong with you?' I asked them baffled by how childish they could be.

'I thought you had gone passed the high school phase already. You are behaving as if you were 15 years old', Maggie picked on them also.

'Oh, look…it seems we have someone new amongst ourselves– and unfortunately for them, they do not know how things work around here. In case you did not know, I am Sarah Hayes. I would say it's a pleasure to meet you, but I would be lying.'

I ignored her comment and helped Annie get her books off the ground.

'Are you alright?' Maggie asked her.

We turned to leave but "Miss Start-a-fight" grabbed Annie by the arm.

'What do you think you are doing?' She said.

'What do you think you are doing?' Maggie snapped at her. 'And now you'd better let go, dollie.'

Unlike Christine who was calm, Maggie was a volcano. She was just like me, but I had learned how to control my temper. I did not want to start a fight and piss her off even more, but Maggie had managed to do just that; this girl was now so angry that I thought she was going to slap Maggie.

'You have no idea what you've just gotten yourselves into', she threatened.

A brown-haired guy who was wearing jogging trousers and a tank top that showed off his well-built body, took that egocentric out of our way and told her to stop.

'But I am having so much fun. Hey, I bet they do not know how to use their powers, since they're new. Let's give it a try.'

'Sarah, give it a rest!' He repeated.

'It's alright Damien. And you' – she pointed to Maggie and I – 'I can hardly wait for our next encounter.'

You're telling me...

'You've got issues, dollie', Maggie said to her being aware that this would piss her out even more.

'You've just won for yourselves a place on the top of the black list.'

'Let's go, Maggie', I told her, while ignoring this annoying girl.

'And you, Annie, we'll meet again and we'll see who stands up for you then! You are more than this Granny-look and I'll prove it!' Sarah said to her, and then left with her friends.

'What was that?' I asked Annie.

'Nothing important. In fact, it's silly. Sarah thinks that I like her Damien. Sometimes, this place is worse than high school.'

'And does he like you?' Maggie asked her.

'What?'

'Damien. Does he like you?'

'No! There is nothing going on between us. I mean, we worked on a project together and that's it.'

'Did that project involve any kissing?' Maggie asked amused.

'Aaa...'

'I knew it! There's no smoke without fire. Haha, dollie is afraid you will steal her boyfriend.'

'It only happened once! It was an accident, really!'

'So your lips accidentally fell on his?'

I could not help myself so I burst into laughter hearing Maggie's question.

'Something like that', Annie said amused and then became serious all of a sudden as she saw Eric coming our way. 'Hello mister Balfour', she said looking at him.'

For some reason, she was intimidated by Eric, and it was obvious that it was not just because of his good looks. She waved at us and left, but not before saying goodbye to Eric in a respectful manner.

'Mister Balfour...Barbara Balfour... the utmost respect and everyone's fear of you...' Maggie babbled. 'Oh God, this is your campus!'

Alright...now this is not something that I was expecting.

I looked over at Maggie and we both become embarrassed. We had both been talking to Eric as if he was someone our age. None of us had showed him the respect everyone else had for him.

I had so many questions about him. This guy was a complete mystery, one that attracted me like a magnet. The prophecy said that we belonged to one another and that we had a special connection. But I did not believe in prophecies, did I?

Chapter 12:

"Getting settled in"

Soon after that, we reached the dormitory. The entry was inscribed with the picture of a white dove with its wings wide open that looked as though it was ready to fly. Under it, it said: "House of the Sun".

When we entered the building, my eyes were drawn to the show of lights on the ceiling and the works of art on the lively coloured walls. This was surreal but it looked much too real. Just by looking at the image of the sea made me hear the waves splashing onto the shore.

I was walking on the big hallway and, as I moved my sight from one image to the other, I was accompanied by the chirp of birds or by the gentle flow of a creek, or invaded by the smell of flowers with their chalice full of golden particles, or by the smell of fresh grass rubbed between the fingers.

'This is absolutely superb' Maggie said. 'I can hardly wait to see my room.'

'I know. I could stay here for hours in a row and enjoy the peacefulness that this place has to offer.'

'Let's go, girls!' Eric interfered. 'You have all the time in the world. You will get bored with this place eventually.'

We got to a large room – probably the girls' living room. Maybe I had not mentioned this before, but we did not stay in the same building with the boys. Our main purpose here was to discover more about magic. We had to work hard to become exemplary wizards and not fool around.

The living room was welcoming and modern. The walls were painted in a light orange – and they were covered in art just like the hallway walls were. There was not much furniture - it was just the way it should be; just one big sofa in the middle, a small glass table in front of it, and a plasma TV. Aaa…and let's not forget about the many bean bags that were spread all over the room.

From the living room you went straight into the kitchen. Great! I started to like this place more and more.

The building had five floors and an attic. We went up on a round narrow staircase and stopped on the first floor. The room that Maggie and I were sharing was the third on the right side. Number 34 – as it also said on the key. Next to the door there was a plaque that read: Katelyn Lambert, Camille Dupont and Maggie Ebenzer.

'I didn't know we would be sharing the room with someone else also', Maggie said.

'Neither did I', Eric said and he seemed unhappy with this.

'What happened?'

'I will ask that they move you two.'

'But why?' I asked revolted.

'What part of "no one must know about you" did you not understand?' You still cannot control your powers and there are many things about you that we do not know and that we will find out along the way. Do you still have nightmares?'

'Well…' I avoided giving an answer.

The truth was that I'd had nightmares every night ever since I had left the island. But what did this have to do with anything?

'Yes or no?'

'No', I lied.

'In any case, we have to be careful. Your magic goes crazy when you are emotionally overwhelmed. We cannot allow that to happen to you when you are with other people, even if that person is your roommate.'

'I agree with Eric', Maggie said.

'I don't! Please, Eric. I promise you that if anything bizarre happens, even the smallest thing, I will let you know.'

'I am sure of that.'

'Don't worry, Eric. I will be watching her. I will let you know.'

She was serious about that. She didn't just say it to get rid of Eric.

'Great, Maggie. Thank you for your concern.'

'Alright, then I am going. And Katelyn, we start the lessons next weekend.'

'I can hardly wait', I told him.

The room was quite spacious and bright, painted in light green; very nice indeed. Three beds were arranged in a line, separated by nightstands; shelves above every bed and a big desk in the corner. We each had our own wardrobe that was quite small to be fitting all of Maggie's clothes, but it was just perfect for me. I had not taken much with me.

Camille was not in the room.

I quickly arranged my clothes into the wardrobe – if you can call that arranging when you just take them out from the suitcase and into the wardrobe. I took a shower and then I put on a long wide t-shirt and jumped in the bed; during this time, Maggie was trying to fit all the clothes in the closet.

I don't know when I fell asleep. But I had been sleeping for – wow – six hours. The clock on my nightstand showed 8.14 p.m. I got my lazybones out of bed and saw Camille as she was rummaging through the wardrobe. She was taking clothes out, studied them carefully with Maggie, and threw them on her bed when she nodded in disapproval.

'Good morning, sleepyhead. I am Camille Dupont. It's nice to meet you!'

She was really nice; dark curly long hair falling on her back, green eyes and a very expressive and smiling face. She had a French accent and by her name you could tell that she was from France.

'Look who's up', Maggie said.

'I'm Katelyn Lambert. It's nice to meet you! Thanks for being quiet. I usually wake up at the slightest noise.'

'Actually, you have been sleeping tight, despite the noise in here. As you can probably realise, there's not much silence in a girls dormitory, not to mention that my phone has been ringing many times. And believe me when I say that it rings very loud and for a long time – that's because I almost always leave it here and there', Camille said.

'Wait', I said baffled. 'Are you joking?'

'Why would I? I also blow-dried my hair and…'

I could not follow what she was saying anymore. I never slept during the afternoon. That's lost time if you ask me. How had I been sleeping for six hours straight? And how come I am still so tired? I feel worse than when I was coming back home from a party in the morning.

'Ouch', I said as I found myself being hit in the head with a pillow.

Maggie laughed.

'Wakey-wakey, sleepyhead.'

'What have you been doing?' I asked.

168

'Camille gave me a small tour of the campus. It's really cool', Maggie said and she seemed very enthusiastic about it.

'Did you talk to Chris?'

'We met briefly in the courtyard. She told me she has some pretty nice roommates. But most of the girls there are a bit too full of themselves. I told her to ignore them.'

'She will get used to them in time. I hope. Camille, what year are you in?'

'I'm a sophomore. It is a bit harder in the beginning, until you get used to it. Well…except for some classes that are a nuisance.'

'I can hardly wait to get the better of those classes', Maggie said.

'I think they might get the better of you, actually.' I said to her.

'Haha, that's funny.'

'And now, can I get back to sleep? I am still sleepy.'

Maggie pulled the bed linen from me and grabbed me by the hand to get out from the bed.

'Don't you even think about doing that! You've slept enough. Camille, the blouse in your hand is a definite no. It's much too flowery and coloured.'

'What is wrong with it? It's lively', she said.

'Maggie is right. I would have chosen something a bit simpler. Wait, where are you going?'

'There is a party in the boys' dormitory on Saturday; it's the remotest building of all. It's a party to mark the beginning of the school year.

'And we are also going', Maggie said.

'Great. I can hardly wait', I said ironically.

With everything that was going on, I did not feel like partying. Although if I think about it, I could try to forget about all the problems and to loosen up a bit, at least for one evening.

'Ethan will also be there. We haven't seen each other this summer. I have to surprise him and I have no idea what to wear.'

'Your boyfriend?' Maggie asked.

'It's complicated. I mean…I don't know where we are at. The fact that we have not seen each other for such a long time has made us distant. From talking on the phone every day, we got to just once a week.

'We sometimes tend to complicate matters when we shouldn't. Be honest with him and tell him how you feel and how you see things.'

'Or not…' said Maggie more to herself. 'Sometimes, saying how you feel can have not-so-pleasant consequences. *Seeing Camille's enthusiasm drop, she changed her idea.* Anyway…I am sure that it will be alright in your case. You are too full of life and you ooze too much positive energy. No way is there anyone who wouldn't like you.'

'That's very nice of you. Thank you.'

Maggie smiled and chose the blue dress, which she handed to Camille. Something was wrong with her. I was curious to know what bad memories haunted her. It was obvious that she had had a bad experience in love. But Maggie was not exactly the person who opens up to anybody.

'It's perfect', Camille said.

For what's worth, she did look very nice in that dress which showed off her legs. This was a summer dress, tight on the upper part and with a few ruffles, and pretty short; too short for me. I would have never felt alright wearing that.

'I take it that none of the teachers knows about the party, right? As far as I remember, partying was forbidden in the regulations.'

'You've read the regulations?' Maggie asked surprised.

I understood why she was reacting like that. I would have done the same a while back. But the new Katelyn is more panicked and slightly more responsible.

It's good to be responsible, isn't it?

'No parties or anything else that might distract you from your initial goal; that of becoming as best as you can and to prove to your parents that they are not paying all that money to keep you in this renown campus for no reason. But what are rules for if not to be broken? This sounded too much like something I would have said not too long before.

'And what do we do if we get caught?' I asked.

'We won't get caught', Camille replied being very sure of herself.

'So, calm down! Take it easy!'

'I'll try. Camille, can I ask you something?'

'Sure.'

'Can you tell me a bit about the campus? I mean, what should we expect?

'I assume that you've both seen the dove at our dormitory entry. It represents innocence and purity that which we all are when we first step into this institution.' *Maggie laughed.* 'It's not what you're thinking. I am strictly referring to magic. We come here to discover ourselves and to grow up. We learn how to love and how to understand those things which seemed meaningless before, and we also learn how to hate. There is always a bad side of things – no matter how small. In Greek mythology the dove is Aphrodite's bird and thus a symbol of love. The Arabs see in this small creature a messenger of love, fortune and peace, of fidelity between the husband and wife, and between brothers. However no matter how it's seen, all things said about it make sense eventually. It will always be a symbol of good. This is how we also are. It does not matter how others see us or how we perceive things. The important thing is how we really are. To be able to look into our internal mirrors and to say that we are happy with what we see. The open wings of the dove represent the flight to knowledge – to a new beginning. Anyway, I'll stop boring you with this. What I wanted to say is that no matter what you find out, no matter what might happen to you, the important thing is to remember who you are – who you truly are.'

I never would have imagined that Camille can be so wise.

'What do you mean to say with this? What do you mean to say with "no matter what might happen" to me?' I asked her.

'I am guessing you were both impressed by what you saw in the hallway. It's all magic. But don't forget – there is no such thing as the perfect place. Wherever there is good there is also bad. Just like...'

She continued to talk although I did not understand much of what she was saying. I did not know where she wanted to get at. She moved from one idea to the other much too fast. I tried to seem surprised about the new information, but still I managed to slip a yawn. Maggie shared my feelings but she did not make any comments.

'Magic was never created for the purpose of harming, but it is being used for that also. There are people who are dependent on power and who end up selling their soul for it. They forget what it means to be human. They become overwhelmed by the wave of power that controls them and by the thirst for "knowledge". And the very special ones are many times hunted down like animals.'

She had finally managed to get out attention.

'These ones find pleasure in others' suffering. They feed on it. As our fear grows bigger, so is their power. There are also those who cannot control their powers – rare cases, obviously.'

Maggie looked at me instantly and gave me an understanding look. She knew about my control problems. I tried to look uninterested but the truth is that I was afraid. What would happen if I ended up not being able to control my powers? I would become a monster. I wouldn't have any more feelings.

'Kate, have you checked your schedule? We'll have all the classes together. We are in the same group.' Maggie changed the subject as she realised that I needed to concentrate on something else.

'Thanks', I whispered to her.

The first glance through the schedule didn't say much to me. I read it again about five times.

1. History of magic
2. Magic for beginners
3. Practice
4. Creatheology
5. Sports
6. Defence lessons
7. Self-deduction
8. Optional classes: fine arts; theatre; creation: prose, poetry; music, musical instruments; archery; fencing.

I had eight classes and the schedule seemed quite busy: six classes on Mondays and Fridays and eight classes every other day.

'Why didn't they call this Moronology? Then at least everybody would have remembered this stupid name. And what's up with the defence lessons?'

Camille started to laugh.

'That's exactly what my first reaction was.'

'How about you enlighten us. A bit more', Maggie said

'Let's see...History of magic. That's interesting, but it can be very boring sometimes. I think it's more because of Miss Grace; she is very demanding. In Magic for beginners you learn about the foundation of magic; a lot of boring theoretical aspects and stuff that is difficult to memorize. Practice is really cool, but difficult. You just do whatever you learned in the previous class – but that's not to say that it's easy or that you can do it from your first try. It takes a lot, a lot of work. Creatheology. It sounds extremely strange. Breeds. You learn everything there is to know about not-so-normal animals. I mean the strange creatures. Defence lessons. Hmm...how to defend yourself in different circumstances.'

'Yeah...that's obvious, isn't it? But what should we be defending ourselves from?' I asked her.

'You two really don't know that much. You learn how to fight off black magic. We are in a constant battle against it. Self-deduction is a bit more complicated. It's more like really bad math. You learn how to anticipate what spell the other one will use; how to calculate the angle, the distance between two objects and other stuff like that.'

'What? I thought I was done with mathematics', I said revolted.

'It seems not. And things are only getting more complicated. I chose fine arts. What are you two going to choose?'

'Aaa, I haven't yet thought about that. Can I choose two?' I asked her.

'Why would you do that?' Maggie asked.

'You have to talk to the headmistress. Normally they don't want us wasting our time. If it were up to them, we would always have to practice – to become better and better.'

'I will choose fencing. I took classes for five years and I quit just a year ago, but I think it's time I started again.'

Before either of us could say anything more, a few girls rushed into our room. After we became acquainted to one another, I found myself in the living room, in front of the TV and with a bag of popcorn on my lap. The girls picked a comedy and it turned out to be a movie worth seeing. I laughed a lot.

Chapter 13:

"Off to a bad start"

I was sound asleep when I heard my name being called over and over by a voice that was becoming really annoying. I finally opened my eyes.

It wasn't even seven in the morning! I could have hit Camille with something. I could see her lips moving but I did not understand what she was saying. I nodded.

Classes were starting at eight and she was already leaving. Maggie was not in the room. How could they be such early birds?

I barely fell back asleep when the message ringtone woke me up. I took the phone from my nightstand - to mute it.

'Oh, no!!!' I shouted and jumped out of the bed.

How could this happen? Had I really lost track of time so much? It was 9.30 a.m. and I had just missed my first class and not just any class but two hours on the History of magic. Could I have had a better start than this? And, on top of that, I was still sleepy.

I threw some books in my bag (I hope I got the right ones), took the fastest shower and put on the first clothes that I could find – some plain tight jeans and a white t-shirt. I did not lose time brushing my hair. On the way there, I tied my hair in a bun.

Great! I was going to look "my best".

What a first impression I would be making.

I started to run hoping that I would make it there in time at least for my second class, Magic for beginners, since I had lost the first one entirely. There were still five minutes left and, with a bit of luck, if the professor would be running late, I would have made it just in time.

As I was going down the hill, I felt I was in the worst physical fitness possible. I almost felt granny-like. Almost!

I wasn't paying attention and I was deep in my thoughts therefore I did not hear the deafening sound – it must have been the bell – which proved to be the horn of a car. I panicked and simply became still in front of the vehicle that stopped just inches away from me. Just a bit more and I would have been...I shook and immediately let that thought fly by.

'Watch where you're going!' The guy behind the wheel shouted at me.

'And you should drive more carefully.' I was about to say something else to him but I stopped when I saw Eric coming out from the car.

He looked at me and sighed.

'Oh...I don't know why but I am not even one bit surprised', he said. He examined me and then concluded: 'You don't look very well. We need to talk.'

I couldn't have expected anything else from him.

'Later. I have a class to go to.'

I was only five minutes late and the professor was already there. Damn it!

I apologised for being late and ignored the blaming look she gave me. I saw Maggie waving at me and I sat on the empty seat next to her.

'What have you been doing until now?'

'I have been sleeping.'

'You can't tell. You have such black circles around your eyes. You don't look well at all.'

Yeah...nothing new about that.

'Is this what you've been doing in just five minutes?' I asked her and felt almost annoyed with the fact that she had already written down half a page.

'Do you have anything to say, miss...? The professor asked.

She wasn't tall; her hair was short and she wore glasses just like Harry Potter's. Uh...really scary.

'Aaa...'

'Name?'

'Katelyn Lambert'

'Miss Lambert, perhaps you'd like to remind us all what I just said.'

Oh God! I won't contradict anyone else who says that short women are scary.

'Well...Aaa...It's not only about the words but also how we say them – how we feel?'

I had just read what Maggie wrote. Thank God her writing was readable.

'You were lucky this time', she said, realising what I had done. 'Now let's continue. As I was saying earlier – and I will repeat that for those of you who were late – we will only be learning the basics for now.

I bet that she wasn't trying to be nice to me; she only wanted to remind me that I had dared be late for her class. Although I should have paid attention to what she was saying, and write down what I should have, it was difficult for me to concentrate. I just could not keep my eyes open.

'It is very difficult in the beginning and that is why you must take everything very serious.' She looked straight at me.

I was officially a target for my professor.

I had not expected this but the class turned out to be quite interesting – the professor had actually managed to keep me focused. She told us about illusions. It was all about concentrating and paying attention. You had to look in the direction where you wanted to create the illusion and to think only about the image that you wanted to project. Then we had to say aloud some words that would normally seem to be harmless and meaningless. In the beginning, illusions appear in a mist and you cannot really create complex images. That is why you need a lot of practice.

There were three things that only the older students managed to do, and not even they could do it so well. The first one was to be able to create the illusion of a person, but not just any illusion; it would have to be one who would look very real no matter from which angle you'd look at it. To give it life through posture, face expression and – most difficult – to make the eyes look alive and deep. The second thing was about creating scenery; you had to manage to make it so that you could feel everything in it, from the strong smell of the flowers to the sound of the sea waves, just as I had felt when I first entered the "House of the Sun". The third one was to hypnotise someone through the beauty of illusions.

The class lasted one hour. At the end, the professor told us to check the book for additional details – she had presented us with the overall ideas – and to prepare for the next lesson.

I checked my messages inbox. They were all from Maggie who kept asking how I was.

'Seriously? Twenty messages?' I asked her while we were heading for the practice class.

'We were worried, Christine and I. We take History of magic together.'

"How is she? Is she alright? What does she think about all of this so far?'

'We didn't manage to talk that much. The professor is crazy. We've been writing constantly, without any break. She saw two students talking and asked them to leave the classroom. Chris seems alright. She is already making friends. You know how she is; nice to everybody; there is no way you won't like her.'

'You're right.'

'We have a break after practice. We'll meet her then and talk more.'

I was entering the classroom when Maggie grabbed me by the arm and pulled me back.

'We have to make a short stop at the bathroom first. Did you even brush your air? You are lucky I have some foundation with me to cover those black rings around your eyes.'

I sighed. It made no sense to try and contradict Maggie so I just let her do her thing.

She brushed my hair and tied it nicely in a ponytail; she put foundation on my face and some blush to give some colour to my cheeks because I was very pale.

'Now it's much better', she said. 'And it did not take long either.'

She was right. I looked a bit more alive now. No black circles and not scruffy hair.

'Thanks.'

Practice turned out to be a complete failure for me. I cannot say the same thing about Maggie who did very well. I tried to concentrate. Really! But my thoughts kept being somewhere else. Moreover, my back was hurting and I was not in the mood for anything.

I did however get support from my professor – luckily, she was quite nice. Maggie and Addison, one of the girls we had met a night before, also tried to boost my morale. It was probably easy for them to say "You can do it, it's not difficult" and bla, bla, bla...since they were doing better than anyone else.

'Is everything alright?' The professor asked me when the class was over.

No, it's not.

'Yes.'

'Are you sure? You are the only one who did not manage to create an illusion, no matter how bad.'

Oh, yes...tell me something I didn't know – please.

'I will practice – I promise.'

During lunch break I met one of Christine's roommates. Beatrice: a brunette with her hair short around her ears, very tall and lean. She wore too much black makeup around her eyes. I liked her haircut; it really suited her although I would never see myself like that. She was alright, very chatty and full of life and she turned out to be one of Camille's good friends. They were both sophomores.

'Isn't that girl Annie?' Maggie said, as she was pointing to a girl who was sitting by herself at a remote table in the corner of the room.

'I believe she is.'

Maggie got up from the table.

'I'm going to tell her to sit with us at our table.'

The lunch break went by very quickly. I wasn't hungry so I barely managed to eat an apple. But the company was quite nice. Annie is also a freshman and is special. She can hypnotise people through music. That's so cool.

Except for the two sophomores, the rest of us went to our last class after the lunch break - Createheology.

The professor was an old grey man, short and with a gentle face. He began telling us about the lubrinsons. They were some cute creatures that seemed to be totally harmless. Their looks however are deceiving one. These animals are very sensitive and as soon as they feel threatened they become extremely aggressive. That's where their name comes from. In Latin *lubricus* means deceitful and *insons* means harmless.

'Excuse me professor', I addressed him before the end of the class.

Yes, is there something that it was not clear?'

'In fact, it has nothing to do with our lesson. I wanted to ask you if you knew anything about the morhs.'

It was as if the sky had fallen – that's how strange he looked at me. His smile turned instantly into a frown. He pondered a bit before answering me.

'I don't know that much about them.' He shrugged his shoulders. 'They are mentioned in some myths.'

Myths? What was he talking about?

'I think you may not have understood me. I said morhs. You know, the living-dead.'

'I understood you just fine, miss. Any other questions? This time about the class.'

What was the deal with that? He was surely hiding something. The problem was that it was only Maggie and I who seemed to realise that. After all, we had had a very unpleasant experience with them.

'But...'

He looked at me and then started to talk again about the lubrinsons, but I could not help it so I interrupted him.

'What can you do if you've been poisoned by one? How do you know if...'

'Enough already, the professor yelled'. You'll get detention after school.

'Detention? You have got to be kidding me. We are not in primary school anymore. We are grownups now' Maggie said, as if to back up what I was thinking.

Her attempt to defend me only got her into detention as well. The teachers here are really crazy, no doubt about it.

Great...a murmur started all over the classroom. "What is she talking about?" or "She's nuts" or other stuff like that. I don't understand anything anymore. Why are my classmates acting like that? The morhs are something important to talk about and we have all the right to be talking about them. I had not hurt anyone. And the fact that we would end up in detention – although we had not done anything wrong – was just too much.

'But it's unfair', I yelled.

The professor couldn't care less.

'Lucas, please take Miss Lambert to the headmistress's office and explain to her what has happened. Miss Ebenzer will follow her shortly.' He said to one of my colleagues.

Maggie puffed and made no further comments; she preferred to ignore the professor.

I, however, could not refrain.

'But it's unfair', I protested.

Despite that, I had to do what he had said. I collected my stuff and went across the room – that seemed to take forever and it was very embarrassing. I went across the room in total silence while all eyes were on me. Maggie would have liked to say something else, but I signalled her to keep quiet.

Good job, Katelyn...

And just when I was getting ready to say that this day could not get any worse, I ran into Eric in the headmistress' office.

He looked at me without saying anything but the expression on his face was not a welcoming one. It was obvious that we would have to have a talk later on and that it would not be a very pleasant one.

'Oh, Eric, you don't need to bother yourself with troubling teenagers', said the headmistress.

'Troubling teenagers? Really?' I said revolted.

'You'd better keep quiet', Lucas whispered to me.

Of course I did not listen to him.

'I am not the problem here, you are' – I continued saying.

The headmistress gave me a nasty look. I thought she was going to have a breakout or something. Instead, she took everything calmly. She gave me this long speech that ended with:

'This is only your first day here and you've started it on the wrong foot. You skipped your first class and I have been getting complaints about you from Mrs. Miller. You were late for her class and she was also disappointed with your activity and your focus in her class. You were a disaster in practice and your mind was somewhere else; and now you're in my office.'

How did she know all of this? Were we all being watched or had Eric had someone watching me in particular?

Lucas interfered and told the professor about my breakout in Creatheology, emphasising my volcanic way of being and then he took off. What a teller.

'Are you at odds with Mister Edison? I cannot believe that. No one ever had any problems with him. He is the calmest person I have ever met. He is extremely patient and tolerating of your little outbursts, and you have managed to be kicked out of his class. Tell me miss, how did you manage to do that?

Eric and she were both looking at me waiting for an answer. Truth be told, I was barely suppressing my laughter. The headmistress' outfit was too out there. She was all dressed in green – a knee-high woollen skirt and a tight top which showed off her love handles. Didn't she realise how awkward she looked?

I tried to compose myself, I really did try it, but when the headmistress got up from her chair and I saw her pink tassel stilettos, I burst into laughter.

Eric continued to be quiet although I was sure that he had a lot to say. I had managed to piss off the headmistress.

'You don't seem to get it, miss. You will only end up getting yourself in a lot of trouble if you continue with this attitude. If you keep this up, you will end up being expelled. For the time being, however, you will have to give a hand in the library.'

I had never imagined that library-duty could scare anyone off; but I was about to find out that this library was hosting several-hundred-years old collections. In time, it had gathered so many volumes that the librarian had had enough of keeping the records and of cleaning the place up. In order to help, and to open up a book every once in a while, the students took turn at doing work in the library. This was such a tedious and unpleasant job, that it had become known as detention.

Eric gave me the once-over and I wondered what he must have been thinking – the expression on his face did not let anything out.

I told my version of the story to the headmistress and when she heard the word "morh", she became pale. Why was everybody going nuts when they heard about the morhs? Eric and she were staring at each other as if they were hiding something. Mrs. Green whispered something to him and then she left, leaving the two of us alone.

I was expecting Eric to become infuriated and to give me a long speech, but he did not say a thing. With the same poker-face he had before, he came to me and stopped just inches away. He gently patted my cheek and his touch made me flinch. Now this was something that I did not expect.

'What are you doing?' I asked him and my voice was trembling.

He did not reply.

I moved back and he followed my every step until I hit the wall and could no longer get away from him. He grabbed me by the shoulders and starred at me. I could feel my heart beat going crazy while I became lost in his deep blue eyes and his face that was so beautiful. I had never before felt so vulnerable in front of a guy – no matter how good looking.

He came even closer to me and I thought that he was going to kiss me. A part of me was disappointed that he did not do it. I longed to feel his fleshy lips.

'You will forget everything about the morhs and about the discussion we just had', he said to me and I could feel his breath on my lips.

His voice was so warm and his smell was overwhelming. What perfume was he using? If there was anything I knew for sure, it was that I wanted to please him.

When I heard him say the word "morh" again, I wondered what it meant.

And just before approving it, an inner voice stopped me. At first I tried to fight it, but then I suddenly woke up to reality – as if someone had poured me a glass of cold water over my head.

'Eric, I cannot believe that you tried to hypnotise me again! Did you expect it to work this time?'

I pushed him away in anger and I left the office without waiting for an answer from him. I was too angry at him. My memories were mine and no matter how awful they may have been, no one had the right to toy with them.

Chapter 14:

"Getting to know Eric's dark side"

The next day I started off in the gym. After a twenty-minutes warming up, the instructor found it amusing to have us run five more laps around the field that was quite large. Obviously, I only managed to do three. My fitness condition was lamer than ever. Whoever thought of the idea of putting two gym classes from 8 in the morning had a bad idea.

Lucky for me, the instructor, a very tough man and much too fat for his job, was most of the time busy reading some papers. So I managed to skip some of the activities without him seeing me.

After the super warm-up, Maggie went for volleyball and I for basketball. I was not too good at it, but I managed. Now however, I did not feel like doing anything, not to mention that my energy level was down to non-existent. After ten minutes, during which I basically did nothing except for walking on the field and passing the ball when it came my way, I dropped it altogether. I found my way out among the others and, before the instructor finished his reading, I left the gym. He had called the attendance list at the beginning of the class and, given how many we were, the chances of him figuring out that I had left were very slim.

Two classes of Self deduction followed afterwards. I thought I was going to go mad. Christine felt the same.

I was not myself. The fact that I felt so drowsy made me feel very peevish. And it was not because of the gym class. Truth be told, I had not been very active either. Moreover, I could not concentrate on anything; nothing important. I could only think of Eric. I had not seen him since the day before and I planned on avoiding him for as long as I could. He had called me several times, but of course I did not answer. Mystic had also called me to check how my first day in school had been. It was an odd conversation. She seemed nervous and she is never nervous. We did not talk that much. She was going to come see me the following day. She told me that I could always count on her for anything I needed. No matter the time of day. That was nice of her, but it's not like I was going to open up to a stranger.

I was sleepy and the only thing I wanted was to put my head on the desk and sleep. But Maggie always showed her intention to give answers in class so the professor had her eyes on us. She loved maths as much as I hated it. When the professor began explaining to us how to calculate the angle we want to choose for a spell, I instantly felt how I got a headache. Of all the theorems she explained to us, the only thing I understood was that any spell is done on a certain perimeter. So, depending on how large you want the area you're making the spell on to be – that's for more complex spells – you have to first calculate the theorems of life.

Christine and I skipped the following Self deduction class. I could not have stand listening to another theorem. I had heard enough for one day.

Finally, the well-deserved lunch break. When Maggie and I entered the cafeteria, Camille waved at us. She was glowing and the boy next to her was the only reason why she was in such a good mood. Christine was already there together with Beatrice, her roommate. We also met Arriana Gomez, a blonde with straight hair down to her shoulders, and Mayte Sanchez, a red-headed who had her hair very long and very straight. They were both much taller than I was. They were Christine's colleagues and they had been best friends since the fifth grade; two goofs who had come all the way from Mexico.

When Nate Pattinson, Ethan's friend, the one that Camille liked, came to our table, the two Mexican girls also began flirting with him, having eyes only for him. It was all about *guapo* this, *guapo* that. In Spanish it means beautiful. Truth be told, he was not at all bad looking. He had green eyes, dimples and a smile that widened every time he looked over at Maggie. She however, paid more attention to the tuna salad she was eating instead of to him. Unlike Christine who was eating chicken thighs with French fries, Maggie was always careful with what she ate. I had to make myself eat the Bulgarian salad I had taken. It was good but I had not had much of an appetite those days.

This was only my second day here and I already needed a long vacation.

Ahhh. And I cannot stand this pesky back pain anymore.

And no, it was not from the morh's poison - I was lying to myself. I was probably being the biggest irresponsible. But, since there was no information about any cure against morh poison, I preferred to just pretend that nothing had happened. Perhaps there was a slight chance that I was not even infected.

'Are you alright?' Christine asked me.

'Better than ever', I replied ironically. 'And don't you dare read my feelings', I warned her. 'This is not my best day.'

'She pushed herself too hard in gym class today, that's why she is so moody', Maggie interfered. Then she laughed and showed off her dimpled cheeks.

'You have a beautiful smile', Nate said to her.

'Thank you.'

She tried to put on a serious face but her smile just became even wider.

'In fact, my sister wanted to say thank you and to tell you that she thinks you also have a very nice smile.'

We all started to laugh, except for Maggie who looked angrily at her sister.

'Look who's there', Beatrice said changing the topic and thus saving Maggie from an embarrassing situation.

When I turned, Barbie was in Damien's arms. They were kissing.

'I still cannot understand how he can be with her', I said to them.

'Aaa…maybe he does not care that the girl has no brain?'

'Haha, Maggie. You are right', Beatrice said. 'Maybe Sarah has other talents though.'

'Yes, maybe she is a real tiger in bed', Arriana said amused.

'I really did not want to get that image into my head. Kate, did you hear what we have to do during detention?'

'Don't remind me, please. But you are a bookworm anyway. You should enjoy it.'

'Yeah…I would rather read the books than to wipe the dust off them!'

The Mexican girls started to laugh.

'Detention already from day one? ', Mayte said.

'Maggie, what did you do? Was the professor upset with you because you knew more than he did?

-Haha Arriana, not funny. Ah, I almost forgot. Kate, Christine, I am really sorry that you two could not stay for the second Self-deduction class.'

'We're not at all sorry', Christine and I said.

'You'll get the next course via email. Since you left earlier, the professor assumed that you knew everything already so you two will be the ones who will present the lesson next time.'

'You're joking, aren't you?' Christine asked.

'This is going to be really interesting. When is your next Self deduction class? I think I am going to pay you a visit.'

'Haha, very nice of you Camille', I said sulky.

'Kate, what happened yesterday? When I met Eric he seemed to be pretty concerned about you', Christine asked me.

'I'm sure he was', I babbled.

Arriana shifted from me to Christine waiting for me to answer.

'Who is Eric? Is he cute?'

'It doesn't matter', I replied.

But obviously that Christine could not help herself.

'Very cute in fact.'

'Is he your boyfriend?' Ethan interfered.

'Oh God, no, no way!'

'It's obvious that she's crazy about him', Mayte teased me.

'That's not true. No! No way!'

'Than why do you get so worked up when we talk about him?' Nate asked.

'You can all believe whatever you want.'

'And yet, who is Eric?' Mayte asked again. 'We also want to meet him.'

Christine laughed.

'Everybody in the campus knows him. Eric Balfour.'

'Thanks, Maggie. You're a sweetheart' I said ironically to her.

'Nooo', the Mexican girls said.

Beatrice was the only one who did not sigh at the thought of Eric's good looks.

'All the girls are crazy about him. But he doesn't care about anyone in the campus. I mean, not seriously. I don't even think that it is allowed for him to be involved with any student, although I am sure that he has been involved with many, but unofficially.'

I was getting pissed.

'I don't care who Eric sleeps with. As far as I am concerned he might as well get involved with all of them.'

'Bien sûr', Camille said. 'Now, leaving dear Eric aside, tell me something. Are we all going to the swimming pool after the classes?

We decided we would all meet up at 5 p.m. at the entrance to the indoor pool in the sports area; this was in the northern part of the campus.

I don't know how that happened but just as I was getting up, Barbie passed by me. Not being able to help herself being a snake, she gave me a gentle push.

'Watch where you're going, Barbie', Maggie said to her.

'Your friend is so dull that I thought she was only a poor illusion. Should I be apologizing for that?' She asked her cohort of bimbos who were always following her.

Arriana got up from the table. She was twice as tall as Sarah was.

'In fact you should apologize.'

'You are *malade à la tête*', Camille said angrily and being aware that Sarah did not understand a word of French.

'I really cannot stand this one', Beatrice interfered.

'Who are you calling "this one"? She snapped, but Nate interfered just in time and came between them.

'Come one, Sarah, cut it out. Must you really pull a scene every single day?'

'Whose side are you on?' She asked angrily.

He took her by the arm and told her something to her ear.

Maggie changed the expression on her face; it was obvious that she had been disturbed with the fact that Nate seemed to be close to Sarah.

She was normally a calm person and had good control over her emotions, but now she looked as if she would snap at the slightest push. And then it came.

'I heard you were supposed to be in detention and that you got into this school because of your connections – magic is not your strong suit. How did you manage to do that? Did you pay Eric in kind?'

I truly could not believe what I was hearing.

'Look here, porcelain dollie', Maggie snapped. 'I've only known you one day and I have already had enough of you and your outbursts.'

'So it is my outbursts that had you in detention yesterday? Please don't tell me that. You got so mad because Eric has a weakness for blondes and chose your friend?'

'Enough', Nate yelled at her; he was visibly disturbed by her comment to Maggie whose face was not a very pleasant one.

'I don't know what you're claiming but you are nothing but a spoiled blonde who craves to be in the spotlight and who won't stop from anything to be in the centre of attention. Channel your energy on something else. If you use it like this, you will only manage to embarrass yourself even more. So next time you decide to pick on someone, think twice before you do it!' Maggie shouted at her.

Sarah only laughed – just like her friends. Anyway, what could I have expected from them.

'I don't understand why you're laughing when you are so damn pissed. 'And no matter how much you want to deny it, I know this because I can simply feel your emotions. Hey, your blonde friend is about to cry – and I think the same goes for you too.'

Sarah did not say a thing. She moved her lips and before I realised what was happening, I heard Chris yelling.

'What did you do to her?' Maggie shouted; this time she forgot all about her good manners and jumped at her. If Nate had not come between them she would have probably pulled her hard by the hair.

'Nothing – just a little illusion...'Sarah replied while Maggie was struggling in Nate's arms.

'Let go of me!' She yelled. '

Christine became still and was staring at a fixed spot. The Mexican girls kept trying to talk to her but to no avail. She just wasn't there with us. Camille and Nate were begging Sarah to tell them what spell she had used so that they might use the appropriate cancelling spell. If they'd use a wrong one, the consequences could have been deadly. Beatrice who was a very fiery person, kept trying to put a spell on Sarah, but Ethan did not let her and interrupted her every time she attempted.

'Just tell us already what damn spell you used', I yelled at her.

Nothing. I looked over at Christine who was crying and I could instantly feel this powerful need to shut Sarah's mouth once and for all.

A dominant thought that made all other thoughts become paralysed in fear.

I was losing my control.

I heard my name being called several times but I could no longer realise what was happening around me, and so I did not reply.

The windows of the cafeteria opened up abruptly and smashed into the wall and an unexpected wind blast entered the room. It became cold and that's when it happened; a flash. With the cold feeling, the thought of making Sarah suffer came to life. The wind picked Barbie up into the air; she yelled so loud that she could probably be heard from all over the campus. She was left suspended into the air for several good seconds, and then she was thrown far away from me and from my friends, smashing into the wall.

Seeing her hurt, my anger diminished and I came to my senses; only then did I realise what had happened, what I had just done. I looked around me and everybody was looking at me terrified as if I were some kind of monster.

"Kate, are you alright?'

I did not reply. There was only one thought in my mind. I had injured a person and it did not matter how much she deserved it – she was still a human being. Could this be the work of someone inside me, and who was just now beginning to surface? What about the feelings? They were so deep. And especially that anger that was so difficult to control. I was simply terrified by the thought that there was a moment when I wished Sarah to become breathless.

'She seems to be in shock', Mayte said. 'Or hypnotised or something...Something was going on', I could hear the despair in the tone of her voice.

'One of you did this', I heard someone say.

And he was right. I had done that. I don't know how bad Sarah had been injured but she had taken a serious fall. People gathered around her. Damien took her into his arms and probably went with her to the medical office.

Wait a minute...they do not know that it was me? This means that I have been feeling so guilty that I thought that all the looks and the offending were addressed to me.

'You will pay for this', several people said.

These were Sarah's best people. Should they not be with her now? Some friends they were – it was more important for them to first spill their venom.

'If you were not so dumb, you would have known that only someone who's specialized in air can make this incantation without using any spell words. Did you hear any of us speak out any words of that sort?

The fight was blowing out of proportion while I was struggling with the feeling of guilt that was becoming more and more difficult to bear.

I am a monster. I was turning into a monster.

I ran out of the cafeteria without looking back.

I wanted to be alone. Just me and my thoughts; no matter how dark they were; they were my thoughts and I had to confront them. I had to take full responsibility for my deeds.

What if that inner force would take control over me every time I got angry?

I could feel the wind better than the others did. I felt how the wind became alive under my command. I had created it and I was the one who was involuntarily telling it what to do.

I was crying and running despite the pain in my back.

I stopped when I found myself surrounded by trees. I was in the middle of the forest and I think that...well...I was rather lost. I did not know where I had come from and nothing seemed familiar to me.

Then someone screamed. It became quiet for a few moments until it could be heard again, this time even louder. If someone needed help then that was my chance to make up for what I had done to Sarah.

And so I ran in the direction of the noise. It did not take long before I found the source of the screaming. A girl was kneeling before him...I could not believe my eyes when I saw who it was. I hid just in time behind an oak and managed to keep away from their sight.

Please tell me this is not real. Around that girl there was Mystic and another man that I did not know.

NO! I almost felt like screaming. Eric did freak me out sometimes and he did have his bad side, but he was not a bad person. I just knew that he was not. I could feel something from him and I am sure that he could feel me. He and I had a connection. And Mystic? I knew her good side. It cannot be that she is so cold and uncaring to the pain of that girl.

They were torturing her. Couldn't they see what they were doing to her? Couldn't they tell how much pain they were causing her? Every scream of hers hurt me deep inside. It was so difficult to watch her pass away.

Slowly...and painfully...

And I was helpless in front of these people who were finally showing off their true selves by taking off their masks.

'Who is that?' Eric shouted thus covering the screaming of that young girl.

When she lifted her head up I froze. It was Annie.

'In your dreams', she said calmly.

Nooo!!! Not Annie! She is such a good girl. How had she gotten herself in such a situation? Why would anyone have any problem with her? She was so innocent.

Eric looked as if he was about to explode. He clenched his fists and a green light began to surround them. From his hating look I could tell that he was focusing all that feeling into the light that grew bigger and bigger.

I turned – realising what was coming next. Annie screamed for a short while and then it became silent. I looked at her and I saw her surrounded by a green light. It seemed to slowly suffocate her.

I hated them; I hated all three of them. They were rubbish.

And that is when I felt the force that was trying to take control over me. This time I did not fight it. After all, it was a part of me and now we both wanted the same thing; to save Annie.

Chapter 15:

"In the wrong place, at the wrong time"

'You are killing her!' I shouted and came out from my hiding.

They were obviously not expecting this; I took advantage of the fact that I had taken them by surprise and I immediately ran to Annie who was now lying on the ground.

'I beg you. Stop!' I said to Eric with tears in my eyes.

I signalled Mystic and the other man to stay out of this.

'Why must you always be in the wrong place at the wrong time?'

'Eric!?' Mystic called for him.

I was unable to control myself anymore and I panicked.

It was clear; I was going to end up in the same situation as the unconscious girl next to me. I wanted to help her. At least she was no longer surrounded by that light – for the time being...But my stupid courage also proved to be my death sentence. And I still could not believe that I had been so attracted to this guy.

'Cut it out', I heard a voice in my head saying.

I was delirious. This was surely one of their spells. I am going to die...I will slowly pass away and...Before I could finish my thought, the voice stopped me.

If you continue complaining like that then you will really end up dead.

Alright...now this was definitely not a spell.

Hey...you are a part of me. Are you my other part; the one that has been trying to take control over me? The one that created the wind, the one...?

Can we leave all this for later?

But... I tried to say.

Shut up and listen to me!

I did not say anything.

You can get yourself out of this and you can also save her. You are very powerful even if you don't realise that. You can kill all three of them, if that is what you want. I know I would love that, but I don't think you share my feelings. In any case, you can distract them. You are very special. In addition to everything else, you also have a sense of all the four elements of nature. You can summon the wind, the water, the earth and the fire. You can control nature – you can create a storm, you can set lightning or...

And how come you know all of this about me and I don't? I interrupted.

Because I am your rational part, I am the magic...I could make sense of what you are able to do a very long time ago. You have used your powers so many times and you were not even aware of that. Some of your dreams were in fact premonitions. You've never paid attention to what was going on around you and the least so to the details. Everything passed you by without you even noticing. You are unique. Your thoughts come to life when you want them to...or I...

Is that why you were trying to take control of me? I asked her ironically.

I was helping you.

This was so strange and crazy to be talking to someone in my head who...was not me. Or was it me? And how was this even possible?

And what is Eric doing? Why is he looking at me like that?

He is hesitant. Since he cannot play with your memories, he is thinking what to do with you. You're welcome, by the way. Thanks to me, he cannot hypnotize you. No constraining spells for you. Well...for us.

Aaa...thank you?

Anyway, Eric would never hurt you. You are too important. Your powers are extraordinary, Katelyn. He wants you for your powers.

Then why did you say I can end up dead if I continue to complain?

How else could I have distracted you? Eric was waiting for you to tell him something. Take advantage of the aces you've got.

Ok...that was weird, very weird. I felt like a crazy person. I was so angry with Eric and shocked at the same time that I did not know what to begin with.

'How can you be so cruel?' I asked him. 'Don't you have any feelings? Don't all of you have any feelings?' I looked at everyone. 'Or has none of you ever felt pain? Do you know how much it can hurt? Because sometimes it hurts so badly that you wish you were dead.'

The stranger looked fiercely at me. Had his look killed, I would be dead by now.

'Did you also feel pain?' the man asked me ironically. 'Or do you want to...'

Eric gave him a nasty look and he immediately swallowed his words. I sighed.

'You have no idea', I whispered more to myself.

But Eric heard me. He was watching me carefully.

I looked over at Annie who was in pain and who was breathing harder and harder. I felt that she wanted to say something to me so I got closer to her. She touched me and that is when I flinched. A series of images flashed through my mind and all of a sudden I was no longer in the forest. This was probably her special power.

I was in a small and dark room. She was having a conversation with a man who seemed to be very worried. He held a picture of me in his hand.

'Bring her to us before Eric finds out about her. We have to help her. To...'

And it stopped. We were now in the forest again.

'Don't you dare', Eric said and pulled me away from her.

I tried to resist but that obviously proved to be a useless effort from my part. Instead, I continued to look at Annie who died before my eyes just a few seconds later.

'Noooo', I yelled as I was trying to pull myself from Eric's strong arms.

'If you knew who she was you would not be reacting like that.'

'It doesn't matter. You've just killed her', I yelled even louder. 'Don't you have a conscience? What is it telling you right this instance?'

'Just shut up already' he said to me.

I shuddered in his arms. He felt that and I knew immediately that he regretted what he had said. The other part of me was right. I was never

paying attention to details. He was looking at me in a strange way. The expression on his face was harsh and impenetrable – but his blue eyes were much too piercing. He was troubled. He was struggling to keep his calm. He who had probably always been in control of the situation was now fighting with the obstacle before him – and no matter how much he wanted to remove that obstacle, he could not. And this made him insane. The fact that I was the obstacle. The fact that he cared about me; well...for my powers.

'And what are you going to do? Are you going to kill me just like you killed her?' I asked him.

'Of course not', Mystic rushed to give me an answer. 'Look, Kate, this is all a big misunderstanding. She is not who you think she is. It is all...very complicated.'

Eric's look confirmed my suspicions. I should have kept my mouth shut. After all, I was meddling in his affairs. A person who takes the life of another should not have any feelings. No matter how curious he must have been about me, I still could not understand his way of thinking. What was he planning to do with me? He knew that if he'd just let me go I would not pretend that nothing had happened.

'Eric, this is too much for her and she won't understand if we try to explain it to her now. Just use your gift and make her forget all about this.'

'Again this forgetting thing?' I asked ironically.

'You are far too serious Mystic', the stranger interfered.

He was not very tall but he was big. He had rough and dark features. He had scruffy black hair and madman eyes. He frightened me.

He came close to me and pulled me out of Eric's arms. Despite my protests, he grabbed me by the chin and gave me a gentle pat on the face. Then he studied my body with this wild look on his face.

'We could have some fun', he said while he was holding me close to him.

'Jamie, cut it out! You are scaring her and you are giving her the wrong impression. Damn it, Eric; just erase that memory of hers already! It's much better than for her to find out the truth. Kate, we are not the bad guys here. Annie was with them. She was just one of their tools. But believe me, you don't want to find out who is behind her.'

What was Mystic talking about? All I knew was that this man who made me sick to my stomach wouldn't let me go from his arms.

'What's so special about her that you are both protecting her like that? You are hiding something from me and I don't plan on letting her go until you've told me what it is.'

Yes, it was about time. I could control nature, couldn't I? And so, what I wanted now was to be at one with the fire. I felt it releasing and spreading into my body; a kind of warmth that you could barely sense; one that was quite pleasant – for me; but not for him. He yelled and pushed me so hard that I lost my balance and I fell. He looked shocked at his burnt shirt and at the burns on his body.

I had done it! Inside me, I could feel my other part; and it was so proud.

'What did you do to me?' He yelled. 'You will pay for this.'

'In fact, I don't think you want to come close to me', I replied in mockery.

'There are other ways. In fact, since you like to play with fire, let's see how you'll manage this.'

He was furious. He had a strange look – full of satisfaction and pure madness. And he was talking to himself. He babbled some words quietly...

I held my breath realising that he was making a spell.

'Don't you dare do anything to her', Eric ordered him.

I was really wondering when he'll show up in the picture. A bit late, don't you think? He could have stopped him from the beginning.

'Jamie, cut it out! You have to learn to control yourself', Mystic told him – he definitely did not like that.

So everything that Eric and Mystic cared about were strictly my powers, I said disappointed. What was I expecting? After everything I had seen I still hoped deep down that they were actually the good guys.

How naive I can be sometimes. I find difficult to believe even what I see with my own eyes. After all, I did not really know either of them.

'Enough, Jamie', Eric shouted again seeing that he was not going to stop.

And that is when I saw them; a blinding light. In fact they were shiny snakes coming my way. I turned and closed my eyes. I could feel the other part of me struggling to come to the surface. I wanted to set it free, to let it take control...but nothing happened. When I opened my eyes, it was only Eric and I. No sign of Annie's body or the two lackeys. They were quick, no doubt about it.

'What were you thinking coming to the forest alone? Are you really that irresponsible? How come...'

'Cut it out', I shouted at him. 'How dare you behave as if nothing had happened? You've tortured a person Eric, and no reason could possibly make that alright.'

'I had no choice! Life is tough, Katelyn. Sometimes, we have to take decisions that we don't like just so that we can get some information. Hypnosis did not work on her, which means that she knew about my special power and that she had a protection charm with her.'

'Protection charm? Should I take it that anyone who has such a thing cannot be hypnotised anymore?'

'It is more complicated than that. Charms are unique. For example, the one Annie has only works against me, because it was made specifically to resist my constraining spell. You should not have seen this. I...'

'In fact, I don't want to know anything else. I just want to forget that this ever happened. Just make me forget. I will not resist anymore. Perhaps it will work.'

I think that he would have been less surprised had I told him that I have wings and that I can fly.

He came in front of me and stared at me; this time I could not feel any influence from him. I could only feel his long and warm fingers on my cheek. I flinched and I involuntarily moved back.

'It did not seem to bother you last time', he said to me.

'Last time I had no idea what a despicable person you are.'

I continued to move backwards.

'Stay away!'

But of course that he did not listen.

I could feel my feet becoming unstable. I hit a tree and before I could make any move, Eric leaned his hands on it on either side of me.

'You are afraid of me', he said and then sighed.

He looked sad and that made me even more confused.

'What a revelation.'

I did not want to seem too vulnerable but his blue eyes – that were fixating me – only made me even more intimidated. I whispered the next words that came out of my mouth although I wished I would have put more strength in them.

'Just do your damn spell from afar...'

'Oh, Kate, I wish there were some other solution. But it is better if you just forget what happened instead of despising me. Nothing is easy in life, and when magic is involved also, things just get even more complicated. The magic world is tougher and sometimes you have to make decisions that you don't like. Do you think that I enjoyed seeing her hurt? It is just that sometimes torture is the best method of making someone talk.'

'Just do your damn spell and after that stay away from me. I don't want to know anything about that.'

I could feel his influence again and that desire to please him; although I did not resist, it still did not work. Or perhaps because, although I did not resist, the other part of me did. That is to say, if the conversation in my mind was not just in my imagination. I really felt I was going crazy.

'Nothing', I said to him angrily and pushed him away from me. Your stupid spell did not work!'

Eric sighed.

'I am sorry; things just should not have worked out the way they did.'

'Just stay away from me. I don't want to have anything to do with you, and I hate the fact that there is a part of me that likes you. Stupid prophecy', I added and went away; I chose the direction I thought was best.

'Katelyn?'

'What?' I shouted.

'You're going the wrong way.'

I turned. He was right. I had no idea how to get out of this forest so I needed him to help me with that.

'Can you walk faster?'

'Why are you in such a hurry?'

'Could it be because I was supposed to be in school right about now? Moreover, I want to spend the least possible time with you.'

'Ouch. That hurt, but I guess I had it coming. Kate, you cannot possibly think that I would hurt you?'

I did not reply because, truth be told, I did not know what to tell him. A part of me was really terrified of him.

'I have done many unscrupulous things. I am not a person that you can trust. In fact, although I will probably regret saying this, I think it is best if you stay away from me. My world is turned upside-down. You would not last for long in my company. But despite everything, I want you to know that I would never ever hurt you. You are tired. Go to your room. You can skip the rest of the classes today.'

I did not know what to say, but Eric was right. Although I was confused, I had to stay away from him. Going to my room sounded like a good option, but I was not going to please him. I built up courage and decided I was going to do it my way.

'I don't need any special treatment from you, Eric. I will be just fine on my own. And if my deeds have not always been the result of the best decisions, I will take responsibility for the consequences. Now, I am going to school.'

I tried to appear as brave as I could. If my mother had heard me she would have definitely wondered who I was and what had I done with her daughter.

'Then take that as an order.'

Oh, he was only adding fuel to the fire.

'You have no right to order me around.'

'You are a student in my campus; I think that gives me the right.'

'Well said; a student, not a slave that takes orders. Next time choose your words carefully. Straight ahead, right?'

'Yes, why?'

'Good. I hope this is our last discussion and that I won't be seeing you any time soon. And if we do see each other, you should pretend not to know me. Good bye, Eric', I told him and then I ran.

I did not know what to do. I wished I had someone to talk to about that. I have a lot on my mind and my heart is aching; I wish I could tell Chris and Maggie all about that – and clear my soul. But I would only prove to be selfish. I did not have to get them involved in this – I was deep enough in it. But shouldn't I warn them about the two?

I don't know what's coming next but, for the time being, I only had two options.

1. Stay away from Eric and Mystic and continue to accept these things and pretend that it had all been an ugly chapter in my life.

2. Find out everything I could about those two and about what they were up to.

The first option did not sound like something Katelyn Lambert would do. The second one was totally crazy and did not make any sense – but it was definitely something that I would have done.

I wanted to go to classes, I really did, but I changed my mind on the way there and I changed direction to the medical office. Luckily I ran into an old lady; I did not need to do much to convince her that I was not well – my noisy stomach helped me with that. And that is how I managed to get the rest of the day off.

Christine was also free. She was alright but just a bit shaken by all that had happened. It is a lot more difficult for her because she must always struggle to keep her control. Otherwise, she would be overwhelmed by the flow of emotions coming from those around her. Thank God, Sarah was also alright, although I heard that she took advantage to the maximum of her victim situation. And there was no news about the person that had hurt her. They were still looking for the guilty one. It seems that I, a novice and doing so bad, was the last on their list. I did not have to worry about that.

Chapter 16:

"Fooling myself"

Already towards the end of the week I felt I was not going to make it. It was Friday evening and I had not finished dusting in the library. I had never before gotten detention and it had always seemed so absurd to me. I felt as if I were a kid again. It did not matter to them that we were adults. Magic is not something to toy with. This was a very serious topic and rebellious students were not accepted in the campus. We had to be taught a lesson...Yeah...what a nice lesson...the cleaning class...But it seems that this was a method that was supposed to make us understand certain things.

In fact, it was worse than high school. Most of the professors were just very tough and absurd.

I had so many shelves left to clean and I could no longer stand the cloud of dust in the air. I was tired, I was hungry and my arms hurt from how much I had scrubbed the floors to get those old stains off it. Only Maggie and I were still in the library. We had spent all week in here after classes, dusting the books and sorting them by year, author and genre. I liked books very much; but only to read them. I won't step into a library any time soon after I've been done cleaning here.

As for school, I managed to do some illusions – poor ones, obviously – and to move some small objects – not more than one at a time. I also found out that sports could be practiced differently than how

I knew. There was an extra something about them. I watched a basketball game between the sophomores. Each person had his own shinning colour. When the ball was passed from one to the other, you could see how the thread of light went towards the other player. This was a game of colours; if you were on the field, you had to be very attentive.

I had not heard anything about Eric since our last encounter, and Mystic had come once to visit us in the library. She was beat down and it was the first time I had seen her without makeup. The big black circles around her eyes covered most of her face. She wanted to make sure that I was alright and to offer herself to take me and the girls shopping in town at the weekend. Maggie was extremely happy with the proposal. I had no choice but to accept or I would have been seen as the black sheep. Chances were high that she was giving us extra attention because she felt guilty. None of us talked about what had happened in the forest.

The most important news Mystic gave me was that on Sunday morning I was going to meet Eric whether I wanted or not. That's the last thing I needed; to have Eric as my personal coach. He was going to teach me how to control my powers and to not let myself influenced by them. And by influenced, I meant to be controlled by them. I am sure that both he and Mystic knew that I was the author of that little show in the cafeteria when Sarah was hurt. Christine and her sister were just as aware of that but they never said anything to me about the incident. And just like that, it seems that I was going to take additional magic lessons with Eric and with Mystic. It did not matter how much I wanted to stay away from them; I did not really have a choice. No one else had to know who I was and so I needed them.

'I cannot stand this anymore', Maggie said.

She shook the dust off the cloth and then coughed. I was struggling to keep my balance on the ladder. I am not a big fan of heights.

'I don't think that the dust in here has ever been wiped', I said when I saw what was on top of one of the shelves.

I took a deep breath in and then I wiped the one-centimetre-thick dust. I started to sneeze and I had to get down from the ladder.

'I am not touching that shelf.'

'Yuck...disgusting! I hate these small legged creatures', Maggie said while she was struggling to broom off some spider webs.

'My nose is itching and my eyes are burning. Let's go! We'll come back in the morning.'

'I thought you were never going to say that. I cannot stand this one minute more', she said and threw away the broom.

*

Waking up in the morning proved to be more difficult than I had expected. While Maggie kept yawning, I was basically tearing because of how sleepy I was. And the worst part is that my back burned and hurt so much that I had to take some painkillers.

'What a bad idea. It would have been better had we finished everything yesterday evening', I said while we were heading for the library.

'I know...we would still be in our warm beds had we done that. At least we are going shopping in the afternoon.'

'Yes...I hope we are still going.'

'Why wouldn't we?'

'Because of the weather.'

It was cold and cloudy and it was very possible that it would rain later in the day.

'It can just as well snow. I don't care even one bit. We are going!'

I did not dare contradict her.

When we arrived, Debbie, the librarian, welcomed us with some coffee.

'You look like you really need it.'

Smiling, as she normally was, she gave us our cups of coffee. She was not older than thirty. Short, brunette, with her hair always tied in a bun; she was much too chatty and too cool to be a librarian.

'Thank you', we both said at the same time.

'I really do appreciate all the help you've given me this week.'

She had been so nice to us from the beginning and insisted that we are not overly polite with her.

'It was a pleasure', Maggie said and forced a smile.

Debbie looked sceptical at her.

'I'm sure.'

'Why is there a flower inscribed on the front door?' I asked thus changing the topic.

I don't know why I had come up with that question. The big flower in the middle of the door had stuck in my mind; it had white petals covered with pink filaments and large stamens and orange sacs.

'It is the Passion Flower. Balfour means passion in Gaelic'

I flinched when I heard Eric's last name.

'Gaelic?' I asked, although my mind was still on Eric.

'It is an extinct Celtic language. Passion Flower...books, passion for knowledge, stuff like that' Maggie said quickly not letting Debbie answer my question.

'Debbie, what do you know about Eric Balfour?' I found myself asking her all of a sudden.

'Eric takes care of everything that has to do with the campus, even if not always in a direct way.'

'You mean to say that he has trustworthy people who work for him', Maggie said.

'Exactly. He is very interested in people who have special abilities. After graduation, the students take part in several competitions and the winner is taken under Eric's wing. That person will work for him and he will give him or her protection. He values loyalty and reacts badly when he is lied to. It is better if you just admit to him that you were wrong to do something. Anyway, he cares very much about his friends. Even if he doesn't show it, he is really big-hearted.

'You seem to know him pretty well', Maggie said while she was eyeing me to see my reactions.

'We've know each other since we were kids', she said and then got busy doing stuff, looking in one of the drawers of her desk.

'Hmm...This means they are pretty close', Maggie whispered to me to tease me.

I made a face at her, reacting like a child.

'I don't know what you are talking about.'

'Did you say something?' Debbie asked.

Maggie refrained from laughing.

'And his family?'

Debbie sighed and cleared her throat.

'His parents, his younger sister and his brother were killed two years ago. Eric suffered greatly especially after his younger sister, Allice. She was everything for him. I know that he and his brother did not really see eye to eye. He was not very close to his family either. But family is family...and such a loss can really affect someone.'

Baldric was not dead and to say that they did not stand each other was far from the truth.

'I'm...I'm sorry' Maggie said.

By the look on her face it was obvious that this had brought back memories about her father's death. It made no sense for her to keep denying that he had never existed in her life and behave as if nothing had happened. I knew that deep down she was hurting a lot. Maggie is much more sensitive than she wants to appear. I also wanted to say how sorry I was but I felt my throat dry and could not say a thing. I had not forgotten what Eric had done. Sadly, there are things that we cannot erase from our memories no matter how much we'd like it; this inexplicable game of perception makes memories stuck in our minds. And the more we try to forget, the more they cling on us and complicate our existence.

I don't know why. I cannot explain why I felt this sudden need to console him. It must be terribly hard to go through such an experience – I cannot even imagine such a pain. I felt sorry for him. Something in me was telling me that I had to help him. To make sure that he was alright. What was wrong with me? Eric had killed an innocent person. I hated this man and yet there was something that drew me to him.

Or...could it be that Mystic was right? What if I had been deceived by appearances?

Nonsense; I had seen with my own eyes what had happened. There is no point in trying to make excuses for him.

Then I remembered about that stupid prophecy that said that Eric and I had a special connection and that we were meant to be together.

'And Eric is hiding behind that tough-guy mask who is not scared of anything and who does not care about anything, but there is more to that. He only appears to be selfish and without feelings, wealthy and egocentric. He has many responsibilities on his shoulders and he has to give an account of his deeds to others also. He is trustworthy and has a wonderful soul.' Debbie said.

By the way that she was talking about him and the expression on her face, it was obvious that she saw him as more than a friend. I felt a bit jealous and I hated myself for that immediately.

'What do you know about prophecies? I mean...are they real? Or are they just stories; bed time stories?'

Maggie looked sceptical at me and Debbie pondered before giving me an answer.

'They are very much true. They have been written by the greatest wizards in history. Truth be told, it is rather difficult to tell what a prophecy truly refers to. They are written very ambiguously so that they won't be understood by just anyone. If they end up in the wrong hands, they can be dangerous. Sometimes it is better not to know what the future holds.'

'In what way are they dangerous? Is there a book of prophecies around here?' I asked.

Debbie burst into laughter.

'There is no book with this sort of things. Some of them are not even written. They are transmitted orally from one generation to the other.

And they are dangerous because, hypothetically speaking, if they tell of the birth of a great witch, with powers even beyond my knowledge, then the life of that person, of The Magic Pawn, would always be in danger. That person would be making enemies without even knowing it. That person would virtually be hunted her entire life by people who will want to have her work for them; or they will kill her for the simple fact that she is more powerful and represents a threat to them.'

I could feel Debbie's words like piercing arrows. Time stood still and millions of ideas began storming my mind. I was a prisoner of this stupid fate, and my mind was running in circles desperate to find answers. I was shaking; I sat on a chair.

'Kate, are you alright?'

In Greece, someone had tried to kill me... and Baldric, Eric's brother, wanted me for himself. Let's not forget that it seemed that I also had a connection with him, even if it was different from the one I had with Eric. The universe was really playing a joke on me. I wondered how many others knew about my existence.

Was this who I was? A weapon? A target? Is that why Eric wants to coach me? So that he can use me later on? I was a normal girl just months before and now I find out that there was a bounty on my head.

'Kate, here you go', Debbie said and handed me a bar of chocolate. Your blood sugar has probably lowered.'

'I am alright.' I lied.

I wanted to stand up, but my feet had failed me just then.

'Eat this and stop fooling around! In the meantime, I will go and get you something to eat. You girls, you do not take any care of yourselves.

'I am alright', Maggie said. 'I'm really not hungry.'

'Don't you even think about saying no. I will be back shortly' she added and then left.

With the chocolate bar in my hand, I continued to look at my trembling hands. Eating was the last thing on my mind.

'I'm sorry, Kate. I realise how hard it must be for you. Not only did you recently find out about magic, but there is also this thing about the Magic Pawn.

Just when I was thinking that my morning could not get any worse, I saw Eric coming our way.

'Good morning, girls.'

I whispered a "good morning" while looking the other way.

'For you maybe', Maggie joked. 'Some of us have been cleaning from early morning.'

'Kate, you are pale! What happened? You don't look well at all', Eric said to me and seemed to be worried. We are going to the medical office. I am sure you haven't been eating these days. You have lost weight. How many kilos do you have? 45? You keep up like that Katelyn Lambert, and you'll be in trouble.'

I looked at him shocked and did not know what to tell him. No matter why he was worried about my health, he was right; except for the kilograms part. I have 50 kilos, not 45. I had gotten on the scale in the morning being upset that the pair of jeans I had bought before coming here were now loose. Maggie had taken the scale with her. She was obsessed with any extra kilos.

'If you cannot take care of yourself, then someone else has to do it.'

'I don't need a babysitter! And you can let go of me. I am perfectly capable of standing on my own.'

Of course, Eric ignored my comment. I don't know what I was expecting.

'Kate, I know that we've both been on a tight schedule due to this stupid detention, but you have been more worked up than me, both physically and mentally.'

'I am sorry I am not as resilient as you when it comes to cleaning the library. Moreover, waking up in the morning has never been my strong suit.'

'It's not funny!'

'Maybe I am a bit dizzy because I haven't been resting properly these past days. I have been busy with classes and detention has not helped either. In any case, you don't have to worry about me. I have some vitamins in my bag. I will take one and I'll feel better afterwards.'

I just wanted to leave this place as soon as possible. Although a part of me longed for Eric, the other part was frightened by his presence. I leaned over to get my bag from the librarian's desk but I only managed to drop it on the floor. I wanted to collect my things off the floor but Eric beat me to it.

'These definitely do not look like vitamins. Painkillers? He shouted and the tone of his voice made me flinch. 'What do you need these for?'

'You didn't have to shout; I am standing right here next to you.'

'When are you going to stop behaving so childish? Life is not a game, Katelyn. Your health is important and if there is something wrong with you, than I need to know that.'

'Why?' I shouted at him.

'Because I want to help you.'

'Why? For my powers? Because I am to have an important role in the magic world? Well, you are wrong. You have the wrong person. I can barely work out a poor illusion. I am not the Magic Pawn. I cannot be everybody's target.'

He looked as if he was about to explode.

'Do you think that I am worried for you because of your powers? Is this what you think? That I want to use you?'

'Yes', I replied, and that is when I could read the disappointment on his face. He sighed and gave up on that angry attitude.

'Alright'. That's the only thing he said and then he left.

He ran into Debbie who was just entering. He whispered something to her ear and then slammed the door behind him.

'Not now, Maggie, please', I told her seeing how she looked at me.

I don't know if it was a good thing or not, but I had to tell Maggie and Christine what had happened with Annie. Perhaps I was being selfish, but keeping everything to myself was simply too much. Too much pressure. Not to mention that Eric had made me even more confused. He seemed really worried for me and no way did I expect him to react like that, after what I had told him. Perhaps the girls would help me realise how things really are. Christine can feel people. Shouldn't she have seen that Eric and Mystic's intentions are not the best ones?

Debbie brought us chicken ham and yellow cheese sandwiches; after we ate, she made me take effervescent calcium. It seemed that we could skip the rest of the detention, so Debbie sent us to catch some sleep.

On the way to our room, I assured Maggie that I was physically alright. I told her that I had a back pain that was probably from all the work I had done those days. To be honest, I was not used to working. My parents had always taken care of everything.

Chapter 17:

"Time to be honest"

Christine woke me up around 11 a.m.

'What are you doing here? Don't you have anything better to do?'

'Is she so grumpy every time she wakes up?' She asked Maggie.

'You get used to it quickly.'

'Come on now; go take a shower and get dressed. The three of us have some talking to do.'

'Do we really have to do this now?'

'Yes', they both said.

'Alright...Where is Camille?'

'She is with Ethan', Maggie replied.

'She is not coming with us to town anymore?'

'Yes, she is. Now move your ass out of bed', Christine rushed me.

I was ready in half an hour. I had put on a pair of high waist tight jeans, a black tank top and some black boots. I had my hair in a ponytail and I was going to take my black leather jacket with me.

'What is this?' Maggie asked pointing to my hair.

I shrugged my shoulders not knowing what she meant by that.

'I understand that you keep your hair in a ponytail when you're going to classes, but we are going out now. Your hair is too beautiful to always have it tied. I think you'd better straighten it and let it loose.'

'But I am just fine the way I am', I fought back, but Maggie had already plugged in the hair straightener.

'And you'd better put on some makeup also. Those black circles around your eyes must be covered', Christine added.

I sighed. I had no chance of getting out of this.

After another half an hour, I was ready.

'Now it is much better', Maggie said. 'You look a bit more alive.'

'Oh, yes. I don't think I have ever seen you so dressed up. You are going to knock Eric off his feet.'

'Errr...Eric? What...what business does he have with this?' I asked stammering.

'Come on...the attraction between you two is too obvious. And I have felt the special connection that you share with him.'

'I don't know what you are talking about.'

They both started to laugh.

'I am glad that I amuse you so much.'

'This is nothing. Wait until the two of you will amuse me today. The way you sometimes act as if you cannot stand each other when in fact all you want is to jump on each other.'

'What? Eric is coming with us?' I jumped as if burned.

'How do you think we can all fit in Maggie's car? It's us three, plus Camille and the Mexicans.'

'Beatrice doesn't like shopping. Can you believe it?'

'And must Eric really come with us?'

'I think this is the last thing he wants to do. Join a gang of girls on a shopping spree', Maggie said amused. 'We'll terrorise him today.'

'I still don't understand why he has to come', I continued commenting.

'So that he can take care of you', Christine said. 'Eric can be so protective when it comes to you. Isn't that nice?'

'NO! Not at all', I said angrily. 'You know very well that I did not ask for this. I did not want to be the Magic Pawn and become a target. Now it seems that I cannot go anywhere outside the campus without having a body guard with me. If Eric had not been able to come today, I am sure that he probably would have had someone follow us. This is the 21st century. Is it a lot to ask for some privacy?'

'Try to calm down. Let's take a walk and have a chat', Christine said. 'There's something we need to talk about.'

'And just so you know, I don' feel like jumping on him. It's more like I want to strangle him.'

They both grabbed my arms and forced me out of the room.

It was a bit chilly but it felt nice. There were not too many people in the main courtyard. Most of the students were probably in their rooms resting after all the partying from the night before.

We spotted a remote bench under a tree and we sat there.

'Now that you're calmer, can we talk like civilised people?' Christine said to me.

'I was calm even before.'

'If this is your definition of calm, then I don't want to see you angry', Maggie said amused.

'I'm sorry girls. It's just that a lot has happened. It's hard for me to get used to all of this. It seems that destiny has played a joke on me, and Eric and I are meant for each other. And, except for the connection I have with him, what is funnier is the fact that I also have a connection with his crazy brother, Baldric, who attacked me back when we were in Greece.'

'When you and Eric are together I can feel the same vibes from both of you, and this has never happened with anyone else. I can simply feel the chemistry between you. You are like a magnet to one another. If I close my eyes and think about you two when you are close to me, I can see rays of light that tie you together.'

'Oh, no...please don't tell me that.'

The last thing that I wanted to hear was that Eric and I were a magnet to one another.

'I still don't understand why you're trying to oppose this connection that you and Eric have. I mean...he looks great!'

'Sister, the outside is not everything', Christine said.

'Yes, fine, he has a lot of qualities also. But he looks greeeat. What does your libido say, Kate?'

'If he is that greeeat, why don't you get him?'

'Do I sense a bit of jealousy?' Christine asked me.

'Well, why wouldn't she be? Eric is a man that many women want. Not to mention the fact that he is an extraordinary wizard and the owner of the campus.'

'Aha...' I said, trying to seem uninterested.

'We have to leave soon. It's time to get down to more serious business. Like the connection you have with Eric's brother', Christine said. 'About that, is there any reason why you'd have to worry?' From what I understood from Eric, when Baldric chose the dark side, he did not realise what consequences this would have on him. He sold his soul for power. He let himself absorbed by hate and now he is no longer capable of any beautiful feeling. Even if he wanted to love, he could not be capable of something as pure as love is. His soul is frozen and that makes him a fierce enemy. He is ruthless and has no kindness left in him. He feeds on meanness. When he took you into his arms, something strange happened. You felt the coldness coming from him; all that avalanche of negative feelings. Nothing out of the ordinary so far. It seems that this is Baldric's special weapon. The problem is that there was some kind of an exchange of energy between you two. For a few seconds you could look into his soul and see how sad he truly is. You gave him the kind of warmth that he had probably not felt in a long time. You managed to crack his shield of ice. To make it clear, Baldric needs you because you might be able to give him what he wants the most: to have feelings once more. The problem is that while this exchange of energy does him good, it is hurting you.'

'Baldric threatened that he will stop for nothing until he has managed to get his hands on me', I said panicked.

'This will not happen. Eric and Mystic will not let this happen. Moreover, you have us also', she said while pointing at Maggie and herself.

'Thank you so much. I really don't know what I would do without you. I don't know what to say about Eric and Mystic though...'

'Are you saying this because of Annie?' Christine asked.

'You knew about her and you didn't say anything?'

'Eric thinks we should not get you worried, but considering that his forgetting spell does not work on you, I feel I have no choice.'

I looked at her and I could not believe it. I wanted to say something but she signalled me to shut up.

'First of all, listen to what I have to say. You can ask the questions later. I know you don't want to be the Magic Pawn and I realise that this must be hard for you. Having one person embody all that power can be overwhelming. You will lead a constant battle with your own magic.

The more your powers grow, the more difficult it will be for you to control them. And if someone becomes controlled by magic, that person will end up like Baldric; having no feelings. Anything you ever knew about that person will not matter anymore once she becomes a pray to her own magic. The Magic Pawn is destined to lead a constant fight between the good and evil in her. It is as if there were two people in that person and each were trying to surface. But Eric and Mystic will not let anything bad happen to you. They will teach you how to control your powers. I know you can do it. You have to! And about Annie; she poisoned a beginner thinking that she might be you. Eric and Mystic did what they had to do in order to find out who was behind her. You are a target Kate and there is a lot of money as bounty on your head. Even if Eric and Mystic's methods are not always the cleanest ones, they are doing whatever they think is best, even if they don't like doing it. '

She took me in her arms; she could sense that I was about to cry.

'It is alright', Christine said when I started to cry.

'It cannot be me', I said and my tears were pouring. 'I do not want that. I did not ask for this. I am afraid. And what's worse is that I am afraid of myself.'

I don't want this! No!

I heard thunders and could feel the cold drops of rain and the wind that made it hard for me to breathe.

'Kate, please try to calm down.'

'I cannot. I don't know how. It is just too much.'

I could feel the warmth coming from Christine, but she was not powerful enough to influence my feelings. Not now, when I felt I was going insane.

'Maggie, call Eric.'

229

'I already texted him. He is on his way here.'

It was raining so heavily that I could feel the drops entering my eyes.

'Let's go!' Christine said.

They dragged me with them and we took cover in the gym; this was the closest building.

Eric and Mystic entered soon after that.

I started to talk about everything moving from one idea to the other.

'I don't know how to make it stop. I am sorry. For everything. I am sorry for what I told you this morning and because I thought the worst of you two. But I do not want that. I cannot accept that. But I felt it. I feel it, damn it. It is there! I have been talking to it. And it wants to do bad. It gloats just thinking about that.

Eric took me into his arms and his grasp had an immediate calming effect on me. All of a sudden, I felt I was safe; I felt protected.

'It is going to be alright! I will not let anything bad happen to you! I promise.'

And I believed him. In his arms, the truth seems easier to bear. Everything seemed easier. I also took him in my arms and I wished for that moment to last as long as possible. I had not realised until then how much I needed this.

'It stopped', Christine said. 'I knew that Eric was the answer.'

I moved away from him and we both turned to her.

'What do you mean to say with that?' Eric asked.

'You have no idea what I felt when the two of you held each other. The positive energy that you release when you are together is...wow. Eric, you are the answer. That is why you share a special connection. The prophecy make sense. You are the one who will help Kate take control of her powers and by that I do not mean the numerous coaching and training sessions. These are also needed, no doubt about it. Eric, you are meant to be in her life because your presence calms her when she gets off track. I don't know how aware you are of that, and you will probably deny it and get on me for what I am about to say, but the love between you is the solution. Even if you have known each other for a short while and you have not been interacting much, the love is there from before you met. Your hearts beat as one in a perfect match. You involuntarily influence one another's mood, no matter if you are together or apart.

I was looking at Christine' I could not believe this.

'You should see how you look right now. The expression on your face says it all. How I like this special power of mine.'

'Well, your senses have failed you this time. There are better chances for it to snow in the dessert than for Eric and I to be in love.'

'She is right. I cannot be in love with her.'

I gave him a nasty look.

'You said it as if there was something wrong with me; something other than the magic.'

'Well, there is. You are completely different from me. You are just a spoiled brat.'

'Nice. And by different, are you referring to the fact that I am not self-centred like you are?

'I am not self-centred.'

'I did not expect anything else from you. Denial and teasing', Christine said.

'Poor them', Maggie added.

'I wonder when they will accept the obvious' Mystic said.

'What? The fact that she is a student in my campus?'

'It is not as if this has stopped you before', I said to him and then I left.

'What was that?' I heard him shouting behind me.

*

We had about fifteen minutes left before reaching the city. Since Eric and I could no longer stand next to each other without being at each other's throats - especially after my last comment – I was now in the car with Mystic and the Mexican girls.

'I take it that you want to buy something for the party tonight?' Mystic asked.

Mayte and Arriana gave me a nasty look.

'It wasn't me!'

'We know everything that goes on in the campus, even if sometimes we act as if we're not aware of things. Moreover, this party takes place every start of the year. I don't see anything wrong with that, except for some people's wish to drink themselves into oblivion. As long as the students don't cause any trouble and they stick to school, I do not care what they do during their spare time.'

'Oh, professor, you are the best', Mayte said.

'Mystic, do you teach?'

'I have a class for beginners; I teach them how to channel the extra energy they have from their special power. I help them control it. Also, one of my many tasks is to find young wizards who have special powers and to bring them to the campus before they end up in the wrong hands. There are people who do not promote white magic. But this is not the time to be having this discussion. I found the girls almost a year ago.'

'We have kept in touch ever since.' Mayte said.

'I don't know what we would have done had you not come into our lives.'

'Arriana, are you turning sentimental or is it just my impression?' Mystic said amused.

'I have my moments now and then.'

'This is what you also said in Mexico, but a moment turned into a week.'

'It was different then. Anyway, this campus was truly the best choice.'

'You two can be crazy sometimes, but you are very dear to me. However, this does not mean that I will handle you with gloves in classes. You will work just as much as everyone else will; perhaps even more.'

'Great', Mayte said ironically and then she changed the topic. 'You have a very nice necklace, Kate', she looked carefully at it for a few seconds. It looks familiar. I think I might have seen it somewhere else. From where do you have it?'

'It belonged to my mother', I said, avoiding at first to give an answer.

'Hmm...where have I seen it before...Arriana? Can you have a look?'

'Professor, didn't you used to have one like that?'

Mystic hit the brakes hard.

'*Que pasa?*'

'It's nothing. I have to make a call. I remembered I have something to fix. You girls can get out. Go straight ahead and you'll see some shops to the left; there are some nice clothes there. I will call you when I am done. Eric will accompany you.'

She tried to look as calm and stress-free as possible, but she looked as if she was about to vomit.

'No offence, but I think we can manage shopping by ourselves. There is nothing that can go wrong.'

'Exactly', Mayte agreed with me. Eric is very *guapoo* and no matter how much I like having him around, I would rather not.'

'Some things are for girls only and I don't know how much he would enjoy shopping with us.'

'You are right; I didn't think about that. I don't know if it makes any sense asking him. He will say no anyway. I will join you. I can take care of my business some other time.'

'Mystic, we are going to be alright', I assured her. We don't need to be chaperoned. Go and take care of your things.'

'Alright, but call me if you feel that anything is wrong.'

'You got it, professor', Arriana said. 'And you don't need to be so paranoid.'

'Kate, there is something in your hair', Mystic told me.

'Ouch', I said as I felt her pulling my hair. What is it?'

'Nothing. I thought there was something.'

After that, she checked something in her bag.

'A message from Eric. He dropped the girls off at one of the shops I was telling you about. Enjoy your shopping!'

'Thank you!' said the Mexicans. And don't you worry, Eric will not know that you were not with us the whole time.'

'I will be quick.'

'See you later. I hope everything is all right', I added before I shut the car door.

Ok...that was strange. I am very curious where Mystic is going.

It did not take more than five minutes before we met with the girls. They were waiting for us in front of a store where they sold dresses that seemed to be very expensive.

Yeah...this was not just an impression. They really were expensive. Maggie picked a dress she wanted to try on. When I saw how much it cost, I realised that I did not have any chance of buying anything from there. Unlike the two sisters, I had a limited budget; by a lot.

Christine was in the dressing room and she was trying on the sixth dress. I hope she likes this one.

'No, definitely not!'

Maggie laughed when she saw her.

'You look radiant. You just need some spangles on the corset...not that there are not enough already.'

'It looked well on the dummy' Christine complained.

Maggie gave me a bunch of dresses.

'What's with them?'

'Try them on!'

'But they are too expensive! I am not going to pay this much for a dress.'

'And you are not going to pay for it', Christine said.

'Yes, we want to.'

They were so excited that I did not dare say no. Moreover, Maggie had pushed me into the dressing room.

After I had tried on about 10 dresses, Christine brought me another one.

'I cannot believe you! Must I really try this one also?'

'Yes!'

The dress was turquoise blue and was the simplest and most beautiful one I had seen so far; no fringes, no spangles, nothing like that; thin straps, and a quite big v-shaped décolletage, tight on the body and long up to just above the knees. It highlighted my figure nicely.

'Wow', Maggie said.

'I was sure! It is absolutely beautiful!'

'Clearly', the Mexican girls said.

'*C'est parfait*, Camille added.'

I don't remember the last time I had been complimented like that, but the girls were right. The dress was very beautiful and it fit me really well.

Simplicity is the best choice.

'Thank you, girls. It really is beautiful!'

My enthusiasm went down the drain when I saw the price tag.

'I am sorry, Christine but I cannot accept this. It is too much!'

'Not at all!' Maggie said.

'Maybe not for you, because you are used to different things than I am.'

We contradicted each other a few minutes but they did not manage to convince me otherwise.

'I really appreciate this', I told them as I was leaving the shop, 'but it really was too much. There are plenty other dresses.'

'But not like that one', Christine said.

The Mexicans had bought the most stuff. Camille and I were the only ones who had not gotten anything. Christine bought for herself only a coral dress with a bit of a cleavage; it fit her nice. Maggie got herself a black dress that was tight on the body. When she put her specs on, she looked like a super-hot secretary!

Oh...Nate is really going to like this!

'I'd really like to know where Mystic went', I told the sisters.

'If she left us alone although Eric had made it clear to her that she should not, that means that it was something really important.'

'Don't you think that he is overreacting?'

'Oooh, yes he is', Maggie said. 'It is just that sometimes it is better to be overly precautious in order to prevent unpleasant things from happening.'

'Yes, it is true that there are many people looking for you, but the chances of them knowing exactly how you look are very slim.'

'Christine, do you think we might do a location spell, a tracking one or something like that to help us find out where Mystic went?'

'Hmm...I could try to locate her car. It would help if there was anything of yours in her car.'

'Perfect! My jacket is there.'

'After I've made the spell we will follow a light and it will show us the way that Maggie took. The light will be denser where the car stopped for longer periods. We won't know exactly where she has been. It might take some time. We will walk. We cannot take a cab and tell the driver to follow a light that only you and I can see because we are the ones involved in making the spell.'

'It will have to do. We'll manage', I said, although I had no idea what was I expecting to find.

'Maggie, if Mystic and Eric show up, text us and stall for time.'

'Alright, but be careful.'

'Girls, Kate has to meet up with a friend. I will join her and cover for her. If Mystic or Eric show up, tell them we are in one of the stores just a few blocks away.'

'What friend? Is he cute?' Arriana asked.

'Aaa...'

'He is very cute', Christine replied.

'Alright girls, you got it. We'll cover for you, no problem', Camille said.

'Couldn't you have come up with a better excuse?' I jumped on Christine as we were getting further from the girls.

'It worked, didn't it? None of them suspected anything and that is what matters.'

'Yeah...you are right...'

Chapter 18:

"At Baldric's mercy"

We walked for almost two hours; we were about to give up when the light became brighter in the parking lot of a large building called Genetic Lab.

'Why would Mystic come here?' I asked Christine.

'I don't know, but let us find out.'

As expected, the blonde woman in the reception office told us with a smile on her face that she cannot provide us with any information, because it is all confidential.

'And now, what do we do?'

'We use a bit of magic.'

'Let me guess. Meya taught you?'

'She also did something good in her life.'

After Christine made her spell, the receptionist became a bit more open to discussions. These are the times when I can say that I love magic.

'Try and see and what you can find by the name of Mystic. Abner?'

'I am sorry. I have nothing by that name.'

'What about if I showed you a picture of her?'

'Of course; I think it would help.'

'Kate, tell me you have a picture of her in your phone.'

'I wish I had. Perhaps we should just forget about it. I don't even know what I was expecting to find anyway. I mean...we should not be meddling into Mystic's life...it is just that...I have this feeling about it...and it is frightening me.

'No way. We did not come all this way for nothing; moreover, I don't want to think that I've missed out on a good shopping session for no good reason. I am texting Maggie; she'll take a picture of Mystic as soon as she gets there, no matter what excuse she comes up with; she'll send it to us.'

'Christine, you are officially the best!'

'I know.'

'Aaa...and what do we tell Mystic when she realises that we are not where we said we were?'

'She won't be able to tell that. We will grab a taxi and be there right away.'

She was smiling.

'I like your optimism. It is really contagious, I might say.'

Half an hour later, we got the photo.

'I remember her', the receptionist said when we showed her the photo. Miss Seamour. 'Lydia Seamour', she said after she checked the computer.

'Hm...so she had used a false name; or was this her true name?'

Christine was no longer smiling.

'What is it?'

'Well...this was Meya's last name before she got married. She kept her husband's name after his death.'

Ok...yes...this is strange, but is does not mean that there is any connection.

'I did not know that. As you know, she and I did not really have a very close relationship and my parents have never spoken to me about her. And now I understand why...'

'Why did Miss Seamour come here?' Christine asked.

'For a sibling test. She wants to find out if she and a certain Miss Katelyn Lambert are sisters.'

I felt my whole world collapsing.

'Can you repeat that name? I am sure I did not hear it right. I imagined it, didn't I, Christine?'

'Sure. Katelyn Lambert.'

'But...that is me...It cannot be...Something is surely wrong.'

'Thank you very much for the information. This is my email address. Please send me a copy of the results when they are ready.'

We sat on a bench outside the clinic.

'Five minutes, not more; and then we leave.'

'It's alright. Take all the time you need. I am here if you want to talk about this.'

The truth is that I did feel like talking to someone. I am not really in the habit of telling others what I have going on, but if I was to, then Christine was the right person to do that.

'I don't know...it is just too much at once. Don't get me wrong; I would be very happy to find out that I have a sister, but it is just that I would have liked it if Mystic had been honest with me from the beginning. Moreover, I don't want to get my hopes up until I have the confirmation. But it all makes sense. Why have I been able to communicate with Mystic back in Greece via this necklace that I am wearing? She has a similar one and when Meya gave it to me, she said that it had been my mother's. And in the car, when the girls told her that she has a necklace like mine, she reacted strangely. There was nothing in my hair; she just pulled out some hairs to have them checked. There is a high possibility that Mystic is my sister.'

'And how does that make you feel?'

'I don no know. It scares me but it also makes be happy.'

'Can I tell you my opinion?'

'Sure.'

'I don't think you should be angry with her for not telling you. She probably just wanted to make sure first. Wait for the results to come and see if she will talk to you after that. She has no reason not to.'

'Yes...I guess...I don't know...it is possible that I might have a sister. Can you believe that?'

'No, but I would be very happy to find out that it is true. You need this.'

'You are right...thank you, Christine.'

'Are you sure you are alright?'

'Under these circumstances...yes.'

'Alright then, let's go! Maggie texted me earlier. Eric is there and he's not himself. She wrote in capital letters that we had better gotten there in five minutes.'

'And when did she text you?'

'Five minutes ago.'

'Oh. It's clear then. He will be pissed and we will have to come up with a better excuse. Why didn't you tell me this earlier?'

'Because you needed some time for yourself. We'll manage with Eric', she said and seemed not to stress at all.

It was almost 8 p.m. and we had already been walking for thirty minutes; we had failed at finding a taxi. It was already dark outside and the empty little street we were walking on did not give me the best feeling.

Even Christine had lost her cool, and she was a difficult person to piss off.

'How is it possible that there is no taxi? And where is everybody? I do not like this street one bit.'

'I cannot believe this.'

'You've got to be kidding me. We walked all this way just to hit a dead end?'

There was a wire fence at the end of the street and the buildings around us seemed to be abandoned; lifeless. No light was on.

'Remind me. Whose idea was it to go on this street? We should have kept walking on the boulevard. At least there we would have been safe.'

'Don't give me that look', Christine defended herself. I thought we might be able to shorten our walk. Moreover, nothing can happen to us. We are witches, remember that?'

'Well, you thought wrong. Is there no spell that you can make to have those lights appear again and help us find our way?

'Yes there is, but that would mean continuing to follow Mystic and we have no idea where she may have been. It might take us a long time.'

'More time than if we continue walking in circles through this small town? If we follow the lights, then at least we know for sure that we will reach our destination.'

'Oh, no.'

'What is it now?'

She showed me the phone. On top of everything else, Eric was now calling her?

'Answer him or he'll go nuts.'

'Yes? And what should I tell him?'

'I don't know. You are the one with the ideas.'

She pushed the answer key on her phone and gave it to me.

'Where are you and what do you think you are doing?' he shouted in the phone.

Yeah...he was pissed.

'Aaa...hello to you too, Eric', I said while trying to seem as calm and stress-free as I could. 'This is Kate; we are fine, thank you for asking.'

'And where do you keep your phone? I have been calling you ten times. What's the point of having a phone if you don't answer it?'

Alright; it was time I worked out my acting talent.

'Yes, that dress looks great on you. Sorry, I was paying attention to Christine. She has been in the dressing room for half an hour and she is still not done trying on. You were saying? Where do I keep my phone? It is in my bag; I did not hear it ring? And there is no need for you to shout. The last time I checked, my hearing was alright.'

'What store are you at? Because you are not at the one where the girls said you were. And I also checked the store nearby that, and I could not find you.', he said in the calmest fashion possible, and then raised his voice all of a sudden, which made me flinch. 'So.Where.Are.You?' He paused after every word, to emphasise it.

'Ah, that one? Yes, we left from there some time ago; and the other stores did not have the underwear we are looking for. Well, girl stuff.'

'You must be kidding me. Just tell me where you are already and I'll come get you, before I get angry.'

Did he think that now he was calm? Did he not realise that I had to keep the phone away from my ear because of him acting like a crazy person?

'Stop yammering! We will be there in ten minutes. And now, if you'll excuse me, I have some bras to try on.'

'Don't you dare hang up on me!'

'Eric, first of all, stop shouting. Second of all, we are alright; we are just a few streets away. We are not as irresponsible as you might think. I will call you if anyone picks on us while we're trying on the clothes. We got separated from the rest because we all have different tastes in clothes and I cannot make the others be in a shop for an hour until Christine and I have made up our minds. And thirdly, today is our shopping day. So just let us do our shopping in peace. Unless you want to come and share your opinion on how the bras fit me, then you had better found something else to do until we are done here. Good bye!'

And I hung the phone on him without hearing what he had to say.

Christine made the spell once more while I was on the phone with Eric.

'You did great, except for the part with hanging the phone. Oh, and the fact that you rather mocked him did not help either. I think he would like to see you in your bra. But anyway, although you made him mad, I am sure that he believed you. And now, let's make a run for it; let's get away from this place and follow the lights.'

'What will we do when they see that we have not bought anything?'

'This Kate is a problem that we will worry about later. For now, we have different problems.'

And by that, she was referring to the three guys who were coming our way.

'I'm sorry to have to say this, but I am not getting any positive feelings from them. Call Eric!'

But just before I could even press the call key, the Christine's phone flew out of my hand and smashed into the building to my right; I could hear it breaking into pieces.

'That phone is not at all cheap', Christine said. 'I don't know what century you were born, but in this one, that is not a way to pick up a girl.'

'Brave. I like her', said one of the men.

That voice seemed familiar to me.

'I am sorry but the feeling is not at all mutual', Christine said.

The unknown wizard flashed balls of fire at us. Christine came in front of me and she was getting ready to make some defence spell. Luckily, there was no need for that. The balls of fire lifted into the air, and remained suspended above us thus lighting up the place. They seemed familiar. This was not the first time I was seeing them.

'This way I can see you better. You are too cute to be left in the dark.'

That voice; from where did I know it?

'If this is how you act with people you think are cute, I don't even want to know how you act with those you cannot stand.'

The wizard laughed. His voice gave you the creeps. He was standing between the two other men; they had not said a word.

'I am happy that I amuse you. And now, it would be nice of you to tell us what you want and get out of our way. If not for anything else, then at least because we are running late.'

I had not seen this side of Christine before. She was so much like Maggie; more than I would have expected.

The man stepped into the light and when I saw him, I froze.

'I told you I will come back for you.'

I chocked and didn't know what to say. If there was any person who could frighten me more than Meya did, it was Baldric. I had had nightmares about him after our encounter in Greece. The thought of him alone gave me the creeps. And to see him now, only three metres away from me, made me paralysed with fear. All that coldness that he had transmitted me last time...the thought that I might feel it again frightened me to death.

'What happened to you?' Christine asked him giving up on that superiority tone.

'I don't know what you mean', Baldric replied.

'How can you stand to be like that? It is too much darkness...too much hatred...and...Oh...my head.'

Christine was staggering and was unable to stand. I grabbed her by the waist and I told her to lean on me.

'What did you do, you bastard?'

'Nothing', he said.

Strangely, I did believe him because he seemed to be in even more shock than I was.

'I am alright; it is just that I am not so good at controlling my powers for too long time...I have never felt this much hatred before. I have never seen anyone who suffered so much and yet not be aware of it. It must be strange not to be able to have even the slightest positive feeling, not to be able to enjoy small things, not to be able to enjoy a sunset, a drizzling summer rain; the sea, the fine sand, a kiss that gives you the shivers, not to mention love. How do you make it when you know that only the pain of others can give you satisfaction? How do you make it without caring for anyone?'

'Enough!'

'You have let darkness control you. It has taken control over you. How could you allow this to happen? How could you lose your soul to dark magic?'

'I told you to stop!' Baldric shouted.

'No! How could you be so coward and let yourself fall prey? How could you choose the thirst for power and give up on anything that makes you human? How could...?

'I told you to stop!'

A green dust came our way and Christine was thrown into the air and into the wire fence. It all happened much too fast. I went to Christine who was lying unconscious on the ground.

'What have you done?'

'She was out of line.'

'Why, Baldric? Does the truth bother you?'

'You don't know what you are talking about.'

'Yes I do know; I can feel it because of the damn connection that it seems I have with you. But she has managed to read you so much better than I have.'

'How did she do it?'

He looked scared.

'It is her special power! I don't know what you did to her, but you make her better again!'

'Hm...interesting.'

He came next to us, squatted in front of Christine and put his hand on her shoulders.

'Be careful! Don't you get her infected with your coldness!'

'Kate, stop with these threats; you are in no position to be making this!'

He studied Christine carefully for a few good seconds; this seemed to take forever but she became better. When she opened her eyes and saw him so close to her, she pushed him away.

'Don't you dare touch me ever again!'

Baldric offered her his hand to help her get up, but she refused.

'I...aaa...I did not mean to do that. I mean...'

'You could not control yourself?' I asked him although I already knew the answer.

'I don't know what game you think you are playing, but I have had enough. So just tell us already who you are and what you want!'

'He is Baldric, Eric's brother!'

And that was the last drop. I don't think I have ever seen Christine angrier than she was now.

'You monster!' She yelled and then she sent flashes of light at him, but Baldric managed to stop them easily. The two other men took out their guns and they seemed to be ready to step in.

'No!' That was the only thing that Baldric told them and they put their guns down.

Christine kept throwing spells at Baldric although she was aware that she did not stand a chance to hurt him. He was much too powerful for her who was only a beginner in magic.

'Stop! You are only wearing yourself down! I don't want to hurt you!'

'You've already hurt me, you idiot!'

'I did not mean to do that! Look, I don't want to be like that, alright? I want to change this and I thought that the only one who can help me is Kate! But it seems that I also need you for that! It seems that you are more special than I had expected.'

'At what cost, you bastard? To destroy her in your desperate attempt to save what's left of you? Well, there is nothing good left in you! There is nothing for you to save!'

'You are right...'

A moment's inattention and the next spell hit him fully making him scream in pain. One of the two men took out his gun and pointed it at Christine; after that, I heard the deafening sound made by the gun unloading. I jumped on top of her and knocked her to the ground but I was not fast enough. I felt the pain from the bullet that touched me as it passed near my waist.

'I told you to stay out of this! And now get lost before I kill both of you!'

'Damn it', I said as I could feel that pulsating pain.

'I did not mean for this to happen.'

'You never want anything.'

'Let me see', Christine said.

She pulled up my tank top and examined my wound.

'That was so close. Thank you for what you did Kate. I am sorry that you got hurt because of me. She took off her blouse in the blink of an eye without caring about Baldric, and put it on top of my wound to stop the bleeding.

'Make yourself useful and go get some help!'

Baldric made a call and in less than five minutes, someone showed up with a first-aid kit.

I screamed when I felt the disinfectant on my wound.

'Damn it, how it hurts.'

The woman dressed my wound and then gave both Christine and me some clothes to change; the ones we were wearing had blood on them.

Baldric turned as we were about to change clothes. A woman came after that with more than ten shopping bags, which she gave to us.

'I did not mean for this to happen. I don't really know how to behave. The idea is that I need you, Katelyn, but you are of no use to me if you are not alive. Have you been felling very tired lately and have you had terrible back pains?'

'What does this have to do with anything?' I asked.

'I learned recently that a morh pushed his claws in your back. Does my idiot brother have any idea how many bacteria the morh's claw bear?'

'Oh no, Kate, please don't tell me this is true.'

'I am sorry, Christine. I...'

'Why didn't you say anything until now?' She yelled angrily at me.

'Let's leave the drama for later', Baldric said. It is possible that aunt Meya may have found out something about this. You see, she was carrying experiments on morhs in her secret lab. Christine, I did not expect you to be so special. I need you more than I thought. I want you to come with me to Kaeillindor to try to find the cure. I need you to get past the barrier. You and Kate are connected to it. Your mothers are some of the wizards that created it.'

Christine and I looked at each other. We could not believe what was happening.

'What do you know about this?' I asked. 'About the barrier? Have you met my mother?'

'That...is a different story...for some other time.'

'What is the cost?'

'Sorry?'

'I know that you do not give a dime for my life. There must be something more to it. What is it that you want?'

'I want you to help me feel again, any small thing. And you, Christine, will be there to make sure that I do not hurt her with my coldness. You will use your special power on me. Eric doesn't have to know anything; he would never agree to this.'

I did not trust him and I had no idea what was going to happen. It was obvious that we would not be getting rid of Baldric. Now Christine had been involved in this crazy game because of me.

'I guess he has his good reasons not to trust you.'

Baldric ignored Christine's comment.

'I will take you to Eric now and tomorrow morning we leave together from the academy. I do not care what excuse you'll give to my brother. I will use a hiding spell and I will be at the party tonight. You have to go; you don't want to raise any suspicion. And I have to be there to make sure that you will come with me, Christine.'

'I will do it', she said. 'But not for you, for Kate. She is too important.'

No, no, no...a disgruntled voice inside me yelled. Something was incredibly wrong.

'But do not forget. Everything comes at a cost.'

'You mean to say that we would become your lackeys, don't you?'

'For how long?' Christine asked.

'Until I am done needing you.'

'Why do I have the feeling that there is more to your plan than what you are telling us?'

'Maybe because there is more', he said.

'You have your business with me, but leave Christine out of this.'

'You do not understand, Kate. I am the element that will help you fight the mass of negative feelings from this monster. Without me, if you choose to help him, you risk becoming exactly like him. And I do not want this to happen.'

'But you don't need to sacrifice on my account!'

'I will, Kate, even if you want to or not. We will get past this too! The most important thing now is for you to stay alive!'

'How do you know that we will live up to our word?' I asked him.

'It's simple! I also have a special power. I control animals. More exactly, I control dead animals. There are different kinds of morhs. They tell me what I want to find out. They are my best spies, but also the best weapons I have. All I know is that we wouldn't want anything bad happening to your parents, would we, Kate? Christine? How is your little sister?'

'You bastard!'

'Don't you dare touch them!'

'This, my dears, depends only on you.'

I hated Baldric and I am sure that Christine shared my feelings. I did not trust him and I had no idea what was going to happen.

Chapter 19:

"Life happens as I wait for a cure"

Eric was waiting for us outside the first store where the girls and I had been. He was alone, angry and the last thing I needed was to have an argument with him.

'Do you have any idea what time it is? And can you tell me why you haven't answered your phone?'

'Well...'Christine began saying.

'Where are the others?' I asked him, ignoring what he was planning to say.

'If you had checked your phones you would have know that they had already left. They were in a hurry.'

I was beat down and I could feel the pain from the bullet wound pulsating with every step I took. I was lucky that it was just a graze.

'Aha.'

'Is that everything you have to say?'

I tried to be as calm as possible.

'Eric, I am tired. You can jump on me all you want tomorrow, but now, please let me be.'

Angry as he was, he grabbed the shopping bags and put them in the car trunk.

'What did you do? Did you buy everything in the store?'

'This? This is nothing', Christine replied.

Eric smiled.

'Did you already change your clothes?'

'We couldn't wait any longer', Christine said and sat in the front seat.

'You girls, I will never understand you.'

I lied down on the back seat and closed my eyes; I was trying to fall asleep. I did not feel like talking to anyone or think about what had happened. I just wanted to sleep and pretend that it was only a bad dream.

Of course, I did not manage to do that. Half an hour later, I gave up. I woke up, leaned my head on the window and continued to stare off at the moon that seemed to be following us.

'I am sorry I yelled at you. It is just that...I was worried and I don't want this to happen again.'

'It is alright. We are sorry we did not answer our phones. We didn't want you to worry', Christine said.

'The important thing is that you are both alright.'

'It's not as if anything could have happened to us', I replied ironically.

'Ok...maybe I overreacted. I shouldn't be so protective.'

'So you know that.'

'Aren't you going to drop that ironical tone of voice?'

I did not answer back.

'Why is she so cranky?' He asked Christine.

'It seems shopping has worn her out more than I had expected.'

'Yeah...it's difficult to keep up with you.'

How could she keep her cool like that? I just felt like screaming. How could she laugh when I could not even manage a poor smile? Christine seemed unaffected while I was just so low.

'Eric, what happens if you get contaminated by the morh's poison?

Christine!!!!

'Where did this question come from?'

'Well...many people were infected in Kaeillindor. What will happen to them?'

'It depends on how many bacteria they have in their bodies. The luckier ones can go on living for a few good months after. The bacteria spread very slowly in the body and their presence is not felt at first. But when they start to make their presence known....I would not want to be that person. In any case, they will eventually die.

I chocked. I really did not need to hear this.

'And is there no cure?'

'I am sorry, but no.'

'There has to be!'

'Not one that I know of.'

'I was talking to Edward today and I found out that a very good friend of mine got infected. If it is possible, I would like to go home tomorrow; at least for a week. I want to see if there really is no cure. I have to do something for her. I cannot just sit around and wait for her to...

She could barely refrain from crying.

'To die...', I said.

'I have to do something, Eric!'

'I am sorry about your friend. Life often takes us on roads we do not want to take. Roads with obstacles...with suffering...Life is not always fair, but we have no choice. We have to keep going forward or we risk being stuck in one place. You can go, but I will send someone with you to make sure that you are safe. And not for more than one week.'

'Thank you!'

'And Christine...I don't want to tell you this but...you had better not get your hopes up. Expectations only bring you disappointments that are even more difficult to bear. You'd better try to accept the truth...There is no antidote...'

'No', I said in hushed tone.

Damn these betraying tears!

'Kate...'

'No, Christine. Just forget about it. We both know what will happen. You will come back with one big nothing. Like Eric said: THERE IS NO CURE! Your friend will eventually die!

'Katelyn Lambert! Eric scolded me. What is the matter with you?'

'What? Should I tell her that she will live, when we both know it's not true? Or should I try to sweeten the truth? Why would I do that? Do you think that it will hurt less if you beat around the bush or if you speak in metaphors? Christine, you know very well what I think about this. You are wasting your time and you are embarking on an adventure that you should not be making.'

'I won't accept that. Do you understand? I just cannot let her die knowing that I haven't at least tried to do something to help her.'

'Fine, do whatever you want.'

'If she has given up hope it does not mean that I will also.'

'She has stopped believing in a good outcome a long time ago...'

'What are you two hiding from me; because I have the feeling that there is more to this?'

'You're wrong', I said.

Christine became quiet.

'Is there anything you want to tell me?'

He looked over at Christine.

'Nothing that concerns you', I said.

"I got it, Kate, but I also want to hear what Christine has to say. So?'

'Well...if you knew the person who has been infected, would that make any difference?'

'But maybe she does not want the others to know!' I said angrily. 'She does not need anyone's pity.'

'What exactly do you want to say, Christine?'

'Would you do the impossible to find a cure if you cared for that person?'

'Yes', he said, 'although I am aware that there is no cure. That is why I've given you permission to leave. Unlike other people – he looked at me – I understand you. I would do the exact same thing.'

'Eric...I am not speaking purely hypothetical...I mean...would you reall...'

'We're finally here', I said and interrupted Christine.

One of the guards opened the gate for us and immediately after we entered the courtyard of the campus, Eric pulled over.

'I am listening, Christine. Kate, you may leave. I guess you know your way back to the dormitory.'

I knew it, but I was not going to let Christine alone with him. Not until I would talk to her first. This was my secret and, even it was wrong that I had decided not to tell anyone, it was still my secret, and it was none of her business. The last thing I needed now was to see Eric behaving nicely to me just because he felt pity. Baldric had warned us not to say anything about the meeting we had had, and nothing about our agreement either. That is exactly what we were going to do; it is just that we had not said anything about who should know that I was infected.

'I am sorry but I have to tell him. He can help us.'

'What part of there is no cure, do you not understand?' I yelled at her.

'Katelyn Lambert, please get out of the car right now!'

'It is not your life, Christine', I said with tears in my eyes. You have absolutely no right!'

I slammed the car door behind me and ran to the dormitory.

There was no one in the room. There was a package on my bed with a note next to it.

"This was made for you; no one else could possibly wear it. Kisses from Maggie and Christine."

I was too angry now to think about how nice the girls had been. And yet, Maggie had not done anything to me and I could not be a jerk; not to mention that I had about five incoming calls from her.

I could hear the loud music when she picked up the phone.

'Wait a moment; I am going out.'

'Ok.'

'Well. What have you been doing? Oh, the two of you are going to be in trouble. Do you have any idea what you put us through? Never mind that now. Come one, move your ass over here. Oh, and you had better wear that dress we got you. You are welcome. Don't you dare not show up. Kisses! Bye!'

And she hung up on me before I could even say anything.

Half an hour later I was on my way to the party; I had to drag myself there and I was trying to keep my mind blank. I obviously could not keep my mind away from the millions of things going on. I had too much information and too many feelings for just one evening and the only thing I wanted was to get rid of them, at least for a short while. I was going to have fun since I was anyway going to that party.

I did not care that this was not the most mature decision; one must not run away from their problems but face them. But tonight, I do not want to know anything; I just want to drown myself in alcohol.

I was surprised to see how many people had showed up and how loud the music was. You could not hear anything from outside – there was probably some spell.

After going around through the crowd of strangers for about fifteen minutes, I finally ran into Maggie and the others.

'Ooo, look who is here, miss Tardy', Arriana teased me.

'And you are wearing the dress we got you. How niiiiicee! Nate, can you please bring me another vodka? With apples.

The critic in me could see that Maggie had probably already had too much to drink; but I did not want to judge anyone.

I had to remind myself why I was here; to forget about my damn problems for one night.

'Bring me one, also, please. More vodka, very little juice.'

I had never before seen Maggie so happy. She had this wide smile on her face and I am sure that it was not the alcohol that was the cause for her good humour. Nate definitely had something to do with it. He'd better not break her heart...or he will have me to deal with. Although I have the feeling that Maggie will be fine on her own.

We all clinked out glasses and then I just poured the vodka down my throat; I felt like the biggest drunk ever. This reminded me of the old times when I was not the best example.

'Take it easy', Mayte said to me.

Both, she and Arriana gave me this strange look; as if I had just escaped from the cage I had been kept locked in until then. To be honest...in a way that was exactly how I felt. Maggie was too distracted by Nate who was whispering something in her ear and made her laugh. Camille was not paying attention to us, because she was too busy scanning the crowd.

'Yes, the night is long', Arriana added.

'You have no idea how much I needed this. Camille, are you going to drink this or what?' I asked her while pointing to the glass she held and which she had not even touched.

She looked at me puzzled.

'Are you going to drink that?' I shouted while pointing to her glass.

'Excuse me; I think I saw Ethan and...'

'Go', Arriana said to her.

'Yes, good luck. Mayte took the glass from her hand and gave it to me. Here you go you little drunk! If you're going to get wasted, then go ahead. You'll be the one with a hangover tomorrow, not us.'

'I have a long night ahead until tomorrow.'

'Still, take it easy. Don't drink this one also in one sip.'

'You've got it. By the way, how did you get the alcohol? Shouldn't all of this be forbidden?' I pointed around me and to the young hormonal people and to all that alcohol.

'There are many things that should be forbidden and yet they happen nonetheless...but don't worry. As long as there are no incidents, then no one has to know anything.'

'Or they know, but they pretend not to', Arriana added.

We left Maggie and Nate together and joined the crowd. We let our bodies move to the sound of a Latino song. The Mexican girls could really dance, no doubt about it.

Seeing Barbie dance trying to draw attention on her, amused me. She wore an extremely short leather dress and a wide décolletage, and she wanted to make sure that all eyes got to see her super-sexy outfit. She was dancing on a table – if that could even be called dancing, since she could barely move in that much-too-tight dress.

I could feel the alcohol rushing through my body and I went out to get some air.

'What are you doing by yourself?' I heard a voice behind me saying.

When I turned, I had the pleasure of seeing Baldric.

'Exactly the person I wanted to see. What do you want?'

He became his sarcastic self.

'Nice to see you too.'

Then he continued looking at me in a strange way, without saying anything else.

'Are you going to tell me what you are doing here or are you just going to stare at me the entire night?'

'I was just trying to figure out how you do it.'

'I don't know what you are talking about.'

'To be so warm. There is so much warmth around you. To have such good control.'

He could probably tell that I was looking at him as if he were crazy, because he continued.

'You are like a volcano, Kate. Be careful; a time will come when that volcano will erupt. Oh, and drinking is not the answer. I know it helps ease the pain from the morh, but the last thing we need is a drunken Katelyn walking around the campus in Eric's sight – and he is no dumb.'

'Give me a break, alright! You don't know anything about me.'

'Maybe not, but there are many things that you somehow manage to transmit to me. When I am around you, all that coldness starts to ease off.'

'And by coldness are you referring to your heart of ice? Because you have given your soul for power?'

He grabbed me by my arm and I moaned as I could feel his painfully cold hand.

'I am sorry...' he said and then let go of my arm...'Sometimes it is very difficult for me to control my emotions...you should know that very well yourself...'

When we touched, the connection set off an exchange of heat between us. I could make Baldric feel again but this came at a cost. In the best-case scenario, I was to become Baldric's female version; a block of ice that did not care about anything because it cannot feel. In the worst-case scenario, I was going to die.

'I am sorry...'I told him and I was amassed by what I was saying. 'Not being able to feel anything must make one feel very alone...And nothing hurts more than that.'

'Where is Christine?'

He obviously ignored what I had said.

'I do not know. I think she might be inside, at the party. Leave her alone, at least for tonight. Shouldn't you two be leaving tomorrow morning?'

'I thought so too, but she told me to meet her here tonight around 1 a.m.'

'When did it get to be 1 a.m.? Wait a minute, Christine wants you to leave earlier? Why? She hasn't said anything to me.'

'See if she is in there and tell her that I am waiting for her outside. I would go myself but I cannot risk anyone recognising me.'

'There is something that I have to do first.'

Christine was going away to Kaeillindor with heartless Baldric and she would risk her life because of me, for me. I took Baldric into my arms while focusing on the warmth he was talking about. It took all the will I got not to run away when I touched him. My entire body hurt because of the coldness and I do not know if it was the alcohol that made me dizzy or this.

When the pain became too strong, I moved away from him and I had to lower myself to the ground. I was too dizzy for whatever reason.

'It scared me terribly when we first touched, but now it was incredible. I should not have let you take me into your arms. You are too weak for this. I knew it was hurting you, but I could not step away. Why did you do that? Are you alright?'

'I did it for Christine. The more you can feel, the easier it will be for her to travel with you. Promise me that you will take care of her.'

'I promise. Wow...this is so strange.'

'What is?

'The fact that I am sorry because you are not well right now...'

I never would have thought that there is anything he might say that would make me feel better, but I started to laugh.

And to my surprise, he also laughed. Not much, but he did.

'I would help you get up but I do not think that I am the best person to do that.'

'I will help her. Are you alright?'

'Christine! Yes, I think I drank more than I should have.'

'Oh, yes. I can feel that. You smell of vodka from a mile away.'

'I had a difficult day', I said in my defence.

'It is alright. I am not judging you. It is just that I thought you are a bit of a control freak. But anyone loses it sometime, right?'

She was talking about herself. I don't know how much she had been drinking but she had.

'What have you been doing?' Baldric asked her.

'I had some fun, I danced, I talked to people and, oh yes, I made out with a guy. Disappointing really, I had to lead him through the whole process.'

I could barely stop myself from laughing. Meanwhile Baldric looked as if he was about to smash something up.

'How much did you drink?' I asked her.

'Not more than you, don't worry. As I was saying, this guy...'

'I really do not want to know', Baldric said and he was visibly irritated. 'If there is nothing else, then I will be on my way. We leave first thing tomorrow morning.'

'No, no. You are not going anywhere', Christine said to him and pulled him by the arm. I need some courage if I am to take off with you, do you understand? And if I don't do it now, I am afraid I will never do it.'

'Finally, we found you.'

Arriana and Mayte were coming our way.

'Baldric, see you outside my dormitory in fifteen, twenty minutes!'

'Are you sure you don't want us to leave in the morning like we had already planned?'

'Yes I am. Now go!'

Baldric left just before the girls showed up.

'Who is that?'

'No one important', I replied.

'Then let us go inside. You are missing all the fun.'

'I have had enough. But you girls have fun. Take care!'

'You go ahead girls. I will take Christine to the dormitory.'

'We will come with you!'

'It is alright. I will be back shortly.'

'Are you sure?'

'Yes Arriana. They have some talking to do', Mayte said and handed us the bottle she had in her hand. Here you go; you had better fix whatever needs fixing.'

'But we are alright.'

'Really? You have been ignoring each other this entire evening.'

'And there is nothing that this whisky cream cannot fix.'

'Alright, alright' I said and took the bottle from her. You are right.'

We walked silently side by side up to the building where her dormitory was; during this time, we had passed the bottle from one to the other.

'Are you going to be alright?'

What a stupid question. I could do better than this.

'The idea is whether you are going to be alright. Your condition will get worse. We have to find out more about the symptoms and know what to expect and what you should do to ease the pain.'

'I don't want to talk about this now...'

'I know, Kate; it is just that I am worried about you. Promise me that you will go to the library and search through all possible books about this. Maggie will help you. I talked to her; I left out the details.'

'How did she take the news? She didn't say anything to me. In fact, she seemed quite happy when I saw her.'

'I think that, of all of us, Maggie is best at hiding her feelings. She is angry with you. In fact, both of us are, because you hid from us something so important. Whatever, the past does not matter now. Maggie decided to let you be tonight. You deserve to have one night to forget about all your problems. But starting tomorrow, I assume you'll have to deal with her.'

'I take it that you didn't tell her anything about Baldric.'

'Obviously not. This man is not right in the head and I do not want to take any risks.'

'Yeah...you are right. Christine...you don't have to do this. You know that, don't you? We can find a different solution.'

'I know, Kate. But for the time being, this is the only option we have. Moreover, I wanted to go back on that island, anyway, to make sure that Edward is alright.'

'We cannot trust Baldric. What guarantee do we have that he will not hurt you?

'Hm...what would life be without some excitement?'

'Christine!!!'

'He needs me; anyway, my powers. So I do not think that he would hurt me. We are his only chances at humanity. It would be stupid of him to hurt us.'

'I don't know...I just don't like this.'

'I know, Kate. But for now we have no choice. See what you do about Eric. He has his eyes on you and he will realise that something is wrong with you.'

'By the way, didn't he say that he was sending someone with you?'

'Yes. I will tell him that I left earlier because I did not need a bodyguard. He will be angry, but he'll get over it by the time I am back.'

'Yes...when you'll be back...

Who knows when that will be...

'It is going to be alright, Kate!'

We hugged each other and I gave her the last sip of whisky cream.

'We'll keep in touch!'

'Take care!'

'You too, Kate!'

Chapter 20:

"Surprise attack"

After Christine and I went our separate ways, I headed slowly towards my room. Everything around me was moving. Getting back to the party did not sound like a very good plan. Moreover, I was no longer in the mood.

I did not want to think about anything. Not now, when I knew that tomorrow I would start worrying about so many things. Consequently, I stopped and lied on the floor. I did not care that I would get dirt on my new dress. I set my mind on nothing and just stayed there, peacefully, gazing at the sky, until someone dared to disturb me.

'Katelyn, what are you doing here?'

When I saw Eric, I realised that it was already too late to try to hide the bottle in my hand. I don't know why I had not already thrown it away. It was empty.

'I am enjoying the nature. You could try doing this every once in a while. It would loosen up that state of constant irritability of yours.'

'In the middle of the night? Is that a bottle of alcohol?'

'And there goes my moment of silence.'

'Stand up! I will take you to your dormitory. You do know you have practice tomorrow from 8 a.m., don't you?'

This seemed to be so funny. I was so calm and he was so agitated. Eric is really cute, damn it.

He leaned over and took the bottle away from me.

'You drank it all?'

I laughed. I could not help it. His serious tone of voice seemed so funny to me. As if I had done something really bad.

'You know, I would get up if I could. But everything is moving around me. This is really cool.' He helped me get up and I stumbled a bit before I could find my balance.

'I thought this teenager time had passed; that you are no longer carefree and that having fun is not your only concern.'

'I am twenty-three, not thirty, buddy.'

'Buddy?'

Eric laughed.

'I am not one of your buddies. I am your professor and your coordinator. You are in my care; you are my responsibility.'

Perhaps I was dizzy, but I was not stupid.

'The coordinator of my magic, better said.'

'Katelyn, I want you to understand that you are not in a normal campus; you are not a normal student; you cannot do certain things. I know this is all new to you, but you are a witch, and not just any witch, but one with great powers. You have to start treating things up to this standard.'

'Aha...' I said ironically.'

'I don't know why I even bother anymore. We'll talk about this when you are no longer drunk.'

I did not say anything. What was the point? Eric doesn't take me seriously under normal circumstances, not to mention now.

'I don't want to see you like this again', he said to me when we arrived at the dormitory. 'I don't want you hurting yourself. You have already been through a lot.'

'Pfff...Don't pretend that you care about me one bit. If there was any way for me to give you my magic without, you know...ending up dead, I would do it in the blink of an eye...and you would no longer need me.'

Eric took me by the arm and pulled me angrily to him.

'You don't know anything, Kate! Don't ever say this stupid thing again!' He said and then he left.

'I will be there at 8 a.m.', I shouted, although I had no idea where 'there' was. 'I mean...text me the location' I shouted even louder, but he did not say anything more.

Why did I not want Eric to know that I was infected with the morh's poison? By the way, my back wasn't hurting me at all. Perhaps it was from the alcohol...maybe my pain became numb. In that case, I should drink more often.

Yes...coming back to Eric. I did not need his pity. Moreover, he could not do anything to help me. He did say to Christine that there is no cure.

Maybe...in fact...I was afraid of losing him...if he knew that I was going to die...his interest in me, I mean in my magic, would be lost...and then we would not be spending time together.

And I hate this...I hate the fact that although he annoys me and I want to stay away from him, I still feel the need to see him. His presence confuses me. It is good for me, but bad at the same time. Like a sugar-craving diabetic fighting his untamable desire for something sweet.

But Eric turned out to be the last problem on my mind; it seems that the night was not over yet. As soon as I opened the door to my room, I was thrown into the wall. I didn't even have time to curse and come to my senses before being sent straight into the wall once more. I landed on my stomach. I could feel everything around me moving. I tried to get up and see who was my attacker, but I felt this strong hit in my head and then I blacked out.

When I woke up, my head was pulsating and I could feel my back burning. But that was nothing compared to the fact that every part of my body hurt. The pain was so bad, that it was hard for me to concentrate on anything. I had this huge bruise on my right arm and scratches on my legs and hands as if my former-neighbor's cat had fooled around with them. It was difficult to get up; I was dizzy and hangover. I was in the middle of the forest. It was day outside but I had no idea what time it could have been. I looked like someone just returning from war; I had had a good roll in the mud. The dress was dirty and my scruffy hair was now nicely accessorized with clogged blood; but this was my last problem.

Today's order of business! Katelyn Lambert, you have got to stop blacking out and waking up in strange circumstances.

After yelling for help for about ten minutes, I realised it was all in vain.

Who had done this to me? I did not have the slightest idea. The real problem was how far away I was from the campus and how would I be getting back there?

I walked for such a long time that I could barely feel my feet, only to realise that I had been going in circles. I was extremely thirsty and I wanted to sit and rest for a while, but it was getting dark and I was panicking. I started to yell for help again but there was no answer. I don't know why, but I was in so much pain, as if someone was making deep cuts into my body. I didn't know for how long I could hold on without going insane. I was about to give up and that is when I realised that I am a witch. Eric was right. I had to start getting used to it. I remembered the spell that Christine had made; the one we had used to track down Mystic with the help of light. I began to mark the way. I was going to make sure that I would not be going in circles anymore. After about half an hour, I finally got to a road. It was already dark outside and had it not been for that light, I would be in total darkness. Now I had to catch a ride. It did not take long before a car drove by. I initially thought that I might end up with some crazy dude, but I was hoping I wouldn't be so unlucky. I was happy to see that it was an old lady who turned out to be very kind.

'What happened to you?' She asked. 'Poor you, hop in, you need some help!

'Aaa…good evening. It…isss…complicated…'

I got into her car. It took some time before I could feel safe, but I became relaxed after that. I don't know why, but my body wasn't hurting so bad anymore. I know it sounds strange, but I felt some kind of healing energy from the old lady. Maybe I was just imagining things.

'Can you tell me where we are? I have to get to the Barbara Balfour campus. Do you have some water?'

'There should be a bottle on the backseat. I am sorry but I do not know what campus you are talking about.'

Ah…what was I thinking? It is hidden, of course, and normal people do not know about it.

'Do you have a phone? Can I use it to call someone to come pick me up?'

'Sure, dear, but on one condition. I want to make sure that you are alright. The nearest hospital is too far from here. We will be at my place in one hour. I am no doctor but I can patch up some bruises. My nephews were the rebel kind. She sighed…I miss them. Then she shook her head as if to push aside that memory. You will take a shower; I will give you some clothes to change, and a warm meal.

'Thank you, but I do not want to intrude.'

'Loneliness is tough to deal with; you would be rewarding me with a bit of company.'

Her offer did not sound so bad and it was perhaps best if I did not get to the campus looking like this.

The problem was that the only number I knew by heart was the landline at home.

'Good evening.'

'Hello, dad', I said, being very happy that he had picked up. I cannot talk right now. I need Christine's telephone number, please. It's urgent. I am alright, don't worry.'

If it had been my mother, she would have had all these questions, but my father gave the number right away and asked me to call him when I could talk longer.

Christine answered the second time I called her.

'It's Kate. Put Baldric on the phone!'

'Hi to you too. Is everything alright?'

'No, I want to talk to Baldric.'

'I will put you on speaker; he is driving.'

'I need your help. I am outside the campus and I have no idea how to get back. I hope you can send someone to get me. I will give you someone who can tell you where to pick me up from. Thank you.'

I gave the phone to the old lady without listening to what Baldric was saying. I was angry enough that I had to ask him for help.

The old lady lived in a modest house that was very well taken care of. In fact, everything looked so new, as if no one was living there. Not even a bit of dust. The tiles in the bathroom were spotless; so was the mirror. I was looking carefully at them while I was in the bathtub with lukewarm water running on me; I could feel the painful touch of every drop. I was in there for not more than five minutes and I thought that was painful; but only until the old lady began to disinfect the cuts on my legs and to put some infusion on them. I probably would have screamed had she not offered me some scotch – much to my surprise. I took a sip every time she touched the cuts. I would have preferred going into an alcoholic coma instead of having to fight the pain. Anyway…not really a coma, but you get the idea. When she was done, the only thing I wanted to do was to sleep. The old lady insisted that she took me into the bedroom, although the sofa was so good. I was so tired and so dizzy that I could have fallen asleep instantly even if I would be lying on the floor.

I fell asleep with the face of a young brunette before my eyes, only to wake up with that of a blonde one. Although I was still very dizzy and I could barely keep my eyes opened, it did not take me long to realise who it was.

'I am either having a nightmare or Baldric is messing with me.'

'You are having a nightmare? Do you think I had nothing better to do than to save your ass?'

I could recognize this voice anytime, anywhere.

'You? Baldric's contact person?'

'Sarah in the flesh, cutie!'

'Cutie? I am the one who hit her head, not you.'

'It's 2 a.m. We have a long trip ahead of us and I have a class tomorrow at 8 a.m., so move your ass.'

'Where is the old lady? I don't even know her name and that's not very nice of me.'

Sarah looked at me with that annoying face of hers.

'There is no one here.'

'What?'

'Do you want me to say that again because you don't hear well or because you are incapable of processing what I just said?'

'But…I want to thank her…She should be back soon.'

'We are not waiting for anyone. Can't you just leave a note?'

'That would not be nice of me.'

'You have five minutes to get out of bed, leave that stupid note and move to the car. I will wait for you there!'

We had been driving for an hour and a half and none of us was saying anything. I did not mind the silence. In fact, this was exactly what I needed. Sarah however, seemed to be pretty agitated and you could see that she was holding back from questioning me; until she no longer could.

'What happened to you?' she asked and seemed to be very worried.

'You are joking, aren't you?'

'What?'

'Don't act like you care. Deep down, I am sure that you are enjoying seeing me like this.'

'What happened to you?' She asked me again, ignoring what I was saying.

'It is none of your business.'

'Look, I know that you do not like me and believe me when I say that the feeling is mutual; but this is my business. I have to make sure that nothing like this happens to you again, or…'

'Or you'll have Baldric to worry about.'

'Well?'

I realised that it made no sense to be at odds with Barbie. I was not in the mood, nor did I have the energy for this. I told her everything that had happened.

'Hm…most people were at the party. I will look into it and see if anyone has left earlier; we will also have to check the surveillance cameras at the entry into your dormitory. Although, it's not that difficult for a wizard to trick some cameras. Let's hope that whoever it was, he did not think about that.'

'It seems that you are not the blonde I thought you were.'

'The question is why would anyone want to do that? I don't know whose toes you stepped on, but it is obvious that they wanted to scare you, really bad. It was surely someone from the campus. If they were from outside, you would not be talking to me right now.'

'I hate this! I hate being a witch! Bad things have been happening to me ever since I found out! If I could get rid of magic without ending up dead, I would do it in the blink of an eye.'

'You are talking nonsense. Do you have any idea how many would want to be gifted with such power?'

'I do not care. The idea is that I do not want it.'

'The more you reject your power, the more difficult it will be for you to control it. I know that this is what happened in the cafeteria. You lost control.'

'I...aaa...I am sorry for that.'

'I appreciate that. But I still do not like you, just so you know.'

She tried to put on her annoying Barbie face but she could not. An almost-sincere smile gave her away. Behind that egotistical doll mask there was a possibility that Sarah did actually have a conscience and that she was a completely different person.'

'How did you end up doing favours for Baldric?'

My question took her by surprise. She gave it a thought before answering. I thought she would not.

'Everything I am, I owe to him.'

'Really? Gratitude? I was expecting him to have something on you.'

'Yes, that would be more like Baldric.'

'He really scares me! He is not really the type of person you would want to be friends with.'

'I admit that there are moments when I am also afraid of him. But I am happy that he showed up in my life.'

'I am guessing the he was not always like this. How did he get to be like that? It is as if he's been locked into a ball of ice.'

'Magic has made Baldric compromise. The reason for him being so tough and scary is that he cannot feel anything; nothing that makes someone human. He never smiles, he doesn't feel pity, he cannot rejoice, he cannot be happy...he cannot love. You compromise and you accept the consequences.'

I was curious to find out what could have made Baldric make such compromises, but I was sure that Sarah was not going to tell me.

'It must be terrible...to have no good feelings in you...'

'It is...it was easy for him in the beginning, but now it is becoming harder and harder. He gets irritated from just anything and it is very difficult to be around him if you have not known him from before. He is very unyielding but he would never hurt the people who have known him back when he was capable of having feelings. Few people can make him feel a bit more human.

'Oh, no, Christine! She is with him and it is only my fault! He might hurt her.'

'It's one thing not to have feelings and another one to be stupid. Your friend has a particular special power. I do not know why, but he needs her. Even if he had not needed her now, he would still keep her. Why it is your fault; and what is he doing in Kaeillindor?'

Yeah...pause...I was not going to answer that. The last thing I needed was for Sarah to pity me. I have a feeling that this stupid pride of mine won't bring me anything good.

'Why is Baldric so interested in me? What does he really want; in addition to wanting to feel something human? I am sure that there is more to his plan.'

'You're answering my question with even more questions? This is not how it works.'

'I am sorry...but I really cannot tell you.'

'Then neither can I, and believe me when I say that I have already been too nice to you. And now I also have to babysit you.'

'Trust me; this is the last thing I want.'

We didn't talk for the rest of the trip.

When we arrived, we had some trouble with the gatekeeper. Sarah flirted with him and tried to sugar-coat him, but to no avail. She got pissed eventually.

'You are so unpleasant. Your colleague, Paul, is so much nicer.'

'I take it that he's the one who let you out, despite the fact that you did not have permission to leave the campus. That's good to know. There is nothing that you can do to make me let you come in, without me announcing the principal's office.'

'Then tell the principal's office already and let us get in', I told him.

'What? No! Don't tell anything to anyone', Sarah became agitated, and gave me a nasty look.

'Mystic! Talk to her!'

They both looked at me strangely as if I had said something weird.

'First of all, you addressed her by her first name and, second of all, I will not be bothering the Miss for this stupid thing.'

'That's a good way of saying it, a stupid thing! Now let us go in!'

So Mystic had really managed to scare everyone. I cannot picture her like that.

The man took out his phone.

'Wait! Who are you calling?' Sarah asked desperately.

'I am definitely not calling Miss Abner. You two are in big trouble for leaving the campus without anyone's permission.'

This guy seemed to enjoy this. He seemed to take delight in the fact that two annoying rebel students were going to be punished.

I was getting angry.

'Look here, you klutz. I am not in the mood for this; I just want to lie down in bed as soon as possible. If you do not call Mystic, then I will.

Give me your phone, Sarah; I will go crazy if we have to stay here any longer.'

'Who do you think you are?' the muscleman shouted at me. 'Don't you dare disturb her and get me in trouble.'

'She is my sister!'

I do not know how I let that out, but I definitely had not thought it through.

'Aha, right. This won't hold, Miss. As far as I know, she does not have a sister.'

'Then you are not well informed', Sarah said.

'I know what you are trying to do, but I won't be fooled that easily.'

'I wanted to take the easy way, but we'll do it your way; suit yourself. Sarah, give me your phone. She doesn't like being woken up and she will be very angry that we called her for something stupid like this.'

I started to dial a random number and just before I pushed the call key, the guard told me to stop.

'Fine, you can go. You may be Miss Abner's sister or not; I do not want to take that risk.'

'I never thought that I would say this, but you were great', Sarah said to me after we passed the guard.

'Aaa...I don't know what to say.'

'How did I not think about Mystic?'

Sarah thought that I was lying. Truth be told, I was not sure that Mystic was my sister. Christine would be getting the results on her email.

'Why do they all seem to be scared of her?'

'Because Mystic is very tough and she doesn't forgive anything. She does not have any friends; she is alone, and she does not seem to want to have friends. And if you dare make any hints about her past, you're a goner. Any insignificant question you might have, you would better keep it to yourself. She goes crazy when you ask her about the past. Mystic is...how should I say it so that you'll understand better...like a robot. She gets the job done no matter the feelings, if she even has any.'

'Ok...I did not expect that. I cannot imagine her like that. I never knew this side of her.'

Then, much to my surprise, Sarah confessed to me.

'Baldric is the closest thing to family for me', she said and then she sighed.

If that heartless mad man was the closest thing to family for her, then this was sad. Perhaps her annoying attitude is only a mask to cover how alone she actually feels.

'You are not as bad as you claim to be either. You know, if you gave up this arrogant attitude that you always have, you might make some friends – some true ones.'

'My purpose is not to make friends. I cannot afford this now.'

'You don't plan to make friends, you just do. You know...aaa...if you need anything...and if I...'

'I get the point but I hope I won't have to. We are here. Do you think you can manage to get to your room, or do you want me to take you there?'

'I think I will be fine', I replied smiling.

'You are not as bad as I thought you were.'

'Neither are you. Thank you, Sarah, for everything.'

'I was only doing what I had to do.'

'That's exactly what I expected you to say.'

'I still do not like you, you know.'

'They are trying to find the cure for the morh's poison.'

'What?'

'Baldric and Christine. This is what they are doing in Kaeillindor.

'But there is no such thing. Wait a minute; who do they need it for?'

'For me. It seems you won't have to babysit me for too long after all.'

Her jaw dropped when she heard that. I think this is the best way to describe how she looked.

She wanted to say something but she did not know what.

'Is is alright', I said to her and then I got out of the car.

Chapter 21:

"When things are getting complicated"

She dropped the juice bottle and then started to run. I went after her; I had no idea what had gotten into her.

When she went out of the dormitory, she stopped for a few seconds to catch her breath and then continued running; she was going towards the professors' dormitory. I thought that I was in a better fettle than before – although I had not done anything to help with that – but I was surprised to see that I was not running – although that was my impression. I was floating above ground.

Beatrice, Christine's roommate, suddenly stopped and exactly when I thought that I was going to run into her, I was shocked to see that I went through her – like a ghost.

'What is wrong with you?' I asked her.

She looked frightened. Her big eyes were desperately looking for a way out.

'Beatrice?' I shouted.

She did not reply. My hand went through her face – still nothing. She could not see or hear me, and I could not touch her.

Was I dreaming?

I saw her lips moving but I could not hear what she was saying. She was looking desperately at the forest and seemed to be crying for help. I wondered what she could see in that darkness – it was almost midnight; I could not make anything out of it.

A red light flashed out of her hand and lifted into the sky speeding up as it went higher. It stopped and then sparked; the entire sky was coloured into tens of colours. After that, the lights in the professors' side of the campus were turned on, one after the other, as did some in the students' dormitories.

That is when I realised that this was the alarm for when something wrong was happening– I could not see anything being wrong; but there was a strange feeling in the air.

I waited impatiently. Shortly after that, it happened. A redhead girl appeared before my eyes; she had taken Beatrice by the arm. They both disappeared in a dense mist that had come from nowhere. It all happened so fast.

Eric arrived at the scene together with some professors. I went next to him and watched carefully. He was angry. He told the others to start immediately the search. I would never had imagined that it can be so fast – faster than I could count to 10; they split into groups and went in different areas of the campus. They were well trained.

I went after Eric; I stood next to him observing all his gestures. He was agitated and angry but I could see a strange spark in his eyes – as if he had been waiting for this moment for a long time.

I was in the forest. You could not hear anything, except for the sound of nature. I could read some of the words from Eric's lips – that was the only thing I was paying attention to – but I was not completely sure that they were correct.

I looked carefully around me. There were three other people – two female guards whom I had seen in the school before, and the Creatheology professor.

Ever since I arrived here, I was curious about this need to have so many guards and so many protection devices. We could not even leave the campus without them knowing. This was because of the very powerful and extremely complex spells around the campus, in addition to the thick two-metres-tall walls.

There is always a guard at the gate; you cannot go in or out without the alarm system going off. I don't know how Sarah managed to get out, but I have this vague feeling that she flirted with the guard.

Lately however, I have seen too many guards patrolling in the campus.

Maybe now – in this dream or reality – I was going to find out the true reason for these many security systems.

Every now and then, I could see a dim fluorescent light at the bottom of every tree trunk. I followed them for some time until Eric and the others changed the direction – I realised that they had not seen them. I was curious to find out where the lights were going, but I decided to follow Eric instead; he had gone ahead of the others. I could see the tree branches moving in the wind, but I could not feel it on my skin.

I sensed a rapid movement through the trees; Eric did not seem to be aware of it. A few second later, he fell on his knees. He seemed to be crying for help. He was fighting something beyond the tangible; I could not see anything. Not long after that, he got up on his feet with great difficulty, as if he was setting himself loose from an invisible grip.

The Creatheology professor was the first one to show up; the two women guards followed after. Eric told them something and then they all left to the place where Eric had pointed them.

Wasn't Eric that person that no one could hurt? Was he not the one who always had some lackeys following him – people that defended him and did his dirty jobs? How had he been caught off-guard?

I went next to him and looked at him from up-close. He seemed to be in pain. He was angry and he punched a tree. I flinched and he turned and looked straight at me, as if he could see me.

He was going through different emotions. One minute he was scared, and the other he would smile. He reached with his hand towards me and I became breathless. I closed my eyes; the image of a very strange symbol appeared in my mind. A sort of an X, but with a circle in the middle; there were four small symbols in each empty space: one that looked like a flame – the only one that had a star next to it – another one with waves; I could not make out anything of the other two.

After that, I heard my name being called, and I woke up with a pillow being thrown at me.

'Look who has finally decided to join us.'

'Now that I have respected your wish and did not disturb you, tell me where you've been. You met Damien, didn't you?'

What were they talking about?

I got out of bed feeling woozy and the first thing I inquired was Eric's whereabouts and if he was alright.

I did not get an answer. Instead, they both looked strangely at me.

'What?' I asked.

'You look...'

I laughed.

'What gave me away? The bruises; the scratches; the bandages?'

'Cut it out, Kate', Maggie picked on me. What happened to you? We thought you had gone with Damien on a little escapade.'

'Damien? How come? And how did you come to this conclusion?'

'We found a note on your bed together with your phone. Since you left your phone behind, it was obvious that you did not want to be disturbed.'

'Where is the note?'

'I don't know', Camille said. 'I think we threw it away.'

'I want to know exactly what it said.'

'You were asking us to find an excuse to get you out of practice with Eric and you said you were with Damien and that you want to fool around with him.'

'You have got to be kidding me. And did you not, for one second, think that it was not me? Moreover, I have barely seen him a few times. And I thought that he and Sarah are a couple.'

'Yes, we did', Maggie said. Afterwards we checked the notes from one of your courses and we compared the writing. It was identical. Well...I don't know what he and Sarah have going on, but we did not think that this would be a problem for you in case you...you know...'

'In case I what?' I shouted. 'In case I wanted to fool around? With Damien who is in a relationship? Who do you take me for?' I asked them and then stormed out of the room slamming the door behind me.

My head was hurting and the last thing I needed was to be asked even more questions. I had to get Sarah up-to-date and to make sure that Eric was alright. And Beatrice, I had to check on her too. I have a feeling that this was more than a dream. It seemed too real.

'Where do you think you are going?' I heard Maggie behind me, which got me to stop. We have to talk to Mystic and Eric who, by the way, is very angry with you. In fact, I think angry does not really describe it enough. What happened to you? Something is wrong and I want to know. I don't like to be kept in the dark like that.'

'What did you tell Eric?'

'That you had too much to drink that that you've been hugging the toilet seat. He became angry...yeah...it does not matter what he had to say. I want to know what happened to you. Faster.'

'Yes, yes...first I want to make sure that Eric is alright.'

I wanted to leave, but she grabbed my arm.

'Eric is alright, I am sure of that. You should worry more about yourself. I won't pick on you now for having lied to me, only because I am really concerned about you! Where were you? What happened to you? I was such an idiot to think that you would go fool around with Damien. It's just that…considering the gravity of the situation you're in, I thought you would like to relax at least for the weekend.'

'The reason why I haven't said anything to you is because I was fooling myself, feeding on false hope. I thought that, since I was not bitten, I was not infected. I don't know if now I have come at ease with the idea or if I am simply desperate.'

'Oh, Kate…I am so sorry. We'll do anything to help you. There must be a cure! You have to tell Eric and Mystic the truth.'

'No, no way! I don't want them to know.'

'But you need them. They have a lot more experience than we do, and they can help us.'

'Damn it, Maggie. There is no cure so it makes no point involving even more people. The last thing I need now is to be looked at with pity.'

'I am sorry, but I cannot accept this. I cannot accept the fact that there is no cure. There has to be something! Your life is at stake now! You cannot be foolish and refuse help just because you are afraid people will look at you with pity. Get your act together!'

'I will think about it', I said just so that I could get her off my back.

'Two days, Kate. That's all you have. If you don't tell them anything, then I will. We cannot afford to waste any more time.'

'Alright. Meanwhile, I want to continue living my student life in the Barbara Balfour campus.'

'I understand. In fact, that is actually a good idea. This will make you forget about your problems and keep you from going crazy. In the meantime, we will try to find more information about the effects of the morhs' poisoning and how to fight it. And now, let's get you changed. I won't let you go out like that. Moreover, you need some long trousers and a sweater, or something. I don't think you want a bunch of nosy people swarming around you.'

'Yeah...you are right...'

'If we are not in class today, we will be in trouble with the Createheology professor. Come on, let's get you ready. You know how he is if we are late. Like all the other professors, for that matter. We will go talk to Mystic and Eric during the lunch break. Meanwhile, you can tell me what happened. I am not letting you out of my sight.

Despite our rush, we were still ten minutes late. Also, I had forgotten my mobile phone in the room. Not that I needed it that much anyway. I had put on a pair of loose jeans, boyfriend style, a black sweatshirt and I let my hair loose to cover up the band-aid on my forehead. After the ton of concealer I had on, I looked relatively alright. We were outside the amphitheatre trying to come up with an excuse; we soon realised that the professor was not in the room.

'Now that's a nice surprise', Maggie said.

'If he has not showed up until now, I don't think he is coming anymore. Let's go! I am not going to waste two hours sitting in the amphitheatre.'

'But maybe he will come.'

'Or maybe he won't!'

I grabbed her arm and took her with me. When I opened the door to the amphitheatre, we ran straight into Eric who did not seem to be having the best day.

'Lambert, what's the hurry?'

'I have to talk to you', I told him silently so that the others could not hear me.

'Yes, we have to! You can go back to the amphitheatre now; you have a Creatheology class.'

'But...'

'Find a seat! Quicker', he shouted.

He did not say anything to Maggie. He only addressed me because I was the one he was angry with. I spotted two empty seats all the way in the back of the room and we sat there.

'Professor Edison will be away for some time. I will be replacing him until we find someone else.'

'Does this mean that he won't be coming back for quite some time?'

'Yes.'

'But why?'

It's not that I liked him that much...but I definitely do not prefer to have the classes with you, I said to myself. It is very difficult to consider him a professor when he is so fine looking. I find it difficult to concentrate when I am around him and I am sure that many other girls have the same problem. It is only physical attraction, and no more! It had to be just that!'

'You have a lot of questions. Why don't we begin the class and focus on that instead?'

It became so quite during the next five minutes that you could hear a pin drop. I stood no chance of talking to Maggie without being heard. Some colleagues were passing notes to each other; I was so curious to know what the note read. It surely had to be something more interesting than what Eric was telling us.

'Turn to page 17', he said. There you will see how these very-agile-and-difficult- to-understand creatures look like.'

I did not even bother taking out the book from my bag. In fact, I don't think that I even had it with me. Anyway, Maggie had taken hers out. I placed my elbows on the desk and laid my face on my palms.

'When they attack, they are so fast that it is difficult for the human eye to track them. The wounds that they cause are not out on the surface, they are not visible. You just end up feeling in pain without having any idea why since there is no scratch on you, although you feel your entire body hurting. The creature messes with your mind. It does not hold physical strength. It is like the wind. No one knows what makes them be aggressive or what is their living environment. They have been seen very seldom. None of them could be captured and studied, therefore we do not know very much about them.'

I really was trying to pay attention. And I was, for some time; it is just that it became harder and harder to keep my eyes opened.

'Don't lose your focus not even for one moment...calm...vigilant...the correct spell...'

His words slowly started to make no sense anymore.

'Lambert!' Someone shouted in my ear.

I got up scared and everybody started to laugh.; except for Eric who looked like he wanted to strangle me.

'Since you are so easily bored, it means that you are probably already an expert on these little creatures. Why don't you continue teaching and tell your colleagues about them?'

'Aaa...I did not get much sleep last night. I am sorry. This will not happen again.'

'I know. I heard about your little escapade with Damien. In fact, we all heard about it.'

I was either too woozy from the sleep and did not understand well, or I was going to punch Damien later on in the day.

I tied my hair in a bun as fast as I could with the elastic band I had around my wrist, and tried to stay calm. I abstained from making any further comments. It made no sense to comment. I absolutely had to talk to Eric.

The girl in front of me passed me a note and asked me to give it to the girl behind me. I could not help myself; I peeked. "Do you know anything about Beatrice?"

I thought of the nightmare I had had the night before. I passed the note; I was shaking. I prayed that this was only a bad coincidence.

'All the pictures we have of them are blurred. They are always moving. They are like the wind.'

I had not paid attention to what Eric was telling us but he had not picked this topic randomly. He had a good reason to do it. He had had an encounter with whatever this creature was, the night before.

'Damn it. It was not a nightmare.'

I ran out of the amphitheatre ignoring Eric who was shouting after me. I closed my eyes for a split-second and I thought that I saw Beatrice on her knees facing a tree that had that strange X symbol I had seen in my dream. I stopped when I got to the exit because I bumped into a crowd. What were they all doing here? Shouldn't they be having classes? I made my way through them, ignoring the comments of those I was pushing aside. I stopped at the bottom of the stairs. The symbol on that tree was in front of the stairs. I rubbed my eyes in disbelief. I went to that symbol, squatted and continued to stare at it as if I was waiting for it to tell me something. It was imprinted on the ground and it looked as if it had been there for a long time. I had seen this same symbol in my dream.

'Oh, no!' I yelled. I could feel my feet weakening. 'Where is Beatrice?' I began to ask around. 'You know her, don't you?'

'What happened, Lambert? Did you run out of pills?'

Sarah; she was together with some of her friends.

'This is not funny' I reproached her. I grabbed her by the shoulders and asked her if she knew where Beatrice was. She shook her head.

'Get your hands off me!'

'I heard that she is sick.' I looked over at the boy behind Sarah. It was Damien. He was exactly the person that I wanted to see; but this was a problem that I would have to take care of later.

'Sick. How is she sick?'

'Theoretically, she has a cold. Practically, she wanted to get a leave from classes. Many students take advantage when poor old Amanda is on duty at the medical office.

'Are you alright?' Sarah asked me after giving me a good head-to-toe scan.

'A...why would I not...be...' I began to stutter. 'Everything is alright; everything is perfect.' After that, I started to talk nonsense in phrases that even I did not understand. 'Dream...not alright, I mean she has to be ok...' I felt this strange need to continue talking. I felt that if I had not done that, then my mind would go crazy.

'Then why are you acting so strangely? And why are you crying?'

I wiped off my tears; I had not even been aware that I had tears in my eyes.

'A...it is from the wind. I always get watery eyes from the wind.'

'What is going on here?' I heard Eric's tough voice; he showed up from behind Sarah.

He did not say anything to me, but as he passed by me, he gave me his "I will deal with you later" look.

I did not think that he could be angrier than he had been today, but I was wrong. He began to yell when he saw the symbol.

'Don't you have anything better to do? Everyone, go to your classes! Now!'

'But we are on break', Olivia said; she was one of Sarah's friends.

That was a bad move. Eric came next to her and asked for her name.

'Olivia...a...Olivia Larsen', the brunette girl stuttered.

'Miss Larsen, since you have nothing else to do, why don't you go to the headmistresses' office? I am sure that she will find something for you to do. Go on now, scram!' He shouted.

I had not done anything bad; at least not during the past 24 hours. But this was not the best time to talk to Eric.

Yet I had to do something before leaving.

'Damien, darling. Can you come here, please?'

'Sure. What is it?'

I did not think that I would do it; not until my fist smacked his face.

'It is much better now', I said; I was smiling with great satisfaction.

'Are you crazy?'

'This is nothing compared to what I had to go through because of you.' I snapped at him and I would have punched his other cheek if Eric had not stopped me. 'I have been hearing that we had a great time together. Really? How come? I don't remember that.' I was struggling to get loose from Eric's grip. I wanted to hurt him. Oh, how I wanted that. 'I was too busy trying to stay alive, you moron.'

'I have no idea what she is talking about. She is crazy', Damien said.

'I will show you who's crazy.'

I was so close to using my power on him but Mystic and Maggie interfered, so I did not stand a chance to do it.

'You! Go away', he said to Damien. The same goes for the rest of you. This is not the circus. I want you to clear this place as soon as possible.'

'See you later', I heard Sarah telling me.

'I was on the verge of losing control, again.'

'I know', Eric said. 'And you would have, if we had not been here.'

'You can let go of me now', I told him.

'Are you sure you are not going to run after Damien?'

I laughed. Strangely, I managed to do that. Being so close to him calmed me.

Chapter 22:

"Confessing my feelings for Eric"

I was in Eric's office. He and Mystic were waiting for me to say something, but I had no idea with what to begin. I did not think that things could be any weirder than they were, but that is when I saw the framed picture on Eric's desk. I took it up to have a better look. I don't know how, but I had seen before the girl who was arm in arm with Eric. In the old lady's house, before I dozed off. They were both so happy. In fact, I have never seen Eric smile with all his heart, as he was in that picture.

'Who is she?' I asked.

'My sister', Eric replied. 'Now please, put the photo back and tell us what happened.'

But his sister was dead...I did not know what to do. Should I tell him that I saw her? I would only be reopening old wounds. He would not believe me anyway. In fact, until now, I thought that I was only imagining it. I was going to tell Mystic later and she will decide what to do with it. She knows him better.

'I don't have all day, you know!' He sounded so cold.

'After you dropped me off outside the dormitories, I went to my room and there...well, there was someone waiting for me. I did not get to see my attacker or attackers. All I know is that I woke up in the woods and that it took me a while to find my way back to the dormitory.' I told the story quite fast adjusting it a bit. If I had told them about the old woman, then they would find out about Sarah and that would lead them to Baldric.

Eric came next to me. He brushed the hair off my forehead and took off the band-aid.

'Ouch.'

'Sorry', Eric said. 'You are hurt. What did they do to you?', he asked me while examining the wound on my forehead. 'Hm...it seems well cleaned but I will still have to take you to the medical office to have it checked.'

'I am alright', I lied and moved back a few steps. 'You don't have to get protective on me.'

Mystic was not saying anything. The expression on her face made me wonder if she somehow felt that there was more to this story than what I was telling.

'I will ask Amanda to have you checked. As soon as she has told me that you are well, that is when I will believe you and I will relax about it.'

'My powers are safe', I said ironically.

'This had better be the last time you say that, Katelyn! Eric has done everything for you. We both have and you continue lying to us and playing the victim.'

'Then we have something in common, sister.'

Her jaw dropped. She was not expecting this. To be honest, neither did I. I had managed to distract them from our main discussion and to make it easy for myself. At least now, I would not have to explain to Mystic why I had lied. Although I have a feeling that I won't be able to avoid this discussion too long.

I could have called Mystic or Eric to help me, but why had I chosen to call Baldric instead? Is it because I did not want Eric's pity? The last thing I wanted was for him to behave nicely to me because he pitied me.

'I am trying to figure out what is going on here', Eric said.

'The medallion was the first thing that made you wonder, wasn't it? You have a similar one. After that, you took the DNA test. I know that because I followed you when we went shopping. The lady at the Generic Lab reception office gave us all the information. Christine cast a spell on her. When are you getting back the results?'

'You followed me?' Mystic said angrily.

'Don't worry. It may be negative.'

'She cannot be your sister', Eric said. 'She would have to be about your age. Moreover, you are the only one who made it out alive back then in Kaeillindor.'

'Apparently not', Mystic said. 'This was the second time I made the test. The first one came out positive, but I had to make sure. You cannot trust just one doctor, can you?'

'What?' I was revolted. Is it so bad to think that I might be your sister that you had to take the DNA test again, hoping that it will turn out negative?'

'Stop being silly. I just wanted to make sure.'

'Really? What? Did you think that the doctor fooled you? And what did Eric mean when he said that your sister would have to be about the same age as you? And what happened in Kaeillindor?'

'I had a sister. She died. And what happened on the island is not your business; not now.'

'It is my business. What do you mean you had a sister who died? I want to know everything. I have the right to know.'

'This is not the time to be talking about this.'

'Why not?' I yelled at her. 'I have the right to find out more about my family. Oh, wait. You cannot give me any details because you don't have the results from the second DNA test. Perhaps you'll get a discount and have another go at it; maybe next time it will come out negative.'

'Why don't you both calm down and talk about this later.' Eric interfered. Meanwhile, you and I will go to the medical office, Kate.'

'Come on, Eric. It's just a little scratch on the forehead; that's it. She probably fell down on her way to bedroom. After all, she was drunk when you met her.'

'I was not drunk! I mean, I was a bit dizzy. Fall of the stairs? What are you talking about?'

'I saw the CCTV recordings from the gate this morning. You and Sarah were both in her car when she drove in.'

Eric lost his temper.

'Are you mocking us, Lambert? I think the problem might be that we've been too nice to you; it seems you don't have any limits. What did you do? In fact, have you really been fooling around with Damien?'

'You're friends with Sarah? Really? Do you know her reputation? I thought you two could not stand one other...'

'In fact, you are not even hurt. What is going on in that head of yours? How could you come up with this story about being attacked? Next time you feel like fooling around and disappearing like that, let us know, won't you', Eric said; he continued to lash out at me.

'We are worried about you, Kate!'

'It's not your powers. We care about you. Is it so difficult for you to understand that?' Eric asked me.

'Don't you have anything to say for yourself?'

I was standing before them and I felt more and more embarrassed as they continued talking. I did not know what to say to them. I could not do this; not now. I would have run and not say anything to them; I would have run and avoided everything like a coward, but I remembered Beatrice.

'I know what happened last night', I said. I thought it was a dream but after that, I saw the symbol. That X. Beatrice set off the alarm and then a young woman appeared, took her by the arm and they both disappeared in a dense mist. I cannot tell you how she looked but she had huge red hair. Then you showed up with the guards. I followed you into the forest. I also saw the Createheology professor. Something happened to him, didn't it? That is why he did not come to classes today and you said he would be away for an indefinite period of time. I saw this creature in the trees; you were not even aware that it was there, until you fell to your knees because of the pain. Saying that I saw it might be an exaggeration. It was more like a flash, a shadow. And I saw the symbol. After that, Maggie woke me up. And no, I was not with Damien. That's all I have to say. It's your business if you want to believe me or not', I said and then stormed out before either of them could say anything more.

Mystic caught up with me. She took me by the arm.

'We have to talk', she said.

'I know...'

'Eric has asked to see all the CCTV recordings from the past week. He wants to go through them personally and take care of this matter with Beatrice. We still do not know why she set off the alarm. The novices are protected. They do not even know about the alarm. We don't want to scare them off from the beginning. Their first year in school is one during which the main goal is for them to become accustomed with things. It is only during the second year that it becomes more complicated. That is why none of the novices knew that the alarm went off last night. Your Creatheology professor went together with some of the guards to check the forest outside the academy. These creatures have been kept under control in the forest by several magic barriers. It seems that some have disappeared and we do not understand how. But these are the problems we have to take care off; you have enough going on as it is. Let's not talk about this now. Let's go somewhere quieter.'

We went in the kitchen of the house that Mystic and Eric were sharing.

'What kind of tea do you want?' she asked me.

'Green tea, please. I could use some energy.'

'Green it is', she said.

'I am tired. All these secrets make me tired and I do not know for how long...' I am going to be alive, I continued saying to myself. 'Yes, you are right; there are some things that I have not told you and that I cannot tell you; I have to make sure that you and my parents are safe.'

'What? Is there someone threatening you?'

'When I woke up in the forest, I did not manage to find my way back to the campus. I eventually ended up on a road and I was lucky to run into an old woman. She took me to her house and cleaned my wounds. She was very nice to me and I did not even get to thank her for that. I called Sarah to come pick me up because I had no idea where I was and this woman knew nothing about the Barbara Balfour campus. I cannot tell you why I asked Sarah for help. Believe me, I would want to be able to tell you. The burden from all these secrets is getting more and more difficult to bear. I asked Eric who was the girl in the photo because I saw her in the old lady's house.'

'What do you mean you saw her? Did you talk to her? I am sure you imagined it because she is dead.'

'How does anyone imagine a person they have never seen before? I have to admit that...I was a bit numb from the alcohol; that was the only thing that the old lady had to give me before cleaning my wounds...but I am sure it was her.'

'You did good not telling Eric about that. The last thing he needs now is to think about his dead sister who apparently is not dead. I am trying to figure out what is going on; it is impossible that she is still alive.'

I wanted to ask how she died but this was not my business. Moreover, we had bigger fish to fry.

'I am sorry...about earlier. It was nasty of me to throw at you the fact that I know you might be my sister. I don't want you to get me wrong. I would be very happy to find out that I have a sister...well...if you are not happy then we can just act as if we didn't know. I think...'

'Don't be silly', she said. 'We will talk about this too, I promise. And I will tell you everything you need to know, even about our sister who died. I am sorry I did not say anything before. I was shocked when I saw the results. My entire world turned upside down. I was very happy, but I did not know how to react. I panicked, and this was something that I had not done in a while', she said and looked shocked. 'That is why I wanted to take another test. If you are alive, then there is a possibility that our mother is also alive. I thought that...you both died.'

'Is there a possibility that mother is still alive? Wow...this is...I mean...are you really my sister?'

'Yes, Kate. It seems I am. Look at me. Can't you see the resemblance? I don't need another DNA test to tell me that you are my sister. It was stupid of me to make another one anyway.'

She was taller than I was, but she had the same natural blonde hair, blue eyes, face expression; her high cheekbones and full lips were just like mine. Why had not I seen before how much alike Mystic and I were?

'Now, I want you to focus on something else. How did the old woman look?'

'Really? This is what's on your mind now?'

'Kate, this is important.'

'Aaa...'

I was trying to remember how she looked but, somehow, I could not picture her at all. The more I tried to think about her, the more my head hurt.

'I don't have the slightest idea', I told her.

'I will be right back.'

Five minutes later, she was back. She had a photo album with her. She showed me the picture of an old woman.

'Does she look like your old lady?'

'I don't know...don't you have a photo with her that is not so blurred?'

'Look closer, please.'

'It is too blurry and the more I try to focus the more my head hurts.'

Her hands were shaking. She poured us some tea.

'What happened?' I asked.

'I think that the person who helped you is Eric's grandmother...and the reason why you cannot remember how she looked is because she put a spell on you. The more you try to remember how she looks, the more your head will hurt. This photo is not at all blurred. It is actually very clear.

'Ms. Barbara Balfour? I know that this campus was named after her. If this was her, why would she do that? Why would she be hiding?'

'Because Eric accused her of his sister's death. He believes that she is to be blamed for Allice's death, even if indirectly. They had a nasty fight and she went missing after that. She vanished. We thought something had happened to her, that she died, since we never heard from her again.'

'But if it does turn out that she is their grandmother, then she must have known that I called Baldric from the car and...'

'Wait! What? Stop! This is Baldric we are talking about. The one who tried to kill you; remember?'

I puffed.

'Believe me; dying is the last thing that Baldric wants me to do. So you don't have to worry about that.'

'But of course I worry. Kate, I don't know what you think you are doing but trust me, you will not be able to fight Baldric by yourself.'

'It is too much and I do not know what to do.'

'Talk to me; let me help you!'

'Betraying tears', I said as I could feel my eyes watering.

'Please, don't cry. I don't know how to act in situations like this.'

'Ouch', I said when she took me into her arms.

She moved back. She was feeling uneasy.

'I am sorry. I thought this is what people do when someone dear to them is crying.'

'No, it's not your fault; it's not because you hugged me. It is only that my entire body hurts.'

'What happened?' She asked.

I took off my sweatshirt and remained in my tank top.

Mystic cursed. The bruises had become darker since this morning. My arms and my abdomen were scratched as if in a regular pattern; there were not even 5 centimetres between the scratches. My right hip was completely blue now.

'I cannot believe this. Whoever did this used "Vex-Insania" on you. This one is forbidden among wizards. It cannot have been a student. How bad do they hurt?' She asked.

'I am alright. It think it's from the painkillers I got in the morning.'

'It is not from the painkillers, Kate. This spell is filling you with deep cuts. On the outside you can only see the scratches but it does not feel like scratches. The idea is not to bleed to death. The spell cannot kill you; it can only make you succumb to pain until you go crazy. Its name comes from the Latin word *vexation* which is suffering, and *insania*, that is insanity. Until you have managed to get rid of the scratches, you will continue to feel as if someone were making deep cuts into your body. *She was shaken up.* The fact that you are still in your right mind confirms my suspicion that the old woman really is Barbara Balfour. I will explain it to you in the simplest fashion. Any spell has one that undoes it. This is exactly what Barbara did. That is why the pain does not make you go insane now.'

'But...who could have done this to me?' I asked while I was putting my sweatshirt back on.'

'I do not know yet, but I will not rest until I find out. Meanwhile, I want you to stay here.'

'Where is here?'

'Move in with us. The house is very big and there are some empty rooms upstairs.'

The thought of moving in the same house with Eric and of seeing him so often did not sound so good to me.

'I do not think this is such a good idea; people will start asking questions.'

'And I will shut them up.'

'I still do not think this is a good idea.'

'At least for some time; until things start to calm down.'

'What will we tell Maggie?'

'The truth. Someone attacked you, and I, as your older and protective sister, want to take you under my wing.'

'I can already imagine the jokes that will be made on my account.'

'It is your safety we are talking about! And you are thinking about the jokes that your idiot colleagues will be making?'

'It is not that. To be honest, I do not care in the least what they have to say.'

'Then what?'

'I cannot; I just cannot.'

'You will have to.'

'I cannot live in the same house with Eric.'

'Why not?'

'Because I am in love with him.'

'What?'

I sighed. I had not been aware of that until I said it out loud. You know there is that part of the brain that stops you from saying what you think? Mine did not work very well today...

'Damn it. I don't know how to explain this to you, but I feel a strong connection with him; and I am not talking about how he looks. He does look to-die-for but it is not that. I think about him too often and the more I try to get him out of my head, the more I want him. When I see him, it is very hard for me not to be attracted to him. I have never felt so secure with anyone as I do with him. Yes, it makes me angry that we always fight and I am aware that there will never be anything between us. I am only that Kate who is immature and who causes only trouble, and who happens to be gifted with powers beyond her ability to understand. He cares about me and he has a duty towards me; that of protecting me. But let's be honest. He would not give a damn about me if I did not have these powers. Oh, and let's not forget about that stupid prophecy.'

'Kate, no...'

'Don't say anything, please. I don't want you to try to make me feel better. I am aware of what I mean to him and, don't worry, I will keep my feelings to myself. But please, don't make me stay in the same house with him. It is very difficult for me to be around him. So close and yet so far...what a cliché.'

'It does not matter if you live in the same house. You will rarely see each other...in fact, I am sure that he will want to stay somewhere else than to share the house with you.'

'He likes me that much...'I said ironically.

'That's not how I wanted it to sound. Things are not at all what you think they are; of course you got it all wrong.'

'Please, I want this to be the first and last time when we talk about this. I will get over it', I said smiling.

'This is not something you get over easily, Kate...'

'I will continue staying at the dormitories.

'Not even Eric will agree to this, once he finds out what happened to you.'

'But he does not have to find out. I would rather have him think that I was fooling around with Damien than to find out the truth. I care about him too much and I do not want him to be hurt. This story about his grandmother...sister...and Baldric...I don't know how it's going to affect him and I do not want to find out either.'

'You don't need to protect him, Kate. He can take care of himself. You were complaining that he thinks you are immature. You can prove to him that you are grown-up by telling him the entire truth. After that, we will see what has to be done and how we can help you.'

'You cannot help me. I am a lost case, really. In fact, I think that the best thing would be for me to go back home. I have no future.'

'What is this silly thing? Stop it!'

'I am sorry but I cannot. I should go home or to Kaeillindor; or, I don't know...somewhere where no one knows me.'

'Why would you do that? Trouble will be there too, no matter how much you're trying to escape from it. Believe me; been there, done that. Running is not a solution. It is only temporary.'

'That is what I need. Anyway, I don't have much time left.'

'What do you mean?'

I got up from the chair.

'I will not let you leave the campus, Kate!'

'And how do you think you can stop me? Will you put me on permanent supervision?'

'Do not test me! I will do everything it takes to keep you safe, even if I have to protect you from yourself. And Eric will do the same.'

'I do not know how much time I have left, ok? There is no point for so much effort.'

'What do you mean?'

'That's all I had to say. Thank you for the tea, Mystic.'

I wanted to leave but she grabbed my arm.

'What are you going to do; keep me here by force?'

'If I have to, then yes', Eric said; he showed up in the kitchen and had a tablet with him. There are cameras in the kitchen and in the living room. I witnessed your entire conversation.'

I was so angry. I wanted to hit someone. Eric had heard me talk about how in love I was with him. Can anything be more embarrassing than this? He was looking at me and I felt so ashamed.

'Did you know that?' I asked Mystic.

'I...'

'I cannot believe this', I said revolted.

I wanted to leave, but Eric got in front of me.

'Move away', I shouted at him. 'I do not want to see either of you anymore. I just want to leave this stupid campus as soon as possible.'

Eric did not budge. Instead, he took me into his arms. He probably thought that this would make me relax; especially now when he knew that I had a thing for him.

'Let go of me!'

'I am sorry'. He said, and moved out of the way. It still hurts, doesn't it?'

'Aaa, I am alright', I said; I was feeling a bit confused. I was expecting Eric to behave differently; to shout at me for having lied to him. Perhaps this was coming next.

'Mystic, bring Doctor Amanda over to have a look at Kate.'

She left and I could hear the entrance door slamming behind her.

'There is no need for that. The one we think is Barbara took good care of me.'

'Exactly. Yet another reason not to trust her.'

I did not know what to say. He was only a few steps away and he was looking at me so carefully. I went to the farthest corner of the kitchen; I did not want to be so close to him.

'And now...what will happen? 'I asked as I was looking out the window. I did not dare look into his eyes. 'I would be very grateful if you could respect my wish to leave from here.'

'Don't you dare do that to me! Do not leave, Kate! I cannot lose you. Not you too. Not now.'

'I will participate in whatever ritual you want me to; I will give you my powers.'

He came next to me and put his hands on my shoulders. I was looking down focusing on the tiles. I really could not look into his eyes.

'I told you never to say that again! IT.IS.NOT.ABOUT.YOUR.POWERS.' He stressed every word. 'It was at first...but now...'

'Now what?' I asked revolted.

'You really don't get it, do you?'

'I cannot read your mind; be more specific.'

'Look at me', he said; his voice was warmer than I had ever heard before. I shook my head and right after that, he took my face into his palms and kissed me. My heartbeat was rushing; this was wrong on so many levels. It felt so easy to let myself go in that kiss' embrace. Touching his soft full lips made me shake and want more. I pulled him closer to me and put my arms around his neck.

'You have no idea how much I have had to refrain from doing this', he whispered in my ear and then kissed me again; that sent a new wave of electricity through my entire body.

It was just the two of us and nothing else mattered. The anger I felt before was now gone. I wanted this man and I could not imagine living my life without him. I realised then, that he was the person next to whom I wanted to wake up in the morning. Having him there made me so calm and I felt so secure next to him. I wanted him so much and this was so wrong. I was a fool to believe that there could be any happy-ending for me, for us. I did not know what I meant to Eric; he was the hot and powerful wizard who was coming from a good family, owned the campus and was a lot more mature than I was in all respects; I was only the rebel trouble-making student. As long as I was in the campus, our relationship would be against the rules, anyway. Not that this was the only problem. I was sick...I did not have long to live. It was so difficult for me to come loose from his kiss. I had to use all the strength and focus I was capable of.

'Don't do that, please, I said and moved away from him.

'I know that this was not the right moment nor the right time, but the thought of losing you...I...Kate...it has been so long since I felt such a strong desire to protect someone. You are so small and fragile and the thought that someone hurt you...and I was not there to help you...is...I am angry with myself. I promise you that I will find them and make them pay. I will not let anyone else hurt you.'

'Why? Why do you care about me if not for my powers? I mean, look at me.'

'I am looking. I do it every time I have the chance. You are so beautiful, Kate. Your beauty is a natural one and you have a smile that could tame any man. I love your long blonde hair and I adore your eyes and lips. People are mean, Kate; they are capable of monstrous actions; and I am not any better. You help me be good. I want to be better for you. You are not the only one who can feel the connection. I feel it too. Moreover, I think we both know that you can be more than the typical annoying teenager you display.'

I memorized Eric's words because I wanted to remember and hold on to them; and I wanted to hold on to the memory of that kiss any time I was going to go crazy and lose control of my powers.

'So I am annoying, huh?' I teased him.

'Obviously, this is the only thing you remember from what I said. You drive me crazy most of the time, Miss Katelyn Lambert.'

'Damn it', I said and then put on a worried face.

'What is the matter?'

Amanda could not check me up. She could realise that I had a morh's poison in me when she was going to see my back. I wonder how long it will take until I begin to feel worse because of the poison. I had to postpone that check-up for as long as possible.

'Nothing important. I remembered there's something I have to do for some classes. I am falling behind and I have quite a few truancies. I have to make it to this class. That medical check-up can wait.'

'No, it cannot! Don't get me wrong. I am happy that you are thinking about taking your classes seriously. You will have lessons with

Mystic and I. We will help you. But, is this what you had on your mind when I was sharing my feelings with you?'

'I am sorry. I would like very much to continue this discussion, but I really have to go to classes. Tell Amanda that I will stop by her office after that. I know that you'll come up with tons of questions about Baldric. In fact, I am surprise you haven't already gone mad for having hidden from you the fact that I talked to him.'

The expression on his face changed when I mentioned his brother's name.

'Your health is more important. First, I have to make sure that you are well. We leave the inquiry and the scolding for later', he said, and then smiled.

'Great. I can hardly wait for that. Now, can I leave?'

'Not before Amanda gets to see you.'

'I told you that I am alright. Why don't you take my word for it?'

'Could it be because you just betrayed my trust and also Mystic's?'

I deserved that, but it still hurt.

'I don't...'

'I don't care why you did it', he said interrupting what I was saying. It is not you who has to protect me. I have to take care of you. It is just like Mystic said: I can take care of myself. I want you to promise me that you will be completely honest with me from now on. As long as we trust each other, we can easily solve any problem.'

'I promise', I told him; I was feeling awful for having to lie to him. Now, can you please call Mystic and ask her when will they be here? I really have to go to class.'

Lucky me, Amanda was now busy taking care of some guys who had managed to crack their heads at a football game. Eric was infuriated; I was a priority to him. He finally agreed that I would go see Amanda after classes.

'Great' I said contentedly.

I gave him a quick kiss on the cheek and after that, I left.

Chapter 23:

"Just another crazy day in the campus"

I did not know what I was going to do with my life. I had to decide what to tell Eric about Baldric. I did not know for how long I was going to be able to avoid that check-up with Amanda. The most overwhelming thing had been the kiss with Eric. I just wanted to be a normal wizard student for one day. Maybe I should do that and enjoy life until...well...until I won't be able to, because I was going to become a victim of that morh's poison...

Miss Schumbar, the defence professor who was a bit over thirty, had a strange behaviour; unlike she had previously had. She had big black circles around her eyes and did not wear any make-up. She normally wore her light-brown hair down, perfectly brushed, but now she had it loosely tied at the back of her head. She looked very agitated throughout the entire class and seemed ready to fight off an attack at any moment. But from whom?

She explained to us how to avoid a fire attack. We should either create some sort of invisible shield whose resistance will depend on the volume and intensity of the flame, or we should use a fight-off spell. But, for those who did not major in water, such a spell would be difficult to control. In addition to the introductory courses, we would have to choose a major based on the elements of nature and depending on our abilities with them.

I had a thirty-minute break until my next class. There was no one in the music room so I took advantage of the silence. It had been such a long time since I had last played the piano. I missed it and needed that. I let my fingers run free on the keyboard and played the first song that came to my mind. One of Yiruma's pieces: River flows on you. This play really touched my soul. I felt each keystroke producing electricity that sent shivers through my entire body. The room became filled with a dance of lights, and colourful lightning bolts flowing out of the piano every time I stroke a key. This was absolutely wonderful. It was as if I were watching a kaleidoscope. I continued playing; I was smiling and could feel the song more profoundly than I had ever before.

When I was done, I heard clapping. I turned and I was surprised to see so many people. The room was soundproof; I thought I could play without anyone nosing in.

'It was superb', Maggie said as she was coming towards me.

People gathered around me and it felt strange to be asked so many questions.

'I have never seen this sort of thing before. Those lights moving as you were playing. It was incredible', said a guy who was two years older than I. How did a beginner like you manage to do that?'

'Aaa...I did not do anything. Is this not a magic piano? Doesn't it do that for every play?'

They all started to laugh. What was so funny?

'I get it that you want to keep this secret to yourself. But this is a normal piano. Magic piano? Really?' Said the guy from before.

'The music was heard throughout the entire faculty. How did you do that?' asked one of Sarah's friends; she had such an annoying high-pitched voice. I think her name was Olivia.

'Why didn't you sign up for the music class, since you are so talented?' Another girl asked.

An older woman whom I did not know came next to me.

'This was magnificent!' she said excited. I could use a student like you. I want you in my class! I will talk to the headmistress to allow you to sign up for my class. In fact, I will go talk to her straightaway.'

And she left without even asking if I wanted to be in her class. This woman was in her fifties. She had big red hair that smelled as if it had just been dyed.

'How is it to feel like one of the privileged ones?' Sarah asked me. Some of us have been trying for a long time to get into Miss Wilson's class; but she is so difficult to please. She is the best.'

'Yes, she is', Nate said; he had just come up next to me. 'The auditions for her class are next week. Sarah and I have been practicing a lot for this.'

'I did not know that', Maggie said. What instrument do you play?'

'Violin; both of us', Sarah replied.

I was happy that people appreciated my so-called talent, but I had not done that much. I did not play something of my own. In fact, I have never been able to compose a play. What's so special in playing songs you've learned from someone else? I was starting to get a headache from all that fussing around me.

'I got goose bumps from listening to that song', Arriana said.

'That dance of lights was incredible', Mayte added.

'You can say that again, *hermana*. It was truly hypnotising.'

'Where did you come from?', I asked them.

'Play that again', a voice behind me said; another and another followed after, until everybody started to ask for an encore.

All those people and the agitation were staring to suffocate me. I rubbed my forehead; my headache was killing me. I was feeling dizzy and I thought I was about to fall down when someone grabbed me by the waist to support me. It was Eric. He had shown up together with Mystic.

'Bring them out from hypnosis', he told her. 'Meanwhile, I will take Kate to Doctor Amanda.'

'Hypnosis?' I asked in coarse voice as we were heading towards the medical office. It was difficult for me to walk, so Eric was still holding me. He would have carried me there had I not argued against it, and if I had not started to shake my legs when he tried to do it.

'I still cannot explain how, but it seems that you hypnotised them. Apparently, magic does not work normally in your case.'

I looked at him and smiled.

'Were you expecting this to be easy? Haven't you already understood that I am like a thorn; I have been causing problems ever since you saw me the first time.'

He seemed worried and older than he actually was. He was beat down; he looked as if he had not been sleeping for several days because of the worries. I did not like seeing him like that.

'Ha! It's not at all funny.'

'It is going to be alright', I told him. 'Somehow, we will fix everything.'

I was not lying to him. At that time, I really did think that maybe, through a miracle, all things will work out fine.

Doctor Amanda was waiting for us. She was alone in her office.

'You can leave now', I told Eric.

'Not until I make sure that you are alright.'

'I need my privacy.'

'A...yes...right' he stuttered. 'I will be outside waiting.'

'There is no need for that. Go and do...aaa...whatever else important you need to do.'

'That's exactly what I will do', he said. Amanda, we'll see each other later. There is something I have to talk to you about.'

'Sure.'

The check-up did not take long because I was commenting on everything that the doctor had to say. I refused to take off my clothes and risk her seeing the wound I had on my back from the morh. That would have made her ask questions and I did not have answers for her. She insisted so much that I thought she would go mad; I finally showed only my arms.

I did not like at all that wonder look on her face.

'I feel a lot better than it looks. Still, could I get some painkillers?'

If my back was going to start hurting again because of the morh's poison, then I was going to need more painkillers.

'From what I understand, the anti-spell was done on you.'

'Aaa...yes, I think so.'

'Honey, it has definitely been done; otherwise, you would not have been able to talk to me right now.'

After that, she checked my pulse and blood pressure. They came out normal. Then she took some blood tests and gave me some painkillers. She would have preferred to give me a more thorough examination but I did not agree to that. Instead, I assured her that I was alright. After insisting several times, she finally gave up and let me go.

It did not take more than twenty minutes, I think. When I came out, Eric was there.

'Why are you still here?'

'You told me to do whatever was more important for me, right?'

'Aaa...I think so...', I said to him; I was slightly puzzled.

'Right now, there is nothing more important to me than to make sure that you are alright.'

'Aaa, ok, I appreciate that but you don't have to exaggerate. Can I go back to my classes? You know...without you holding my hand. I can take care of myself.'

'I noticed that', he said ironically. 'I noticed how well you can take care of yourself. Now, if you are done with this childish attitude, let's go pack your stuff; you're moving in with Mystic and I; temporarily', he added as he saw how dissatisfied I looked.

'I am sorry, Eric, but this won't happen. I am...alright...', I lied.

'You don't look very convincing. If it makes you feel better, Maggie can move in with you too. There are many protection spells on my house. If anyone tries to get in, other than those of us living there, I will know it.'

'But what will the others say? Everyone will gossip if we move in with you. They will say that we are being favoured and talks about this will escalate.'

'Seriously, Lambert? Your life is in danger and you worry about gossips? Let me take care of that. Now, go to classes since you are so anxious to do that. I will ask Mystic to take care of your luggage; you and Maggie will come straight home after that. Your new home!'

'I got it', I said, realising that I was not going to win against Eric. He would have done it his way, no matter what.

In the History class, Miss Grace, who is always extremely happy to share her knowledge, talked to us about the great magic discoveries. She told us about objects that would increase your powers if they were in your possession – which would make your spells stronger. There were crystals, hidden in the most unexpected and dangerous places – protected by all sorts of spells – that were supposed to never get into the hands of those who wanted to use them for evil – this was why they were hidden. In time, many of them had been destroyed. No one knew if there was any crystal like that left.

It was obvious that in the past there had been people who used magic for evil, just for fun or out of desire to lead; could it be that there were still people like that? The professors surely behaved as if there were. The problem was that we did not know anything about it. Well, some of us knew that Baldric existed. He was definitely a bad guy.

But, come to think about it, why would we even have defence classes if we did not have to practice it on any given day? If you ask me, this thing about competitions did not sound too convincing. Let's all learn how to defend ourselves so that we can practice what we've learned in different contests. Yeah, right...this was all there was to it.

That's it, I told myself as we were approaching the end of the class.

'Miss Grace, I have some things to clarify about one of the lessons we had before. Could you...'

'Of course', she said with a smile on her face.

I was certain that this would be her answer. I had gotten to know her quite well in the short time we had spent together. She was always so excited when a student showed interest in her lessons. It did not even matter if I had questions regarding past lessons, as long as I knew how to go about that.

'When you were telling us about the great wizards, you said that some of them have gotten to a level of practicing magic that no one would have ever imagined – just by thinking about what they wanted to do. Are there any persons today that can practice magic like that? Can you bring your thoughts to life without knowing it?'

'Hey, Lambert, you don't need to worry. You are definitely not one of them', Bill commented; he was one of my "dear" colleagues. I had never had any business with him. In fact, I don't really have any business with any of the students in my group, except Maggie. Bill was one of the filthy rich guys who were also quite brainless. His body – he was about my size and chubby – did not really help, despite the Armani he had on. He was the exception to "you are what you wear"

'By the way, how is moving the objects working out for you?' Another colleague added; he was sitting two rows away from me. Matt, another idiot of the same kind. Unlike Bill, he was good looking. He was tall, had dark hair, and was the type of guy that every girl was after – I, however, could not stand him. Moreover, I thought that he was working out in the gym too much.

As usual, Miss Grace did not know how to act in situations like this. Quarrels between students were not her strong suit.

I was about to turn to say something nasty to them, but then I realised I had something more important to do. I had to get some answers that would help me understand myself better.

Bill and Matt became silent; they were obviously pissed that I had ignored them.

'As far as we know, there is no one as powerful as that nowadays. You cannot practice magic without being aware of it. In order to bring your thoughts to life, you need a lot of practice. In fact, it is almost impossible.'

'But can you be born with it?'

The professor laughed.

'We wished. Moreover, only those that have an affinity for one of the elements – of the four – can practice magic like that.

'I don't really understand', I said puzzled.

'Thoughts come to life only if they are about the affinity you have: for water, fire, air or earth. This is the maximum performance anyone can get to – although, to be honest, I don't think that there is anyone nowadays who can make that possible.' She sighed. 'With all the technology that is available, students have other things to be passionate about. All the other special talents, like the one that your friend Christine has – of being able to feel a person's emotions – can be done without the use of key words.'

I had gotten the point, but Miss Grace was like a train; you could not get her to stop once she started.

When the bell rang, the professor rushed out of the classroom. I had not even managed to collect my stuff when Bill popped up next to me together with his friend.

'What's the deal, Lambert? Why are you so interested about this? Seeing how well you do in practice...', they both laughed.

'It's none of your concern', I said to him harshly and pushed him out of my way.

'Hey, Kate', Stella shouted. She was tall and so skinny; her voice was high-pitched and extremely annoying – the type of person who is all about gossiping and who comes up with a lot of crap just to meddle or to harm others. 'Can you tell us what's the secret for Eric and Mystic's favouring of you?'

'What is your problem? Are you so bored with yourselves that you have to pick on others?'

'The lioness has taken out her claws', Bill said.

Most of the others in my classroom had already left. Only a few friends of these ones were still there, and they were not capable of saying anything. They were just watching with their mouths wide-open as if this was a circus. Of course, there was no one left in my corner. Maggie had not showed up for the class. Eric had probably held her behind to talk to her about moving. I took the most mature decision I could take and I left.

The next hour – and the last class I had that day – I had Practice and no way was I going to let my mind be occupied with such nonsense. I was the poorest performer in the entire group. I still could not work out the illusions and moving things was another milestone I had to make. I could barely move a small object while others were already moving several at the same time. And that was because I had never been able to concentrate enough and to clear my mind of all the things that were distracting me.

When I got to the classroom where we were having the Practice lesson, I was disappointed to see that it was full of beginners, and not just those in my group. I managed to spot Maggie among all those students. She came to me and pulled me away from the crowd.

'Kate, I am so sorry about everything! Mystic told me what happened to you. I still cannot believe that someone in the campus would use a forbidden spell against you.'

'What's done is done. I don't want to talk about it now.'

'Sure, I understand…Regarding that other problem, I will go straight to the library after classes. I hope to find something, anything that could help us with you know what…'

I knew very well. I wished I were as optimistic as Maggie was but, in all honesty, the odds were not in our favour. The only thing we could do was to go through all the books in the library and I doubt that, even then, we would be able to find anything. If there was even a small chance that there was an antidote for the morhs' poison, then there would not have been so many dead in Kaeillindor. Still, a part of me hoped. I was going to hang on to that with all my strength, hoping that we would eventually find the cure and that everything would be alright. I know that there was a long way to that but the result was entirely worth it.

'Thank you, Maggie. I appreciate that you are there for me and I am sorry if sometimes I am a bit bad-tempered.'

'It's alright. Now, let's listen to what the professor has to say; we will talk later.'

'You are probably wondering why there are so many novices in the room. We have a special guest today – who wants to see how well you perform' – the professor said; her voice resounded in the room. 'He is already well informed about those who do very well and about those who – she coughed – don't do well at all.'

I was in the second category. I rose up on my toes trying to get a better look on who she was talking about.

Eric. He had a casual outfit: a pair of jeans and a polo t-shirt – he was armed with smiles and really looked extraordinarily hot.

Then the professor continued to praise the Great Wizard and Owner of the Campus, none other than Eric Balfour. After that, she told us very enthusiastically to begin.

Anxious as she was, Maggie got down to business.

'Why are you standing?'

When had he gotten behind me?

Indeed, I was the only one who was not participating in the Practice class, but that was because it made no sense for me to do it. I had made a few attempts, but after seeing how badly I'm performing, I was not going to embarrass myself in front of all those beginners – oh...and in front of Eric.

I turned and saw those deep blue eyes. His presence had an immediate effect on me. As always, he clouded my judgement, and the fact that I was agitated in his presence made me mad.

I was in a corner of the field, further away from all the fuss and the enthusiasm. I did not want to be mean and I am not the jealous type, but it made me mad to see how well the other novices were doing.

One part of the field was buzzing with illusions while objects of different dimensions were ricocheting into the air on the other part of the field. A very tall and skinny guy whom I did not know, got a tree branch over his head. Maggie, whose performance I thought was amazing, lifted several stones into the air giving them the shape of a star.

'I cannot do anything', I finally said.

'Maybe you should try harder.' His voice was warm and nice.

Some girls were giggling behind me. I ignored them, as I was also trying to ignore Eric's disturbing looks – I just was not getting it right.

'But I tried...' I think I wanted to tell him something else but I got distracted.

Susan – a short red-headed girl, with her hair down to her shoulders and a ton of make-up on, had managed to make an illusion similar to Eric's. This translucent shape that had an impenetrable face, looked like a ghost. However, to create the illusion of a person – even if a poor one – is quite a performance for a beginner.

'Impressive' Eric said aloud as he clapped his hands together with some other novices.

She, of course, enjoyed her moment of glory but her lack of attention did not come cheap. The illusion evaporated into the air right away; that made me laugh.

'Oh, yes...that was truly impressive', I babbled. I could not stop laughing as I saw Susan's red face; her moment of glory had not lasted long. Aware of the fact that she had become nervous in Eric's presence, she hid immediately amongst her friends.

'Do you find that funny? You cannot even create the illusion – he pondered a bit – of a damn chair', Eric scolded me – as if that was what I needed. *I don't like it at all when he acts the professor with me; the less so when he raises his voice at me – in fact, I never liked anyone who did that.* 'If you continue like that, you are going to flunk the exam that's coming in a weeks' time.'

I opened my eyes wide.

'There is still plenty of time until then, my friend.' I pat his shoulder; only afterwards did I realise what stupid gesture I had done. Eric was not at all my friend and I was definitely not his equal – theoretically, I was only a poor student and he was the owner of the entire campus. Eric flinched when I touched him but he did not budge.

'Miss Lambert, I don't think we are on first-name basis' he said to me. What? He was acting strangely. Was this because of the novices that were watching us? 'And you, stop starring and get back to work', he snapped at the novices who had stopped practicing. 'You should take your friend Maggie as an example; she is doing great.'

'Well, I am not her', I commented.

He did not reply immediately.

'That's right. You are very immature. Moreover, I think you are going to fail in the exam, and that will not help you at all. The academy does not waste its places on students who don't take care of their business.' I remained perplexed, staring at him as he turned his back on me and got lost in the crowd.

I was angry. I crossed my arms over my chest.

Where was this change of attitude coming from? I assume that he had done that intentionally to stop the gossiping, especially now that I was moving into his house.

'Hm, I puffed. What can I say? As if he knows anything about me. How m...'

'Who were you talking to?'

I looked over at the girl next to me and I tried to figure out why she seemed so familiar; I then realised that I had never seen her before. She was about as tall as I was, with red hair and a smiling face.

'Do I know you?'

'I am sorry if I've bothered you. I am Monique', she said with a French accent.

There was no one else around me except her. The others were probably crowding around Eric.

'Anyway, what do you want? Don't you have anything else to do?'

'I...', her smile disappeared from her face. Maybe I was being mean and was taking it out on this poor girl, but I definitely did not need any company now. 'You know Eric well, don't you?'

'Give me a break', I replied.

There were only fifteen minutes left until the break – it seemed like a nightmare – and since there were so many novices, I thought no one was going to miss me; I decided I could leave earlier.

I had just closed the door to the gym when I saw Monique behind me.

'Are you following me?' I jumped at her before giving her the chance to explain herself.

'I...want...to talk to you...', she stuttered. She was looking down at the ground. Her face was sad and I could not ignore that. For a moment, I felt bad for the way I had treated her. But my compassion soon vanished after I remembered the discussion I had had earlier with Eric.

'I need your help', she said.

'I am sorry but I don't see how I could help you. I cannot even help myself. I need to be alone, I am sorry', I said and then left.

I was too caught-up in my own drama to feel like talking to a girl that I did not even know. Still, I don't know why, but something about her intrigued me. Although I had never seen her before, she seemed familiar.

Chapter 24:

"When you would rather be lied to than find out the truth"

I kept trying to remember the route of the fluorescent lights that I had seen in my dream, but I could not recall much. I hoped I was in luck and that the lights I had seen at the bottom of the trees were still there. However, I was curious where they were going. I was at home when I decided that I was going to go into the forest; I hoped I would remember more while I was there. I did not know what to expect but Beatrice was smart; perhaps, with a bit of luck, I was going to find some sign…something left behind by her that would take me to the place where she was now. I went towards the professors' dormitory and then up the hill following a narrow track. The forest was on the other side of the hill. I felt a chill down my spine. Perhaps I should have brought company.

I flinched when I heard someone calling me.

'What are you doing here?' Debbie, the librarian asked me.

She did not look well at all. Normally, she was the one who always had a smile on her face but now she was frowned. She had big black circles around her eyes; she did not seem to have had much sleep lately. The question was: what was she doing here? I thought she was a library mouse who never leaves her books.

'Aaa…I came out for a walk.'

'So far?'

Damn it; I had been caught in the act.

'Look, Debbie, can you please mind your way and pretend you haven't seen me?'

'No', she snapped at me and grabbed me by the wrist.

I pulled myself from her grip and moved backwards.

'What has gotten into you?'

'I am sick of you and of the fact that everybody does favors to you. Why are you so important to them? I would like to know why Eric cherishes you so much; I have my suspicions, but I would like for you to confirm them for me.'

I did not understand this change in her behavior, or what she was talking about; but this was the last thing I needed.

'Mind your own business and let me be' I told her. I tried to leave, but a strong wind blow came out of nowhere and threw me to the ground.

I looked at her. I was shocked and could not understand what was happening.

'I thought I would get rid of you. I did not think you would come back after I attacked you nd threw you in the forest.'

What? How? Why? I was struggling to get up, but the more I tried the harder the wind blew and pressed on my chest; that made it difficult for me to breathe.

Debbie answered the questions I had not even asked.

'Surprising, isn't it? Yes, I have the affinity for air; I can make you suffer by playing with the wind as I feel like.'

'Why?' I asked in coarse voice. I tried to say something else but the pressure was too strong and I felt I was suffocating.

'The more you agitate, the worse it will be. It's simple. Eric. Ever since you appeared he has changed. Nothing is the same anymore. He is completely absent. But we love each other; I know he loves me just as I love him. As soon as I get rid of you, he will become once more the loving and affectionate Eric that I know.'

What??? I could not believe it. This must be a nightmare that I will soon wake up from. She is crazy. She is lying. It cannot be.

'I can see the surprise on your face. But you do not believe me, do you?' The wind blow disappeared. She came next to me and gave me a phone. 'Feel free to check out the photos and the messages.'

I stood up, took the phone from her and gave it back.

'I do not want to see anything; I do not care.'

She came next to me and turned on the phone; she went straight to the photo gallery.

'Oh, but you will look, or else I will use the wind on you. I don't think you want to suffocate, do you? Listen, I tried to hurt you once, I do not want to do it the second time. I just want you to see how much Eric and I love each other and then I want you to leave the campus, and from Eric's life.'

'Let's go back six years ago.'

I looked at the phone. I was shocked.

'Yes, we have known each other for a long time.'

Who still keeps photos in their phone six years later?

She obviously had a separate album with pictures of herself and her great love. She scrolled through the hundreds of photos to the most recent ones. There were so many with them hugging, kissing or gazing into each other's eyes like...any girl wants to be looked at...just like two people who are in love...At the seaside, in the mountains, hiking, in an amusement park; and the photos kept rolling before my eyes until I threw the phone; I could not take it any longer.

'What do you think you are doing?' She snapped at me. 'Let's get to the more recent ones. From a week ago.'

She put the phone in front of me. It was a selfie with her cuddling on Eric's chest in the bed.

Seeing Eric with someone else had a great impact on me; greater than I had expected. Knowing him with a crazy woman hurt me even more. What kind of person could live with someone like her? He had told me that he cares about me and I, like a silly person, believed him. It had always been only about my powers.

'Don't be upset', she mocked me.

'I have seen enough, Debbie. Please, just leave me alone.'

'But I still haven't showed you the messages. Look, this one is from last evening: "We cannot see each other at my place for some time. Mystic's sister and her colleague are moving in. She wants to keep her close. We will speak more when we meet." 'And this one is from this morning: "I will come to your place tonight. I expect a nice welcome." 'Or...'

'Enough', I interrupted her; I took the phone from her hand and threw it away and then I started to run. I could hear her laughing behind me.

I do not know for how long I ran but I stopped only when I could no longer feel my legs. I found myself thrown in this thick and foggy forest.

"I expect a nice welcome."

Everything was a lie! I am only an instrument!

'Damn it', I yelled and pushed some leaves aside 'Don't cry, don't cry, don't you dare cry.'

My back hurt because of the effort and I felt a bit dizzy. I wonder how much time I have left until the morh's poison gets to me? I leaned on a tree, put my face in my palms and let myself drop to the ground.

'And now; what do I do?' I shouted hoping that the forest would give me an answer. However, the echo was the only thing I heard.

I have to call Baldric and leave this place.

Someone put his hand on my shoulder.

'Oh, no, not you again...' I got up angry and ran into...Eric... except for Debbie, he was the other person that I did not want to see.

'Who were you expecting to find? What are you doing here?' he said angrily.

Then he looked at me and saw that I had been crying; he changed the tone of his voice and pretended to be worried.

'Are you alright? What happened? I am sorry I yelled, but the thought that something might happen to you...You should not be here.'

'Eric, move out of my way!' I snapped at him. 'And stop pretending for one second that you care about me. I think it is time we were honest to each other.'

'What are you talking about? Look, I am in a hurry. I have to be somewhere this evening and I do not have time for your moods.' He grabbed me by the arm. 'I will take you safely back to the campus.'

'Do not touch me!' I almost screamed at him. Don't worry about me; I am sure that your girlfriend doesn't want you to be late, so you had better left.'

'What are you talking about?'

'Just stay away from me' I said to him and then I ran away.

It was getting dark and the forest looked even stranger. I stopped. The only noise I could hear was my footsteps. It was awfully quiet.

A crow – a very big one – flew less than a meter away from me; the next thing I heard was my scream that resounded throughout the entire forest.

I started to laugh when I realised that I had been scared by a mere crow.

Something strange happened after that. The forest was no longer quiet. Footsteps could be heard all over the place as well as different sounds – it was either the noise made by a crow or a barely hearable scream, or sharp voices or deep footsteps.

Why did I have to use my vocal cords to the maximum? I sat with my back against a tree-truck; I put my hands over my chest and waited for the quiet of the forest to come back.

It did not happen, however.

Eric jumped out of a bush and before I could react in any way, he put his hand over my mouth and stopped me from screaming.

I had a feeling of exaltation. Oh God, I cannot believe that I am so happy to have Eric around me. In fact, I was angry that my body had had this reaction from seeing him. Although I did not want to admit it, I felt a lot better now that he had showed up.

'Let's go', he said to me firmly. Until one of those appear...'

He took my hand and pulled me with him.

'I can walk by myself', I protested.

A big and very ugly creature appeared; it was green and oozed a terrible smell. It was less than a few meters behind me. It reminded me of a troll I had seen in a fantasy movie. I could feel its foul breath. It was nothing like a morh but at least I had heard about the later. I knew what to do had I met a morh. I knew the run-and- don't-look-back type of action. Instead, I knew nothing about this awfully smelling strange being. Should I start running?

'You don't know what it is, do you?' Eric asked me; he looked more serious than he had ever before.

Oh, no. This is bad.

I looked up and frowned at him.

'Do you think I would be shaking so much if I knew what this is? What is that noise? It sounds like someone rattling his throat. There is more than one, isn't it?'

'How strange. You suddenly need me. Why don't you go back and check yourself?' He put his hands on my shoulders but before he could make one more move, I said no vehemently.

'Alright...they are very dangerous, very and...'

'Then why don't you make them leave already?' I yelled at him.

Oh, no. I could feel the breath of that creature even closer to me.

'Alright. I am sorry. Are you happy now?'

'Shouldn't we test your talents on something actual?'

I instantaneously said no.

'This is the best practice.' I continued to shake my head repeatedly.

'Alright, Tyr. You came just in time. Well, Katelyn Lambert, I think you've learned your lesson. You won't be coming alone to the forest any time soon.'

'What do you mean?' Only after that I realised how stupid I had been. I moved away from him. 'Do you mean to say that this ...thing is harmless?'

'In fact, my name is Tyr. I am named after one of the bravest gods in the Scandinavian mythology.'

'Am I still in a state of shock? Is it talking? Wait, stay away from me.'

This big creature I was so afraid of was in fact one of the supernatural guards of the campus. How should I have known that there are also good supernatural beings? I did not have wizard parents to teach me about these things.

It seems that Tyr came from a family of trolls. And I thought they existed only in stories and movies. It immediately felt my presence in the forest – although I don't know how it can have such a fine sense of smell with that foul odor surrounding it. It had come to escort me out of the forest. There was also a sort of a dog with it. I am saying 'a sort of' because it looked slightly different; or a bit more. Although it had the body of a dog, it had as many legs as a spider. It was simply repugnant to look at and scary. Who knew that there were giant spiders who could mate with dogs?? Yuck…gruesome.

In any case, I hate spiders.

After we said goodbye to Tyr and his buddy who never left the forest, I promised myself that I will never come back to this place.

Now that it was just me and Eric, I caught my breath. Although I was extremely angry with him, I thought it was better to just keep my mouth shut. I went ahead of him and as I passed by, I gave him the nastiest look I had. I slowly picked up the pace until I could no longer hear him behind me.

Then, I heard another strange noise. Ok, if Eric was trying to scare me again, he wasn't going to succeed. But it turned out to be Debbie. Crazy Debbie, again.

'Not you again. What do you want now?'

'I don't think we finished our discussion.'

I ignored her; I was distracted by a spot of color that was behind her.

I heard Eric shouting for me and when he showed up next to us, Debbie's face and attitude changed completely.

'What are you doing here?' he asked her. 'And you, Kate, why did you run off again?'

'I was looking for Kate. I am worried about her.'

'Give me a break', I picked on her. 'I am out of here. One more minute in the same place with you two and I'll throw up.'

'Kate, what was that?' Eric picked on me. 'We start all over with this immature behavior of yours?'

'I won't even bother answering that', I said as I tried to keep as calm as possible.

Then I saw the spot coming closer to us. The closer it got, the more it started to look like an animal. Hey…it was a deer. Its purple eyes were shining; so was its turquoise fur that had a few black spots on it. So different and yet so beautiful.

Its eyes were so gentle that I could not resist the temptation of getting closer to it.

'Kate, stop', Eric shouted at me. 'It's dangerous.'

I started to laugh.

'It's a deer. Well, it is different but it looks innocent. Look at it! How could it harm anyone?'

Debbie came next to me. We were both in front of the deer.

'Kate, do not move; its looks are deceiving. Eric, I am too close to it' she said quietly. 'Make a spell; faster.'

'There really is no need to exaggerate', I told them.

Debbie took me by the arm. 'Let's go, slowly, before we scare it off and it attacks us.'

'Get your damn hands off me', I yelled and pushed her; that is when the deer, or this animal that looked like a deer, showed its true face. Its fur turned black and its eyes became red as blood. In a split second it threw Debbie to the ground and pressed its fangs – since when do deer have fangs – into her arm.

Eric sent a green light towards the creature; it ran. He then yelled at me.

'What did you do?' he kept yelling. He seemed maddened. I don't think I had ever seen him so angry. 'Don't just stand there!' He threw his phone to me. 'Call Mystic and tell her to prep the emergency room. And tell her to get in touch with Tyr. Tell her that Debbie was attacked by a lubrinson. She will know what to do.'

That is when my mind put two and two together. If I had paid more attention to classes, I would have been able to tell from the beginning that this was a lubrinson.

To Eric's surprise, I did not budge.

'Call Mystic' he yelled at me even louder.

Nothing. That was surprising. A part of me was happy that Debbie had just been attacked, and this scared me. But this crazy woman had it coming; she deserved the worse.

'Debbie, open your eyes, please. I know it hurts and that you are dizzy but try to keep your eyes open.'

Right then, no one else seemed to matter to Eric. The way he looked at her...it hurt me to see him like that.

'You have to fight, do you understand?'

Seeing the look on Eric's face had a great impact on me. He was so sad and yet so angry. His eyes were shining. Tears; Eric was crying? He...he really loved her.

That is when it all became clear to me.

'It's burning' she whispered and her face grimaced from the pain. 'Make it stop.'

'Hang on a bit longer', he said and then took her into his arms.

He passed in front of me and looked angrily at me.

'You still haven't called her?' He snapped. 'Do it! Faster!'

'No', I told him; I was angry.

'What? What do you mean?', he yelled at me.

He looked shocked. I don't think I had ever seen him so angry. He looked as if he wanted to hit me.

'Eric, I will do nothing to help your crazy girlfriend.'

'Call her now', he said again, pretending that he had not heard anything from what I said.

'No!'

I felt the earth quaking and I fell on my back. A light passed by me leaving a choking smoke behind it.

'Call her or you will have to deal with me.'

I was shocked and unable to say anything more; my hands were shaking. I took the phone. Eric had just tried to hurt me. I...was nothing to him.

'I am not doing this because you scare me', I said to him. 'I am doing it because I am disappointed. I will call her, you have my word.'

Eric went away running with Debbie in his arms; he did not say anything else. I called Mystic and told her what had happened. She did not even ask me if I was alright. That was when I realised how truly alone I was.

I was trying not to think too much about what had happened. I left towards the campus. I had to call Baldric.

Damn it; all my stuff was now at Eric's place, including my phone where I had Baldric's number.

I knocked on the door hoping someone will open for me; Luckily, Maggie let me in. She looked worried.

'Are you alright? You don't look very well.'

'To be honest, I don't know what I feel anymore.'

'Kate, I am worried about you. Is something wrong?'

'Yes, but I don't want to talk about this now. I have to make a phone call first'

I went upstairs. Maggie showed me my room. It was a lot more spacious than what I had imagined but this did not matter now.

This was the tenth time I had called Baldric and no answer. It is hot. When did it become so hot? I went into the kitchen to get a glass of cold water. I finally decided I was going to leave him a message on his voicemail.

"Baldric, this is how it goes. I do not have much time left. I am feeling worse by the day. You had better gotten that cure as soon as possible!"

Only afterwards did I realise that there is not phone reception in Kaeillindor. That meant that for the time being I had no chance of reaching Baldric or Christine. I took a cold shower and then hit the bed. I did not know what I was going to do next. For now, I wanted not to think about anything else and just sleep.

Chapter 25:

"When you think it cannot get any worse"

I got off from the bed. I was feeling dizzy. I went out on the balcony to get some fresh air and I saw Eric. He was leaning on the railing and had his head in his palms; he was only two rooms away from mine. This man, who was so foreign and yet so present in my soul, and who did not give a damn about me, was now suffering. No matter what was the reason for that, it still hurt.

Then I felt that same terrible smell, of morhs. I could never forget it. Moreover, the pain in my back pulsated worse than ever. It burned. I felt my body moving as if I was floating. Something, a force beyond the tangible was pushing me, trying to get me thrown over the railing. I hung onto the bar as tight as I could, trying to resist the push.

'What do you think you are doing? Is this your new way of getting my attention?' Eric shouted.

I ignored him. I was trying to fight off that force. My hand slipped and in a split second, I felt how I was falling into thin air. I heard Eric swearing and I waited for the fall; but it did not happen. When I got close to the ground, I floated above it until I made it down safely.

'I do not know what is happening.'

After that, I fought my own body; I felt my legs moving by themselves and taking me God knows where.

'You are joking, aren't you?' I heard Eric shout.

'Does this look like I am joking?' I yelled at him while still fighting my own body.

Then I heard it; the other part of me.

Stop fighting.

I let myself go; the further I went, the stronger the smell of the morhs was. The lights of the campus faded much to fast in the dark of the night. I realised that I had stopped walking. My body was simply floating above ground. All of a sudden, several balls of fire lit up; they were following me and were shading some light on the surroundings.

I was in the forest. I was floating so fast that I could barely see the trees fading behind me. A person walked by me; that is when I stopped. I turned. I was scared and did not know in what part of the forest I had gotten to and how long had I been floating. An old woman came close to me.

'Hello, Kate. I am sorry that I frightened you and that I had to bring you here like this.'

How come she knew my name? Who was this woman? But her voice…her voice sounded familiar; and then I knew.

'You…you are Eric's grandmother. Did you bring me here? But how? Why?'

'Yes, it is me. But this is not what's important now. I am sorry you had to go through so much; and there is a long road ahead of you with so many obstacles. You don't deserve this. You are a kind-hearted girl. I have to show you something. It is important. Everyone's life is at stake.'

'What is this about?'

She signaled me to follow her.

'Where are we going?'

'Kate, you have been poisoned by a morh. A connection has been unavoidably created between you and them.'

She got closer to me and put her hand on my forehead.

'Poor girl, you are burning up; and I am sure that your back hurts. I realise it must be very hard for you. You're lucky that your magic is fighting off the poison every day; otherwise you would feel so much worse. There is a power in you that you do not acknowledge and perhaps it scares you, but it takes care of you every time. It just has to be fed, or else…'

'What do you mean that it has to be fed?'

'This is something we will talk about another time. As I was saying, the reason why you are feeling worse than before is because there are morhs prowling around the academy; every night, they try to break the spell that is keeping them away.'

That is when I saw it: an aurora borealis filled with explosions of lights and the morhs dying as they tried to get past it.

The smell was difficult to bear and my body was burning.

'Let's get closer to them. I want to show you something.'

I looked very skeptical at her.

'Don't worry; they cannot pass over the barrier, for now…'

When I got closer, I could see that there were numerous morhs.

'How many are there?'

'Many, and more of them will come. The spell will not last for long.'

'But where do they stay during the day? Doesn't light kill them?'

'Oh, dear Kate, there are so many things you do not know. This place has so many hidden underground areas and so many caves. That is where they hide during the day.'

'But why now? Why do they want to attack the campus?'

'That, Kate, is something that we have to find out. Now, I want to test a theory that I have. Come closer to the barrier. Do not be afraid.'

My body was burning even worse with every step I took. I was sweating more than I did in the sauna. I saw the multitude of morhs as they struggled and filled the place up with their smell. They were so disgusting that it made it difficult to look at them.

I stopped and that is when something strange happened. The morhs were no longer struggling. They came close to the barrier and bent over as if they were taking bows; then they remained like that waiting.

'This is incredible', Eric's grandmother said and then she came closer to me. That is when the morhs got into an upright position and started to growl; their wings were aiming at Barbara.

'What is happening', I asked flabbergasted.

'You have created a connection with them. The morh that poisoned you was their leader. Don't give me that look. There are hierarchies among animals.'

'Animals? These are monsters, not animals.'

'You get the idea. They worship you; they feel the presence of their leader within you. They would never hurt you.'

'Do you mean to say that I have a connection with these awful smelling creatures? Oh, no. When has my life taken such a strange turn?'

'You might be one of the reasons why they keep trying to enter the campus. They feel your presence.'

'But how is this possible?'

'Everything is magic, Kate, including their poison. The morhs however, are a topic surrounded with so much mystery that there is very little we know about them. I suppose Meya found out more, but she wanted to use them for evil purposes.'

'How do you know about Meya?'

'I know everything that has to do with my nephews, and with you for that matter.'

'Why haven't you spoken to Eric?'

'This, my dear, is none of your concern. Let's go!

As soon as I moved away from the barrier, the morhs began the aggression again, trying to get past the barrier. For the time being...

'I take it that everybody in the campus is in danger because of me.'

'Don't say that. It is not your fault. It is just that indirectly, you are the reason for the morhs' presence here.'

'But what do they want from me? Can these beings communicate?'

'I do not know that.'

'I am afraid...'

'We will pull through.'

'How? I do not even know how much time I have left. Moreover, I just found out that I have the morhs to worry about. I have to leave. But does this mean that I will always be on the run because of them? Does it mean that I will not be able to settle in one place? And if Baldric does not find the cure...'

'He will find it. He will surely find something in the files he got from Meya's laboratory.'

'How do you know that?'

'I told you...'

'Oh, yes, I forgot that you know everything. What can you tell me about him?'

'What do you want to know?'

'Why do I have a connection with him?'

'You are the wizard that is born every thousand years, Kate. You hold the power of a thousand years of spells. But it takes many things, many efforts and compromises in order to control it and to make it surface.'

'But it cannot be me. I cannot even create a poor illusion. Why?'

'Because in your case, magic does not work if you do not feel that. You do not need magic words in order to do something. You are the Magic Pawn.'

'But I do not want that. I did not ask for this.'

'I know…and I am sorry. You did not deserve this.'

'Does Eric know about the morhs? That they are hovering about the campus?'

'No, and that is exactly the problem. You are not the only reason why they are here. Someone has hidden them. A wizard is involved in this. You have a personal connection with them; except for you, no one else can feel or see them unless they are on the other side of the barrier. And if anyone would go past the barrier, the morhs would kill them and they could never tell the others. The reason why I know about this is that no spell works on me, not even the hiding one. I have a special power of my own.'

'We have to tell the others.'

'Yes, you will tell them.'

'You're not coming with me?'

'It is not yet the time for me and Eric to have a face-to-face discussion. I will take you close to his house and then I'll be on my way.'

'But I do not know what exactly to tell him. Moreover, he does not know that I have the morh's poison inside me…'

'You have to tell him.'

'I am sorry but this will not happen. If you want me to warn him about the morhs, I will do that, but not more. This is not my battle; I cannot do this; I did not ask for this. I just want it to be over as soon as possible', I said. She could probably feel the despair in my voice. And it is so hot.

'I am sorry, Kate, but you will begin to feel worse. You have to tell the others. You are going to need them.'

I sighed. This was too much to take in for just one night.

'I do not know what will happen. I want to sleep, that's all. I am very tired.'

'And you will start to feel even more tired. You need to start eating better. You need to strengthen up.'

'How can I get in contact with you?'

'You don't need to do it. I will. Take care, Kate', she said to me and then left;

Luckily, the door to the house was open. It was pitch dark and total silence. Eric was probably with crazy Debbie, but unfortunately, I had to talk to him. Or maybe not? Could I warn Mystic and could she then tell Eric. I tiptoed to my room but as I went through the living room, someone turned on the lights.

'What do you think you're doing?' I heard Eric say in a not-so-friendly voice.

'A…'

I did not even know how to begin.

'It's 2 a.m. Where were you?' He got up from the armchair and came towards me. 'Why do you make me worry about you? What happened to you today; why did you refuse to help Debbie?'

'Debbie? Here we go again.'

He sighed. He wore an Adidas t-shirt and some jogging pants; his hair was scruffy. He had this look that I could not decipher.

'I do not know what is going on with you, Katelyn Lambert, but I hope you will come to your senses.' This time his voice was warm. 'You make me so mad sometimes, and other times… Do not make me worry about you again', he said and then came to grab me into his arms.

He must be kidding. Where was this change of attitude coming from?

'Do not touch me' I said and pushed him aside. 'Stop pretending and stop lying once and for all!'

'You should stop behaving like a child.' He took my arm and pulled me towards him. 'You are burning up', he said. He put his hand on my forehead. 'Kate, you are really burning up. I think you might be coming down with a cold. Let's go into the kitchen. I will give you a pill and make you some tea.'

I was furious at him and I would normally have said no; but now, we needed to talk and if I had continued with this rebel attitude, I would only have proven to him what a child I was.

I was on the sofa in the living room, drinking the forest fruit tea with extra lemon that Eric had made for me.

'I do not want to get angry anymore. I have enough to worry about. Now, can you tell me, please, where you ran barefoot in the middle of the night?'

'We have problems; big ones. There are morhs hovering about the campus trying to break the protection spell. And there are many, lots of them.'

Eric sighed and took his fingers through his already-scruffy hair.

'If this was happening then I would know about it already, believe me. My people would have told me. And the morhs are legendary creatures; there are not so many left.'

'But I saw them. I saw how they disappeared in an explosion of lights when they tried to get past the barrier.'

'What do you mean you saw them? Kate, do not lie to me just to get my attention. You could not have made it to the barrier by yourself. You would have had to go through the forest, which is much too dangerous at night. Moreover, the forest guards did not tell me of any foreign presence.'

'But I am not lying. The others cannot see them because someone has hidden them with a spell.'

'And why would you see them?'

'Because…'

Ah…I cannot do it, I cannot tell him the reason. I do not want him to know, not him.

'I am sorry, Eric, but I cannot tell you why or how I got there. You will have to trust me. Just have some people search the area in more depth, alright? And have them make spells to cancel the hiding one. I think that can be done, can't it?'

'I am also sorry, but your past actions do not prove to me that I can trust you.'

'It is because of Debbie, isn't it?' I said angrily. 'Yes, yes, I found out that you two have been together for years.'

'Is that why you did not want to help her? Jealousy? You shock me, Kate. Not to mention that there is nothing more going on between Debbie and I.'

'What? I cannot believe what you just said. Stop lying to me! "I expect a nice welcome". Does it sound familiar?'

'Where did you read this?'

'Crazy Debbie showed it to me and she forced me to look at your beautiful photo gallery, and then she threatened me to stay away from you. And she was the one who attacked me that evening.'

'She was right.'

'What?'

'Debbie. She told me that you would try to blame her. She said that you stole her phone, but I did not expect that you would go through her messages. I found her phone in your room.'

'But it cannot be. She is lying!'

'You are the one who's lying! I've known Debbie for so many years and she has never betrayed my trust; meanwhile, you disappoint me every day that goes by.'

I sat on the sofa with my elbows on my knees; I wrapped my arms around my face.

'This is too much for one evening.'

'Stop playing the victim! This is what happens when you are caught lying.'

'Please don't say anything more', I said to him while sobbing.

'I will go check on Debbie. I am done with you. We'll talk more tomorrow, when you'll come to apologize to Debbie.'

I removed my hands from my eyes and I starred him down. I wanted to scream; I had so much I wanted to tell him but nothing would have been enough. Instead, I got up, passed by him and went to my room; I had never felt so miserable.

I checked my phone; nothing from Baldric. I tried calling him again but I no longer had reception. I was impatient. I could not just stay like this. I had to do something. I went out of the house and sat on the front steps and called Christine. I knew that she would probably not answer but I had to do something.

Just as I was about to hang up, she picked up. That meant that they were no longer in Kaeillindor.

'Baldric, what are you doing answering Christine's phone? Especially at this hour.'

'Hello to you too, Miss Katelyn.'

'Give me a break. Did you listen to the message I left on your voicemail? I called you. What have you been doing? How is Christine? Put her on. I want to make sure that she is alright.'

'She is in the shower.'

'In the shower? What do you mean she is in the shower? Do not touch her with those damn hands of yours!'

'I did not touch her; or at least not how you imagine. In fact, she was the one who wanted to touch me.'

'Do you think I am in any mood for joking?' I shouted at him.

He laughed. Baldric could laugh? Since when was he in such a good mood?'

'She is sleeping', he said.

'And what are you doing with her phone?'

'I am making sure that she does not say anything without me knowing it. You were saying something about a voice message.'

'Yes, Baldric, and it is urgent. A lot has happened since you left.'

'I had a full day. Tell me what happened' he said.

He was no longer laughing. He seemed worried. Not for me, obviously. Everybody cares only about what I can do with my powers.

'Please tell me that you've found the cure or that you are almost there. I do not know how much time I have. I am feeling worse with every day that goes by; especially now when the morhs are outside the campus and your dear brother is not doing anything about that, because he thinks I am a liar. His crazy girlfriend, Debbie, was the one who attacked me that evening when your grandmother helped me. Go figure, I am the black sheep. I know I also have this connection with the morhs. Why did it have to be their leader the one who infected me with poison? They will be after me for as long as I live. Wait, this is saying a lot; in fact, I do not know how much time I have left.'

'Barbara told me about the morhs. I will sent someone and we will see what needs to be done. Debbie? Are you sure? She would not even kill a fly.'

'Yes, Baldric, I am very sure that it was Debbie. Please don't start, not you too. You did not find the cure, did you? How much time do I have? I want to leave from here. I do not want anyone seeing me in the final stage.'

'No! You will not die! I will not let this happen!'

'I would like to say that I am impressed by your apparent concern, but, just like your brother, you also only care about my powers. Tell me. Did you find the cure?'

'Not yet, but…'

'But what, Baldric?' I interrupted him. 'What are the chances that you will find it? You have already left from the island. Having these morhs around is making me feel even worse, and I cannot continue living in the house with Eric. I want to go away from here as soon as possible. I want to go home, to my parents. Oh, wait, I cannot, because the morhs are after me.'

'Calm down; try to get some sleep, alright? Sarah will contact you tomorrow and she will help you with everything you need.'

'I know that you cannot feel anything, and that you do not care about anyone, but please take care of my friend.'

'I am. Christine is a girl full of surprises.'

'And Baldric…'

'Yes, Kate?'

'I am scared.' I told him in trembling voice. 'I do not want to die and…'

I could not believe that I had just poured out my heart to Baldric, as if he was my friend.

'Cut it out! Stop whining like a baby', he snapped at me. 'Don't you dare leave! You will fight until we find that damn cure, alright?'

'I will do my best.'

'You had better.'

'Baldric? If by any miracle you find the cure, I will come with you; I will help you, but please let Christine go.'

'Good night, Kate', he said and then hung up on me, ignoring what I had said.

I sighed. I wanted to pinch my arm and realise that this was only a nightmare; a never-ending one.

Chapter 26:

"When the man you love ends up hating you"

'Good morning, dear.'

The first face I saw in the morning was Debbie's. She showed up behind me in the kitchen.

'What are you doing here? I thought you were supposed to be in bed, in the emergency room', I said ironically to her.

'Eric made sure that I got better sooner. Last night, he got me out of that depressing room and brought me to sleep with him. He personally took care of me, if you know what I mean.'

I tried to ignore what she had said to me but it obviously hurt. Then I realised that Eric had a surveillance camera in the kitchen. Perhaps I could get something out of her. It did not matter anymore if Eric believed me or not, since he had doubted me the first time, but at least I would be shutting this crazy woman up.

'Debbie, I really don't give a damn.'

It was time for me to stir her up a bit.

'I don't think you don't care.'

'I am curious about something. How did your phone end up in my room?'

'That is something you should tell me.'

'Come on, Debbie. It's just us two. You don't have to pretend around me.'

She threw her glass of water on the table and came towards me.

She grabbed me by the neck. She probably wanted to sound even more menacing. I did not fight back. She would not risk hurting me here.

'Listen to me good, little girl. Eric is mine, do you understand? You had better move your stuff from his home and get lost from this campus asap.'

Then I felt her fingers squeezing harder and harder. Debbie was crazy and she did not care about the consequences. I tried to push her away but, for some reason, she was very strong. It felt as if I was fighting a tough man, three times my size. I cried for help and that made her very amused.

'Go ahead and scream; no one is home.'

I looked desperately around the kitchen trying to think of a spell or something so that I could fight back; I just did not know enough about my magic. Moreover, it had acted on its own most of the times. I had sliced up a lemon for my tea and that meant that the knife had to be on the countertop behind me. I reached and grabbed it before the crazy one realised what I was doing; I stuck the knife into her abdomen.

'Let me go, I said in coarse voice.'

The crazy woman continued to squeeze. It was either me or her; without thinking it further, I pushed the knife into her and blood came out instantly. She looked at me shocked. She had expected me only to threaten her and not do anything. She took her hand off my neck and put it on her belly trying to stop the bleeding.

I could not move. I remained there with the knife in my trembling hand. Debbie deserved the worst but I did not want to have another person on my conscience. I took a towel from the kitchen and gave it to her to press on the abdomen. After that, I took the phone and called for help.

Eric picked up immediately.

'I need help. I mean, Debbie needs help...'

I did not get to say anything else; my phone flew out of my hand and straight into the wall turning to pieces.

'It's all your fault', she said and a rainbow of lights headed my way. The impact was so powerful that I was unable to get up off the floor; I felt my body immobilized.

'If I leave, you're coming with me!'

Then the second wave came towards me. A black suffocating mist. Just as I thought that I was going to be left breathless, this curtain of chocking dust disappeared; I took a deep breath in; I felt released.

'No one touches my friends', I heard a voice saying and then I saw Sarah in the kitchen. I felt the wind against my skin and then a wave was formed that lifted Debbie into the air and threw her sharply on the floor. I heard her bones cracking when she landed on the tile floor.

'Eric will never love you anyway. You are only a weapon to him', she said.

Sarah gave me her hand to help me get up.

'You really don't manage without me. Baldric was right.'

'You have no idea how happy I am to see you.'

'Are you alright? How do you feel? Show me your back!'

'But, Debbie?'

'She's gone.'

She stood in a pool of blood. Her eyes were closed.

'No', I yelled.

I got down on my knees next to her and checked her pulse.

'She…she is really gone…I said in trembling voice.

'She had it coming', Sarah said. She sounded so cold.

'No one deserves to die, no matter how bad they are. This is the third person who has died because of me.'

I took her into my arms; I did not know what I was doing; I just yelled at her to open her eyes.

'Cut it out, Kate. Life is tough. Welcome to the magic world. Now get up; We have work to do.'

I got up and only then I realised that I had blood all over me. I washed my hands; I was feeling miserable.

'I don't know what hurts more; the fact that Eric will hate me his entire life or the fact that he will suffer because Debbie died.'

'How are you feeling?'

'I don't know… I cannot describe how I feel.'

'Kate, the morhs will soon get past the barrier. You will begin to feel worse; I cannot give you painkillers because I need you lucid. Let me have a look at your back', she said.

She came next to me and when she lifted my t-shirt, she cursed.

'Kate, I did not know it was so bad. How are you holding on?'

'It's hard', I said to her. I reached for my back and felt the deep cuts into my skin; it burned.

'Baldric had better hurried up with that cure. Now let's go.'

'Where? We cannot leave her like this. I have to call Mystic.'

'Kate, trust me. Debbie is your last concern. By the looks of your back, you are heading for the final stage. The fact that the morhs are so close is only accelerating your condition.'

I took a deep breath in. I did not know what to say. I continued to look at Debbie who was lying dead in front of me. Then I looked at myself; I was covered in blood. And the icing on the cake was that Eric had showed up.

'No', he screamed when he saw Debbie

Then he looked at me with icy eyes. He was shaking.

'This is your fault' he said; He was coming towards me but Sarah got between us.

'No, Eric. Debbie did this to herself.'

'What are you doing here?'

He pushed her next to me, grabbed my shoulders and squeezed tightly.

'Why?' he said while he shook me.

I let my head down and sighed. I did not know what to say.

'I…am sorry.'

'It is not her fault' Sarah said, trying to defend me.

'It does not matter', I said. The woman he loves is now dead; Of course he is angry.'

'You don't know anything' he told me and squeezed even harder.

'Eric, you are hurting me.'

'I was so wrong about you. You know nothing. You are no good. You do not deserve to be The Magic Pawn. Yes, I did care about her and I neglected her because of you, because I became fond of you. But you do not deserve anything good in life. You are just a troublemaker.'

I did not know what hurt more; the wounds on my back or his words. I tried to refrain from crying but I could not.

'It should have been you, not her. Get lost! I do not want to see you again.'

This was too much. I could not take it any longer.

Sarah pushed Eric away from me and grabbed me by the waist.

'Let's go, Kate.'

Eric kneeled down next to Debbie; I could hear him cry as we were going away.

Then something happened. I felt as if someone was pulling the skin off my back from where I had the wounds. I screamed because of the pain. Then a mist came before my eyes. I saw the barrier disintegrating and three morhs getting in. It was during the day. These were probably the morhs that Meya had made tests on. If the barrier had disintegrated, did that mean that the morhs I had seen the day before were going to invade the academy during the night?

The vision stopped and so did the pain. I woke up on the sofa; Eric and Sarah were staring at me.

'Are you alright?' Eric asked.

'Morhs...the barrier. They are coming to the campus...3...', I babbled. I tried to get up but I was so dizzy that I felt back on the sofa.

'What are you talking about?'

'Eric, are you deaf? You really don't see what the real problem is? Kate was...'

'No', I yelled. 'I don't want him to know.'

'What don't you want me to know? What are you talking about? Is this another one of your games?'

'Yes, it is time' Sarah said. 'I don't care what Baldric has to say.'

'What does my brother have to do with this? What business do you have with him?'

'We don't have time for that now', I said. 'They have managed to break the barrier. It was three of them; I am guessing they were some of my aunt's experiments.'

Eric looked skeptical at me. He did not understand what was happening. Sarah moved away from us to make a call.

'What are you doing?' I shouted at him. 'Your students need you. I know you hate me and that you do not trust me or my visions, but you cannot risk the life of your students.'

'This is the last chance you get. If you are wrong and make me disturb the peace of my students for no good reason, you are leaving this campus and I do not want to see you again.'

I sighed when I heard his harsh words.

Eric called someone and the tone of his voice became more serious. Then he looked at me shocked; he had realised that I was right. Morhs or not, something had disturbed the peace of the forest. Eric called Mystic and gave her a quick insight about the morhs telling her to get her best men and defend the academy. After that, he called the headmistress and told her to take all the students to the gym and that they should all make protection spells to defend the building.

'You might be right, although I don't know how the morhs that your aunt has been experimenting on, have made it all the way here.'

Sarah came next to me and handed me the phone.

'How are you feeling?' I heard Christine' panicked voice.

'Forget about me. How are you? How was your trip?'

'I am alright, Kate. We are on our way to the academy.'

'Did you find it?' I asked her. I sounded desperate.

'Who is she talking to?' Eric asked.

'It is a bit complicated', Christine said. 'I will give you Baldric. He wants to talk to you.'

'My men are on their way there. They will come to help defend the academy. Listen to me, Kate. I do not want you to play the hero or get yourself in danger. I will ask Sarah to lock you in your room if I have to.'

'But this is my fight', I told him.

Eric grabbed the phone from my hand.

'Who is this?' he asked aloud; he became angry when no one replied and threw the phone back at me.

He looked towards the kitchen and sighed.

'I will take care of Debbie later', he said and then left.

'Kate, I hope you heard Baldric well. Go to your room and stay there until you hear from me.'

'But I cannot just sit and do nothing. The morhs are here because of me.'

'There is nothing you can do to help us so you'd better stay out of our way. I mean it, Kate. Baldric would go crazy if something happened to you. I really do not want to see him infuriated, so please, stay here.' She was leaving.

'Wait', I shouted after her.

'We cannot leave Debbie like that.'

'She is dead. What does it matter?'

I remained on the sofa thinking about the twist that my life had taken. Sarah was right. I was weakened and could not do anything. The thought that I was so useless was driving me crazy.

I went into the kitchen to get some water and to look for some painkillers. I froze when I saw Debbie. I looked again at me. I was covered in blood and I was feeling miserable.

'I am sorry', I said while I was crying. 'I did not mean to hurt you.'

I tried to not look at her. I looked around the kitchen for some painkillers but I could not find any.

'I don't need cold medicine', I yelled and then threw the bowl of drugs on the floor. 'Damn it; it hurts so bad.' I sat with my knees up to my chest and leaned my head on them. I began to cry thinking about Debbie who was lying dead in a pool of blood next to me. I could hear the thunders, the lightings, and the drops of rain that began to pour. I don't know for how long I sat like that. At some point, I could feel a calming warmth. Then two pairs of arms got me up. Christine and Sarah. Baldric was also in the kitchen.

'Have you been here since I left?' Sarah shouted at me.

I looked at Christine. She was using her power on me trying to get me to calm down.

'I am so happy to see you', I said to her in coarse voice.

Baldric came next to me and wanted to touch me, but he stopped.

'The weather doesn't help at all', he said. The sun weakens the morhs. You have to calm down.'

'I don't know how to make it stop.'

'I could help you, but I am afraid that you won't resist if I touch you. You are too weakened now to send you my coldness.'

'Where is Eric? What happened to the morhs? Please tell me that he is alright. I know that he is suffering a lot.'

Baldric puffed when he heard his brother's name.

'He is fighting the morhs; he is trying to keep them away together with some of the professors and Baldric's men', Christine said.

'Did you find the cure?'

Complete silence. I asked again.

'I am sorry that we've disappointed you', Christine said. Baldric looked at her immediately to see her face. 'Our last chance is Baldric's grandmother. We had to come back earlier because of the morhs.'

There was something different about her and I was trying to figure out what it was. Baldric was looking at her in a strange way. His face was normally without any expression, but I could sense something. Could it be that, thanks to Christine, Baldric felt something human during the trip?

'You should be fighting with them. Eric needs your help. I should also be there.'

'Kate, the morhs do not care about the students. They will attack them only if they get in their way. It is you they want. We are here to protect you.'

Christine and Sarah grabbed me by the waist.

'Let's go and get you showered. Baldric will take care of Debbie.'

'Cleaning up the mess has never been my business. I don't mind if she stays here.'

'But I mind', Christine snapped at him. 'Now move'. To my surprise, Baldric laughed.

'Alright', he said. 'I don't want to upset you.'

Something was fishy. Since when was Baldric listening to Christine?

I woke up and I was feeling dizzier than I had been before going to bed. I could hear screams and things breaking.

I got off the bed. I was still dizzy. I went into the living room to see where that noise was coming from. I stopped in front of the stairs. Eric and Baldric were fighting. Lights ricocheted from one corner to the other destroying everything in the way.

'Where is Debbie?' I heard Eric yelling.

'I told you already. I am here to help you. Her body is somewhere safe', Baldric said as he moved away from an attack.

Eric was the aggressive one. Baldric instead, was trying to duck.

'You never help without wanting something in return.'

'What I get in return is not you concern', he said.

'That's it. If you won't leave my campus willingly, then I will have to make sure you do.' Then he began drawing up some shapes into the air and sending them in Baldric's direction.

'No', I yelled and went down the stairs.

I knew what he was about to do. No one stood a chance against Eric's special talent. Baldric had been caught off- guard. Or perhaps he wanted to appear off-guard. I got in front of Baldric hoping this will make Eric stop but it was too late. I heard both of them cursing.

'I cannot help you', Baldric said. 'If I touch you, it will only be worse.' I heard Baldric talk as if with an echo. 'Do something, Eric; because if anything happens to her...'

I saw Eric coming towards me, and Baldric going aside. They seemed to be moving in slow motion.

Then it all became clear. All of a sudden, it was not Eric who was coming to me, but me. The same clothes, the same hair, the same body and the same girl but with a different face expression. She had a mean look and I was getting so many negative feelings from her: hatred, disdain, indifference and selfishness.

'Look, this is the improved version of you. Just let yourself controlled by the magic that flows through you.'

I was hypnotized. I could not understand what was happening. Then she touched me and that was when all my nightmares amplified. That Kate who was me, but not really me, had showed me a vision. I saw fragments of images with my friends who had been injured, many morhs around me and myself standing powerless before them. Then I saw Eric in a pool of blood and that is when I screamed. 'Get away from me!' I said and then I tried to grab her but she was too strong.

'This is what will happen if you do not let magic help you. You have the power of a thousand wizards. You do not need a cure against the morhs' poison; you just need to let yourself controlled by magic; to let it envelop you and fill you with power. This is the only way you can save yourself, your friends, and the man you love.'

'At what cost?' I asked. 'And how to I do it?'

'Look at Baldric and you will know what the cost is; but do not worry, it is wonderful. Power changes you but it also saves you. Accept it, Kate, and you will never suffer from love; you will get rid of those tormenting feelings and your power will be the only thing that matters.'

'But what is the point of living without love?'

'You weak being', she said and then squeezed my arm tighter. 'You will accept it or we will both die together with your stupidity.'

'Who are you? You are not me.'

'I am your improved self', she said and then got into me.

I screamed. I could feel the coldness.

'Let go, stop fighting!'

'No', I yelled. 'No, no, no.'

I closed my eyes. I could feel the coldness. When I opened them, I was in Eric's arms hitting him in the chest. I stopped as soon as I realised where I was. I was shaking uncontrollably and did not know how to stop that. I looked at Eric. Because of the tears, I saw him as if through mist. I put my arms around him and hugged him as hard as I could. I was going to miss him so much. He did not react at first, but then he also hugged me.

'I am sorry', he said as he ran his fingers through my hair. 'I do not know what you saw but you looked terrified. It did not last more than a few seconds.'

'I saw myself', I said and then came loose from the embrace.

'What do you mean you saw yourself?', Baldric asked me. 'You are not afraid of yourself.'

'The 'me' that is controlled by magic frightens me', I said and then quickly changed the subject. 'What do you think you two are doing? You are acting like teenagers showing off their manliness. I do not know and I do not care what you two have to share, but it will soon become dark and the morhs will attack the campus.'

'You have to take me away from here, Baldric. I have put all the students in danger.'

'What do you mean that Baldric should take you from here? Since when are you two friends? What business do you have with her?' he yelled and then positioned himself in front of me in a protective manner. 'You are not leaving, Kate!'

'I thought you had preferred it was me, not Debbie' I jumped at him. 'All of a sudden you are my protector again? Moreover, I am not your property.'

'I was angry', he said. 'I don't have to explain myself to you. I will be watching over you all the time and no way am I going to let you go with crazy Baldric.'

'Hey, I am right here' he said. 'And yes, the feeling is mutual. Now that we can talk without you throwing spells at me, tell me if you are going to let me help you.'

'You never help. The only way you can help me is by getting lost from here as soon as possible.'

'No, no, no. You can peacock later. For now, put your egos and disagreements aside. We need a plan and all the help we can get if we want to make it out of this alive.'

'Does he know?' Baldric asked me.

He was referring to my wound.

'No, and I do not want him to find out.'

'Find out what? What are you talking about?? Since when do you, Kate, keep secrets from me? Not to mention that they are shared with my brother. Tell me know what this is about or...'

'Or what?' I interrupted him. Then I heard the entrance door slamming against the wall.

'It is too late for you to leave now', Christine said. 'We will have to protect you here.' Maggie was with her.

'They have passed over the barrier and they are many', Mystic said as she was going towards Eric. 'I have spoken to all the professors and...', then she stopped when she saw Baldric. 'What are you doing here?'

'Some of your men will come here to help Kate in case they get to her...', Sarah said.

'Exactly how many?'

'Five of them. The other 27 will be waiting at the exit from the forest.

'They are too few. We need more men here.'

'We cannot let them come so close to Kate. They will become crazy when they get to her.'

'Why are they after her', Eric asked. Should I take it that you are the reason why my students' life is in danger?'

Ouch. That hurt.

'Eric, not now' Mystic scolded him. She grabbed his arm and pulled him next to Baldric.

'Tonight, the two of you are going to shake hands. After that, you will decide what to do; you can pull out your eyes for all I care.'

Baldric reached out his hand, but his brother was hesitant.

'Eric', Mystic yelled at him. I flinched. I had never seen her so angry; now I knew why everybody was afraid of her.

'Fine', he said. He reached out his hand and gave Baldric a firm handshake. 'This does not mean that all is forgotten and that we will become brothers again.'

'I did not even expect that', Baldric said. 'I have to go get my animals. I will have them stay in front of the gym. You make sure that we don't run into any lost student on the way'. After that, he left together with Sarah.

I was wondering what animals he was talking about, but then I remembered the living-dead crows and dogs that Baldric was controlling back in Palaiochora. Could this have been his special power?

'I don't know how we got in this situation, but after tonight I am going to need some answers, Kate. You are not getting off so easily', Eric said.

'You two stay here with Kate', Mystic said to the two sisters. Eric's house is protected by some very powerful spells.'

Chapter 27:

"The battle"

I remained in the house with Christine and Maggie. I knew I could not just sit and wait while the lives of all the others were in danger.

'I have to go', I finally told them.

'You are not going anywhere. The morhs are crawling through the campus; you cannot take such a big risk.

'I am coming with you', Maggie said.

'What is wrong with you girls?' Christine picked on us. 'We are not powerful enough. We are only going to screw things up.'

'The morhs will not hurt me. They think I am their leader and that means that I will be safe.'

'No, no, no. This is totally wrong.'

'Come one, sister. Stop trying to act the grownup. Tell me you don't want to get some of the action.'

'Fine. If Baldric asks, at least he'll know that I tried to keep you girls in the house. We need a plan. If we meet a morh and Kate's tested theory works, then there will be a moment when they are in a trance, taking bows and all that. Maggie and I will take advantage of the situation and kill them; we'll take them by surprise.'

'I can also kill them', I said.

'No, you cannot. If you attack them, there is a chance that they might regard you as an enemy and that will be the end of our upper hand.'

'Ok', I said. 'Let's go. It is just that...'

Maggie asked the question we all wanted an answer to.

'How do you kill a morh?'

'Do you take his head off?' Christine asked.

'These are legendary creatures. It is going to be rather difficult to get close to them and cut off their head, sister.'

'What about if we do the spell that crazy Debbie used against me? This will weaken them. We take some sharp objects and use magic to send them straight into their necks. Maggie, you are very good at moving objects. Take a bag and put in it all the sharp objects you can find in the kitchen.'

'I know what spell Debbie used against you. Baldric taught me, although it is forbidden to use it. He said that this is the best way of putting your adversary to the ground. He taught me some other tricks and spells.'

'Good', I said '... I think that ...we can go.'

Two minutes later, Maggie came with a bag flying after her. I looked skeptical at her.

'What? The extra time I have been spending at the library has really paid off. I am a witch. Do you have any idea how heavy this bag is? I'm guessing you don't want me to carry it.'

'I am the only one here who doesn't know any spells?'

'Kate, you only have to feel, you don't need to learn spells. You can do anything, don't you forget that. Moreover, I will help you. I will use my power to make you feel better. You have to get ready; you will feel worse the closer you get to the morhs.'

'When we left the house, we could feel the air imbued with the smell of the morhs. I was already so used to it that I could actually refrain from puking. We ran into Baldric's men who were standing outside the door.

Oh, I had forgotten about them.

'What do you think you are doing? We got strict orders not to let you go away.'

'We have to talk to Baldric urgently. Can either of you send him a message from us?' I lied. That was the first thing that came into my mind.

'I am sure it can wait. As I said, we got strict orders that neither of us should leave from here.'

'Look', I said angrily. 'Either one of you goes to find Baldric and give him our message, or I leave, no matter what you say. I am sure that Baldric told that you could not touch even one of my hairs, or else. So that means that you cannot stop me with magic.'

'Are you threatening us?' this two-meter tall guy asked me. He was quite a colossus. He came next to me.

'Count to three', I heard Maggie say, 'and then run.'

What the hell, I did not see her move her lips.

'Escero vista', she said and a curtain of dust lifted into the air and surrounded Baldric's men, making them close their eyes.

I started to run after Maggie, through the trees, passing by the gym. I saw some people standing at the entrance; the headmistress was there as well as many of my professors. They were tense, waiting for the morhs.

They had still not gotten so close. Eric and Baldric were probably fighting them at the exit from the forest.

We passed the gym. I could feel my back burning worse. We were getting close. Then, it felt as if someone had set my back on fire. I clenched my fists as hard as I could in order to keep myself from screaming. But this was not enough. As I looked towards Maggie, I realised that the screaming had actually come from her. A morh was just a few meters away from her. In a second, it was right in front of me.

'Don't move!' I told them.

The morh seemed to ignore the girls. He was focused only on me. The smell it oozed was terrible, but bearable by comparison with how bad my back burned. Maggie however, did not resist; she vomited. Christine came next to her and I thought that the morh will be distracted by them, but it continued to look at me. It let his wings down and wrapped himself in them. Then I felt something. It's icky look was hiding a pair of eyes that seemed human. Sad eyes, filled with sorrow, and covered with mist so that you could not tell their color. Then it looked down. I looked at Christine who was babbling something; she was probably getting ready to make the spell. I took a step towards the creature. Unaware of what I was doing, I touched its face. I felt its rough skin that was full of small veins. It looked up at me and that is when I froze. I tried to pull back my hand but I could not.

It seemed I was in Kaeillindor but it was different. I could tell it was different from the tress I had seen when I first got there. This was not something that I could forget. There was a dim light outside and the sky was cloudy. I went past the screaming tree and I saw why they call it like that. Screams that seemed to express the pain of a crowd were coming from it; a mix of male and female voices. Around the tree, there were stones sunken into a pool of blood. The screams stopped and spots of light began to come out from the tree, turning into human shapes beyond the tangible – ghosts. Tormented souls that could not go across the barrier.

Then the image changed and I woke up in an old house. A girl was writing something at the light of a candle. She did not seem to be aware of my presence. I got closer to her to see what she was writing.

" The only element that I am missing is to find the spell that ties lost souls to the lifeless bodies of the dead. The Grimoire that is hidden in the place where magic was born, will be the answer to creating the living dead. I will have my own army and I will be able to get rid of the tyrants that are against magic and will not let us use it. "

Then the image disappeared and I woke up in a dark cold. A strong light came out of nowhere. It went up into the air and lit the cave that I was apparently in. I saw someone blonde in front of the light. I got closer and saw a big book; light was coming out of it. The woman who was making the spell had a half-moon on her right arm. I saw a multitude of bodies on the ground, and then it all flashed before my eyes. Lost souls began to appear one at a time in the light emanated by the book, and lifeless souls were coming out from the ground. Each soul was entering a body; when they touched, the contact was as striking as the smell. I heard howling as they grew wings while they slowly turned into …I chocked…morhs. The blonde head turned and I screamed when I saw that it was I.

I woke up. Maggie and Christine were standing next to me and a beheaded morh was in front of me.

'What happened? You looked as if you were in a trance.'

'What were you thinking? Why did you touch it?' Christine picked on me.

I looked at the morh in front of me asking myself what had happened with the soul that was in it. There were so many things that I had to find out.

'I…had a vision, I think…about how the morhs were created.'

'What? How?' Maggie asked.

'Not now. Let's go.'

When we finally found the others, I realised that we had no chance to get closer. You could see them fighting on the hill behind the boys' dormitory. So many spells were being made and the smell of the morhs was so striking.

'How will we get closer?' Maggie asked.

'They are too many', I said. 'It is…too much. My back is burning.'

'Too many emotions', Christine said; her voice was trembling. 'I cannot control my power very well.'

'We cannot get closer without being seen by the morhs.'

'It is what it is; we will fight', I said…', they need our help.'

When we came closer to the battle field, I saw the full chaos. I froze when I passed by the History professor; she was lying in a pool of blood. Several girls whom I had seen in the campus on several occasions, were also lying there; they were hurt. Then I saw Eric. He was full of blood and I prayed that it was not his. He was surrounded by morhs and I could not see him having any chance. He kept sending spells at them but they were too many to fight off.

'I need a bow and a quiver', I yelled as I was running towards Eric.

Immediately when they felt my presence, the morhs became numb. This was their moment of dormancy.

'Now', I shouted at Maggie and Christine.

Baldric showed up behind me.

'What do you think you are doing here?'

'You seemed to need my help', I said.

Christine did the spell on two morhs and Maggie sent two knives into their necks.

I screamed together with them. My back was burning even worse.

The moment of dormancy was now fading. The morhs began to feel more and more confused and attacked again; they were coming my way.

'What were you thinking coming here?' I heard Eric say when he came next to me.

I looked at him. He had so many scratches on his arms.

'Eric, I hope that…'

What if he had been infected with the morh's poison?

'I am alright', he said. He gave me such a cold look.

A morh jumped on me but Eric pushed me to the ground and hit the morh.

Baldric sent a spell in the morh's direction. Eric managed to get the morh off him and stand up. Meanwhile, another morh came to attack Baldric, but Mystic saw the happening and set it on fire. The creature began to scream and squirm, and then it ran to the other creatures. Together we formed a circle. Mystic, Baldric, Eric, Maggie, Christine and I were now surrounded by the morhs that were trying to get to me. I did not know for how long we could resist. I looked carefully at all of them; Eric seemed to be the only one who had been touched by the morhs. I saw a bow and a quiver and I concentrated on that. The next moment, they flew over the morhs and straight to me. I was shaking. I took the bow and put on the arrow. When I touched it, the arrow became powerfully lit.

No one touches the man I love. I shot a morh that Eric was fighting. The arrow hit it like a lightning bolt.

Then something strange happened. I felt the coldness and the spirit of the morh coming closer to me.

'Thank you', it whispered to me, 'for releasing me.'

'Wait, don't leave', I said and all the other turned to me while continuing to send spells at the morhs. 'I want to know more.'

'The arrow' it said, and then left, leaving a clod breeze behind it.

What did it mean?

'I don't think I can keep like this for long', Christine said. During this time, she continued to make the same spell that Debbie had done on me.

Baldric's animals came next to Christine to help her. They were biting all the morhs in their way. However, they were not such a big obstacle for the morhs. Compared to them, the animals' power was insignificant. But at least it distracted the morhs long enough for Maggie to take their heads off. Knives were flying everywhere and were sticking deep into the morhs; they were falling in a pool of tar that was running from their necks.

I heard Christine screaming when a morh jumped on her and wrapped her with its wings. It was holding her put while it looked at me, almost as if it was waiting for something. But what was it waiting for?

'No one touches her', I heard Baldric shout while he headed towards Christine; but the morh pulled her even closer to it.

He could not make any spell because he risked hurting Christine also.

'Let me go', Christine yelled. You could see the disgust on her face as she struggled with the creature.

Mystic joined Maggie. Eric could barely hold on. We were outnumbered. This was obvious. I blinked and in a split second all my friends had become prey to the morhs; they were holding them wrapped in their disgusting wings. They were like in a cocoon.

'This is entirely my fault', I said and I watched the chaotic imagine before my eyes.

I was angry; I took the bow and I started to shoot at them until I could no longer feel the muscles on my arms; that's how much strength I put into every arrow. They ricocheted from one morh to the other, killing them one at a time. But it was too much. I could feel every soul leaving the body and coming next to me to say thank you. With every soul that was being release, I could feel how my power became stronger and how I was accumulating coldness. My back did not burn that much either.

Nothing mattered except for the life of my friends. I looked over at Eric and Baldric. They were struggling in vain to remove themselves from the wings of the creatures.

They were too many and I was not going to be able to deal with all of them by myself.

I reached for the quiver and realised that I had no arrows left.

'I cannot breathe', I heard Christine say; the creature's wings were squeezing her tighter.

'That's it', Baldric said and the sky became filled with so many crows. They all attacked the morhs that were holding them and began to pluck big parts from their flesh. Then I saw Sarah and balls of fire being thrown into the air.

'I am sorry I was late', she said and then went to help Baldric.

'No, go to Christine first.'

When she touched the morh, it wings turned red and the creature let go of Christine. She did the same thing with the others. As soon as Eric was released, he came next to me. Then he told all of us to come as close to one another as we could.

'Activate all the protection spells you know. We need to have a shield until we come up with a better plan.'

'What do they want from you?' Mystic asked me after the shield was up.

The morhs attacked it but they were thrown back. They screamed because of the pain they were caused when they touched the shield. However, it was not going to last for too long.

'I don't know that much either', I said. 'I had some visions...I mean...'

'What visions?' Eric asked.

'Why did you not remain in the house?' Baldric became agitated as he looked at Christine.

'I think I know how the morhs were created; every one of them has a soul. I think they come to me to set them free. Every time I kill a morh, I feel a spirit that comes to me to say thank you for having set it free. But there is so much coldness; I do not know if I can last for long.'

'What do you mean coldness?' Maggie asked. I ignored her question but everyone was staring at me.

However, Sarah understood that I did not want to talk about that. 'What do we do?' she asked.

'There are too many morhs, but if we fight as a team, maybe we have a chance. The problem is that if they all attack one of us, then there is nothing we can do.

'How do you all feel?' Eric asked. 'Are you up for some more fighting?'

'I can call some more animals. In the meantime, I will help Christine with the forbidden spell that I taught her.

'And I will help Maggie and Sarah', Mystic said. 'Girls, get ready to use all the attack spells you know.'

'Kate, you stay next to me. I did not know you can shoot so well.'

'I don't have any more arrows', I said and a part of me was happy I didn't.

I did not want to kill any more morhs; I was afraid that if I did it, I was going to fall even more into the magic and the coldness.

'No problem. I can fix that', Maggie said and several quivers filled with arrows appeared next to me.

I grabbed one of them. I was breathing heavily.

'Ok', I said to Eric but I was unsure of my words.

'Get ready', Mystic said.

A part of the shield opened up and the morhs jumped in. Christine and Baldric stopped them. Maggie took some arrows and used magic to send them into their heads. I got goose bumps when I heard how they screamed. Sarah set fire all around us and blue lightning bolts were flashing from Mystic's hands.

'Don't come close to me' she said and then moved aside. 'Sarah, I need you to cover me.'

Those two seemed to team up well. Baldric was managing and so was Maggie. Christine, however, was getting more and more tired and you could see that she had a hard time.

Eric was throwing spells and was pushing them away from us. They would come back soon after, but they were weakened.

'Kate, what do you think you are doing?' He yelled at me.

I was the only one who was not fighting. I put on the arrow and shot a morh that was much too close to Eric. The effect was immediate.

'Thank you', another soul said to me and then went away filling me with coldness.

I could feel the other part of me gloating. This was the part of me that wanted power.

'Keep up the good work, Eric said.

I put on another arrow and when I took the shot, instead of breathing out, I continued to hold my breath. I knew what was going to happen. Another soul came to thank me and that was too much; I fell down on my knees.

'I cannot do it anymore', I said and threw the bow and arrow.

'Mystic, take it from here', Eric said and came next to me.

He took me by the waist and helped me get up. I screamed when his hand touched my back. I could barely stand having the shirt stuck to me.

'Are you alright?'

'Please…don't make me kill another morh. I cannot do it anymore; it is too much.'

He took his hand off my back and looked at his palm that was covered in blood.

'This is not my blood', he said and then checked my back. 'What happened to you? Did you get hit while I was not paying attention?'

'Please, don't', I said and moved away. 'I don't want you to see.'

Eric used a spell to immobilize me. When he lifted the t-shirt off my back he cursed.

'When did this happen?'

'Please don't make me kill another morh. I cannot do this anymore.' I continued to say; I was confused.

'Does it hurt?' He asked. 'It's alright if you are not fine and cannot fight anymore. Stay next to me and I will protect you.'

'I…'

I was no longer thinking about my back. I was too afraid that I would end up like Baldric; without feelings, captive to my own magic.

'Watch out!' I heard Mystic shout.

But it was too late. The morh jumped on Eric and bit his hand.

'Noooo', I yelled. I grabbed the bow and shot the creature in the back. 'No, no, no', I continued to shout and shoot it until I felt again a strong coldness.

'Thank you for setting me free', it said and I felt a kiss on my cheek. That is when a part of me froze. I could not stop anymore.

I continued to shoot one arrow after the other, one lightning bolt after the other, one saved soul after the other, and I was feeling less and less human.

'Kate, stop; they're gone', I heard Mystic saying.

Eric came and took the bow and arrow from me and threw them away.

'It is over, Kate', he said and took me into his arms.

'I don't want to end up like Baldric', I said and then I fell unconscious into Eric's arms.

I touched my cheek and felt the cold kiss of that soul. I saw myself in Eric's arms and the others standing next to him and shouting after me. I saw tears. Eric laid me gently on the ground and was now checking my back. After that, I saw all the souls coming closer to my body.

'Come', one of the souls said as it came behind me. 'Now you are like us, a ghost in the sky trying to find its way to peacefulness.'

I looked at my body that was now fluorescent and was floating above ground.

'Do you mean to say that I am dead?'

'No, Kate, but you are between life and death. It's up to you what happens next.'

'How did you get here? I asked her?'

This was a woman in her thirties who had short hair.

'It's a long story, but you saved us', she said. 'Come.'

We got closer to the other souls; I was surrounded by them.

'How did you get into the bodies of the morhs? I had a vision and I saw myself, but I cannot believe that is possible.'

'There was a time when wizards were harshly persecuted. You are the wizard that holds the power of a thousand years of spells. You saw yourself in the vision because the morhs were created by a Magic Pawn.

'But why did he create them? I never thought that these creatures had a soul. And what connection do I have with them? Is it because one of them bit me? Does this mean that the morhs will be after me all my life? How will I be able to save myself from the morh's poison? And how will I save Eric?'

'Take it easy. There are too many questions and we don't have time for all of them. The one who created the morhs wanted an army to help her fight against the tyrants who were killing the wizards. She did not think about the consequences. We are the souls of the wizards that were burned on the pyre and who could not find their peace. The hatred, the revenge, the negative feelings, the dead human bodies, the ground, us and the right spell were the elements that made the living-dead. But we have become uncontrollable. In the beginning, we were fine with that, but we did not expect to turn into such monstrosities. The thirst for revenge was too strong and we could no longer control ourselves. After we became monsters, the only thought we had was to kill for blood. Then you showed up; our salvation. The Magic Pawn created us, cursing us as he did so. Therefore, he is also the one who could help release us. You set us free and we owe you for that. Tell us what you want the most and we will make your deepest wish come true before we take off into the infinite sky.'

'I want the cure against the morhs' poison. Eric and I are injured.'

'There is not cure against that; none that we know of, but you can try to find something in the Grimoire that is hiding in Kaeillindor. But you must be very careful. As soon as you have that book, you will become a target and all the power-thirsty wizards will be after you. The Grimoire in Kaeillindor is the most powerful book of spells that ever was.'

'I want to know how I can save Eric and how I can save myself!' I said. One could hear the despair in my voice.

'Your magic is the only thing that can save you. Unfortunately, the only chance Eric has is for you to find that Grimoire.'

'But I do not want to become like Baldric. And what if it will be too late for Eric until I find the book?'

'Unfortunately, letting magic take control of you is a big risk that you have to take. You can be a great witch without having to lose yourself. When the thirst for power begins to control you, think about what you love the most and how that makes you feel.'

'And Eric?'

'We will help him with some spells. We can slow down the effect of the poison, but I cannot do more than that unfortunately.'

'How much can you slow it down?'

'It depends', another soul said. 'Everything comes at a cost.'

'I can slow it down even by half a year, and make him feel nothing. The trouble is that we all have to cross over at some point; once our business has been terminated, we have no choice but to leave this world forever.'

'And then...'

'One of us can stay behind to observe Eric and make sure that the slowing down spell is done every day. But in order to do that, she or he will need energy, life, feelings. We have to feed on something.'

'And what does that mean?'

'It means that the one who will stay behind, will visit you occasionally to fill up on energy. Every touch from that person will release even more of your magic but it will also make your soul colder. It will be just as when Baldric touches you. The person becomes more human, while you...'

'I become more and more like him...'

'And that depends on how much time it takes you to find the Grimoire.'

I saw a blinding light in front of me at the entry into the forest.

'You have to decide, Kate, until it is too late.'

'Alright', I said. 'Anything to save Eric.'

'I will stay behind' a young blonde woman said. 'I know what it means to lose the person you love. You saved me and that is the least I can do for you.'

'And the rest of us will give you the energy you need to wake up to life.'

I felt a cold wind coming towards me.

'Don't try to fight it! Close your eyes, accept the magic, and learn how to live with it. It is your salvation.'

Epilogue:

"Eric"

When I thought that it could not get any worse, she showed up. I had not seen her. I could not have, I was surrounded by morhs, but I felt her ever since she came close to the battlefield. Her perfume is like none other. Because of the connection that we have, I can feel her when she approaches me. How did she think that I could focus when I knew she was there, being in danger, close to the morhs. This stubborn girl was never going to learn her lesson. I am so angry with her. We need to have a serious discussion. Although I do not want to admit it, I cannot get this troublemaking immature girl out of my head, no matter if it is because of the prophecy or not.

I don't know what happened, but the morhs stopped fighting. I took advantage of their moment of weakness and, just as I was getting ready to make my next spell, I heard her scream. I panicked. Since the start of the fight, this was the first time I was panicking and feeling nonplussed. I always had everything under control. I rushed through the morhs who were no longer reacting and went to her.

I looked at her head to toe. She seemed to be alright. I respired realising then that I had been holding my breath. She was alright. For now...

'What were you thinking coming here', I yelled at her.

She looked at me and fixated her eyes on my arms. I had some scratches from the morhs; they hurt a bit but there were only scratches and a bit of blood. I have been through worse.

'Eric, I hope that…'

That what?

'I am alright', I answered in a cold voice.

Then I saw it coming her way. I instinctively put myself in front of her to stop the morh and threw her to the side. She will probably get a nasty bruise. Not more. Bruises don't last very long. The morh was more powerful than I was expecting; before I could make any spell he threw me to the ground. I thought it was going to bite me but someone had acted just in time and sent a forbidden spell at it. It was Baldric. I never thought that I was going to say this but I had to thank my evil brother. Deep cuts began to appear one at a time on the creature's body and a black liquid started to run from it. It howled and I took advantage of the fact that it was in pain. I made a spell; I used the force of the wind to throw it far away from me. After that, I got up.

I was now in a circle together with the others, and we were surrounded by morhs. I continued to make one spell after the other against the morhs that were standing in Kate's direction. We weren't going to last long. They were too many. On our side, it was only Baldric, Mystic and myself who could lead an actual fight against them. Kate had too much energy in her but she did not know how to use it.

It was difficult for me to pay attention to the morhs and concentrate on the spells while also keeping an eye on her. I would have done anything to protect Kate. Although I am angry and I do not understand why she has been acting like that, I would go crazy if I lost her.

I was concentrating my attack spells on the morhs that were approaching Kate. Then I saw a shining arrow that left a trail of light behind it. It went straight into the morh's chest making it fall to the ground. I turned and saw Kate with the bow in her hand.

This was something I was not expecting. A part of me was proud of her, but the other one was furious because she had hidden from me the fact that she had such a special talent like archery. This girl was full of surprises and it seemed that they were not all bad.

'Wait, don't leave', I heard her saying.

Who was she talking to? I could not pay too much attention to her but she looked frightened.

I realised that something had changed in Baldric's soul when a morh captured Christine. The way he had acted so protective proved that it was possible for Baldric to care for someone else and not just for himself. But why Christine; and what was this connection between them?

The unavoidable happened. I was in the arms of a morh, wrapped in its wings. The smell was awful. I could not bear the fact that I was powerless. There was nothing I hated more than this. Perhaps just Baldric, but he was not the enemy now. And Kate was alone, powerless; she was probably going to be to next victim. I tried to fight the creature but its wings kept me so tight that I could not make any spell. I could not concentrate. The smell was terrible and a spell wrongly said could have consequences. I could not risk hurting Kate.

'This is entirely my fault', I heard her say. I could feel the bitterness in her soul. It was not her fault. I wanted to comfort her.

Then she took her bow and started to shoot arrows filling the sky with lightning bolts. The morhs were dying one after the other. She was wonderful. I had never before seen her like this, so brave and so powerful. Magic radiated around her. She was using her powers and this was only a small part. You could see that she was getting tired but she did not stop until she finished all the arrows.

Then Baldric's crows showed up as well as Sarah. I was shocked to see once more my brother whom I knew to be heartless, telling Sarah to help Christine first and then him.

I did not know much about Sarah and I did not have the slightest idea that she worked for my brother. She was probably his spy, but I thanked her when she helped me get away from the morh's grip.

Time was not a friend. Moving quickly was of the essence, so we decided on a plan to fight off the morhs. Until then, I had not realised how frightened I was. I had not felt like this since my childhood. I was not afraid for myself and I was not afraid to fight. I had fought so many times. I was afraid for Kate. I never would have forgiven myself if something happened to her because I could not protect her. She is difficult and annoying but she is mine. That is what the prophecy said. I began to fight and I was focusing on Kate and me. She was not fighting anymore and I did not understand why since she had done such a good job before. She was not injured, she looked …ok…I think…at least on the surface.

'Kate, what do you think you are doing?' I snapped at her. I immediately felt guilty for the high tone of my voice.

She took the bow and I could see that her hand was shacking when she put on the arrow. There was no way that she could hit the target, but she did; straight into a morh's neck.

'Keep up the good work', I encouraged her.

'I cannot do it anymore', she said and then fell down on her knees.

I asked Mystic to guard our part and went to help Kate. Something was going on with her and I wasn't realising what. I grabbed her by the waist to help her get up, but I froze when I touched her back. I could feel the cuts on her back through the wet tight t-shirt she had on.

'Are you alright?'

What a stupid question. She was obviously not alright. How could I have been so blind? I had blood on my hand and it was not mine. It was hers, from her back.

'Please, don't make me kill another morh. I cannot do it anymore; it is too much', she said with tears in her eyes.

'This is not my blood. What happened to you? Did you get hit while I was not paying attention?'

This was entirely my fault. I wanted to lift her t-shirt to see the wound but she refused. What a stubborn girl; you cannot stop her from being her annoying self even when she is hurt or sick.

I obviously ignored what she said and used a spell to immobilize her for a moment; otherwise, she would have just continued to resist. When I lifted her t-shirt, I could not help myself from cursing. She had deep cuts in her skin. You could see that this was an old wound but it had reopened and her entire back was bruised.

'When did this happen?'

'Please don't make me kill another morh. I cannot do this anymore', she kept saying.

This was my fault. I had forced her to fight although she was physically unable to do that. I tried to remain calm, as calm as I could, buy I was terrified. I could not lose her.

'Does it hurt? It's alright if you are not fine and cannot fight anymore. Stay next to me and I will protect you.'

That was silly of me. Of course, she was hurting. She had been in pain ever since she arrived, but I had been too blind to realise that. She had been in pain ever since that morh had injured her back in Kaeillindor. How could I have been ignoring all the signs? Was it possible? Could she have been infected with the morh's poison in Kaeillindor?

That was when it all became so much clearer to me. Christine had gone to Kaeillindor to find the cure for Kate.

No!!! I screamed inside of me. Kate had been poisoned by the morh. I was going to lose her and it was entirely my fault. No wonder she had been acting so strangely. She had been in pain all this time. She fought by our side and I yelled at her when she stopped fighting; I had no idea how difficult it must have been for her.

'I...'

That was the only thing she said. Could she not speak anymore? Was it difficult for her to speak?

'Watch out!' I heard Maggie shout.

The morh jumped on us and I got in front of Kate. It bit my arm and I screamed. I felt like a child. I was not the type of person who screamed. I had been tortured before and still I had not made any sound. How could I have been so weak to scream in front of Kate? This must have made her even more frightened. No matter how much I tried to refrain from doing it, I could not. The impact was crushing. I felt my whole body catching fire when the morh's bacteria-filled teeth pierced my arm.

I heard Kate screaming. Then I saw a white light and the arrow striking the morh in the back; it died before my eyes. She continued to shoot until there was no morh left. But even then she did not stop. With her shaking hand she continued to shoot the same morhs that had already died.

I went to her and took the bow from her hand; I tossed it away.

'It is over', I said and took her into my arms.

'I don't want to end up like Baldric', she said and then fell unconscious in my arms.

'No, no, no, this is not happening.'

I took her into my arms and lifted her to my chest. I pushed her hair aside and looked at her. How had I not seen until then just how frail she was?

The others came next to me; except for Baldric who went to make a call. I did not know what I was doing. This was the first time when I had no idea what to do. I would have done anything to help her and still it would not have been enough. She had been poisoned by a morh. I was aware that there was no cure, but I could not accept that; I could not lose her; not now.

'What are you looking at?' I shouted at them.

Mystic put her hand on my shoulder.

'She's going to be alright.' she said to me.

I did not need to be comforted.

'How? I do not know what to do; I feel so powerless.'

'Put her down', Baldric said while he still held the phone to his ear. 'I have to check her back.'

'Is it Barbara?' Christine asked.

Grandmother? What business did she have with this?

'I don't want to let her go', I said. I was panicking at the thought that I would be losing her. I squeezed her tightly. I could barely feel her breathing on my chest.

'Come on, Eric, I have to check her back and tell Barbara how it looks to see if there is anything we can do to slow down the process.'

I did as he said. I never thought I was going to listen to Baldric.

'It doesn't look good, not at all', he said. 'I will send you a photo. And hurry', he added before hanging up.

'Mystic, call the doctor and tell her that...'

'We have someone who has been infected with the morh's poison', Maggie continued.

'Noooo'; I heard Mystic shout. 'I cannot lose her. I just found her. She is the only family I have. I have to...aaa...I will call the doctor to get the emergency room ready. It's going to be alright, It's going to be alright. It has to be alright', she said as she tried not to panic.

I got up, while still holding Kate.

'Thank you' I said to them. 'And Baldric, you are not as bad as I had expected you to be. Mystic, let's go! The rest of you, you had better not come back without a cure.'

After I laid her gently on the bed, it seemed to me that she whispered something. I took her hand and squeezed it softly.

'No', that was all that she said.

'No, what?' I asked.

I sat on the bed next to her and gently stroke her hair.

'Kate?' I called her name hoping she would answer.

'Eric, we should let the doctor do her job', Mystic said. 'The rest of us should see how we can help her.'

I kissed her on the forehead and got up. I was feeling worse than I had ever before. This was such a peculiar feeling. I was not used to this and I did not know how to react. The prophecy said that we were meant to be together and share a special connection. Now I had to see how the person I loved was dying before my eyes.

I had done it. I had finally come face to face with the truth. I realised that I truly loved her, even though my actions had previously suggested the contrary. Now I desperately wanted to let her know the depth of my feelings, to guarantee that she would no longer go through life's ups and downs alone. The opportune moment had, pathetically enough, come and gone; but it was too late now.

'Lay her gently on her stomach and tear off her t-shirt. I have to disinfect the wound and see what we are up against.'

I did as she said. When I saw her back, I froze. This was such a strange feeling and I was not used to it. For how long had she been like this? I had yelled at her; I said to her that she was an awful person and she did not say anything to me. Why?

'Eric, you were bit. We should have a look at you also', Mystic said.

'I am not the important one now.'

'But you were bit. What if you also got infected?'

'I am alright', I yelled at her. 'Take care of your sister!'

'Eric, I hope you are aware of the fact that we cannot do much for her', the doctor said while she was preparing some mixture.

I was aware but I did not want to admit it; I could not even think it, not to mention saying it aloud.

'It is entirely my fault. I told Kate that I wished it were her and not Debbie. But I did not want that. I was angry. I was nasty to her and now I don't think I will ever have the chance to at least say that I am sorry.'

'I am her sister, Eric, and I ignored her. She was sick all this time and we were there but none of us saw anything. This means that we are both equally guilty. Why didn't she say anything to us?'

'Because she was scared and didn't want to get us worried, Christine said as she entered the room with Barbara behind her. 'As shallow and selfish a child you think she is, in fact she has a kinder heart than all of us together. I know that because I can read people's emotions and I can see into their souls. She has these mood swings more than others because the inner battle is more difficult when one has a soul as kind as hers. Not to mention all that magic that she holds.'

Christine was right. I felt her words like slap on my face. I was worked up with regrets. I would have done anything to make up for it but it was too late.

As for Barbara…I was so angry with this woman and she had so much explaining to do; but this was not the time. If she could help Kate, then I would have to give up on my ego.

'I will take it from here', she said. 'Come Baldric, I need you.'

'Do you think there is something more you can do? I gave her something to ease up the pain and disinfected the wound; but more than that, unfortunately…', the doctor said.

'I said I will take it from here' Barbara snapped at her. 'I'm guessing you know that this is my campus, don't you? You can leave now.'

The doctor left. She was pissed. She slammed the door behind her without saying anything else. In any other circumstances, I would have picked on her for behaving like that with Amanda who had always been so nice and such a good help for the campus. Now however, I did not care about anything else except for Kate. I treasured her and I wanted this girl. Yet, I had not done anything to prove to her what she meant to me; not when I had the chance. Quite the contrary, I pushed her away; and she continued to protect me choosing to go through this torment alone.

'I thought you had died', I told Barbara in a cold voice.

'And I thought that you could do better than that. Let me alone with Baldric and Kate.'

'I am not going to leave Kate with the two of you.'

Barbara shrugged her shoulders. She looked at me as if to say 'you are so stupid". I knew what she thought of me. We had not seen each other in two years. I don't think she had changed her opinion during this time.

'Fine. I said this for your own good but it seems you are still as stubborn as a mule. Are you sure you want to see what happens next?'

'I am not leaving. Go ahead. If there is anything you can do to help her, then do it.'

'This is only a theory', she said. 'Unfortunately, I don't have more than that. Kate has a connection with your brother. When they touch, an exchange of energy takes place. This makes Baldric feel more human, and Kate...'

'She will become more and more like you', Eric said and looked angrily at Baldric.

It all made sense. I went towards him. I wanted to punch him but Christine got in front of him.

'So this is why you need her, you bastard. Move out of the way, Christine!'

'Eric', Mystic yelled at me. 'This is not the time.'

I needed to break something up and I wanted to start with my brother's head. Then, all of a sudden, I felt how I slowly calmed down. Christine was using her power on me.

'I will use Baldric as a bridge to take out the poison from Kate.'

'Does this mean that there is a chance that he will also be infected? I'm fine with that', I said.

'No, that's not a possibility', Barbara replied. 'It is about the energy. But there can be consequences.'

'Like what?' I asked.

'The Kate that you all know might be gone.'

'What do you mean to say by that?' Mystic asked.

I knew what she meant.

'It means that her soul will be touched by the darkness in Baldric. I cannot let you get your hands on her.'

Mystic came to me and grabbed me by the arm.

'Eric, there is no other way. This is better than her dying.'

I released my arm and went next to Kate.

'No, don't say that. She will not die.'

Mystic and Baldric came next to me. I could feel Christine using her power on me more and more. I sat on the bed next to Kate and I began to draw shapes into the air.

'Stay away from her!' I said to them.

'Eric, cut it out. This is absurd', Barbara shouted at me.

Mystic came next to me and took my hand, thus stopping me from making those shapes in the air. My special power was to make someone consume himself even to death because of his or her own fears that became reality, or better said, illusion.

'We all want what is best for Kate. You should know that there is no other solution.'

'But I do not want her to become like Baldric.'

'Why, Eric?' Sarah asked.

'When did you get here?'

'Why?' she asked again. 'Are you scared that she won't love you anymore? Are you willing to lose her just to satisfy your own egocentric self? You had the chance to have her for yourself. She would have done anything for you. This girl loved you so much; she was destined for you in a prophecy, and you know how rare prophecies are; and what did you do?'

She was right. I left Kate and went out of the room. This was the first time I hated myself. I leaned on the wall next to the door; I was fighting off those betraying tears. I was a grownup and I thought I knew better than to cry. I cannot tell for how long I stayed like this. It seemed to me like it had been an eternity, but when I checked my watch I saw that it had only been five minutes. My arms burned, but the morh's bite hurt even more. However, I was used to physical pain; I could control it. What I was not used to was the pain in my soul. I took out my phone to check the video recordings from home. Maybe something from them would make me understand Kate better.

I saw her going out one evening. She stopped on the front stairs. I thought it would upset me when I saw that she was talking to Baldric, but the dominant feeling was in fact that of disappointment. She preferred to trust him. She had asked him for help instead of me. Just as I thought that I could not feel any worse, I saw the recording from the kitchen, when she was fighting with Debbie. I leaned on the wall and let myself drop; I hated myself more than I had ever before.

I became even more afraid when I heard her screaming. I rushed into the room and saw Christine and Mystic holding Kate on either side of the bed, while Baldric had his hand on her back. Barbara was saying a spell that I had not heard until then; objects were flying around the room. The wind was so strong that it made the windows slam into the wall.

'What are you doing to her?' I screamed maddened and went up to her. I duck just in time to avoid a blood pressure monitor.

I was ready to step in but when I got close to her, I saw her back regaining its normal color. Baldric however looked more fazed than ever; who knows what he was fighting.

'Stop', Kate said. It broke my heart to hear her coarse voice full of pain.

I took her by the hand and, to my surprise, she squeezed it.

'Don't go', she said to me.

'I am here and I am not leaving anywhere. I promise you. It is going to be alright.'

The chaos in the room and the weather outside were the results of Kate's uncontrollable magic.

'Make them stop. There are too many negative feelings.'

I wanted to tell her that I can do that, that I can make her pain go away, but sadly, I could not do anything to help her. I was powerless and that was driving me insane.

'I know it hurts but it won't take much longer.'

I heard the door slamming and saw Maggie entering the room.

'Let her go', she said. That is enough. You are only going to make her worse if you continue.'

'How do you know that?' Mystic asked.

'I don't know how, but I could hear her thoughts.'

'You are a mind reader', Barbara said and then stopped immediately and took Baldric away from Kate.

'She is the only one who can save herself now. If you had continued, she would have ended up worse than Baldric who still has a chance of being human.' added Maggie

I looked over at my brother. He was shaking and then he fell. Christine immediately ran to him.

'He is going to be alright. It was too much also for him', Barbara said.

I looked at Kate. She got up in a seated position. She looked around the room and seemed to be very confused.

'Are you alright?' We all asked her.

She did not say anything. I grabbed her hand but she pulled it back.

'Kate?'

'She is not here anymore. I am Lotherien. Nice to meet you all.'

If you enjoyed **The Discovery**, you don't want to miss **Two Worlds Apart**- volume 2 of the Magic Pawn series.

What happened to Kate? Will Eric be able to rescue her?

Two Worlds Apart

"Katelyn wakes up and finds herself floating above her own body. She is now in the other world, a place for lost souls. Her only comfort is when she can see her dear ones, even though the images come up blurry and they are not aware of her presence. Poisoned by the morh, Eric has come to terms with his fate and is now focusing only on bringing Kate back.

Despair…hatred…torture, a rush for power and, last but not least, sweet revenge. The world beyond can be a true nightmare and when the Lord of Darkness develops an interest in you, there is no way to hide anymore. Things at home are not better either. Those dear to you are struggling with their own battles and no one is the same anymore. Being left with no other options, they decide to travel to Kaeillindor. But complications arise as soon as they reach the island. Facing one attack after the other, every day becomes a fight for survival. Will Kate be the same after the losses she has suffered?"

Made in the USA
Monee, IL
12 February 2024

53330157R00236